A GLOW FROM THE WINDOW

A GLOW FROM THE WINDOW

C.P. DU TOIT

ISBN: 979-8-88785-058-0 (Paperback)
ISBN: 979-8-88785-059-7 (Hardcover)

Any references to historical events, real people, or real places are used fictitiously. Names, characters, and places are products of the author's imagination.

Book design by Allison Chernutan.
Edited by Emily Kudeviz.

Printed in the United States of America.

First printing edition 2025.

emily@fracturedmirrorpublishing.com
Fractured Mirror Publishing
Knoxville, Tennessee

www.fracturedmirrorpublishing.com

To Han,
I never believed in fate,
and then I met you.

PART 1

THE DRESS WAS THE COLOR OF SMOKE, THE CHAR THAT still marred the palace walls. It was the color of my heart, battered and bruised after Finn's death.

It was perfect.

I looked at myself in the mirror—a young woman, a daughter, a friend, a queen.

The last descriptor landed hard. After everything that had happened, this was the aspect of my personality that was both the truest and the most difficult to accept.

From somewhere behind me, Mara asked, "Which crown, Your Majesty?"

Mara and her twin sister Kaiht had been with me since my first day in this kingdom. Loyal servants and, more importantly, companions, they were the two I relied on as an anchor in the storm that was my soul. Soft brown eyes met mine in the mirror, and they waited for my response.

It had been two weeks since Finn's death, two weeks since the explosion that had physically and emotionally rocked the palace. But today was the first day I would be back at court.

All this time I had remained holed up in my room. I let the light spilling in from the wall of windows warm me. The verdant ferns provided all the life I needed, the framed maps of Izwe a reminder of the nation beyond. The high thatch roof above my head filled the space with a sunbaked timber smell. A new desk sat in one corner, paper and pen ready—my link to the outside world.

This space had become a balm to my senses, overwhelmed as I was by the sudden devastation that was my abduction and Finn's violent death. I had long ago admitted that I never loved him, but his passing still rocked me. It was not fair that I had survived, but he had not. The fight was mine, my family's.

He had been my truest friend in Izwe. His only misfortune was to get between me and my enemies.

For the millionth time, I shook my head. It did little to dispel the guilt and sadness that seemed to linger over me these days. I struggled to refocus my attention back on the mirror, the crowns being held up behind my head in question.

The gold one reminded me too much of the dainty tiara I had been wearing that night…I quickly looked away from it before the jagged memories could come rushing back.

A more traditional crown in some sort of silver was the other option. "That one," I said, nodding over my right shoulder at my choice.

"Very good, Your Majesty," Mara replied. Her servant-brown skirt swished as she approached, going up on tiptoes to place the crown on my head. It was heavy and, nestled in my bound curls as it was, it did not need any pins to secure it.

"Thank you," I murmured as she stepped back. I smiled but I feared the expression did not reach my eyes.

There was nothing left to do. I had delayed all I could.

No, that was not true. I had not been delaying these past weeks in my room; I had been mourning.

I mourned Finn. I mourned a sort of innocence I had somehow retained this past year despite the attack on Ukuwela.

I mourned the girl I had been before my power flamed white in an unstoppable barrage of death and destruction.

For the millionth time in the last weeks, I looked down at my hands. I spread the long, tan fingers wide as if some answer, some trace of power hid in the webbing between each digit. But of course there was nothing there—no clue to guide me, no explanation of what it had been, and certainly no guide to how to do whatever I had done again.

That was most assuredly for the best.

I closed my ordinary hands and smoothed them against the gray gown as I took a deep, resolved breath. Today was the day that I left these four walls. The Council demanded my presence, and no amount of pleading or ordering could hold them off.

Oh, I had tried. Roland, the closest thing I had to a father, had tried. But at last even he appealed to my sense of duty when he said it was time I faced the Lords. They needed to know what happened from my lips since no one else could tell the tale. I knew Roland had told them as much as he could. But, like any good game of telephone, I was sure things were less clear than when I told them to Roland and Eliza in those first few days after the palace attack. There were gaps only I could explain and clarifications only I could provide.

And now, it was my time to face the Lords.

My hands shook at the thought of standing before those twenty men of the Council. I stuffed my hands into the pockets I had expressly ordered for this gown and, before I could delay any longer, I turned towards the heavy wooden door.

"Are you waiting for Lord Roland, Your Majesty?" Kaiht asked from where she stood by the wardrobe. Her chocolate hair was pulled back from her face in a low bun. She and Mara may have shared the same features but the intensity that shone from Kaiht's eyes set the sisters apart.

I shook my head. "No. I'll see him there. It's better I go now—while my nerve is up."

Kaiht's lips compressed into a line, but she did not say

anything else. She and Mara had sat with me every day of the last weeks. They had listened as I thought aloud, dry-eyed and teary-eyed. They knew the fear and the dread coursing through me. And they knew the only way out was through.

"Good luck, Your Majesty," Mara called.

I stalled just long enough to whisper, "Thanks." Then I forced my feet to move, one in front of the other, my hand to reach out and wrap around the doorknob, my arm to pull open the door leading to the hallway that would lead me out of my rooms—what had truly become my sanctuary.

I pulled my shoulders back and stepped over the threshold. My Vikela, the Queen's guard, fell in behind me.

It was strange to walk through the hallways that nearly felt forgotten. Locked in my room, I had become accustomed to the quality of light that streamed through the windows, the feel of the worn hardwood floors upon my bare feet. I had forgotten the sound of my heels clipping on the polished checkerboard marble of the palace hallways. The sound echoed with those of the guards who followed behind me. It set my nerves on edge, and I willed my steps to be quieter.

I did not want to draw attention to myself. After so long in hiding, I wished to blend into the very wood of the paneled walls, the portraits of past Izweian rulers.

Hiding. Mourning. Whatever you wanted to call it.

Ultimately, I did not feel ready to face my Court and the Council. My mind still spun about that night. Questions of where I had gone, what I had done, and how I had been saved plagued me. And then there was the ever-present thought of Finn.

I was more apt to call it a memory, gone as he was, yet I struggled to bring myself to accept that. I had stood at his grave, held the hands of his grieving parents but somehow, I could almost believe I would find him if only I made my way to the training grounds.

No, he would not be there. He was gone, and my destination

was the Council Chamber where I would finally face the reality of that night.

Chatter floated in the air as I approached a turn in the hallway. I forced myself on, even though my heart raced in trepidation and fear. As I expected, the turn brought me directly to a crowd of *bright* courtiers. There were no more than normally lined the halls of the palace. But, unaccustomed as I had grown to their absence, their colorfully wrapped *chitenge* cloth gowns made them seem larger and more numerous.

My legs screamed at me to stop, to turn and flee back to my rooms. Safely cloaked within the gauzy canopy of my bed, I would not have to contain my sorrow or school my face into a semblance of queenly neutrality. But I had made a promise once. I swore to Finn that I would not run, and I was going to stick to that—or at least do my very best in trying.

My right hand moved automatically to my left wrist where Finn's thin silver bracelet laid across my skin. I turned it around once, twice, the only outward sign of nerves I would allow. Then I carried on.

I did not meet the eyes of the courtiers around me. Sunk into their reverential bows, it was easy enough. And I was grateful for that small mercy. I swallowed against the discomfort.

Painted lips greeted me with, "Your Majesty" and "Queen Sahle." One courtier remarked, "A pleasure to see you."

I knew I should smile. I should respond. But my own lips were frozen. Any words I could say had shriveled on the back of my tongue.

Luckily no one stepped into my path. None reached out in greeting. Perhaps they knew I would need time to find some semblance of normalcy. For that, I was also grateful.

But if I had feared the courtiers, it paled in comparison to the terror of facing the Council. The floor-to-ceiling wooden doors to the Council Chamber loomed in front of me, and I focused on the pattern of the stone floor as I took each step, one at a time. I focused on the painted images of graceful kudus and watchful lions and disapproving monarchs lining the walls. I focused on anything other than the reality that in a moment, I would stand before twenty noblemen and relive the most horrific, traumatic moment of my life.

The beginning of panic bloomed through my chest, a tightening of my muscles and skittering of my pulse. I turned the bracelet again and again around my wrist. And when I finally stood before the great towering doors, when two servants dressed in brown uniforms pulled those doors wide, when I finally gazed down the long Council table at all twenty Lords seated, I prayed.

I prayed to Finn.

I prayed to any force that would or could help me.

Please. Please give me strength.

I stood frozen in the doorway while the Lords of the Council stood from their seats and bowed. Some averted their eyes while others peered up at my still form from their lowered positions.

A moment later they rose, and I forced myself to enter the Council Chamber.

My footsteps on the polished floor charted my movement, echoing loudly around the silent room. I knew the Lords had wanted to see me, but I did not expect the shocked silence that surrounded me now. I wondered if I had changed so drastically in the weeks since my twenty-first birthday.

No one spoke until I reached my throne-like seat at the head of the Council table. I arranged my gray skirt around me as I sat, nestling my hands into the folds to hide any shaking, should it start. And then I addressed the men.

"My Lords," I began. "It is a pleasure to see you all. Thank you for your patience these last weeks."

Roland's gaze caught mine from two seats down the table. He gave me a small, reassuring smile just as he had done many times before, during the years he had pretended to be my father in the Humanrealm.

Lord Grimly, the most senior member of the Council and Chief Advisor, stood and cleared his throat as if he had to force words past his surprise at seeing me here in the flesh. "Your Majesty, we are most grateful to have you join us today."

I nodded as I looked from face to face around the table. It was as if I were seeing each of them anew. I had been in the Alterealm for just over a year yet so many of these faces were foreign to me.

Yes, I had seen them at this table or in passing in the halls, but I had never really *looked* at these men. I had never thought to speak to them or inquire about their lives. To me, they had always been people I tried to avoid.

But now, I was both afraid to share such painful memories with them and somehow hopeful that in doing so, they could help me make sense of what exactly had happened. Fear and hope warred strangely within my chest. I tugged at the hope, wishing I could drape it around me like a cloak so these men would not see the cowering girl I felt inside.

One face gave me pause. I met the unapologetic gaze of Lord Anson, the Council's second in command and Lord of War, where he sat midway down the table. His dark eyebrows pulled low above his bright eyes, and I watched as he ran a single hand through his dark hair dismissively.

There was no kindness in those green eyes but that did not surprise me. Animosity spread out between us like a deep well, starting from the first moment I had laid eyes on this man, in this very chamber, one year before. It had continued to grow in the many months since with every slight he cast my way, every incredulous look, every attempt to undermine my decisions.

I knew where it came from—his family had ruled Izwe before mine had conquered—and despite everyone believing him the most loyal of subjects, I had my doubts. He had advocated for me to never return from the Humanrealm. He had sent me out into the garden with Finn *that* night.

Yet, I also had not imagined Lord Anson coming to my chambers in the days immediately after my ill-fated birthday party. He had given me Finn's gift, and he had treated me with a kindness I could not place in the unimpressed look directed at me now.

I took a breath and forced my gaze past Anson's.

"If it pleases Your Majesty," Grimly continued. "We have several questions for you."

The words pulled me out of my musings and a sharp spike of trepidation hit me. I was sitting here. I had made it this far, but I was not ready to speak. I was not ready. Not yet.

I swallowed thickly before responding. "Lord Grimly, before I answer the Council's questions, I would like an update on what has occurred since the…explosion."

In my peripheral vision, I thought I saw a few of the Lords exchange glances but my focus was fixed on Grimly. He bowed again, the vibrant orange of his jacket strangely at odds with the graying of his hair. "Of course, Majesty. After the explosion, and your return, the Council has been primarily occupied with two pursuits. The first is repairing the damage done by the blast itself. The second, of course, is identifying the culprit behind the blast and dealing with them."

I nodded. It felt like the correct thing to do.

Grimly seemed to agree. He carried on. "In the first pursuit, we have conducted an assessment of the damage done to the palace. The Great Hall took the brunt of the blast. A wall collapsed. The windowed balcony doors blew out. The main fireplace crumbled in place. Then, of course, there was a fair bit of charring on the paintings in the Great Hall. Several chairs and benches broke, not so much in the blast but in the general chaos that ensued once the blast occurred."

Thinking about the chaos, as Grimly called it, sent a chill down my spine. I had been so focused on my own pain over Finn's death that I had not thought a moment about the courtiers who had been in the hall when the blast went off. Eliza and Roland had not said anything and thus I had assumed that all was fine. Perhaps that was not the case.

"And those in the Great Hall?" I asked quietly. "Were there any injuries or deaths?"

Grimly shook his head. "Luckily no one was killed in either the blast or the veritable stampede afterward. Healers treated several scrapes, bruises, and a dozen or so fractures but nothing more severe."

I let out a relieved exhale. "That's good news."

"Yes, Your Majesty. It could have been much worse," Grimly agreed. "Repair work has already begun on the wall that sustained the most damage. Unfortunately, it will take several more weeks to complete as it was a load-bearing structure. The rest of the repairs will come along quickly after that.

"But as to your question, Majesty. The fact that no one was killed in the blast leads us to our next area of focus. The blast was almost certainly meant to be a distraction. Had it meant to be deadly, more would have been injured and killed."

In all the weeks sitting about my room, running my mind over the moments before and after the blast, I had wondered exactly that. If it had been a distraction meant to draw attention away from the real prize—taking me *wherever* it was I went—the next question was clear. "Do you have any idea who would have done such a thing?"

A quiet scoff sounded from midway down the table. "Apart from the obvious, Your Majesty?" Lord Anson asked.

I squeezed my hands together, buried as they were in the skirts on my lap. I knew Lord Anson had been too quiet by half today, but it seemed I must wait no longer.

I did not look at Anson but rather addressed the table broadly. "I am well aware that Trina Cheile is our enemy. What I'm asking is if we have any idea who *exactly* within that kingdom would be so bold as to attack our palace?"

Grimly threw a look at Anson but seeing the latter was not going to respond, the former did. "That is what we are working to discern. And it is what we need your help with. We are hoping that the details you provide—what you saw, what you encountered—will give us something more to go on.

"What Trina Cheile risked with the explosion and your attack," Grimly paused as he shook his head. "It's the most we've had to go on since your parents were killed twenty-one years ago. It could help us figure out a target, finally."

"I understand," I responded. And I did. It was why the Lords were so anxious to have me back in this chamber, providing answers. "Shall we begin with your questions then?"

"Certainly, Your Majesty," Grimly responded. "Let's start at the beginning. The last we saw of Your Majesty, you were being accompanied outside by Commander Finn."

My hands twitched at the name spoken aloud, and I clamped my lips tighter together. I could do this. I could listen to this and explain what had happened. I had to. "That's correct," I replied curtly.

"What made you decide to leave the Hall that night?"

I thought back to the evening. The taste of passion fruit *konstans* wine prickled on my tongue, the memory nearly as sweet as the reality. I could hear the pounding of the *djembe* drums and sounds of an *umtshingozi* flute in the air. And I could almost feel anew the need for fresh air in the press of courtiers' bodies and the thick smell of roasting meat. "I wanted some fresh air and was headed towards the balcony when…"

My eyes shifted to Anson, and I recalled in vivid detail his suggestion that I might enjoy the jasmine's fragrance in the garden.

Anson stared back at me, utterly unconcerned. I could find no fear in his eyes, no hesitation about his role in this, and so I said the truth of what had happened. "Lord Anson suggested I visit the gardens."

Part of me expected shocked gasps, pointed fingers, and words of accusation directed at Anson. He had sent me out there, and perhaps he had meant to—exasperated as he always seemed by my mere existence.

But Grimly nodded simply. "Lord Anson told us that. We are led to believe that whether you had gone to the balcony or the garden, the same would have happened. Did nothing prompt you to leave the hall, though?"

I thought back and could identify no such thing. I had merely wanted air, as I did most evenings spent in the Great Hall. I said as much to the Lords.

"Hmm," Grimly murmured. One wrinkled hand rubbed at his chin in contemplation. "Perhaps whomever attacked had simply observed your routine before and knew to expect you outside at some point."

"It's possible," I replied, disconcerting though it was that someone or someones had been watching me intently enough to pick that up.

"And once the blast went off, what happened?" Grimly asked.

I took a deep, steadying breath. "Finn…Finn and I ran to the training ground. He felt it would be safer for me the further we got from whatever was happening in the palace."

"Unfortunately, that was exactly what Trina Cheile wanted," a Lord at the end of the table added.

Grimly nodded in agreement. "It would seem as such. When you got to the training grounds, what happened then?"

"We went somewhere," I said immediately. I did not struggle to recall that. I could too clearly see the odd purple tint to the sky wherever Finn and I had been taken.

A stillness settled on the room, as if twenty pairs of ears focused in more closely. But it was Grimly who parroted back, "You *went* somewhere? What do you mean?"

"I mean I blinked and suddenly we were there but not there. The training ground looked the same. The soldiers' *rondavel* huts looked the same, but the sky was different. It wasn't the blue of daytime or the black of night, but a purple that seemed to glow."

Hushed, surprised voices floated to me. I blinked rapidly as if to keep my sight here, on what was in front of me, rather than to see that eerie purple again.

"Then what happened?" Grimly plowed on.

"Strange creatures materialized—a dozen, maybe two dozen—and Finn and I had no option but to fight," I said. I noticed a Lord lean in as if to try and hear me better, so I cleared my throat and spoke louder despite the press of fear that was inching up my neck as the memories flooded back. I could almost feel the desperation once more as I realized Finn and I were running out of time, as I told him over and over I did not have magic. "We fought and hoped that someone would find us wherever or whenever we were. And then Finn...one of the creatures struck him down—"

"You keep saying 'creatures,' Your Majesty," a blonde Lord interjected. Evan, I recalled suddenly—that was his name. "Yet when we arrived, there was only you and the Commander around burnt heaps we could not identify."

I was grateful for the interruption; it gave me time to try and pull my nerves together for what had to be said next. "I'm not sure what else to call them. They were humanoid—two arms, two legs, a head—but they were not *right*. Their movements were jerky and fast. One spoke to us and told me I would die. But when Finn fell, I...I don't really know what happened."

I took a breath, looking down at my hands where they twisted and twisted in my skirts. When I looked back up, I said the words not that were most painful in this story but that I was most afraid of. They were ones I had been denying so vehemently in the days and weeks past. "One second I was screaming and the next, everything was white and blazing. The creatures were burning as if from the inside out. When they were dead, Finn was still there. He had not been burned."

There was silence around the room, stunned silence. I could feel it, heavy and oppressive like a thick fog drifting over the Council table.

I did not look up. I did not want the Lords to see whatever monstrosity lived within me. For I knew that light had come from me. Just as I knew, deep in my bones, that my name was Sahle, that I lived for the taste of fresh bread, and that the sound of a solo cello made me cry. I also knew that light had been some innate part of me that Finn had been trying to pull out for nearly a year.

But it had not surfaced soon enough to save him.

I swallowed at the thought. The guilt and shame lapped at my mind, but I pushed it aside. There would be time to wallow—oh, there was always time, especially during sleepless nights—but now, before the Lords, was not the moment.

Then, to my surprise, a Lord laughed. My eyes whipped up at the sound, and I watched in shocked outrage as Anson's head tipped back at whatever it was he found funny. Several other Lords joined in with their own chuckles, and my brow pinched in fury.

"I see nothing amusing," I bit out, louder than I intended.

Anson wiped at his eyes in what looked almost like a stage gesture, overly animated as it was. "My apologies, my Queen. I do not laugh at you, though I understand that it might appear that way from where you're sitting."

I glared daggers at Anson, but he did not seem to notice. He continued, "My laughter is in relief and joy. All of us at this table have long hoped that you had powers of any kind. Even a minor ability like being able to light a candle or heat a cup of water would have been welcome. But this? What you just described is power unlike anything the Alterealm has seen in generations. This is fantastic news."

I itched to jump to my feet, to scream in his face in outrage. Instead, I simply said, "Nothing about what happened is fantastic."

If Anson could see the monumental effort it took to keep myself in check, he did not seem to care. "I admit it must have been a trying ordeal, Your Majesty, yet look what has come out of it."

My eyes widened in disbelief. I had no words for him. I sat, flabbergasted and silent. Then I shook my head and shut my eyes. After a moment I opened them once more, resolved to not look at Anson ever again.

I knew he was not a kind man but there seemed to be no limits to the horrible words he could say to me. I glanced at Roland and was slightly comforted by the narrowed eyes turned in Anson's direction. At least someone, anyone else seemed to think Anson was out of line.

"Your Majesty," Roland chimed in, clearly intent on changing the subject. "When the Lords and soldiers arrived, you were in the training grounds here. Do you know how you came back from wherever you were?'

It was a good question, and one I had not considered. I had been too distracted and distraught to notice where I was after Finn fell and the creatures burned. "No, I don't know. I assumed whoever rescued me came and got us back from wherever we went."

"We did not," Anson called. He had been there that day, and he had been the one to pull me away from Finn's body. "Without knowing the magic of the one who transported you, it is hard to say exactly where you went. But between the creatures and the oddly colored sky, my guess would be that the wielder moved you to an in-between space. In those spaces, life is not life as we know it—which would explain why the creatures looked human but were not and why the training grounds looked normal and at the same time felt different. Perhaps your use of magic broke whatever power held you in that border place."

"That's a thought," Grimly said.

Silence fell in the chamber once more, as if every Lord was mulling over what this magic could mean.

I waited for them to finish their questions. Surely they wanted to know how bravely Finn had fought or how he had urged me to use the magic they found so remarkable. Surely they wanted to know how he had died a valiant death, battling for the life of their queen.

But when Grimly spoke again, that was not what he said. "Given this news of your power, I will begin at once in securing a new magical trainer for you. If there are no objections, I believe that covers all of our questions, Your Majesty. We understand that it has been a trying time for you, and we thank you for joining us today."

I knew the sound of my dismissal. On any other day, I would have stood from my seat and made my way from the room. Today, though…today the panic and fear of reliving that night coalesced into righteous anger.

I knew I had a temper, and I knew it was something I would always work to check. But right now, anger felt better, felt easier than the raw nerves and sadness. I glommed onto that anger, fully acknowledging the crutch that it was.

I lifted my chin, and I did not stand.

I was the Queen here and I would not go. Not yet.

"Do you not have any questions about Finn?" I asked levelly. My voice did not betray my emotions, but I was sure anyone looking at me could see the fury churning behind my eyes.

"We know of his death, Queen Sahle," one Lord replied.

I turned to look at the Lord. "You know of it," I echoed. "And I ask again: You have no questions? Not about his bravery or his sacrifice or his attempt to save his queen up to his last breath?"

The Lord looked from me to the faces around him, confused.

"Queen Sahle," a patient voice called from nearer to me. I followed the sound of the voice to Roland. "Commander Finn was a valiant soldier. He was a great asset to the kingdom, and it will be difficult to replace him when we select a new commander. I believe I speak for everyone here in saying that his death in service to the crown will not be forgotten."

I stared at Roland. I knew what he was doing. He was saying the words I wanted to hear in order to placate me. And they were the words I wanted—the words I needed—to hear at this table. Yet I feared it was futile for me to wish anyone else had said them.

There was so much I regretted when it came to Finn's death: my promises of love, my magic which came too late, the fact that he was outside of the palace with me that night at all. But I understood that it would be up to me, not these Lords, to keep his sacrifice alive.

"It certainly will not," I replied. "I know many of you were less than enthusiastic about our relationship. But all of that aside, Finn died a hero's death and will be acknowledged with all the respect that entails. Do I make myself clear?"

Heads nodded the length of the table, even if a few moved sluggishly. "Yes, Your Majesty" echoed around.

It was as much as I was going to get. I knew that, and so I stood at last.

I looked to Lord Grimly. "I am eager to meet your candidates for magical trainers, Lord Grimly." He had said nothing about presenting me with candidates, but I was in a bad mood, and I wanted to remind him that I was ultimately the one in charge here.

I did not wait for an acknowledgement from him before I said to the rest of the Lords, "A pleasant day, gentlemen."

And then I was up and moving once more, needing to put as much distance between me and whatever arrogant, ridiculous atmosphere existed in this room.

I could not get out fast enough.

"Come. Get up," Eliza prodded me with a finger.

"Ow," I exclaimed, though my heart was not in it enough to truly be outraged. I just felt tired, slow and listless and aimless in a way that had become all too commonplace these last weeks.

Eliza, alongside Roland, had been my rock along the way. But then again, they always had been that for me. As the two people I had once believed were my parents, they embodied calm and stability in the twenty years I had lived as their supposed daughter.

Since becoming Queen and coming to the Alterealm, they remained the people I could rely on, yet they had also necessarily taken a step back. They were overly conscious of how it would look for them to be seen as too close, too influential to the Queen. As a consequence of this, they had retreated to their country estate, only to visit me in the palace—never to stay.

Yet the last weeks since the attack, since Finn, since everything, they had stayed. It was a cautious thing done with particular care and delicacy. If so much as one courtier raised an eyebrow, I knew they would leave again. I earnestly wished that day would never come. Having them with me had become indispensable as if, once more, I was a toddler dependent solely on their love and care and affection to survive.

Courtiers be damned.

Eliza poked me again. "You're doing well, Sahle. You made it to the Council. You've told them everything. You've done too much to settle back in this room to mope."

I raised an eyebrow from my half seated, half lying position on the bed. "Mope? Is that what you think I've been doing all this time?"

Eliza sighed, her faux-cheery smile suddenly dropping. "I'm sorry. That was a poor choice of words. I only meant that you've taken the first step to ending the mourning period you've been in." She settled beside me in the blankets, tucking her powder blue *chitenge* cloth skirts around her before looping an arm across my shoulders. "I know it's hard, Sahl, but you have to keep going. Your Court needs you. Your kingdom needs you. You understand?"

I looked at her in profile, the high bridge of her nose, her blue eyes, her blonde hair piled atop her head. I loved this woman, and I trusted her as much as any child could love and trust a mother—biological or not.

I nodded. "I understand. It's just easier said than done. Going to the Council Chamber yesterday…" I swallowed and I was sure Eliza could hear the motion. "It was overwhelming and scary in a way that reminded me of my first days here in the Alterealm. Having to explain everything that had happened was a lot. And seeing those men's reactions to Finn's death and my power, it was all disconcerting and made me feel what's up is down and what's down is up."

"I can imagine," Eliza replied. A stray curl had snuck out of my bun, and she wrapped it back into place. "I know it's hard but the only way to make it better is to keep going. That means keep facing your court. Keep dealing with their reactions. The more you see it, the less it will shock you."

I did not want to imagine the days and weeks it would take, the number of distasteful words I would have to stomach. Still, I agreed. "You're right."

Eliza smiled. "I know. A mother always is."

"I wouldn't go that far," I quipped back with a small smile.

"Right," Eliza said, squeezing my upper arm. "Let's go."

"You were serious about that walk?" I asked, glancing at the wall of windows. I could see the leaves of the silver trees outside blowing in a brisk breeze. I shivered as if I could already feel the bracing air across my cheeks.

Eliza tracked my gaze with her own. "Sometimes a walk is the best medicine, especially in the right amount of cold."

I huffed, even as I pulled myself to my feet. "Sounds like an old wives' tale to me."

We bundled up in shawls and a set of leather gloves each. Then I followed Eliza back down the dreaded staircases and hallways of the too large palace with the too watchful courtiers. It seemed almost silly to me that this palace with all of its polished wood and ornate maps, its white plaster and leafy ferns was mine. I could burn it down, paint it neon pink, decide I actually wanted to live in a glass dome, and it would be done. Thus was the power and the influence of the monarchy.

Yet because of who I was and the crown I wore, I would never be truly comfortable in this "home." I would always be observed and remarked upon. I would always be followed and waited on. Even now, four members of the Vikela floated along in Eliza's and my wake.

It was a strange juxtaposition to have and yet never to be able to truly enjoy the power one wielded.

Or maybe it was just me. Maybe I was still too timid, too conscientious of the eyes and opinions swirling around me. I could not imagine a time when I would no longer care.

I kept my eyes trained on the checkered hallways, the state portraits, even the mounted heads of *insephe*, *kudu*, zebras, and lions as we passed through the palace. It was easier to focus on these oddities that had somehow become familiar, rather than meet the eyes of the Lords and Ladies who bowed before us. I hoped they interpreted my lack of interaction as aloofness rather than fear.

I knew little of being a Queen, but I knew one thing—it did not do to have your subjects know you feared them.

Soon enough, we exited the palace and stepped out into the pale sunlight of the blustery day. Not a single rainbow-dressed courtier lined these cold garden paths and, perhaps for the first time, I thought what good sense they had. I pulled my shawl closer around my shoulders as I followed after Eliza.

She did not say anything for some time. We wound our way through the expansive garden, passing the church-like Yesonto and heading out into an area I had rarely visited. Tall silver trees lined the path, their thin leaves flapping in the wind. Stone benches sat here and there. I eyed one longingly, but Eliza moved past it without a second glance.

A small clearing opened before us, and I realized we must be near the far perimeter of the palace estates. A wall made of mortarless stone climbed before us and I reached out to touch the cool surface as we neared it.

"Your ancestor created this wall," Eliza said.

I turned to find her watching me. "It was not here before?"

She shook her head. "Perhaps some sort of wall was, but the style of this one—with rock but no mortar—that's something Manelesi brought with him when he came here. I'm sure you saw the same style of wall in Ukuwela when you visited a few months ago."

"Yes," I replied, thinking back to the border town I had ridden to after it suffered its own attack. Their mortarless stone wall had risen high out of the red Izweian soil, but it had not stopped Trina Cheile from killing nearly fifty of its citizens.

"It's just a wall of course, but Sahl, it's also your destiny."

"A wall?" I asked with a quirked brow.

"No, not just a wall," she smiled. "The legacy you inherited in your blood. Yes, there is a prophecy which says you'll do great things. But even without that, just because of who you are, which family you were born to, you have an inordinate amount of potential. You do realize that, Sahl?"

I turned to look at her now, not hiding my emotion, not letting my queenly mask disguise my true feelings. "You say that. The Lords say that…Finn said that. But no matter how many times I'm told it, it doesn't change the fact that I don't *feel* like a special, mythical ruler."

Eliza glanced around her, checking that we were alone. Only the Vikela lingered here. Then she reached out a hand to clasp my own. "What do you feel like?"

I shrugged. "Broken, sad, lonely, uncertain. There are a whole host of emotions I feel these days, and none of them are good or brave or strong. None of them are conducive to being some all-powerful ruler."

"But you saw it, Sahl," Eliza whispered, suddenly serious. "You saw your power with your own two eyes. You are the most powerful wielder that has ever lived, except for Manelesi."

I blinked. "So they say."

"One day you'll have to believe it."

"And maybe one day I will. Today, I'm just trying to survive in this palace."

Eliza was quiet then. The breeze stirred the fine blonde hairs that framed her face. "Is it really so bad? I know I've never asked you that, not since we brought you here a year ago. I…I guess I just thought you'd need time and then you would fit in here as if you'd never left."

My brow knitted and I hesitated, the words ready on my tongue. If I said my true feelings, if I spelled out exactly how hard the last year had been, I would hurt this woman who meant so much to me. And no matter how broken and lonely and inconsequential I felt, I never wanted to make Eliza feel those things.

And so I shrugged once more. "There was no reason to ask. It's not like there was a choice to return to the Humanrealm or not.

I won't lie and say it has been easy. It's been difficult. Especially once you left—" Eliza opened her mouth as if she would protest, but I hurried on. "No, you don't need to apologize for that. I know it was necessary. But still, it was hard feeling abandoned by the only people I knew in this place.

"You know I made friends, though none that the Lords would consider worthy. Kaiht and Mara and Finn, they've been lifelines for me here. I did everything I could to learn as much as possible about the Alterealm and my responsibilities. I just—in the wake of everything—I feel like I failed."

Eliza's hand tightened on my own. "Why would you have failed, Sahl?"

I looked at the stone wall once more. I let my eyes trace the gaps where mortar should have rested, where instead a sort of lingering ageless magic held the stones together. "Because if I had tried harder from the start, maybe I could have prevented what happened here."

The stones blurred as my vision clouded with tears. I hurriedly brushed them away. I had cried enough in the last weeks.

Eliza turned me towards her and held my gaze as she said, "Sahle, none of what happened was your fault. Do you hear me?"

I blinked but could not nod. It would be a lie to nod. "If I had not been so adamant that I did not have magic, Finn would still be alive. And maybe, if I had mastered my magic early on, I could have even prevented the attack on Ukuwela."

"Stop it, Sahl," Eliza bit out. "You cannot change what happened. You could not have changed it then had you had your magic. What is fated in this world will always come to pass."

I rolled my eyes. The petulance felt good, anything to push the melancholy away. "You sound like the Masters in the Yesonto."

"If I do, it's because the Masters are wise. You should try listening to them."

"You know I don't know if I believe any of that—the God and gods ideology," I muttered. I glanced back to where I knew the

Yesonto stood beyond the trees, all white plaster and windows aglow with eternal flame.

"I know, but whether you believe it or not, believe what I told you. What has come was always meant to. Not even you could change it."

I nodded then because I did believe in something like that. At least I used to. I had always felt an overwhelming sense that fate or God or the universe—whatever name people interchangeably applied to it—put things in motion for a reason. I had just never applied that belief here in the Alterealm, or in any context of the God and gods of Izwe.

"Fine," I said eventually. It was as good a word as any to tell Eliza that I would think about it.

She seemed to accept that single syllable. She took my hand again and began walking along the perimeter wall. "Good. I know you only just left your chambers yesterday for Council and now for this walk but think about getting back into your training. Go for a run. Take one of the zebras for a ride. Visit Ruth in the library and take up your studies. All of that would be a good first step in starting again, after everything."

"And Council?" I asked.

"You should try to be more involved, Sahl. Especially now that you've proved to the Lords how powerful you really are, they will want you there to voice your thoughts and weigh in on decisions. It doesn't need to start today, but you should start going regularly."

As much as it rankled that this newfound power somehow earned me more respect, I knew Eliza was right. "Sure," I murmured.

"I'll host a tea soon, as well," Eliza added, more to herself than to me.

I groaned. "Please, no."

But Eliza just laughed. "Seriously, Sahl, you would think that teas were a form of torture. They aren't so bad. It's just you and a few Ladies discussing court gossip."

"Fine," I repeated. There was no fighting Eliza on it. I knew she would get me there whether I wanted to go or not.

"Good, good," she said, patting the back of my gloved hand. "Keep moving forward, Sahle. It's the only thing to do now."

I nodded again, as much to myself as to Eliza. She was right, of course, as mothers tended to be. The only way to get past Finn, the attack, everything was to keep moving, keep training, keep learning, keep fighting. Muddled as the past weeks had been, I had the utmost clarity about that. If I did not fight, more would die.

And soon, that *more* would also include me.

I took Eliza's words to heart.

Although I avoided the crowds of courtiers who amassed each evening at dinner, instead taking meals in my room as I had grown accustomed to lately, I did venture out more frequently.

I told myself it was baby steps. Go stroll through the gardens one day, attend morning prayers in the Yesonto another. Ask Lisideria, my old etiquette tutor, to lunch one afternoon, sit in on a Council Meeting the next.

Each moment out of the safety of my room challenged me. I forced my expression into the shape of queenly composure, the angles and planes of my face setting in what I imagined was a wooden mask. I pulled that mask on whenever I came across a courtier on the garden path, as I sat on the dais before the Lords, as I listened to Lisideria prattle on about the weight of nobility in the Alterealm.

And every time I schooled my emotions behind that front, it became a little easier. Oh, the emotions never faded. They refused to. The nerves and anxiety, the overwhelming guilt and quiet sorrow—those were constant companions.

I only learned to hide them more effectively while I was out in the world.

No matter how good my mask was, it did not make the experience any less fraught. Ghosts appeared in places I expected, and those I did not.

One ghost in particular.

The memory of Finn seemed to flash before my mind's eye at every turn. And each time, I worked to push past the guilt that cloaked him like a shroud. Instead, I let him guide me. I let his faith in me embolden me.

As I sat at a wicker table in the leaf-lined solarium with Lisideria, Finn's face popped into my mind. His belief that I was more suited to rule than I realized shot through my mind. And I let this long-gone encouragement move through me as I told Lisideria that I would no longer keep regular lunch appointments with her.

I appreciated Lisideria's instruction and her experience, especially after being raised as Grimly's daughter and navigating the court since infancy. She had been important in my learning the veritable ropes of the Alterealm's culture during my first year here. But now, I knew all I needed to know. I trusted Finn when he had told me I was capable, and I found myself thinking of him as I thanked Lisideria and told her I would reach out should I ever need her again.

The library was its own sort of horror. Something about the quiet and the dim light startled me. I had thought it would have the opposite effect, after the roaring of light and magic and monsters.

But in the quiet of the library, the monster's voice seemed to laugh louder in my memory. The crash of glass breaking and walls blowing out was not dulled by the constant chatter of gossiping courtiers. The silence heightened the memories so much so that I had come to my usual spot at the low table in the belly of the library, only to hurry back out in horror, my breath panting from the memory of blood and power and danger.

And then there was the training ground. With its brown, thatch-roofed *rondavels*, the red dirt training circle, the jacarandas ringing it all, there were far too many memories here—both good and bad.

Finn had been alive here. *I* had been alive here, in this place where I had faced so many inner demons and found a true friend. He had also died here, or a version of here, just as a part of me had died.

My return to the training ground was one I had been dreading, but one morning I awoke and knew it was time. I marched through the palace, down the stone steps that wound to the Vikela's training ground. I ignored the passing, surprised, awed faces of soldiers around me.

And when I stepped into the training circle, kicking up red dust with each movement, I forced my face into that wooden mask. Tears burned in the back of my eyes, and I felt my knees loosen, wanting to buckle. But I held the emotions back. By sheer force of will, by the memory of Finn's laughter and lectures and spinning sword in this space, I beat my reaction back.

I took a deep breath. I made myself see the red dirt for what it was—dirt. The *rondavels* were just *rondavels*. The bench where we had once sat and talked of sun ribbons was just a bench.

Finn was gone, a part of me with it, and I owed it to him to soldier on. He would expect no less.

I was not sure how long I stood in the center of the training circle. A fierce sun beat down on me from the sapphire of the Izweian sky. At some point, I began to feel the gray of my gown heat as the dark color absorbed the rays. The smell of roasting meat and laundered clothes wafted in the breeze. And my ears attuned to the sounds of whispered words behind me. I realized I was not alone and, willing my face to remain still, I turned towards the people.

A small crowd of Vikela stood outside of the ring, almost as if they were afraid to step within the bounds while I stood at its center. They bowed on instinct, dropping low and reverentially.

I instantly said, "Rise." I did not want to see this group of men bow. It cut something in me, something I did not want to explore.

But when the men rose, when the weight of their gazes landed on me, I panicked. They waited, as if I came here for a purpose.

Had I? I could not remember suddenly. And so I said the first thing that popped into my mind. "I need a new trainer."

The soldiers looked between themselves, the brown linen of their uniforms pulling over honed muscle. Any of them could train me yet none of them stepped forward.

They looked back at me. They waited.

Directly across the ring stood a young Vikela. I had seen him interact with Finn before. I remembered Finn saying he was something of a prodigy with a sword, skilled beyond his years and mature to boot.

Caleb. That was his name.

With his dark hair and rounded face, this soldier seemed earnest in a way that I found *safe*. He was not all lean muscle and blonde hair and straight talk as Finn had been. I did not know how I would handle training if it were with someone who resembled him. And in noting the difference, a certain sort of relief flowed through me.

"It's Caleb, isn't it?" I called out.

His surprised eyes shot to mine, then back to the ground he had been so studiously watching before. "Yes, Your Majesty."

"Commander Finn spoke highly of you. I'd like you to be my new trainer."

Caleb's throat bobbed but he did not say anything.

I smiled at that. I was not sure why. "Would you accept?"

That seemed to surprise him for his eyes whipped back up to mine. "If Your Majesty requests it."

"She does," I replied simply. "I will not need all of your time, but I will send word when I would like to train."

"Yes, Your Majesty," he said.

I looked at him a moment more. I looked at the men surrounding him, questions painted across their faces. And then I said to Caleb, to all of them. "Thank you."

THERE WAS SOMETHING ABOUT THE QUALITY OF THE AIR this morning in the Yesonto that soothed me.

It had been just over a week since that walk with Eliza and perhaps my second or third morning back in the hallowed circle of candles. Whether or not I believed in Izwe's God and gods, I still found solace in the church-like structure and atmosphere of the Yesonto. And so I rose from my bed before dawn, dressed in a simple gray gown, and tiptoed through the quiet palace and even quieter garden paths to the sanctuary.

As usual, there was no official program. No priest stood before congregants and espoused the word. Rather, the Master and those courtiers who felt compelled gathered somberly and quietly. They took their bare wooden seats amongst the candles. They bowed their heads and prayed.

I may have been unsure to whom I prayed, but that did not mean I did not use the time in contemplation. Some mornings I thought. Some mornings I hoped. Some mornings I begged. Today, I asked God, the gods, the universe for guidance.

So much had happened in the last weeks and the overwhelming emotion that rose to the surface of the complicated mire of my thoughts was fear. I was afraid of the bright, blinding light of the Great Hall explosion. I was afraid of the purple sky that haunted my nightmares. I was afraid of the voice that goaded me, and the too-wide mouth that voice slipped out of.

I was afraid of death, and the finality of that place for Finn. And I was afraid of myself.

I had been so convinced I had no power. No matter how many times I tried, I could not feel the ribbons of the sun when Finn asked me to pull them. I could not heat the cup of water clasped in my hand in the Vikela's mess hall.

Yet somehow, I had been able to burn each and every creature that surrounded us that night. And I had had enough specificity with my power that Finn had not been among the carnage.

A different kind of carnage had claimed him.

I wondered if another queen would have been proud of herself. If the Lords and all the books were right, power of this magnitude had not been seen in Izwe since Manelesi himself. Perhaps another monarch would feel vindicated, joyous, ready to seize the world—or rather, crush it with the sheer capability and unfettered power within them.

But not me. I did not feel pride or confidence or invincibility. All I felt was the icy, slick fingers of fear. I was afraid of what else I could do and what it all meant for my reign.

I bowed my head further, and I prayed for guidance. The Lords had said they would seek out another teacher for me, one who may have some idea of how to harness the unfettered power that swirled in my veins.

I shook my head gently, eyes closed. I prayed that teacher was out there, even as logic told me that if power like mine had not been seen in generations then no one would have the knowledge to share with me.

The sun broke over the ledge of the window sills in the Yesonto and shone in angles through the wide room. I felt the rays on my cheeks and slowly, gently, blinked my eyes open. Those around me did the same.

When the sun entered the room, the liminal space between daybreak and morning passed. The time for prayer had ended. The day had begun.

Quietly, each courtier and Master rose to their feet. A few who made eye contact with me bowed; I nodded in acknowledgement.

I made my way towards the exit, but a voice halted me.

"Your Majesty, a blessed morning," a Master said. Bare-foot and clad in red and cream robes, the lead Master stood before me.

"Master Edgar. And a blessed morning to you."

He bowed his head. "We have enjoyed having you back in the Yesonto these last days. After your ordeal, we were unsure how long before you resumed your usual routine."

"I felt it was time," I replied tightly.

"Of course, Majesty," Edgar replied with a slight smile, one that said all too well that he knew I did not want to discuss this. "If you have a few moments, there is something I would like to speak with you about."

"Certainly," I said. I expected Edgar to lead us back to the circle of chairs before the ever-burning flames. Surprisingly, he motioned towards the Yesonto's door. I followed.

We stepped out into the garden and kept walking. The further we moved down paths lined with vining jasmine and studded with pink protea flowers, the quieter it grew. When no courtiers or Masters were in sight, Edgar finally turned to me.

"I thought this was a conversation best had without an audience," he explained as he motioned to the empty garden paths around us.

I nodded, even as I crossed my arms before my chest. The bite of morning's chill hung in the air. "What exactly did you want to discuss?"

"A few days ago, the five members of your Senior Council approached me for advice on finding a new magical teacher for you. I understand Commander Finn had been training you but given the circumstances…"

"Given his death, you mean," I replied before I could help myself.

Edgar bowed his head. "Yes, Your Majesty. And my deepest sympathies about his passing."

I bit the inside of my lip. "Thank you."

"Given the Commander's passing, you are without tutelage in a time where it is evident you need tutelage and a great deal of it.

"The Council told me privately—though I feel it necessary to share with you—that they are struggling to find a teacher suitable to instruct a wielder such as yourself. It is why they approached me about something unorthodox."

That caught my attention. "Unorthodox how?"

Master Edgar glanced around him once more. Seeing that we were still alone, save for the Vikela trailing behind, he explained, "The Council, or the Senior Council at least, consider whether channeling God may not be the best option."

"I'm sorry, what?" I breathed. Channeling God? To channel anyone or anything was a huge question mark in my mind. But God? They could not really mean—

"Manelesi," Master Edgar broke through my questioning thoughts.

I stared back at him for a moment before finding my words. "I'm sorry. Let me see if I have this right: You would contact my ancestor, Manelesi, in order for him to teach me how to control my powers. And you'd do this through something called channeling?"

Master Edgar nodded simply, as if this was the most commonplace of occurrences. "Yes, Majesty. It is a controversial and rarely-performed rite, but it is possible. It would require many Masters to lend their strength in a ceremony, calling down the essence of Manelesi and capturing that essence within a corporeal form for a time."

"A corporeal form?" I echoed. "You mean a body, a person?"

"Yes, Majesty," Edgar confirmed again. "As a vessel of magic and the gods and God, one of the Masters would willingly offer themselves up for this."

My mind spun. I knew a good bit about magic in the Alterealm. I understood the difference between elemental and non-elemental magic and their wielders. I had read about how the ability moved through blood lines. I even knew a good deal about the Masters' ability to draw upon a sort of borrowed magic for ceremonial purposes, though they were not wielders themselves.

Never in a million years would I have guessed at being able to call forth Manelesi—*the* Manelesi—and have him trapped within a Master's body. And especially not to be my teacher.

Speechless, I stared back at Master Edgar.

"I understand that this sounds a bit odd, but after some contemplation, I tend to agree with the Senior Council that it may be our best and only option for teaching a wielder as powerful as you. None living will be able to understand or instruct on a power like yours. But your ancestor, whom you have received this gift from, would be able to. With that in mind, Majesty, I approach you now to ask for your blessing upon this."

I started. "My blessing?"

Edgar inclined his head once more. "Yes, Majesty. As you may know, to channel the dead is forbidden in Izwe. Once a corporal form dies, the soul moves on to the afterlife and this afterlife is sacred. It is forbidden to contact the soul, much less to draw it back to the living plane through channeling.

"Such an act is punishable by death under Izweian law. To undertake this act, then, would need to be done with your express request, blessing and, I would humbly ask, pardon for the Masters who participate."

"An exception would need to be made," I murmured through numb lips

"Yes, Your Majesty."

"And afterward?" I asked, trying to wrap my head around the strangeness of being able to talk to the dead, much less bring them back in a human form. "What happens to the person's body being used? What happens to the soul that is brought forth?"

"The particulars are not relevant, Your Majesty," Edgar replied with a little wave of his hand, as if to bat away a pesky gnat.

But I wanted the details. I wanted to know the full weight of the decision I made. "They are relevant to me, Master Edgar."

"Very well," he replied with the slightest sigh, barely a whisper in the morning air around us. "The soul of the vessel remains within the body but in a state of hibernation while the channeled soul makes use of the body. When the channeled soul returns to the afterlife, the vessel's soul would take residence once more."

"No one would be harmed then?" I asked.

"No, Your Majesty. From my research, some vessels report feeling out of place in their bodies for a time after the channeled soul departs. But that passes and the vessel's soul goes on normally."

"From your research," I repeated slowly, skeptically.

"Being a banned rite, none that I know of have seen this performed. We would have to follow the accounts and instructions found in literature."

I rubbed my chin, casting my gaze along the empty garden paths as I thought. "So really, no one is supposed to be harmed but it's possible since this would be a new rite for everyone present."

"There is an element of risk," Edgar agreed. "But I would urge you to consider, Your Majesty, as this appears to be your only option. Were you another person, perhaps you could consider the risk and decide you do not want to undertake the rite for fear of how it would affect the vessel. But—and I hope you will forgive the impertinence of me saying this, Majesty—your need to harness your power is all important. It is worth risking one life, five lives, perhaps even half the lives within your kingdom if it would preserve the other half.

"There is a moral imperative, in my view, for you to have whatever you need to control and wield your power. Your servants, and especially your Masters, understand that and would do anything necessary to see you succeed. That includes risking their own souls."

My eyes tracked Master Edgar's face. I wondered how old this man was, lined as the pale skin at the corners of his eyes was. I considered his words.

They may be impertinent but there was a brutal, honest truth in them. A nation relied on me. And if I were to be the strongest Queen possible, I needed to understand how to control this awesome power I seemingly held. I did not want to harm another person in that pursuit—not after Finn, not after everything— but I also knew how many lives would be at risk if I did not.

I closed my eyes at the horrid, utilitarian idea of risking one life to save more lives. And when I opened them again, I nodded resolutely at Master Edgar.

There was only one choice here, really.

"I'll do it," I decided. "I'll bless this rite. Do you need me to approach the Senior Council with the request?"

Edgar replied solemnly. "Yes, Your Majesty. That would be best. From there, the Senior Council and I can determine the appropriate vessel and timing for the rite."

"Fine, Master Edgar. I'll see that it's done."

Master Edgar bowed low, his cream and red robes brushing through the dust of the garden path as he stooped. "Thank you, Majesty. It is for the best."

I took a deep breath. "I certainly hope so."

I found Grimly later that day, as the sun sank towards the horizon and the courtiers gathered together for the nightly festivities in the Great Hall. He was easy to spot as the Lords and Ladies of my court habitually flocked to him. It made sense. The Chief Advisor was the second most powerful person in Izwe, after myself, of course.

All eyes turned my way as I entered the wide, ornate room. It had been weeks since I joined the Court for dinner and I took in the state of the space, knowing the repairs that had been ongoing since the blast.

The windowed doors to the balcony had been replaced, the stone surrounding the tall fireplace rebuilt. Panels of wood that shined a touch more brightly with polish than their neighbors pointed to where parts of a wall had been reconstructed.

I was relieved to see the state of the room. I was less relieved to see the crowd of courtiers staring back at me. Their bubbling conversations trailed off as they took me in. In a single sweeping move, knees bent and heads dipped as their colorfully clad bodies bowed. The room paused, then a moment later, the festivities resumed. The laughter of the courtiers spiked and chattered like background noise, mingling with the clinking notes of the marimba.

And I was entirely forgotten.

I loved this moment just after all acknowledgement of my presence ended. For one brief second, I almost felt like a normal person and not a queen.

Almost.

I made a beeline towards Grimly, nodding at a few courtiers who caught my eye as I walked past. When I approached his group, Grimly turned to me with a smile.

"Your Majesty, a lovely evening," he said in greeting.

I nodded at him, at the curious eyes circled about him. It was not every day that I willingly approached the milling groups of Lords and Ladies, much less members of the Council while in the Great Hall. "Yes, it is. Lord Grimly, I have a matter to discuss with you."

Grimly's eyes widened just slightly. But then his face smoothed into a neutral calm. "Certainly, Queen Sahle."

I turned on my heel and began making my way towards the head table. I had considered the balcony for this conversation but the head table was as good a place as any—quiet as it was and private with only myself and members of the Senior Council permitted to approach.

Grimly pulled out my seat for me and, once I was situated, he dropped into the chair to my right.

I angled myself towards his questioning face. "I had an interesting conversation with Master Edgar after Yesonto this morning."

Like a puzzle piece clicking into place, recollection shone in his eyes. He pitched his voice low so that I alone would hear him ask, "About channeling Manelesi, I take it?"

"Yes," I said just as quietly. "I did not know something like that was even possible but Master Edgar assured me it was. Although he did say that it would require a special request and blessing."

"And pardon," Grimly added.

"That's right. Pardon, too." I paused then, wondering. "Is all of that really necessary?"

"Oh yes, Your Majesty," Grimly replied solemnly. "It is taboo to interfere with the dead. Only an express request, blessing, and pardon from you—all three officially documented, of course— make the rite permissible."

I nodded, realizing anew the seriousness of what we were considering. "If it is so taboo, is it really the best course of action? Surely there is *someone* who could teach me."

But Grimly shook his gray head. "Unfortunately not, Majesty. The Council has searched high and low this past week. We've contemplated every scenario. No one within Izwe's border has the skill necessary to instruct you. This is our only option."

I bit my lip as I let that sink in. Between the risk to the Master who volunteered his body, as well as the general seriousness— crime almost—in the act, I was hoping there would be an alternative. Yet it seemed none were to be found.

"Majesty," Grimly called. He glanced around us furtively once more. "Every member of the Senior Council has agreed, though we have not taken it to the broader Council. It may be too delicate of an item for that. But we would like your say before we proceed any further."

I could feel the tension pulsing off him, the nearly perceptible aura that spoke of how dangerous and forbidden and *wrong* this was. But I believed him and Master Edgar when they said it was the only path forward. Even after a year here, I could only know so much. I had to rely on those around me to lead me down the right path.

"Alright," I whispered cautiously. Servants carrying trays of steaming food approached, and so I hurried my words. "I agree to this. You said my consent needs to be documented. How do we do that?"

Grimly waited as a brown-clad servant laid a gravy boat filled with some sort of spiced sauce before us. When the man turned away, Grimly replied, "I'll have the documents brought up. There will be three individual pieces for you to read and sign— one for the request, one for the blessing, and one to pardon all those who take part in the rite."

I nodded. "How soon would this all happen?"

Grimly's eyes tracked the rest of the Senior Council as they detached themselves from the courtiers and made their way to their seats at the head table. "I'll discuss it with the rest, but I would imagine we could have the documents to you by tomorrow. The rite would take place on the next full moon."

"That's in two or three days," I replied automatically. I had gotten used to watching the moon. It was as good a pass time as any during my sleepless, guilt-ridden nights.

If Grimly was surprised at my astronomical knowledge, he did not show it. He nodded to Lord Anson and Lord Marcus as they took their seats further down the head table. "Then that is when it will occur. We do not have another month to wait."

I nodded, smiling slightly at a servant who poured *konstans* into my glass. The orange liquid glittered in the candlelight. "So be it."

My smile felt forced. There was nothing nice or good about what we were about to do. The seriousness of our task settled over my shoulders like a mantle as I looked at a green soup steaming before me. I took a bite and did not taste it.

All I could see and taste and smell and think about was fear—fear for who I would get killed next in this high stakes game of ruling.

4

the great one

I RACED PAST LINES OF TALL, PURPLE-FLOWERED jacarandas like the mounted Vikela at my back were chasing me. My breath sawed in and out of my chest. The muscles of my thighs screamed and trembled with the task of holding my legs steady in the saddle.

But through the quaking muscles, the tight grip around the rough weave of my reins, the attuned nature of *feeling* the zebra under me, a sort of relief began stealing through my veins.

That was why I had climbed onto this animal after all.

I did not *dislike* Izwe's overly-tall zebras. I had learned to ride one soon after arriving in the Alterealm. They were sweet enough animals with mild temperaments and beautifully striped coats. But at the same time, I had never been a horse girl in the Humanrealm. I had never had little toy ponies or pretended to be a princess galloping off into the sunset. It just was not me.

No, enjoyment was not why I found myself on zebraback today.

After the conversation at dinner, a new sort of fear had stolen hours of sleep from me. When I finally fell into an exhausted, fitful rest, it was close to dawn. My mind immediately began to race. My fingers twitched. My legs ached to be stretched and challenged. And so I had asked Kaiht and Mara to help me into a dark riding habit before I hurried to the stables that were housed near the training grounds.

Now, I sat astride my zebra and met each of its furious, thrusting gallops with a complementary pitching of my body. I let myself move with the animal, back and forth, back and forth. I let my lungs expand to take in the warmth of the midday air. Strands of my hair whipped about, stinging across my cheeks.

Behind me, a small contingent of Vikela followed suit. But it was my zebra that led, racing up the winding red dirt path that took us to the farthest reaches of the palace grounds.

As the earth sloped upward, I slowed my zebra into a trot. I leaned towards its mane as the animal pitched its body forward. My hands tightened on the reins, readjusting my grip as we made it to the top of the small hill.

Then I looked out before me.

Silver trees and jacarandas covered the outskirts of the palace grounds in haphazard placements. The palace gardens broke the vast wilderness with its manicured, planned lines and colorful blooms of proteas and jasmine and strelitzia. The training grounds and the Yesonto stood on far ends, and at the center of it all was the palace of Izwe.

The white plaster and dark wood accents rose out of the greens of the brush, the red of the earth. It stood apart from the sapphire sky. It dwarfed the ever-glowing windows of the Yesonto.

I sighed looking at the palace. I had lived under its high thatch roof for over a year, and while I knew the layout, how to move from room to room, it still did not feel comfortable and happy as a home should feel. I wondered if it ever would.

I had thought it was slowly becoming a sort of home. I could remember considering it as I dressed for my birthday party mere weeks ago.

But, back then, I had friends, a man who cared for me, a naïve idea that I could avoid my responsibilities. I did not have power—that I knew of, at least.

This was now, where Finn's last words clanged guiltily in my ears, where my make-believe idea that I was any other woman had been blown apart by the blinding evidence of my magic. This was now, when fear and guilt and desperate need coalesced in my veins. It coalesced in that palace.

My throat constricted at the swell of emotions and I cleared it roughly. I took a deep breath.

"Your Majesty?" the closest Vikela asked.

But I shook my head. I turned my gaze to look past the palace walls at the brown plaster rondavels of the city, at the faint lines of smoke rising from hearth fires.

Nothing was wrong. Everything was wrong. As Queen, I was the only one who could right it.

And soon I would have the tools. I would have a teacher to help me understand my power. My power would help me protect this place. It would help me establish stability in a land that had been without for years.

I thought back to Grimly's words, his statement that the channeling of *God* would happen on the full moon. Above my head, a shadowy outline of the celestial body hung pregnant in the blue sky like it would mock me, like it would taunt and say, "See me, even in daylight. See me, even when the sky is bright."

I blinked at it. "I see you," I whispered to the hidden craters, the faintest of dark crescent at its edge. "I'm ready."

If my Vikela heard my breath of words, if they watched me speak to the moon above us, they did not comment. No, they merely followed behind as I took one more glance at the city beyond the palace walls and then turned my zebra back towards the palace.

A knock at my door sounded around three o'clock in the morning. I was sitting before the fireplace in my room, watching the wood sizzle and pop in bright little sparks of shimmering orange. Mara sat in the chair opposite me, sewing some sort of decorative border on a red handkerchief. Kaiht sat, legs curled under her, on the rug between our chairs.

Both women looked at me the moment the knock echoed through the darkened room.

"Shall I answer it, Your Majesty?" Mara asked, setting her sewing aside.

I nodded.

I knew who it was. I had signed the channeling orders mere days ago. The moon hung full in the sky. And this evening Grimly had leaned towards me over a plate of wild boar, whispering, "The channeling will take place tonight." Still, a shot of adrenaline coursed through my veins at the secretive, shadowy nature of this rendezvous.

I rose from my chair, smoothing my gray skirt with slick palms. Mara pulled open the door with a brief curtsy to the two men standing in the doorway. Then all eyes turned to me.

"Your Majesty," Grimly called with a bow. Beside him, Anson mirrored the gesture.

"Is everything ready?" I asked as Kaiht set a black cloak about my shoulders. I secured it with a small silver clasp at my neck.

"It is, Your Majesty," Anson replied. He extended his own cloaked arm, a gesture that we should be on our way, and it was then that I realized both men were dressed in black.

That was nothing new for Anson. I had noticed early on that he never wore the brightly colored *chitenge* cloth of the other courtiers. He favored dark blues, dark grays, dark greens. The less pattern the better.

Yet Grimly was usually dressed as festively and loudly as any Lord and Lady in my Court. It was a shock seeing him so soberly clothed.

I padded on leather-booted feet towards the door. "You're both in black. You never wear black."

Anson raised one brow, but it was Grimly who spoke. "This is not an occasion to draw attention."

I looked between the two men as Kaiht lifted the hood of my cloak for me. I had removed my crown some hours ago and the wool sat low over my forehead.

"It would appear so," I murmured as I followed the men out. But two steps later, I turned my head again. It was not a noise that caught my attention but rather a *lack* of noise. No footsteps echoed behind me. Not a single Vikela followed us.

I turned back to Grimly and Anson where they had paused further down the corridor. "Why aren't the guards coming?"

"Your Majesty, the less witnesses to this rite, the better," Anson replied. His face was uncharacteristically serious. No mirth shone from those sharp eyes tonight.

I swallowed, the anxiety pulsing through me once more. On tentative feet, I neared the two men. "Is it really so dangerous?"

Anson glanced at Grimly before replying. "It's dangerous and ill-advised and taboo, Your Majesty. I will not sugarcoat it."

I reached out then, grasping Grimly's forearm. "And yet we need to do it?" I asked.

My mind raced. I knew this was dangerous. Both Grimly and Master Edgar had both urged and cautioned me towards this moment. But being told and experiencing the reality of it were two different things. I could feel the tension in the air, the fear, the need to be as secretive about this as we could be.

Even with the request, blessing, and pardon I had signed days ago, this was a grave thing we were doing.

"We need to do it," Anson continued over my shoulder. I dropped Grimly's arm as I turned to him. He met my gaze head on. "There is no other option, Your Majesty."

I blinked at that—not at his words but at the tone of his voice and the expression on his cruel face. He looked resigned, sure, but more than that, he looked concerned. Perhaps concerned that this was too big of a risk, but for who?

Certainly not me.

"We'll be late, if we do not hurry," Grimly breathed, glancing down the dark corridor before us.

I peeled my eyes away from Anson as I nodded. "OK. Let's go."

We wound our way through the still halls. This time of the night was unique in the palace. It was the dark and quiet of deep night, when even the bubbliest of revelers had tucked themselves into their beds.

The halls seemed unfamiliar at this hour, like a different world entirely cast in muted grays and blacks, cloaked in shadows and rays of moonlight that filtered through the windows. We did not dare light a candle. Even with hoods drawn, that could give away our identities.

At one of the doors that led outside to the gardens, two guards stood watch. I dipped my head lower, hoping to remain obscured, as Grimly murmured something. The guards pulled the door open and the three of us slipped outside silently.

It might have been my imagination but I could have sworn all three of us exhaled a collective sigh of relief on making it out of the palace. We were much less likely to be seen in the gardens at a normal time of day, let alone now. We allowed our steps to make more noise, rustling as they did on the alternately red dirt and gravel paths.

I followed just behind Grimly and Anson. I had agreed to this plan. I had signed all of their documents, but I had not asked particulars. Now, I wished I had. The lack of knowledge about where exactly we were going and precisely how this rite would occur gnawed at me. I took a deep breath to steady myself.

Soon I began to recognize the route. Even bathed in moonlight as it was, I knew this path. It was the one I took to the Yesonto each morning. A handful more steps and the roofline of the sanctuary rose before us. Its white plaster walls and curved windows showed the orange glow of eternal flame within.

Yet when we reached the Yesonto, we did not enter the sanctuary's main door. Rather, we wrapped our way around the side until we came to the back. I had never noticed a separate structure there before, not in all of my times walking this garden, running the grounds with Finn, or coming to the sanctuary for morning reflections. But here it was, decidedly humble in stature. It must have been painted gray or some muted brown for it did not reflect the moonlight as the Yesonto did. And strangely enough, it seemed to have no roof.

I peered up at the line where roof traditionally met wall and could see nothing. I felt my hood begin to slide back on my head, but then it stopped.

"Careful," Anson whispered from my right. He tugged the wool forward into place again. "We wouldn't want you to be seen."

If it were anyone else, I would say thank you. I would feel grateful for his watchful eyes. But his tone irritated me. It always irritated me, smug as it was. Even now, with the tension in the air, the promise of forbidden things, those words held a needling edge.

I leaned away from his touch and turned to where Grimly stood before the building's door. He knocked three times, paused, and then knocked once more.

And then the door opened.

I could see nothing past that door. In fact, it looked as dark inside as it was outside. A shiver ran through me as Grimly motioned me forward. With a hesitant glance back at both men, I stepped across the threshold.

I instantly knew why the inside had seemed the same as the outside. I looked up once again at where the roof should be. But there was no roof. I did not bother to hold my hood on this time as the wool slid back, not as the door behind me snicked shut, nor as Grimly and Anson removed their own hoods.

There was not a single cloud in the night sky. In the light of the full moon and glittering stars that fell through the open ceiling, I could make out shadowy figures lining the walls. My breathing hitched. I had not seen them before but of course someone, many someones, would be in here. The door had opened inward at the knock.

I willed myself to breathe in and out.

This was fine. Everything was fine. I had asked for this, had I not?

My eyes blinked at a sudden flare of light. Three candles were lit and a golden glow drifted through the strange space.

"Good morning, Queen Sahle," a man said. It was Master Edgar. I could see his face clearly, stark shadows cast over the angles as he held the candle at chest-level. Like the others around me, he was dressed in dark colors. It, too, seemed out of place on him, accustomed as I was to seeing his red and cream Masters' robes.

"Good…morning," I replied. I did not know whether *morning* was the correct term in the case of mid-night, but now was not the time to remark on such fine points.

Other more important, more perilous things were about to occur.

"Thank you for joining us," Edgar continued. The shadows from the walls shifted, drawing in. I could make out the faces of other Masters from the Yesonto as they neared the candles' glow.

It was quiet then and I had the sense that the men were waiting for me to lead. I cleared my throat hesitantly, the sound loud in the otherwise silent space. "Thank you for arranging this."

I heard someone scoff quietly from behind me.

My cheeks burned in embarrassment but I forced myself to banish the thought. Now was not the time to let Anson get under my skin.

Edgar bowed. "We are loyal servants of the crown, Your Majesty. Anything for our Queen."

"Thank you," I repeated.

"If you are ready, I see no reason to delay."

I nodded. But then realized no one could make out that motion in the low light. "Yes."

The Masters moved as one, arranging themselves in a circle and placing the candles on the ground before them. I saw Master Edgar move to form part of the circle. Then a single Master stepped into the center. I thought of a hurricane, and he was the eye of the storm.

Edgar motioned towards the lone man. "Master Gilman has volunteered to be the vessel, Your Majesty."

I looked at the man again. I did not recognize him, though it was hard to tell in this light.

From what I could see, he was young, perhaps no older than I was. His hair was fair, perhaps strawberry blonde, and he was slight of build.

He seemed wholly too young for something this dangerous. I thought of all I had been told—about his soul lying dormant, about residual feelings of disconnect for months after the channeled soul departed.

And seeing this man, this boy, before me, all of my concerns rose to the surface once more.

I opened my mouth, but then a voice was at my ear. "Your Majesty, the man has volunteered for this," Anson said quietly.

I turned to him, trying to make out his eyes. He was near to me, closer than I had realized and our eyes met and held. The lack of light stole the green from his gaze, but I could see the intensity simmering just fine.

And hating him as I did, I do not know why I let his words placate me. Maybe I just needed someone, anyone to reassure me in this moment.

I held his gaze. I focused on the calm, steady energy that emanated from him. I begged myself, the gods, God for even an ounce of Anson's resolve.

"Fine," I whispered back at him. The word sounded harsh to my ears.

I thought about calling to Gilman, telling him thank you

before all of these gathered men. But the Masters had joined hands. They were chanting.

The rite had begun.

Just like at my coronation, the words the Masters used sounded like English, but it was not English. It was some sort of tongue once removed, a generation too distant for my ears to make sense of.

They intoned these foreign words as one, hands linked, eyes closed, heads bowed. Then they repeated a single word—one I knew all too well: Manelesi, Manelesi, Manelesi. They repeated it, growing louder and louder with each utterance.

The candle flames began to flicker. Several of the Masters' shoulders and necks seemed to shudder and twitch involuntarily.

I watched with wide, curious, dread-filled eyes as the call rose higher and higher, as it took on a keening sound closer to a wail than a call.

When I thought the pitch could rise no higher, when I was sure all in the palace would wake at the noise far out in the garden, it suddenly stopped.

The candles stilled. The Masters' limbs ceased twitching.

And then everything went black.

I gasped. Instantly, I felt a hand at my lower back. But standing between Grimly and Anson, I was unsure who reached out to me.

As quickly as the candles had guttered out, the light flickered back to life. The hand at my back dropped away.

My eyes widened, trying to take in more of the sight before me.

Gilman had been standing tall before, but the Gilman in the circle now was kneeling. One knee was planted on the ground, one hand fisted beside it. His head bowed forward.

Slowly, it rose.

My exhale was one of fear and wonder both. Even before the eyes met mine, I knew that Gilman was no longer Gilman. It was in the set of the shoulders, the arch of the neck, the haughty angle of the head.

This was Manelesi the King before me, and I suddenly balked at the unmistakable presence.

The Masters dropped their hands and melted back into the shadows. With them out of the way, I had a direct path to Manelesi. A shiver ran through me as this being's focus narrowed in on me.

"Young woman," the Gilman who was not Gilman spoke. His voice was deep like the bottomless depths of the sea floor, cracked like the harshest of desert soil. He rose to his feet in a stiff way, as if he had long since forgotten how to command corporal limbs. "You dare to disturb me."

I felt like a gazelle picked by the lion, a seal singled out by the shark. There are moments in life when your gut tells you to run, when for whatever instinctual reason, every cell in your body shouts YOU ARE NOT SAFE. I had known a few of those instances: a particular alleyway in a Humanrealm city where, as a teenager, I had turned down but abruptly backtracked out of; the backseat of a boy's car I had taken one glimpse of, and promptly untangled myself from his cloying arms. The moments were few and far between but when they struck—when my soul cried *no*—I listened.

I listened now.

But unlike the other times, I could not leave the alley or walk away from the car. I had a duty to my people and I needed this man, this being, this unfathomable *god* to help me. And so I faced him.

"Manelesi, yes. My name is Sahle, daughter of Bekha, current Queen—"

"I know who you are," he hissed. His eyes narrowed. "Do you not know that as God, I see all?"

I nodded quickly. "I do know. Of course."

"Then tell me why I am here."

A million thoughts ran through my head. If he saw all, he must have seen my discussions with Grimly. He must have known there were no other teachers. And if so, what he wanted was an admission from me that I needed him.

I glanced around subconsciously, at all of the Lords and Masters gathered. Then I took three steps towards Manelesi.

"Your Majesty," Anson said quietly, but there was warning in his voice.

"I'm fine," I replied over my shoulder. And then I crossed the final distance to Manelesi.

Standing before Gilman who was not Gilman, I looked up into Manelesi's eyes and said honestly, "I had you brought here because I need you. I have power, your power, and no one knows how to teach me to use it. Such a power scares me beyond measure—both at what I can do and what I may never do if I do not learn to use it. I have already been the cause of death and I refuse to be it again. Please, I beg you to willingly help me. You're the only one who can."

Manelesi looked at me. His eyes dropped and his gaze dragged over every inch of me as if he was weighing up whether the being before him was worth his time. I was his kin but, hundreds of years after his earthly life, I did not know whether that fact held any weight for him.

Whatever he saw in my face must have been enough. It must have told him that I was worth the trouble of existing in the land of the living.

His eyes seemed to relax and he nodded. "Fine, Daughter. I will help you." Turning his head, he then called, "Masters."

Each man dropped to their knees.

"Master Edgar," Manelesi continued. "Your spell cleverly set the period of this channeling for four months. Is that not so?"

"Yes, God," Master Edgar replied. I could hear the waver in his voice, so different from his usual, confident tone. I wondered if anyone else could hear it.

"And you did that because?"

Master Edgar bowed his head. "To ensure you return to the land of the dead."

"You mean to ensure her reign is protected," Manelesi bit out.

My eyes widened. I had no idea about this end limit, or that the Masters and Lords had apparently put in place contingency plans on my behalf. I looked at Master Edgar, curiously.

"You are clever, Master Edgar," Manelesi continued, his voice suddenly light. All traces of anger dissipated. "And you look after your Queen. I appreciate that, even if it does suppose the worst of me."

"I would never—" Master Edgar started but then stopped.

Manelesi had raised his hand and pinched two fingers together. And at that exact moment, Edgar had been cut off.

The sheer power on display startled me. I took a half step back.

Manelesi held his hand up another moment before dropping it to his side. Master Edgar took in a deep gasping breath on being released. Then Manelesi said, "I require no further words from you, Master Edgar. I am tired. It has been some time since I have existed in a body. You will show me a place where I can retire. Now."

Master Edgar hopped to his feet, bowing to Manelesi repeatedly and then to me. The other Masters followed suit. Wordlessly, Edgar motioned for Manelesi to follow him out the door.

Manelesi smiled, looking back at me as if he and I shared some sort of joke. If he thought I found his use of power and intimidation amusing, I did not.

His too-knowing eyes tracked over my face, and his grin widened. "Until tomorrow, Daughter."

Moving with stiff limbs, as if each joint was awkwardly fused, he followed the Masters.

The door shut behind him with a decided snap, and I let loose the breath I had been anxiously holding. Anson and Grimly materialized at my side once more, and I turned to look at each of them in the moonlight.

"This is good, right?" I asked them again. "We did the right thing here?"

"Certainly, Your Majesty," Grimly replied. But the answer was too reflexive, too quickly produced. The quality of the sound was too hollow.

Their minds were equally as conflicted as mine was.

By the time Grimly, Anson, and I had righted our hoods and made our way back to the palace, it was nearing four in the morning. Kaiht and Mara were asleep before the fireplace where I had left them, Mara leaned back in the wingback chair and Kaiht curled up in a blanket on the floor. For a split second, I debated waking them and asking for *rooibos* tea and a few rusks. Perhaps I should merely get going with my day.

But the soft glow from the fireplace was too comfortable, especially how it lit up the downy, white covers on my enormous bed. Dawn was still a few hours away and I had no plans to attend prayers. I had seen enough *divinity* for one day.

Balancing on one foot at a time, I pulled my leather boots off before tiptoeing towards the bed on silent feet. I shrugged off the dark cloak and gown, letting them fall in a heap. Then I crawled into the covers.

Yet, try as I might, sleep evaded me. My heart seemed to race too quickly. The blankets that had looked so soft were now too warm. The air alone was too cold. My mind buzzed with thoughts of what I had just seen.

I doubted the wisdom of our actions. I asked myself why, why, why had I agreed to such things. I railed against Grimly for suggesting it. I even mentally swore at Anson for choosing this moment to seemingly stop telling me I was doing something stupid.

I could have used those words a few days ago. I could have benefited from him explaining that I did not know the sort of power I was playing with when it came to channeling my ancestor.

Because I was certainly out of my depths.

Until I had seen Manelesi standing there before me, cloaked in the skin of another, I had not truly understood how terrifying, how all-powerful, how world-altering he and this moment would be.

It all suddenly felt wrong. I turned over, my back to the fire, and squeezed my eyes shut tighter.

What had I done?

But I knew what. I knew why. I needed Manelesi. He was the only answer to solving the mystery that was my power.

Both things terrified me—him and this intangible gift—and it seemed oddly poetic that I would have to face one in order to harness the other. The one fear was the only answer to the other fear.

I turned over again, facing the fire this time.

I thought about tomorrow or, rather, the hours after dawn broke. Manelesi had said he would see me then and I would go. I had to.

I did not know how far his powers could extend. I did not know what he could do if I displeased him, and I had no desire to find out.

I would go to him, and I would begin this absurd training with this absurd teacher.

I had no other choice.

Despite my best efforts to sleep, I pulled myself from bed at dawn, restless and anxious. I woke Kaiht and Mara, dressed, and headed back to the Yesonto on swift feet.

The morning prayers were concluding when I arrived, and I waited at the back of the sanctuary for Master Edgar to notice me.

Of course, I was hard to miss, what with everyone bowing and scraping the moment they laid eyes on me.

"Good morning, Majesty," Master Edgar said as he broke out of the circle of candles. His eyes looked as weary as my soul, and I knew instantly he had slept as little as I had after our experience just hours earlier.

"Morning, Master Edgar," I replied. I glanced around to make sure no one else was near. "I've come to see our…new friend."

Edgar's eyes flicked to a door along the far wall, one I had never passed through. "I have not seen our God since we took him to a room to rest. I can lead you there, if you would like to speak with him."

Edgar's last words were pitched somewhere between a statement and a question, and I could read how little he truly wanted to face Manelesi again—even if he did want to be of service to his Queen.

"No need to take me there. If you just tell me where to go, I am certain I can find my way."

Edgar nodded, the relief evident in his eyes. "Through there," he said, pointing to the door I had noticed moments before. "There are stairs that lead up to the living quarters of the Masters. If you take them all the way to the top floor, there is a single door. That is where our God rests."

"Thank you," I answered. I signaled to the two Vikela who had followed me from the palace and now lingered silently near the building's entrance. "I'll see you later, Master Edgar."

I made to walk away but Master Edgar's voice called quietly. "Your Majesty…"

I turned back to him.

The Master's gaze flitted here and there—anywhere but directly to me. And then he bit out curtly, as if the words themselves pained him to utter, "Please be careful, Your Majesty."

My brows rose. "Is this not the God you pray to, Master Edger? Do you not trust him?"

I did not know why I asked those questions. Of course Manelesi was his God. Manelesi and service to Manelesi and the crown were what this man had molded his life around. Yet I needed to know why his voice again wavered, why he seemed afraid when he should be joyous to see God in the flesh.

I knew why I was afraid, but I was curious why Edgar was.

Edgar suddenly bowed, bending at the waist abruptly. Then he rose and his eyes glistened fervently. "Oh yes, Majesty. It is truly our God. I trust him with everything, but I would be a fool to not balk in the face of such power, to not quiver in the presence of a supreme being.

"You are his kin, and his representative in the land of the living. You are our Queen. But as much as we would like to know what God thinks and what he believes, we do not. How can any of us understand the inner workings of omnipotent beings? It is for that reason I ask you to be cautious."

"Are you saying I'm in danger, Master Edgar?" I asked, my voice pitched low in the echoing room.

"No, I would never presume to say that God would be malevolent towards you—"

"But?" I cut in.

Master Edgar finally met my eyes. "But there is little we know about channeled, all-powerful beings. And you are the last of your line. At the risk of overstepping, I simply urge you to consider your safety at all times when with him. He is an unknown."

I nodded at Edgar, unsure of how to respond. Edgar looked at me a moment longer before bowing once more and moving back towards the center of the Yesonto and the ever-burning candles there.

I headed up the stairs, and with a single moment's hesitation more, I knocked on the lone door on the Yesonto's top floor.

I expected to hear the shuffle of feet from the other side of the door as Manelesi approached, but to my surprise, the door opened instantly and silently.

Manelesi sat in a chair far into the room. Only a hand was raised in my direction.

"Hello again, Daughter," he remarked as he lowered the hand to the chair's arm. "Enter."

Eyes wide, I looked once more between the door and him before gingerly stepping into the room. It was surprisingly bare of furnishings—not at all what I would expect for Manelesi, God, the former King, or whatever else the Masters considered him.

There was a sparse, low-profiled single bed pushed to one wall. A table on which a humble earthenware jug sat alongside a basin of some sort. The chair Manelesi sat in was plain and wooden, just like the many that filled the sanctuary space below. The only ornamentation, the only beauty in this room were the four windows carved into the white plaster wall. Through them, morning light spilled inside.

"Your guards may wait outside," Manelesi added.

I clamped my lips shut, trying to silence my immediate and instinctual protest.

But Manelesi saw it. As if he could hear every thought turning in my mind, he grinned. "You come here hesitantly. That is wise, Daughter, to approach the unknown with care."

"And yet you would tell me to leave my guards outside? Surely you understand why I would want them with me," I answered, slowly.

Still seated, Manelesi inclined his head. "I do, but I promise you they are not needed. I assure you I will not harm you. You are of my blood. You rule in my place here. Your guards protect against enemies, of which I am not."

"Do you swear that?" I asked quickly.

Perhaps it was too impertinent, too presumptuous for he blinked with the slightest amount of incredulity. But then he stood from his chair, placing one hand over his heart. "I swear it, my daughter. No harm will befall you by my hand nor by my will."

I looked at him a moment longer. Like last night, his movements were stiff, as if he were not yet comfortable with commanding a physical form. Still, he held himself tall and kingly. He had a stateliness to him that Gilman, in the moments I had seen him before he gave his body over, had not had.

"Thank you," I finally said. I motioned to my guards to stay outside, then I pulled the door closed behind me.

Manelesi watched me walk awkwardly into the room, glancing around, unsure of what to do or where to go in this sparse environment. Finally, he pointed to the bed. "Please have a seat."

Gingerly, I sat on the corner. The thick, woven blanket rustled under my fine skirt. "I apologize for the room. I'll see to it that you're relocated to a more fitting place."

Manelesi smiled. "Thank you for the thought but I am most content here."

"Really?" I asked quickly and disbelievingly. Then I bit my lip. I needed to learn some control over my mouth.

Surprisingly, Manelesi laughed—a short, barking sound. "Quite. The Masters are my servants in the land of the living. They are an extension of myself. It is natural for me to live amongst them."

"But you are—were—King. Surely I can at least get you some softer bedding?" I asked. I rubbed my hand along the scratchy blanket in illustration.

He inclined his head. "If you insist, Daughter. I thank you."

"I'll have it delivered as soon as I leave."

Silence settled around us as we took each other in. It was frightfully unfair. He could see me, all of me, both inside and out. But I could only see a glimpse of him, a shadow soul shimmering behind unnatural silver eyes.

We watched each other for a few moments, and then I cleared my throat. "If you don't mind, I thought we could jump right to it. As I said last night…er, this morning, I mean…I need your help to control my power. Perhaps we could start with some training exercises, if you're not too tired from your ordeal coming here?"

But Manelesi's eyes regarded me cooly. "I do mind, actually."

Surely I had not heard him right. "Excuse me?"

He walked the few steps back to his chair and sat. One leg lifted, pulling the Masters robes taut, and he balanced an ankle on the opposite knee. "I said I do mind. We will not begin any training today."

I bit the inside of my mouth to keep myself silent. No, I did not want to push this man, this creature. I had seen how effortlessly he had silenced Master Edgar in the roofless building. I had no desire to see that sort of treatment turned on me.

I spoke hesitantly, warily. "Alright. What do you propose then?"

Manelesi leaned back in his chair. "Let's converse. I would like to know you better."

The smile I gave him was pinched. "Surely, as an omniscient being, you know all there is about me."

He merely shrugged. "I may know you but I am interested in how you know yourself, how you consider your own actions and decisions. Mortals are so fascinating in that truth often does not align with how they see the world or their place in it."

"Are you saying we lie to ourselves?"

"No, not consciously at least. But the mortal mind is a malleable thing. To you—" he waved in my direction "—knowing and truth are only as good as opinion."

It was hard to not take that as a slight. I crossed my arms in front of my chest, even as I decided to play along. "What would you like to know, Manelesi?"

"Please. Call me Father."

I balked at him. My mouth opened and shut and opened again.

"You do not like that. Why?"

I took a breath, asking myself the same question. "I…I have a father," I replied finally.

"The man you believed was your father, or the one you never knew?"

"Both," I shrugged. "I have had two fathers. It does not feel accurate to call you that."

Manelesi regarded me thoughtfully. "Still, it seems much too complicated to call me great-great-great-great-great-great grandfather. Thus, I would have you call me Father."

I met his gaze and nodded stiffly. With Master Edgar's warning still ringing in my ears, I had no desire to upset this being. "Of course…Father."

"Anyway, where were we?" he mused to himself. "Oh, yes. You asked me what I would like to know."

I nodded again.

"I would like to know about your first twenty years, the ones you lived in the Humanrealm. What were they like?"

That question was enormous. How did one describe two decades of experiences, lessons learned, friends made and lost in just a few words. I took a breath.

"They were happy," I finally said. "Roland and Eliza—the two tasked with being my protectors in the Humanrealm—created a life for me that left nothing to be desired. There was always enough. I was always comfortable and warm and safe. I had friends. I went to school. I had crushes, boys I thought were cute. I had successes and failures. I lived a life."

"And then you were brought here," Manelesi added when I paused, lost in thought.

"Yes, and then I was brought here and I learned everything I thought I knew was a lie. The girl I thought I was—she did not exist, not really. And the Queen I was expected to be—she did not exist either. I was both and neither. It was a lonely existence."

"Is it not anymore?"

I sighed, turning to the window. I did not know how much I wanted to share, but if Manelesi really knew everything then I supposed nothing could shock him. "I found a way to not be lonely. I made friends. I had a boyfriend, I guess you'd call him. He died recently."

"Ah, yes, Commander Finn."

My head snapped back to Manelesi. "Yes."

"He was a good man. You could have done much worse for yourself."

I stared back, surprised. "I would not think you'd approve of such a relationship."

Manelesi scoffed. The sound was harsh and I forced myself not to flinch. "You are the Queen of Izwe. You can do anything you like, my daughter. That includes spending time with whichever men or women please you."

My brow raised at the liberal sentiment, but I carried on without remarking on it. "Since his death, it's been lonely again. Eliza and Roland have tried to spend as much time as they can with me. My friends—"

"Your servants, you mean," Manelesi interjected.

I held firm. "My *friends* as well as my servants. They have been around but the loneliness I feel now is altogether more. It's deeper and darker and hopeless in a way that it never was before."

"That's because it's not loneliness, not really."

I paused, struck by those words. I felt myself lean forward subconsciously. "What do you mean?"

"What you feel is not loneliness. It's fear and sadness. Yet none of it truly matters. All of those are useless emotions."

"Useless? How so?"

"They do not serve you," Manelesi said simply. He rocked back slightly on his chair once, twice. "Others, yes. But you are not them. You are powerful. You are a child of the Great One. You are above petty emotions."

"If only it were so easy," I muttered to myself.

But Manelesi heard me. Of course he did. He scoffed again. "Daughter, tell me of my kingdom."

I had no idea how he made the leap from my near-depression to wondering about Izwe. I took a breath and answered his questions once more. "It is beautiful and unique. The people are resilient. In truth, I am still learning it. I have left the palace only a handful of times in this last year. But everything I see of it is amazing."

Manelesi considered that. "Much power went into making this land what you see around you. It once looked like every other nation in the Alterealm, yet I had a vision for what it could be. I made it that, single-handedly. Thus is my power. And yours."

I focused my gaze on him. "About my power—"

"We'll save that for another day."

I opened my mouth to protest. Then shut it and shook my head slightly.

Just breathe. Just go with the flow, I told myself. I tamped down my confusion and annoyance. It would do nothing but endanger me here.

Whether he ignored my internal somersaults, or merely did not notice them, it was impossible to tell. He carried on. "And you are yet unmarried."

It was a statement, not a question. I knew he was all too aware of my relationship status. I simply nodded, hoping that would satisfy whatever curiosity he had about the subject.

But my luck was not that good.

"And why is that?" Manelesi asked, brusquely.

A million words flooded my mouth, including several curses. I did not say any of those, though. Instead, I folded my hands politely in my lap and replied, "Apparently I have not found the right match."

Manelesi watched me for a moment without speaking.

I swallowed instinctively, unnerved by the severe way he seemed to read every private thought, every past and future action from the mere expression of my face.

Then Manelesi added, "It is no matter, my daughter. You will be married soon enough."

This time, I could not master my mouth. I fairly sputtered, "I'm sorry?"

But Manelesi, damn him, just smiled. "Oh, yes. It is unsuitable for a Queen, powerful though you are, to be alone. Especially in your circumstance."

A million questions came to my mind. Did he know something? Had he seen something? Was there a man there, just around the figurative corner for me?

I opened my mouth to ask one or all of these questions, but Manelesi held up a hand. "No, Daughter. I have already said too much. I will not speak anymore of it. In fact, I will not speak anymore at present." He rose from the chair, pulling himself to his full height. "We are done for today."

I felt my lips part in the slightest of o's. My mind spun on the questions about the Humanrealm, those on Izwe, those about Finn, and finally the few words about me marrying. I could not seem to grasp how any of it was connected or why any of it mattered to Manelesi.

And I sure as hell had not received so much as a smidgen of a lesson about my power.

I shut my eyes briefly. I took a deep breath. And then I pasted that practiced, wooden smile across my face.

I rose in a fluid motion, my hands clasped before me. "Very well, Father. I will plan to return tomorrow, if that suits you."

Manelesi's eyes twinkled as he took in my too-serene face. "Certainly, Daughter. I look forward to it."

I wanted to shake my head, stomp my feet but instead I inclined my head stiffly. "I'll send up that bedding."

"Thank you. Until tomorrow then."

I smiled *that* smile, the one reserved for courtiers and, it appeared, for Manelesi, too. Then I echoed, "Until tomorrow."

6
flail

I DID NOT HAVE TO WAIT LONG FOR MANELESI'S WORDS to bloom in fruition. Really, it took only a handful of hours—time in which I did not once think about Manelesi's words on marriage. I sat with Mara and Kaiht. I attended dinner. I tried to calm my anxious thoughts during the lonely dark of night.

But then I walked into the Council Chamber the next day and heard the first words out of Grimly's mouth.

"Your Majesty, the Council has been discussing something of import and we'd like to bring it to your attention," he said, pausing then for my reaction. I waved my hand to signal him on. He continued, "Queen Sahle, we would like you to consider the idea of your marriage."

I stared back at Grimly in disbelief. "Excuse me?"

And I could almost see Manelesi high up in his room in the Yesonto, smiling.

Grimly looked around at the other Lords, as if begging one of them to repeat his words. Seeing no takers, he cleared his throat.

"Your marriage, Your Majesty. We feel it would be most prudent to discuss the possibility of it, as well as potential suitors."

"Potential suitors?" I parroted. I shook my head slightly as I looked around at the table of Lords. Each of them wanted to see how I would react—if my hackles would raise in defense or if I would sweetly acquiesce. They waited with bated breath.

Just like when Manelesi had mentioned it, the thought of marriage made me shudder. It felt like too much of a coincidence that this conversation was happening now, just after Manelesi's odd musings on the topic. The muscles of my legs bunched, ready to spring from the throne, run to the Yesonto, and ask that man—that *being*—how he had influenced the Lords.

Instead, I forced my legs to stay still under the drapery of my thick skirts. I pulled my spine up a little straighter and stared back at the eagerly watching Lords. Unconsciously, I twisted Finn's bracelet around my wrist once, twice.

"Alright," I began. "I'll hear you out. Start by telling me why I should consider this?"

Someone scoffed from further down the table but I knew which snide Lord that was. I handily ignored him.

Standing as he still was, Grimly was the one to respond on behalf of the table. "It is something that has been discussed since your arrival in the Alterealm, Your Majesty, but we felt that you might first benefit from a period of getting used to your surroundings."

I nodded, funny though it was to consider any of the upheaval of the last year with the words "getting used to."

Grimly carried on. "You are more settled now and the threat to Izwe is as marked as ever. Although it is an uncomfortable idea, there is only a certain amount we can do internally to protect ourselves from Trina Cheile. We must consider what else is possible, and the best hand to play is to wed a powerful ally.

"Both symbolically and practically, it will make Izwe stronger. We would have more soldiers at our defense, more weapons, more ships. We would be a more fearsome adversary with the might of two nations. And Trina Cheile would have to consider that any attack on us would be an attack on a larger foe, including our and this potential partner nations' allies."

"It is a deterrent," Lord Marcus, one of the Senior Council, clarified from the other end of the table.

I took in his calm face, the no-nonsense set of his jaw. "I see," I replied. And I did see. I could understand just how beneficial a strong ally would be, in light of our recent attack. Yet more than one aspect irked me: the timing and the concept of marriage itself. The timing I could only discuss with one being, so I filed it away for later.

But I could ask about the marriage.

With a smile, demure in its mildness, I questioned, "And in terms of this marriage you propose, what are you thinking?" I was not ready for a fight, though I felt the whispers of it rise in my bones. Still, I wanted to hear what these men had in mind for me. I wanted to know the depth of outrage that was warranted before I reacted.

"I'm glad you asked, Your Majesty," Grimly said. "There have been several contenders for some time, including Prince Joachim of the Kingdom of Niel, Prince Alfred from the Kingdom of Wynsum, and Lord Pierre from the Empire of Royaume."

I barely tracked the names of the men and their nations. My mind stuck on one word in particular. "When you say *contenders*, do you mean that they have voiced their interest? This was brought to them before it was brought to me?"

I could hear the edge of outrage in my voice and I took a deep breath to calm my beating heart.

It was Lord Anson who stood now. "If Your Majesty allows?" he asked with the smallest of bows.

"Lord Anson."

Anson smiled at the telling tone of my words but did not seem to be cowed. "Your Majesty must appreciate that a female heir to Izwe would be considered as a possible match since her birth."

I raised my brows, not entirely understanding.

Seeing this, Anson continued, "The sole child of Bekha and Otto would, of course, be an eligible match for any Prince or Lord in the Alterealm. Since you were a baby, this Council has received proposals for your hand, granted they all came with stipulations that the marriage would only occur after your twentieth birthday."

"Was this not something you should have told me about sometime in the last year?" I asked. I met a few of the Lords' eyes. Others avoided my gaze.

"No, my Queen," Anson replied simply.

My gaze snapped back to his. "Why not?"

"As Grimly has already explained, it was not something to be considered until you had settled into the Alterealm. Truly, I think you would be hard-pressed to find a single Lord around this table who would say you are fully ready now but—"

"And you mean what by that?" I bit out. The hackles I had tried so hard to calm were raising, and raising quickly the more Anson spoke.

But Anson being Anson, he smiled serenely, ironically before answering. "It means that you continue to flail—"

"Flail?" I interjected again.

Anson paused for a moment to see if I would add more. Seeing my shocked expression, he eventually said, "Flail, yes. That is the word I used. And before you ask, I meant it. You have been flailing your way through this past year as Queen. By all accounts, you have been resistant to understanding our ways—"

"Whose accounts?" I demanded. I twisted the bracelet around my wrist faster and faster. I felt an angry, embarrassed flush rising to my cheeks.

"Lady Lisideria, Lady Mary, Lady Genevieve," Anson replied simply, rattling off some of Eliza's closest friends and those I had taken tea with occasionally. "Just to name a few. You have disregarded customs such as touching the people in Ukuwela and at Commander Finn's funeral.

"While your studying has been admirable—Librarian Ruth has told us of your steadfast dedication in that regard—you have been resistant to implementing what you have learned. For too long your powers went untouched. Commander Finn's reports were clear on that point. Only his death was enough to prompt you to actually use—"

"That is enough," I finally said. Loudly and sharply.

As Anson had spoken, my breath had become more and more uneven. My heartbeat had increased until the mention of *that day*, the moment Finn died, undid my control.

With surprise, I realized I was standing. My fingers curled into balled fists at my side, and my chest rose and fell in quick succession.

Anson quirked a brow at me, and self-consciously, I sank back to my chair.

"Of course, I mean no disrespect," Anson continued. I scoffed. "But, Your Majesty, I meant to illustrate that you were not settled enough to consider marriage. It is debatable whether you are now, though the Council realizes we no longer have the luxury of waiting."

I glared daggers at Anson but forced myself, through my anger, to ask, "Has something happened? Has another threat occurred?"

Anson shook his head and a tousled lock of his dark hair fell over his forehead. He pushed it back with a hand. "No, my Queen, though we risk it with every day that passes. As such, the Council believes it is time."

It was my turn to shake my head. The idea of marriage was so outlandish in my mind. Even in all of the days and nights with Finn, in every touch and discussion, the idea that I would marry him or anyone never seemed an immediate reality. Oh, I knew I was a Queen. I had assumed I would one day need an heir, and that meant a marriage and a husband and children.

But that had seemed like a distant concern. Never once had the Council mentioned suitors. Never once had they brought up the idea of a wedding. And I certainly had never met a man who caught my eye, captured my imaginings, and made me yearn for forever with him. So I had ambled along believing I was far, far away from that moment in my life. I was just Sahle, and I was Queen Sahle, but I was not bride-to-be Sahle.

Lord Grimly stood, and I watched with a sort of weary relief as Anson took his seat once more. "Your Majesty, what Anson has not mentioned is that the three suitors listed before are those who have recently renewed their proposals. They, or their fathers on their behalf, submitted proposals years ago but have contacted us since your return to the Alterealm to remind us that they continue to be hopeful you will select them. Accordingly, the Council would like to bring these three suits to you and ask for your consideration of them."

"You want me to pick one?" I asked. My lips felt numb, detached.

"Yes, Your Majesty." Grimly turned to snap his fingers at a set of servants lingering along the walls. The two men in their servant-brown disappeared. "We have taken the liberty of asking each of the suitors to send a portrait of themselves. We also have their latest missives which we can read to you."

My eyes widened as I watched the servants return. Each of them carried an easel and a picture frame, turned so that the back was outwardly displayed rather than the picture encased within. A third followed with the same items. To the side of the Lords' table, the three servants set down the easels and, one by one, turned the picture frames to me.

My eyes tracked across three painted images. Each was a simple portrait of a man ranging from my age to middle age—though that could mean anything from twenty to one hundred fifty years old in the Alterealm. Two were fair-haired and one was brunette. One was a bit pudgy through the cheeks, so much so that I wondered what the rest of him outside of the tight frame would look like.

A little hysterical giggle threatened to crawl up my throat but I forced it down. The absurdity of the scene struck me.

How had it come to me picking a husband just by looking at framed paintings?

Lord Grimly walked to the three images and pointed at the pudgy-cheeked man. "This is Lord Pierre of the Empire of Royaume. He is first cousin to the Emperor of Royaume which, as you well know, Your Majesty, is our largest ally geographically." Then Lord Grimly pulled a piece of paper from his jacket pocket and unfolded it. From where I was sitting, I could see a heavy seal pressed into the back of the page.

Grimly cleared his throat. "Lord Pierre of Royaume writes—"

Horrified that whatever words the Lord had surely meant me to hear would be read out loud to these twenty men, I cut him off. "If you don't mind, Lord Grimly, I would appreciate reading the letter at my leisure."

If that request fazed Grimly, he did not let on. He merely bowed from the waist as he refolded the letter and returned it to the original pocket. "As you wish, Your Majesty."

Grimly approached the second portrait. "This is Prince Joachim of the Kingdom of Niel. While Niel is not the largest of our allies, they are known to have a particularly skilled and sizable military. Prince Joachim is the youngest son of the King of Niel and is rumored to be the King's favorite."

I ran my gaze over this portrait, taking in the blonde hair, the slight upturn of the mouth, the particular softness of the eyes. It was a painting so I knew much of what I was seeing was an image translated through the lens of the artist, with all the biases and likes and dislikes of that person ingrained into each brush stroke. Still, there was something about Joachim's eyes that made me pause. They seemed...kind.

Grimly moved to the final portrait, the other blond man. "And this, Queen Sahle, is Prince Alfred of the Kingdom of Wynsum. Wynsum is our nearest ally, sharing a portion of our northern border. We share many similarities in customs and history, and many Izweians have family in Wynsum. Prince Alfred is third in line to the throne."

I looked at Alfred's portrait another moment, noting the long blonde hair, the high forehead and the serious set of the jaw. I knew nothing of this man but the idea of him being an outdoorsman popped into my head. It was in the strong set of his shoulders, the golden hue of the skin of his face.

Then I looked back at Grimly. "Thank you for presenting these suitors. May I have their letters?"

Grimly came forward at once and I took the letters from his hand. They were heavier than I imagined; a few must be pages long. But I did not open them now. I merely placed them in my lap and turned my attention back to the Lords.

If the Lords thought I was flailing as a Queen, I would show them just how Queenly I could be.

With my polished, neutral smile, I raised my voice so that every man in the room would hear me. "Thank you, all of you, for bringing this topic to my attention. I agree with you that a marriage to a strategic ally would be a wise move for Izwe. I will read the letters and take it under consideration."

My nerves had ricocheted around this afternoon. I wanted to stomp up to Manelesi and ask what he had done. I wanted to run my hands down the portraits of the men and consider which face I might look at for the rest of my life. I wanted to laugh at the concept of me, who felt like a child most days, getting married.

I was about to climb to my feet when Anson cleared his throat.

I reluctantly turned my attention to him. "Yes, Lord Anson. Did you have something to add?"

"If we did not make it clear, we feel that any of these three would be a suitable Consort for the Queen of Izwe. Other suitors have also put forward their hand and we have deemed them unworthy. These are the best options, Your Majesty, and we would ask that you select one. Not just *consider* them."

I swallowed, my gaze flickering back towards the painted faces. Their eyes seemed lifelike as they stared back at me.

"I understood that perfectly, Lord Anson," I replied shortly.

"Very good, Your Majesty," he replied, Then he turned to the servants who had once again melted back towards the walls. "Please have these portraits delivered to the Queen's chambers at once. I am sure she'll want to examine them further."

Anson's eyes met mine once more. My own eyes narrowed as I watched that glimmer of mirth flicker in his green gaze.

"Thank you for that, Lord Anson," I called as I stood. I tucked the letters under my right arm.

Each of the Lords rose and bowed, and as I passed Anson's seat, he replied, "Anything for Your Majesty."

My eyes rolled of their own volition.

I tossed the letters in my chambers and headed back out, even before Kaiht could finish her question of, "Your Majesty, where would you like these paintings? They've just been delivered."

But I did not have time for the paintings. I did not have time for the letters, dropped haphazardly onto the clean, pressed covers of my bed. I needed to speak to Manelesi. I had a sneaking suspicion that he had something—*everything*—to do with this sudden discussion of marriage.

Sure, it made sense that a Queen needed a partner and a Consort. Sure, I was not getting younger and the strength of my kingdom depended on me eventually producing an heir. I knew all of this at heart. Yet I was not ready, not yet, for the reality of it.

And with Manelesi taking an odd interest in the topic yesterday and the Lords bringing it forward today? More was at play.

I was convinced of it.

Clad in my usual gray, I stormed through the hallways of the palace. Courtiers scooted quietly out of my way. Maybe they saw the concentration on my face. Maybe they saw my pace. Either way, they scooted and bowed, bowed and scooted. I made it to the garden paths that led to the Yesonto in a blurred rush. I bustled into the sanctuary, barely acknowledging the Masters buzzing about. Then, holding my skirts clear, I took the stairs two at a time up to Manelesi's room.

Before I could knock, the door opened of its own accord, just like yesterday.

"I was wondering what was taking you so long," Manelesi said, instead of a "Hello" or "How are you doing today?" He stood just inside the doorway, dressed in a simple pair of dark pants and a white button-up shirt. The white made his blue-gray eyes seem to radiate.

I huffed as I stepped into the room, shutting the door behind me. "Father. What makes you say so?"

"You said you'd be back tomorrow and already it is afternoon. I was beginning to fear you had forgotten me."

"Never," I replied seriously. How did one forget a divine creature you had summoned from the afterlife to be your own private teacher? Especially one who seemed to be influencing important moments in your life? I opened my mouth to ask what he had done but he beat me to words.

"Thank you for the bedding, by the way. I had forgotten little luxuries like soft sheets. When one does not have a body..." he trailed off with a small shrug as if I could relate, as if it were a normal thing to talk about being a divine being without physical form.

I glanced at the bed and then back to him. My eyes narrowed. "Are you trying to distract me?"

His brows rose. "Me? Why would I do that?"

"I don't know. If you know all, you know what you did and what I want to speak about now."

"The Council Meeting," Manelesi answered. It was not a question.

I took two steps to the lone chair and sat heavily. "I find it a little too coincidental that, yesterday, you took an interest in me marrying and, today, the Lords on my Council seem taken with the idea of me choosing a husband."

Manelesi looked back at me levelly. "Did I not tell you that you needed a husband?"

"You did."

"And now you will have one. I see no problem."

"The problem," I started to say, my voice pinching in a way I knew spelled disaster. I forced myself to pause. This man, this being did not seem like one to get into an argument with.

"The problem," I continued after a calming breath. "Is that you sought to influence as you saw fit, rather than allowing it to come along in its own time."

But Manelesi smiled at that, a smile as ageless and deep as an ancient lake at midnight. "Daughter, all is because I will it to be. You seem to not understand the nature of God, if you realize so little. I will have to discuss your religious education with Master Edgar."

Yet as he rambled, I looked back at him with a sort of dawning horror. All did come because of him. He might be in a physical, tangible form now but his ability to influence had not changed. He was still God, Lord of the lesser gods. And whatever he wanted to occur did occur. It was simply strange, oh so strange, to be able to discuss the points with him before he willed them into being.

"Perhaps," I conceded. "Did you put it into their minds, or did you merely tell a few of the Lords what you wished?" I did not think he had left his room in the Yesonto, but you never knew.

"It is the same, is it not?" he replied with a small shrug.

I stared back at him. I guess it was the same for a being such as he. My head ached with the sheer scale of that limitless potential.

He continued, "I take it none of the Princes or the Lord caught your eye?"

I laughed, a humorless little sound that well communicated my annoyance. "If you know all, surely you know the answer to that. Actually, surely you know exactly who I will marry. Why don't you save everyone the time and trouble and just tell me."

"Ah, ah," Manelesi replied with a wag of a raised finger. "That's not how this works. The realities of existence arise out of the interplay between my will and your choices. To tell you what I would see in this realm is not the same as telling you what will ultimately occur. Yet, if it makes you feel better, we can change the subject entirely. We can pretend to forget that I can influence you and everything in this way."

I exhaled, trying to grasp the concept of what it would be like to exist as I did, yet also control everything. The idea was beyond my comprehension. "Fine. Let's change the subject. Should we discuss my training?"

Manelesi clapped his hands together. "What a lovely idea."

I was not sure whether we were joking or not.

He sat down on the edge of his bed, much as I had yesterday. "I'd like to hear more about your power, my daughter. And before you snidely answer that I already know everything about it, I mean that I would know your thoughts about the power—what makes you like it, what makes you fear it."

Already, he knew me too well. I *had* been about to ask him exactly that. Instead, I decided to put snide remarks aside. "Well, I've only ever controlled it once—and I'm not sure I'd call that control, necessarily. It...erupted out of me when Finn was struck."

"Yes, so what was different about that moment compared to all of the other times you tried to summon your magic?"

"My fear," I replied immediately. I did not need to rack my mind to answer that. I lived the horror of that moment over and over daily. "My fear and my anger. I think a part of me had accepted that I might be hurt or killed by the creatures that night. But I couldn't bear to see Finn injured. And when it happened, I don't know. I just lost it."

"Lost it," Manelesi repeated. "Or lost your inhibitions?"

"You think inhibitions have been holding me back?" I asked with raised eyebrows.

"Inhibitions, self-doubt, fear. All of those are potent emotions that will quickly and readily stop you from meeting the true potential in you. When Finn fell, though, there was no time for doubt or fear, was there?"

"No," I said quietly, glancing down at my clasped hands. But I was not really seeing them. No, in my mind's eye, I was watching that moment when Finn fell again. "I did not think of anything then. I merely acted."

"Exactly," Manelesi said with a solemn nod. "You have power. You have my power, in fact. The having is not the problem despite all of your protests in the last year. The problem is quieting that inner monologue of yours—the one that blocks your mind from your power. That is our real task."

"Perhaps *you* can just will away my doubt," I muttered quietly enough that I thought Manelesi might not hear it.

He did, of course, and his eyes shone menacingly. "Careful, Daughter. I like you and so I allow a good deal of your impertinence. Rulers should be allowed such things, after all. But do not push it. While I cannot will away your doubt and fear, I believe I can help you overcome them."

"How?" I immediately asked. Maybe I should have been more afraid or ashamed to be chastised but I was still seeing Finn's too-calm face. I was still seeing my golden hem progressively soaked with blood.

"We'll figure out where the blocks, for lack of a better term, are. Then loosen them. Of course, I should not imply that it will be easy. Wielding power is as much about force as it is control and finesse. We'll have to free your power and then help you learn to wield it accurately. Tell me, when it unleashed itself before, what was affected?"

The purple sky flashed before me, the standing thatch-roofed huts of the Vikela, the untouched blonde strands of hair on Finn's head. None of that had turned into the ash piles that had been my attackers. "Only the creatures."

"Yes," Manelesi said thoughtfully, almost to himself. "So you have inherent control. That is good. We can work with that."

And I wanted to work. I wanted to be able to control this, and I wanted to be able to control it now. "When do we begin?"

Manelesi tsked once more. "Patience, Daughter. We have all the time in the world."

I was about to snip back that in fact we did not. There was a literal clock ticking on Manelesi returning to his godly plane. Trina Cheile was breathing down our necks. I needed to learn as much as I could—now.

But Manelesi saw all of those thoughts. He saw and he added, "Trust me. There is time. Come back tomorrow and we can begin."

I opened my mouth to argue but closed it again. I tried to conceal my sigh even as I felt it shiver through me. I was grateful for Manelesi and his help, but his omniscience chafed.

"Alright," I finally said. I stood from the chair. "Tomorrow then."

"Get a good night's rest," he said with a smile. "You'll need it, Daughter."

As I left the room and headed back down the stairs, I realized I had lost all of the anger about the suitors. Whether he had willed it from me, or I had simply and quickly accepted, I did not know which. What I did know was that I had decisions ahead of me.

Decisions and training and oh so much more.

I opened the door to my chamber to find Kaiht and Mara staring at the portraits. They—or whoever had delivered them to my chambers—had set them up along the wall of windows. It was a beautiful backdrop for a very un-beautiful thing I was being asked to do.

Both women spun and bowed as they heard me come through the door. "Your Majesty," they said in greeting. When Kaiht rose from her bow, a wide smile painted her lips.

"Are you two enjoying yourselves?" I asked as I made my way to them and the portraits. Five sets of eyes stared back at me.

"Of course, Your Majesty," Kaiht replied. Her cheeky grin rose to her eyes. "The servants who dropped them off mentioned they're suitors. How could we not take a look?"

"And?" I replied. "Any favorites so far?"

My question took them off guard. They looked between each other before nodding resolutely.

But it was Mara who answered. "Oh yes, Your Majesty. We each have a favorite."

I angled myself to get a better look at the portraits. "Wait, don't tell me yet. Let me try and guess."

I approached the nearest painting, that of the pudgy brunette man. His eyes were slightly too small and gave his face a piggish look.

"That's Lord Pierre of Royaume," Mara added. I followed the line of her slim finger as she pointed to the name plate attached to the bottom part of the frame.

I nodded, recalling what the Lords had said. He was cousin to the Emperor, a powerful man surely, even if he was only a Lord. I looked back at his eyes, the curved slope of his cheek, the lack of neck that connected head to shoulder.

I sighed.

The Lords mentioned that Royaume was our largest ally geographically, but did not implore me to consider him otherwise. I turned my head to the next painting, all too content to discard Pierre.

The next portrait was of a blond man. My eyes dropped to the nameplate. Prince Alfred of Wynsum. Ah, that was right. I recalled the Lords saying Wynsum bordered Izwe and that Alfred was third in line to the throne.

I ran my gaze over the fair hair before moving to the face.

Alfred had struck me as an outdoorsman the first time I had seen this portrait. Looking at him now, I was not sure if that was it necessarily. He was certainly strong—the cut of his jaw severe, the span of his shoulders wide. Yet nothing about that said he enjoyed hiking or fishing or skiing. Perhaps he was more of a military man.

Attractive as he was, nothing in his face drew me in. He seemed too harsh.

I turned my attention to the last man, the other blonde, Prince Joachim of Niel.

The Lords had said Joachim was the favorite child of the King of Niel. Looking at the portrait, I could believe it.

His eyes had captured my attention in the Council Chamber and they did again now. Something about the set of them, the rich hazel color, seemed kind and understanding. It was a lot to assume from a portrait. That I knew. But if this was all I had to go on, then it would have to do.

I turned questioning eyes to Kaiht and Mara. Their bright, eager faces looked back at me.

At least some of us were enjoying this.

"Let me guess. Do you both like Prince Joachim?" I asked them.

The quiet Mara nodded enthusiastically. It was so out of character that my eyebrows rose.

"Well actually," Kaiht jumped in. "Mara prefers Prince Joachim, but I personally like Prince Alfred."

"Why?" I asked them. And I genuinely wanted to know.

I had heard what each of these men would bring as Consort. I had seen the portraits. But now I wanted more. I wanted opinions. I craved the long-gone moments from the Humanrealm when I could sit with my friends, Mer, Cecily, and Jenna, and gossip about a guy. It was a simple thing yet the lack of it was just one of the ways I felt so alone in the Alterealm.

Kaiht and Mara were only too willing to oblige.

Kaiht jumped in first. "Prince Alfred is strong and handsome. He looks like the sort of man who could command a room. That strength would be an asset to you as Consort."

I nodded, glancing back at the portrait. He did seem like someone the Lords would respect. That would be a plus. Yet a part of me also wondered whether strength like that would eclipse my burgeoning command.

"Mara?" I asked, turning to the other woman.

"I prefer Prince Joachim because he seems…understanding. He seems like a man who would listen to you and support you."

I looked at Mara a second longer before reaching out and squeezing her forearm gently. "We're assuming a lot from portraits, but it does seem like that, right?"

She nodded earnestly. "Yes. And, if you don't mind me saying, Your Majesty, perhaps a friend is what you need right now."

I looked between both women before reaching out to Kaiht, as well. "Thank you both for your opinions. I don't know who I'll pick but I've been advised to choose one."

Kaiht broke away from our small group and came back with something in her hands. "Don't forget about these, Your Majesty. They could help."

She held out the letters from these suitors.

In my hurry back to my Chambers and then to Manelesi, I had forgotten about them, hastily tossed on my bed. I took them from Kaiht with grateful fingers.

"Thank you. Now, if you would excuse me, I'd like some privacy."

"Certainly, Your Majesty," Kaiht replied. Mara nodded. Then they both melted away.

I held the bunch of letters gingerly, as if they were explosive, as if something terrible would occur if I moved too quickly or spoke too loudly.

The fireplace was gently glowing and I ignored the two wingback chairs in front of it. Rather, I walked to the burgundy rug before them, before the fireplace, and sank to the ground in a heap of gray skirts.

I fanned the three letters out around me and sighed. Choosing a husband at this point in my life was laughable. I had railed against the proposition, yet even in the few hours since the Lords broached the topic, a sense of duty had settled in me.

It was not about want or love. This was about considering what was necessary. And if I were entertaining this path, there was no point in delaying.

I tore into the nearest letter.

7
arena

AS REQUESTED, I ARRIVED AT THE YESONTO THE NEXT morning dressed in my soldier-brown tunic and pants.

I shrugged my shoulders against the weight of the brown cloth. It was just fabric, I told myself. But every time I put on the outfit, the feel of the linen against my skin brought forth phantom memories.

Bright sunshine glinting off Finn's blonde hair.

Sweat stinging my eyes as I threw a punch.

A furtive, stolen kiss.

A heap of brown, discarded garments strewn beside my bed.

I blinked against the rush of emotion. Then I knocked on Manelesi's door.

Silence greeted me.

I leaned closer, angling my face as if the extra inch closer would allow me to hear infinitely better through the door.

I knocked again. And again, there was no response.

"Manelesi? Father?" I called, raising my voice to be heard through the dense wood.

"He's not there," someone said behind me.

I whirled to find a young Master standing on the top step of the stairs, watching me. The young man bowed hastily. He lowered his eyes in an embarrassed hurry before he added, "God has asked me to tell you that he awaits your presence in the arena."

"The arena?" I replied. Whatever or wherever that was, it sounded ominous.

The young Master nodded in a hurry. "Yes, Your Majesty. You'll recall it from the night of the channeling?"

A wide building with no roof immediately dawned in my mind's eye. "Ah, yes. Thank you."

"If you'd like, I can guide Your Majesty there?"

"That won't be necessary," I called over my shoulder as I took the stairs back down in a hurry. I knew where I was going.

I nodded at the bowing Masters again as I passed them in the Yesonto. Then I broke outside of the sanctuary and made my way quickly around the back, where the ceilingless building stood.

I shook my head at the thought of it. I had been coming to the Yesonto, strolling the gardens, and running the grounds of the palace for a year. In all that time, I had not noticed—or cared to notice—that strange building. And now, I was going to it twice in one week.

The building in question rose before me and I quickly made my way to the plain, weather-beaten wooden door. The hinges creaked as I opened it.

Then I stepped inside.

Manelesi stood in the center, as he had on the night of the channeling. He turned at the sound of my entrance. "Daughter. Good day."

Instinctively, I began to bow, knowing I was in the presence of a much more powerful being. But I stopped myself.

I was Queen.

I was Queen.

It was funny how I still had to tell myself that, after all this time.

"Good morning, Father," I replied with a nod instead.

Just like on the night of the channeling, I dropped my head back to look up at the space where a roof should have been. A brilliant, deep blue sky stared back at me.

And for the second time I wondered why this building had been made.

"What is this place?" I asked, as I approached the rounded wall. Like most buildings in Izwe, this building had the sloping shape of all the roundhouses. Yet where most were topped by thatch, this one was not.

I studied the place where roof should meet wall, and it did not look as if there was once a roof. There was no sign of joints or a lingering ceiling structure. I did not think it had fallen away or been burned. No, this building was built without a roof.

"We call it the arena," Manelesi said. His voice was closer than I expected. I turned to see him standing beside me, looking up at the same spot on the plaster wall. "It was built in my time, under my direction, for this express purpose."

"The practice of magic?"

Manelesi inclined his head. "Yes, I needed a place that could be walled off from those who would seek to look in," he said with a wave at the literal and figurative wall. "But that still retained a direct connection to the stars."

"Why the stars?" I asked. I looked back at the wide expanse of blue above us. If I squinted just so, I thought I could barely make out the faint arc of that teasing moon.

I felt Manelesi's questioning look. "Do you not know that our power comes from the universe, Daughter?"

"I…" I began. In truth, I had never thought of it. All at once, the glow of Eliza's stone linked with the glow of the stars. The glow of the stars linked with the white light that had lashed out of me.

"Our power is a heavenly gift, given by the universe itself. It is made up of the dust of planets, the remnants of stars. And in it, we can command all things."

I nodded. "No one has ever put it like that before."

"That is not surprising. The history books only contain what the authors perceive. Nothing more.

"Our power is a fundamental connection to the heavens and the earth. We can wield it any time we like but we are most in control of it when we are in direct contact with the natural world.

"Have you ever walked in the woods barefoot and felt the tingling life of the soil on your soles? Have you ever held the leaf of a tree in your hands and felt the heartbeat of its essence? Or stood in the midst of a tempest and felt the sheer fury of the wind?

"That is the essence of the world. That is our power. It is one and the same. And so I built this place, simple as it is, to allow for better connection to it even as I kept prying eyes out."

"I understand," I said, though I had more questions than anything. Would this place have helped me with my powers before? Would I have learned to pull them out and control them months earlier had Finn known all of what Manelesi said?

There was no way to know any of that. And, in truth, I did not think any of that would have mattered.

I had tried my power over and over again outside and inside, in direct line with the sky and inside the closed walls of the palace. Nothing had seemed to work—until suddenly, it had.

Manelesi's voice pulled me from my thoughts. "Show me what you can do."

It was a command more than a request, and I turned my gaze to him. "My power?"

"What else?" he asked with a smile.

But I shook my head. "I can't.

He stared down at me from only a few paces away. Those blue-gray eyes seemed to swirl as if they were a portal to the real being trapped within. "What do you mean? You know you have powers. You've seen it. So why do you say you can't?"

"I don't know how," I replied simply, quietly, my gaze pitched anywhere but Manelesi's face.

A sharp laugh broke out, and I snapped my attention back to him. My emotions swung quickly from embarrassment to anger. "I don't know why that's funny."

Manelesi's laugh continued. It was a deep laugh, a belly laugh as if what I had said was the funniest thing he had heard in many years. As it died down to a chuckle, he raised his hand and wiped at his eyes. He looked at the mirth-filled tears gathered on the back of his fingers as if surprised at the moisture there.

Wiping the tears on the leg of his drab pants, he focused on me. "I find it humorous that the most powerful ruler in my line has no idea how to call forth that power."

"Perhaps you could help me," I suggested pointedly. I wanted to add "rather than laugh at me," but I bit my tongue. Those would not be wise words.

"Yes," Manelesi replied. "I'd say that's imperative, would you not?"

I nodded stiffly as I folded my arms in front of my chest. It may have been a defensive, impertinent action in itself but I had to do something. My fingers twitched, as if my annoyance were a physical force running along my skin. Fidgeting made me feel better.

"Let's try this, then," Manelesi continued. He walked a few paces away, seemingly looking at the sloped walls around him. Then he strolled back towards me with purpose. "Think back to the night of the attack in the palace."

Instantly, my mind rebelled. I did not want to think about smoke and screaming—mine or others. I did not want to think of the exact deep, dark shade of ruby that was arterial blood.

Whether he saw it or felt it in whatever link that existed between my soul and his, he knew I was not cooperating. "You're fighting it," Manelesi said. "If you push back against the emotions, you can never use them to harness your power. You need to summon that fear and dread, not hide from it."

I looked at Manelesi again, but I did not really see him. I saw horrors and white light and too-still fingers. Distantly, I watched as Manelesi nodded. "That's it. Close your eyes and let yourself *feel.*"

I obeyed. My eyes shut, and instead of the veined yellow-red of seeing through eyelids, there was the rushing, jolting look of the training grounds as Finn and I ran through them. There was the overwhelming boom and then silence of the first explosion in the palace. There was the look of those creatures, whose heads fell back like sickly music boxes.

There was that voice that taunted and told me I was going to die.

I felt it all. I saw it all. And for the first time since that night, I did not push back against the memory of it. I let myself *live* it again.

From close yet far away, a clapping distracted me.

"Daughter, your fingers are glowing," a voice called.

It was Manelesi's voice and I let the memories fall away as I opened my eyes.

Manelesi beat his hands together once, twice more. "Look."

I lifted my hands, turning them to see front and back. And to my surprise, there was the faintest glow as if some light from under the skin had been turned on. Yet as I watched, as I marveled, the glow faded.

"Where's it going?" I whispered.

"It's in time with your emotions—your heightened emotions," he clarified. "As you came back to a level head, the power faded. But there, you see. It is in you. You just need to learn how to call it forth."

I kept staring at my fingers. I turned my hands over as I had done in the carriage after the coronation, after I had seen the Masters' symbols sink into my skin. My hands looked the same, mine and not mine, and I could not stop staring.

"Your hands aren't going anywhere," Manelesi said.

I looked up quickly. I dropped my hands.

"The key for you will be learning to summon those emotions or an approximation of them whenever you want access to your power. Unfortunately for you, too, that means we'll be spending quite a lot of time exploring unpleasant moments from your life."

"Great," I murmured, even as my heart picked up in pre-emptive trepidation. I had a feeling the next weeks would not be pleasant.

"Let's try something else," Manelesi said as he brought a finger to his chin. "Tell me about your journey here."

"To the Alterealm?"

"Yes," he replied with exasperated patience. "Tell me how it happened and what you felt."

I looked at him for clues as to how I should begin. Seeing none, I decided to start from the moment I arrived home from my twentieth birthday party. "Well, I walked into my house and found Eliza and Roland sitting on the couch with bags packed. It was the middle of the night so I knew something was wrong. They were acting strange. They brought me to the backyard and Eliza pulled out a stone from her locket. She used it to call some sort of magic that netted over us. Then suddenly we were here and people were bowing and calling me Queen."

"Not just anyone," Manelesi interjected. His eyes shone knowingly.

Eliza and Roland's faces flashed in my mind. "No, not just anyone—my parents, too."

"And how did that make you feel?"

"Confused and frightened," I admitted. "And angry. The more they told me, the more I learned, the more I realized they'd spent twenty years omitting a very big fact about who I am."

"Good," Manelesi replied. I raised a questioning brow at the smile on his face.

"Use that bewilderment now," he added. "Close your eyes and let that feeling enfold you."

"What if I don't want to?" I muttered under my breath even as I shut my eyes.

"Hmm?" Manelesi asked.

"Nothing," I replied. I screwed my eyes shut tighter and took a deep breath. Then I thought back on that night: Roland's fingers biting into my arm as he forced me into the backyard, my shock as Eliza dropped into a bow, the sheer overwhelm of being there and not and everywhere on the journey to this realm.

I let the feelings move through me. I let the emotions burgeon and fill and hollow out. And when I thought I could take it no more, when I felt confused and angry tears prickle behind my closed eyelids, I heard Manelesi exclaim, "Marvelous."

I opened my eyes and found Manelesi staring back at me. I glanced at my hands, my forearms where the soldier brown did not cover. The glow was back and brighter than before. Yet as I looked, the skin returned to the color of caramel.

"That does it, too. And those emotions were more focused on confusion and overwhelm than fear and sadness, as with the attack. It seems any large emotion can pull forth your power."

"Is that so different from yours?" I asked, suddenly curious about Manelesi's gift and especially what I may have inherited from him.

"Daughter," he sighed heavily. "It has been hundreds of years since I discovered my gifts. It is difficult to recall a moment before my gifts flowed effortlessly upon my command. Let me think."

I waited as his eyes took on a distant look.

Then he sighed again before he began. "I was a child the first time I used my gifts—at least the first time that I remember. I was in my village with my mother and my sisters. My father was gone, perhaps repairing something on our house or gathering food in the forest. In either case, he was not there.

"He was not there when they came, nor were any other of the men. Perhaps the attackers timed it to be like that, so that the women and children would be the only ones in the village. It would be easier to attack people who were defenseless.

"I remember them breaking down my door. My little sister was screaming and my mother was hugging her to her chest, trying to quiet her. But I…I stood up from the hiding spot my mother had pulled us to. I stood in front of the door and stared at each shuddering of wood as the attacker beat it from the outside.

"When the door finally splintered and fell in, I did not think. I did not move. All I remember is that they were there and each one who tried to step through the door fell instantly. I can remember the empty look in their eyes, how they were dead the moment they hit the ground. And I had not lifted a finger."

Manelesi's eyes focused back on me and I swallowed as I met that blue-gray gaze. "Where was that?" I asked. Images flickered in my mind: *rondavels* built against the heat of a bright sun dawning, the haze of red dust moving over brush land, a family with skin generations darker than mine.

"That is a story for another time," Manelesi replied quietly. The quality of his voice, the tone in which he spoke made me focus my attention more squarely on him. He was…earnest, wistful. It gave me pause.

"It wasn't the Alterealm, was it?" I pushed, even when I knew I should not.

His eyes met mine levelly but there was a cool wariness in their depths. "No."

"You haven't told anyone this. That you're from another realm," I guessed.

He shook his head, eyes flicking away. "No, at the time there was no reason to explain, and later, well, it did not seem to matter much after I had taken over a people, installed magic, and forever changed the social order in the Alterealm."

I blinked at how simply he stated such world-altering truths. "You would think it would be mentioned in the histories, at least."

"It would have, if I saw fit to explain it. Yet, I did not. And none asked, not after what they saw me do."

"And what was that?" I asked reflexively. Even as the words left my mouth, I was not sure I wanted to know—not really.

Manelesi, in his way, saw all of that flit across my face. He smiled a knowing smile. "I think that's enough for one day."

"Alright," I replied. I tugged on the hem of my tunic, pulling the fabric back into its proper place.

"Tomorrow, Daughter. We'll meet here once more."

"Of course, Father."

Manelesi did not stay any longer to small talk. He did not ask me to walk with him, or to be shown the palace or the grounds.

No, he simply watched me a moment longer before heading out of the arena's door and back towards the Yesonto.

I let out a breath I did not know I had been holding.

Through the doorway, I watched him disappear back into his sanctuary.

From that point on, my days seemed to find a routine. I spent hours in the Yesonto each morning, sitting or kneeling on the floor. I had never been one to pray, but since coming to the Alterealm, I noticed that had started to change. I still did not know what I necessarily believed in, but the fact that a mythical God resurrected from the dead was literally floors above me seemed as good a reason as any to believe in the God and gods.

Unlike others, I had actually met a divine being.

I also found peace in the Yesonto. Especially after Finn's death, after sleepless nights and days filled with ghosts, there was something simple and delicate and peaceful about sitting in the Yesonto's golden glow. I relished the quiet. I relished the warmth of the candles in the cold moments before dawn.

After Yesonto, I usually went for a run. I found Caleb and asked him to train. Unlike Finn who had been singularly tasked with training me, this Vikela had other duties. But he never failed to drop whatever he was doing when I arrived.

I knew I could command him to focus on me, command him to be my dedicated trainer. But, in truth, I could only stomach sparring across the red dirt training ground for so long before a specific maneuver brought up a flash of Finn's arms, a particular spin resulted in shock when I found brown eyes close to mine rather than blue ones.

No, the training ground was something I could only face on my strongest days. Those were few and far between.

I also always made my way back to the arena to see Manelesi—at least on the days he told me to come back. We had determined that strong emotions triggered my magic. It was what brought it to the surface. The problem now was that I needed to learn to direct the magic once it swirled around me.

This was proving more difficult than I had expected. Over and over, we tried. I endured Manelesi trudging through my memories of adolescent fear and anxiety. I relived Finn's death more times than I ever wanted to. I even had the pleasure of experiencing anew the burning humiliation of Anson embarrassing me before the Council.

I was left shaken and scarred whenever I left the arena, hidden in the shadow of the Yesonto. And I was loathe to return. But Manelesi told me we were close. In whatever otherworldly sense he had, he seemed to think I was mere moments from a breakthrough.

I doubted it.

And then there was Prince Joachim.

The three portraits sat before my windows for a single night before I instructed Kaiht and Mara to get rid of the other two. Prince Joachim was my favorite of the suitors the Lords had presented. Though that did not mean I *accepted* Prince Joachim.

No, I needed time and so I kept the portrait with his kind eyes in my room. I studied it while Kaiht and Mara laced me into my dresses each day, while I sipped my *rooibos* in the afternoon. I paced in front of it before I headed to a Council session, debating with myself if I should bring the topic up with the Lords.

I was being silly. I knew that. A queen did not choose to marry for love, not unless she was the luckiest queen in the world. A queen had to marry for the safety and surety of her kingdom. In that light, I began to gaze upon Joachim's face with a new perspective. And in the end, it was the eyes that did it.

Mara had said he had kind eyes. It was the first thing I too had noticed, and the thing I focused on now. He had a defined jaw. His hair looked full. His cheeks seemed rosy. I supposed, if the portrait was accurate, that he was an attractive enough man. But the kindness in the eyes made me believe that maybe, just maybe this man could be someone I could build something with.

I read and reread Prince Joachim's letter while I left the other two discarded near the fireplace. I was certain the other men had not written the notes themselves. They were both too flowery and too detached as if they were a sort of form, fill-in-the-blank Valentine's card.

The only one that was not was Prince Joachim's. Somehow, I was convinced his own hand had penned these words. There were certain lines struck out. There were slightly odd turns of phrase. There was authenticity woven into the imperfections.

And there was the same sort of kindness that sat in Joachim's portrait's gaze.

With those hazel eyes in my mind, I came to a decision, though it was not what the Lords would have preferred.

Dressed in my formal charcoal gown and a low circlet of a crown, I strode into the Great Hall for dinner. My step was determined. The heavy skirts of my gown moved around me. My courtiers fell into bows as I passed, naturally creating an aisle from the Great Hall's door up to the head table. Several Senior Council Lords were waiting there but I was seeking one in particular: Grimly.

Several courtiers rose as I moved through the hall. Perhaps they wanted to say something to me, knowing that once I was seated, tradition would not let them approach. But the look on my face must have deterred them.

"Your Ma—" one began.

"Queen Sah—" another started before abruptly cutting short.

I had no time for them and I would bet a pretty penny that my expression communicated that clearly.

I stepped up on the raised dais and took my seat besides the Lords. Several of them murmured, "Good evening, Majesty." I inclined my head in acknowledgement but turned directly to Grimly.

In a voice lowered so only those nearby would hear, I said, "I have come to a decision about the Consort."

From the corner of my eye, I noticed a few of the seated Lords' cups still. Anson's dark head turned in my direction.

Grimly was more composed. He set his glass down after a sip of *konstans* and then angled his body towards me. "That is good news, Your Majesty. Who have you decided to marry?"

"None of them," I said simply. I swear I heard a choking cough from several seats down.

"None of them," Grimly echoed. His intonation was slightly higher than usual but that was the only indication that he was as surprised as the other Lords. He was a seasoned politician. He had long ago learned to school his face, and that face showed no emotion as he trained sharp eyes on me.

"No, at least not yet," I continued, smoothing a napkin across my lap. The servants had begun to bring out trays of steaming food. The scent of roasted butternut wafted my way. "I am partial to one but I would like to meet him before I make a final decision."

"That is most unusual, Your Majesty," Grimly replied simply.

But that was nothing new. Not for me. "I figured as much."

Grimly leaned forward an inch to hear me better. "Excuse me?"

I shook my head. "Never mind. Regardless of how unusual it is, I would like to invite Prince Joachim here. A portrait can only say so much."

"And a letter?" Grimly asked pointedly.

My brow rose. It was unusual for Grimly to be contrary, but I brushed off the slight edge to his voice. "Yes, a letter can only say so much, too. Send for Prince Joachim, and if he is anything like he is in person, I will consider accepting him."

Grimly thought for a moment, running his finger absently over the stem of his wine glass. "It is most irregular but not entirely unheard of. I believe the King of Niel may be persuaded to allow it, though if his son is here longer than a few days, Niel as well as the Court will believe you have accepted Prince Joachim."

I waved my hand at Grimly, half listening as a servant speared several plump shrimp and deposited them on my plate. I thanked the servant with a smile before turning back to Grimly. "Yes, that's all fine. I'd just like to meet him. Would you arrange it?"

"Certainly, Your Majesty," Grimly replied with a nod of his head.

"Wonderful." My words were muffled by a mouthful of seafood.

And it was wonderful. I had bought myself more time. I would have an opportunity to meet the possible Consort, rather than pick him based on a painted portrait.

This was good. And if—a major *if*—Joachim was as kind as his painted eyes looked, perhaps I would have a partner to sit beside me as I ruled. Perhaps I would have a partner to walk through life with.

Then again, perhaps I would hate him.

At least then I would have a reason to say no.

8
the prince

"The Prince has arrived, Your Majesty," Grimly called as he strode through the doors of the Great Hall where I was waiting. The courtiers around me fairly buzzed with energy, even as I braced myself for the unknown about to appear in my doorway.

It had been just five days since I had told Grimly that I wanted to meet Prince Joachim. I had asked Grimly to arrange it, but even I had not expected him to bring the Prince of Niel in such a short time frame. Apparently, our messenger had gone to Niel and Prince Joachim had set off just a day later.

I rolled my eyes internally at that. Had the man never heard of playing it cool?

But perhaps that was a Humanrealm sentiment. I supposed when the hand of a queen was at stake, it was different than meeting someone in a bar or, God and gods forbid, on a dating app. In those situations, being aloof had always served me well.

Yet now I was Queen. I would never chase a man again, not after coming here, not after Finn. All the suitors I would ever have would see me as a means to an end—the end being their own power as Consort of Izwe. And in this, pulling out all of the stops seemed to be the best way to win their future position.

I only hoped Joachim knew I was not easy to impress.

"Thank you, Lord Grimly," I replied as he tucked himself back into the small contingent of Lords who stood on either side of me.

I straightened my spine, steeling myself for what was to come. Who was to come. In the year since arriving in the Alterealm, I had learned about our allies and enemies yet I had never met any of the leaders in person. Today, I would.

I was anxious to meet another ruler, especially one I was considering marrying.

Even past the lilting notes of marimbas, past the chatter of voices and warmth of the grand fireplace roaring, I could hear the sound of a small crowd approaching the Great Hall. I glanced around once more. The five Lords of the Senior Council were by my side, as were Eliza and Roland. The other fifteen Lords of the Council were in the room, scattered among the courtiers but watching regardless. Six of the Vikela stood by, just in case. And all of us were dressed in our Sunday best—or, in this case, our trying-to-win-allies best.

I rubbed my palms against the front of my own burgundy gown. It was a more vibrant *chitenge* cloth than I would normally wear. Eliza, Roland, Kaiht, and Mara all insisted on this dress, though. They had each separately and together urged me to lay aside the gray dresses for this one night.

Apparently mourning was not sexy.

Instead, they had wrapped me in this burgundy *chitenge* gown composed of fine interlocking patterns. It had a standard bodice yet the flow of the skirt and the way the long sleeves fitted around my arms made it appear like the dress was merely cloth draped across my curves. It was both formal and suggestive in a way I was not entirely sure I was comfortable with.

I was Queen. Yet tonight, I was also here to entice, to offer myself up to the man about to walk through this door.

Rather than dwell on that thought, I focused on the crown I had selected for this evening. While Eliza had tried to urge me to wear a dainty tiara, I refused. I might wear this silly dress but I insisted on a traditional state crown. I picked a tall, golden one studded with rubies.

If that did not remind this Prince who I was, nothing would.

The doors to the Great Hall opened and the music of the marimbas swelled. A group of five men walked through the open doors, escorted by a small army of Vikela at their back. I was impossible to miss, standing before the high table. It was no surprise then when the men beelined towards me, a path clearing through the Great Hall.

As each of the five men sank into deep bows, I instantly knew which was the Prince. Of course, his own crown gave him away, but the solid set of his shoulders and broad stance of his feet confirmed it. There was an ease to this Prince that I envied. I wondered whether I would have commanded such innate confidence had I been raised in the Alterealm.

The man standing to the right of the Prince stepped forward. "Your Majesty Queen Sahle of Izwe, I am Lord Robert of Niel. May I present His Royal Highness Prince Joachim of Niel."

Prince Joachim met my eye before bowing at the waist once more. "It is a pleasure to meet you, Queen Sahle. Thank you for inviting us to the Kingdom of Izwe."

I tracked my gaze over his face, taking in eyes that were bright. Under the crown sat short, wavy hair that landed somewhere between blonde and brunette. His build was average, not skinny but not fat, not tall but not short. In fact, it appeared he was the same height as me.

The portrait had done him justice.

It was hard to get the read of a man in a moment, but he seemed friendly enough. I nodded my own head in acknowledgement to him. "Prince Joachim, you and your companions are most welcome. May we interest you in dinner? You must be hungry after your journey."

"It would be my honor to join you, Your Majesty," Joachim replied with a smile.

Distantly, I was aware of Grimly and a servant approaching the four men with Joachim and directing them to where they could go. I noticed the three silent members of the group exit the Great Hall. Soldiers or servants, then. Of course Grimly would not welcome them to sit beside the Lords at the long tables.

"If you'll follow me, Prince Joachim," I said, gesturing with one hand to the head table. I was about to reach out for my ornate chair, when Joachim's hand grasped it first.

"Allow me, Your Majesty," he replied with a smile.

I forced my lips into a matching expression, though I hoped it was more convincing than it felt. I took the offered seat and he settled into one on my left.

The marimbas continued their tune and the constant background chatter of the courtiers filled the space. The smell of fragrant roasted meat and curried vegetables wafted in the air as servants arrived bearing platters of food.

I sipped at my glass of sparkling *konstans*, unsure of what to say or where to even begin. It felt like I was a contestant on some Humanrealm reality matchmaking show, and I had a sudden, inappropriate urge to laugh.

"If you don't mind me asking, Your Majesty, what amuses you so?"

My eyes swung to Joachim instantly. "My apologies. I didn't realize I was making a face."

"I'd hardly call a smile *a face*, Queen Sahle. But please, enlighten me. I'd like to know what makes you smile so that I can note it for future days."

At that, I did smile—a great, large smile. Coming from any other man, that line may have felt forced or slick. But something about Joachim made me believe he really meant it.

I took another sip of wine. Eliza had fed me a list of twenty questions I could ask this man, as well as a dozen more topics for if the conversation waned. None of those had included acknowledging how awkward our situation was. But I could not stop myself.

"You know, I'm sure, that I was raised in the Humanrealm?" I began.

He inclined his dishwater blonde head. "Of course, Your Majesty."

"There they have what we'd call reality television shows. Essentially, it's real life that is recorded so other people can watch it. One of these shows is about matchmakers, women whose profession is setting up couples. I just had the absurd idea that we were one of those couples."

Joachim chuckled. "It certainly feels like that, what with your Court watching like hawks."

I had been so deep in my own mind that I had not paid any attention to the Court. I looked now and saw exactly what Joachim meant. Though they sipped at their wine and held conversations with their peers, each set of eyes flicked towards us every few seconds.

The Lords who typically sat at the high table had moved to the lower tables with the rest of the court, presumably to give us some privacy in our first interaction. It only heightened the feeling that we were on display.

"I apologize for them. They are not the most subtle of people."

"No need to apologize, Your Majesty. They are merely curious about who is courting their Queen."

I grimaced. "While we're on that topic, perhaps we could have a frank conversation." I waited for Joachim to nod before continuing. "Can I ask whether you actually want to be here?"

If I thought my question would faze Joachim, I was wrong. He smiled and it was a jovial thing filled with warmth. It reached right up to his hazel eyes. "I would not be here if I did not want to be, Your Majesty."

I studied him a moment longer. Maybe I was flabbergasted that anyone could be so sure about this when it had been such an internal struggle for me. "You mean that, don't you?"

"Of course," he replied. He looked away just long enough to pick up his wine glass and take a sip. Then he met my gaze once more. "When your advisors wrote to us, asking if we remained interested in an alliance through marriage, I will admit that I was uncertain. My father was eager, you see, but he would never ask this of me if I were not willing.

"So I decided to do some research. I asked after you. I tried to learn what I could. Everything I heard endeared me to you. You seemed a remarkable leader for someone so young and so new to this world."

"That's it?" I said, handily ignoring the very nice compliment. "I sounded like a good leader and that was enough to convince you to shackle yourself to me for the rest of your life?"

Joachim's light brown brows rose. "Is there something else I should have considered?"

"Whether you liked my personality, whether you found me attractive, whether you could see us together?" I replied with only a hint of snark.

But Joachim just smiled again. "I don't mean this to sound harsh, but those things do not matter—not for people like us, Your Majesty. When Queens and Princes marry, we decide the fate of nations and the people in them. Your goodness as a ruler was the only thing that mattered in that consideration. You seemed principled and caring, and I would hope that through marriage to you, you would consider Niel with the same care as your own country."

I stared at him, unsure of what to say.

He was right, of course. There were larger forces at work and more potential for disaster for people like us. But no matter how many people told me a version of this reasoning, I could not seem to shake the feeling that my marriage should be more. My marriage should be everything.

Joachim's voice broke through my racing thoughts. "Of course, now that I've seen you, I can also add that I do find you lovely, Your Majesty. You are a beautiful woman. Any man would be a fool to refuse you."

"And my personality?" I asked, again leaving the compliment unacknowledged.

"Ask me once I've had a chance to get to know you," he replied, a playful glimmer in his eye. "And you? I take it from this line of questioning that you are not entirely sure about this suit."

I paused for a moment before nodding. "You've been honest with me and so I'll be honest with you. My advisors tell me this potential match is the best thing for Izwe but I struggle with the idea that I'm to marry a stranger. I know it's for a larger purpose, but the concept is so foreign to me that I instinctively shrug against it."

Joachim tapped his fingers on the arm of his chair, an unconscious motion as he mulled over my words. "If you were not raised with this understanding, it makes sense that you would feel this way, Your Majesty. But perhaps we can strike a deal?"

My brow rose warily. "What deal?"

"For the time I'm here, try to suspend your disbelief," he replied. I had to tighten my grip on my wine glass to keep it from falling. Those were nearly the exact words Roland had said upon my arrival in the Alterealm. The fact that this man would think along the same lines as Roland made a sudden warmth flow through my chest.

Joachim continued, "Let's try to get to know one another. Allow me to show you how Niel could help Izwe. Open yourself up to the possibility rather than railing against it each step of the way. Would you do that for me?"

Still surprised at the sudden comfort I felt at his words, I nodded. "I don't see how it can hurt."

Joachim smiled again and I allowed myself to smile back at him. "That's the spirit. The worst that can happen is that we hate each other, and then you'll never have to worry about being married to me again."

I laughed despite myself. And, shocked though I was to think it, I…*liked* this man.

It had been a long travel day for Joachim and his companions so they made their excuses soon after their plates were cleared. I did not take any offense and, as Joachim bowed over my hand and pressed a kiss to my fingers, he promised to see me tomorrow.

Assuming that was acceptable to me, of course.

I gave him one last smile and a promise that I would send him a note in the morning. Then he left the Great Hall, Lord Robert melting in alongside him.

The next morning found us walking side by side down one of the palace's garden paths.

The sun hung low in the sky and the slightest chill floated in the breeze. I instinctively tightened a knitted navy blue shawl around my gray-clad arms. Kaiht and Mara had vocally—respectfully, but still vocally—urged me to wear anything else but one of the gray gowns for this walk. But Joachim had asked me to try at this, to give him a real shot. I assumed part of trying was being myself, mourning dresses and all.

"How did you sleep?" I asked Joachim, turning my head to better see him where he strolled on my left.

If the prince was weary from yesterday's travel, he did not look it. His head was bare of a crown and his dark blonde hair, manicured as it was, seemed impervious to the breeze. He wore a fitted long-sleeved emerald top with a high collar and fitted tan pants. Tall leather boots rose nearly up to his knee. All he needed was a helmet and he could have been a Humanrealm polo player.

"Very well, Your Majesty. Thank you for asking. I will admit, those birds that start squawking at dawn—"

"The *hadedas*," I provided.

"Yes, the *hadedas*. They were the only thing that disturbed me."

"On behalf of the kingdom's *hadedas*, I humbly extend my apologies."

Joachim chuckled and sketched a small bow from the waist. "I accept your apologies on their behalf. Unfortunately, I am led to believe you'll be doing much apologizing over the coming days if their display this morning is typical."

I sighed. "Sadly it is. But if it's any consolation, you do get used to it."

"Perhaps in time," he replied, glancing to his right. Our words implied there might be time. They hinted that he could be here for a while. I held his gaze as his eyes met mine. I refused to look down.

"Yes," I finally concluded. "I've gotten quite used to them in the year I've been at the palace."

Joachim shook his head. "It still bewilders me how you've been here just over one year. Tell me, how has it been—adjusting to the Alterealm, meeting your court, assuming your role?"

"Hard," I sighed. A part of my mind wondered if I should be diplomatic and say something light and noncommittal about my experience. But I did not want to. If I were to take this man as a husband, I did not want to lay a foundation of lies.

I continued, "I'm sure you can appreciate how having everything you know ripped out from under you can be wildly disconcerting. Suddenly my entire world changed. The people I thought were my parents were not. I had this great responsibility of leading a kingdom. Not to mention, a pressure on me to develop magic. Still, some days I feel like this entire realm is a dream. I don't know if I'll ever not feel like that."

Joachim nodded thoughtfully. We came to a bend in the path and he extended an arm to signal me to turn first. "I cannot speak from personal experience of it, of course. But I'd imagine that as the years tick by, as the portions of your life here begin to stretch out as long and longer than your time in the Humanrealm, the reverse may be true. Perhaps one day you'll feel like the Humanrealm is but a dream and this is and has always been reality."

"Maybe," I replied. It was something I had considered but it scared me—the idea of my childhood home, my suburban town, my friends Mer, Jenna, and Cicely all floating away over the years. I did not want to forget, even as I tried my best to immerse myself in this strange world.

"Regardless, Your Majesty. I said it last night but it bears repeating: I find you remarkable. To have gone through such a thing and to be leading as you are leading…it's simply stunning."

I shrugged, unable to find the words to respond to that. There were many things *not* stunning about my leadership. We had just recently cleaned the rest of the blackened walls of the Great Hall from the explosion's ash. A grave in the soldiers' graveyard—and nearly 50 more in Ukuwela—existed because of my actions.

"You do not see yourself as a great leader," Joachim guessed at my silence.

We turned down a garden path and a small pavilion came into view. I led us under the vine-covered roof and to a large wooden bench. I sat before replying. "I see myself as a leader who is doing the best with what she has. And while I understand why the Lords decided to send me to the Humanrealm as a child, I cannot help but think that there should have been more…preparation given to me before I returned.

"Could my protectors not have begun laying a foundation of who I was or what would be expected of me? I trust them with my life and I know they did what they thought was best, but I just wish they had found a way to better prepare me for this life. Sitting in university classes, listening to opera, and reading Shakespeare did nothing to ready me."

Joachim stood before me, gaze cast down to meet my eye. "While I do not know those Humanrealm things, I do take your meaning. I cannot pretend to understand your protectors' rationale—I have not met them, after all—but perhaps there's something to be said for giving you two decades of normalcy?"

I looked up at Joachim as that question clicked into place. The fact that they might have taken advantage of the distance, the different realm, to allow me an upbringing where I was just a kid had never occurred to me. Not once.

Seeming to understand how his question jumbled my mind, Joachim sat. "Your Majesty, perhaps I crossed a line with my question…"

"No," I replied quickly. "I just never considered that they might have purposefully kept me clueless so that I could experience a regular life."

Joachim nodded. "Again, I do not know them but I do understand the life of a monarch and that of a royal family. There is no privacy. There is no selfishness. There is only duty to one's country, and the overwhelming knowledge that every decision you make affects lives. To be spared that weight and scrutiny for twenty years…I can only dream what that must have been like."

There was a wistfulness in Joachim's voice that made me turn to him on the bench. "I take it being a ruler in Niel is just as stressful then?"

He chuckled. "I'd imagine the weight of it is much the same everywhere."

"Tell me about Niel," I said.

The corners of his lips lifted, the skin around his eyes crinkling in a way that said this man was one of smiles, of laughter, of easy joy. "Niel is beautiful. Its interior is filled with low mountains covered in forest and verdant valleys filled with wildflowers. Along the coastline are both cliffs above blue oceans and beaches of yellow sand. It's softer than Izwe.

"Coming here, Izwe seems stark. It's beautiful in its own way but the ground is red, the flowers are not delicate but tough—"

"The pink ones? Those are called proteas," I interjected.

Joachim nodded. "Yes, the proteas. The birds call in sounds I've never heard. Zebras and horned deer and all manner of creatures roam. Even your palace and houses seem stark, just different and stronger than Niel."

"Do you think much of the Alterealm is like Niel, rather than here?"

Joachim replied instantly. "Without question. Your ancestor, when he came to this realm and took control of this land, kept his influence within the borders of Izwe. The rest of the Alterealm seems homogenous in comparison.

"Of course, that's not to pass judgment on Izwe. With your line's power, Izwe is arguably the strongest of the nations—at least historically. And with power comes the privilege of being able to be different."

"Hmm," I murmured. It was interesting seeing Izwe through the eyes of another foreigner, granted one that had known the Alterealm far longer than I had. "You seem to illuminate much for me, Prince Joachim."

He raised a brow. "What do you mean, Your Majesty?"

"Only that you've been here hardly a day and already you've changed how I think about a few things."

"Happy to be of service," he replied with a smile.

I looked at that smile, at the man sitting next to me, and I allowed myself to smile back.

It was not until much later, once the day had wound down and the white-lighted stars had come out, that I realized the extent of my smile.

I was laying in bed, tracking the lines of the gauzy canopy above me through the haze of candlelight. And I was thinking back to our walk in the garden.

There was something about Joachim that made me feel comfortable, something that made me feel safe enough with him to speak my mind and voice my thoughts freely. I was sure the Lords would think I overstepped on several occasions. I was sure Eliza and the Ladies she took tea with would tell me I was being too serious, not coy or flirtatious enough. I was supposed to be wooing a man to my bed after all.

Yet, when I was with Joachim, I felt a freedom I had not felt in some time.

I turned on my side as Finn's face flashed in my mind, and I asked myself if I could imagine Joachim in the way I had come to imagine Finn—as lover, friend, companion.

Try as I might, the word lover did not stick. I was comfortable with Joachim, but the nature of the budding relationship was respectful and *friendly*.

My mind skipped back to a conversation I had had with Mer years ago. We had been perched along a stone half-wall on our college campus and she was telling me everything about a date she had recently been on. At the end of the play-by-play, she sighed and said, "But it's no use, really. There was just no *awareness* between us."

Of course, I had questioned her and she had explained that, to her, attraction was subterranean. It was a subconscious vibration that said you and that other person were sexual beings attuned to the same frequency. Even if a great spark was not there, the awareness was bound to be. And with this boy, there had been no awareness.

I thought of Joachim then and the same description applied. Though he said I was beautiful, though he praised my rule, the compliments felt hollow. He meant them but they were stated as facts, not deeply, passionately held beliefs.

I smiled and laughed with him but my skin did not tingle when he was near. My stomach did not hollow.

I sighed. There was no awareness between us.

I had never asked Mer if she thought awareness could grow. Maybe it was something that, inexistent as it was today, could suddenly appear tomorrow.

As I blew out my candle and shut my eyes, I hoped that was so.

PRINCE JOACHIM'S ARRIVAL IN IZWE HAD LIT UP THE palace. The courtiers in their bright colors were always festive—so much so that I often wondered if I had missed something notable like a high holiday or another national event. But Joachim's arrival was something else.

The excitement was palpable. It hummed through the air and felt like little tremors under my satin-slippered feet. There was a heartbeat to the palace, and the beat thumped out a tune that asked, *Is he the one?*

It was a good question, one that I asked myself each day I awoke. I let that question echo in my mind as I wandered to the stone arena to train with Manelesi. I asked myself in every silent moment there.

Even Manelesi noticed my distraction.

"What is on your mind, Daughter?" he asked me one day as I tried to push my power out, as I tried to do something more than make my fingers glow.

Manelesi had set up a pile of rocks in the shape of a cairn and asked me to topple them. I turned from the mock-cairn with a raised eyebrow. "Nothing. Does it seem like there's something on my mind?"

Manelesi merely raised his brow. "I would not ask if I did not think so."

"That's true," I grumbled. I flexed my fingers absently, as if the movements alone would coax the power free. Then I responded. "I'm preoccupied with Prince Joachim."

"Ah, the potential Consort," Manelesi replied. This was the first we had broached this topic, though I knew Manelesi was well aware of Joachim's presence here.

The same could not be said in reverse. The Lords of the Senior Council had laid down strict *guidelines* that I should, under no circumstances, mention the channeling to Joachim. The court was blissfully ignorant, the wider Council remained so, as well. The last thing we needed was another country knowing.

I nodded. "Yes. He has been here for a few days and…"

When I did not seem ready to continue, Manelesi guessed, "And you cannot find anything wrong with him?"

My eyes narrowed in his direction. It was always unsettling that Manelesi could read my mind. And I still was not sure if it was simply because we thought along the same lines, or if he really could see every thought that existed between my ears.

"No. Yes." I crossed my arms in front of my soldier brown-clad chest, uncertain. "He is kind and caring. He is comfortable. There is absolutely nothing wrong with him and yet—"

"And yet there is nothing right?" Manelesi interjected.

I took a deep breath before I nodded. "Yes. He's lovely, of course, but nothing in me says 'he's the one.'"

Manelesi took a few steps in my direction, his red and cream Masters' robes shifting over the lines of his limbs. His movements had become more normal, more fluid in the past weeks. It was almost possible to believe he was a common man now. "A word of advice, Daughter? Queens rarely find more than that. You should be pleased that he is not awful."

"Is that all I can hope for then?" I replied immediately. I was not sure I truly wanted an answer.

Manelesi raised his eyes at me. There was something moving in their blue-gray depths, some knowing, some words yet unspoken, but I could not put my finger on it. "There is much in store for you. All I can tell you is that Joachim would be the easy path."

"That's not really an answer to my question."

"Yet it is the only answer I am prepared to give."

I *hmphed* at that and I watched as Manelesi flicked his wrist towards the cairn. It toppled effortlessly, the rocks rolling away in all directions.

With a snap of his fingers, the rocks gathered themselves and reformed their towered structure. Manelesi turned to me expectantly. "Your turn."

But no matter how much my fingers glowed, no matter how many times I relived the moment that Finn stopped breathing, the rocks stayed right where they were.

Without fail, I always left the Yesonto's arena disgruntled and unsettled. I moved quickly, as if I was a spy sneaking away. I let this scratching feeling of doing something wrong, something scandalous, push me to the training grounds. Sometimes I sought out Caleb to spar with and other times I went for a run on my own—I was already dressed in soldier browns after all. Other times, I headed right back into the palace and let Kaiht and Mara change me into one of my gray gowns.

The Lords seemed to have cleared the Council schedule in an attempt to give me more free time with Joachim. I took advantage of it. Instead of sitting on my throne and listening to reports on Trina Cheile's movements or a trade negotiation in progress, I sat on quilted picnic blankets in the garden beside my suitor. Some days, we had lunch in the solarium where I used to meet Lisideria. Other days, we wandered the halls, whispering about my favorite Izweian books or the unique musical instruments in my kingdom.

But I never took him to the library. For some reason, that was too intimate.

One afternoon, Eliza invited us to tea and I gladly accepted. Joachim and I arrived to find Eliza and Roland alone in their palace rooms. I had expected Eliza's tea ladies—as I had come to think of them—to be there, too, but it was just the four of us.

I had the absurd idea that I was back in the Humanrealm and bringing a boyfriend home to meet the parents. Only this time, the power dynamic was drastically different with me being a Queen, Joachim a prince, and Eliza and Roland mere nobles. It was also different because Joachim knew all about Eliza and Roland's place in my life. He had studied me, he had unabashedly explained one day as we walked in the garden. All of the eligible young men of the realm had. I was, after all, the most eligible woman across any kingdom.

While I appreciated Eliza and Roland's opinion on Joachim, I also knew that their opinion did not hold the same weight as it would if we were just normal people back in the Humanrealm. I had a kingdom's future to consider, not just my own. I had my people's lives to consider, not just whether my father found the guy respectful.

Still, the four of us fell into effortless conversation. We laughed. We shared stories. And when Joachim and I eventually finished our tea and stood to leave, the look Eliza aimed at Joachim was genuinely warm and hopeful. Roland bowed to him with a seriousness I did not expect.

And I knew Eliza and Roland's opinion. They had chosen their Consort, even if I had yet to decide. I feared the whole palace had.

"HOW MANY TIMES MUST WE GO THROUGH THIS?" Manelesi sighed in exasperation.

Sweating and annoyed, I turned towards him. "I guess again."

Manelesi merely looked at me a moment and then sighed once more. "Pay attention," he barked.

We had been in the stone arena for God and gods knew how long. I was sure Joachim would come looking for me at some point and the worry of discovery only served to distract me further from my task. Regardless of how distracted I was, Manelesi would take no excuses.

No, I had shown him my glowing hands weeks ago. I had proven to him and myself that I could summon my magic. Apparently I just could not direct it at anything.

The hot Izweian sun beat down on my head, the ceilingless building providing no protection. My hair was wound in a braided circle but I could feel the bright rays on the skin visible at my middle part. It itched with the first prickling of sunburn.

"Focus, Daughter," Manelesi replied. I forced my eyes to settle back in the present, shaking off the there-but-not-there stare I had been looking at him with.

"My apologies," I replied.

But Manelesi did not acknowledge that. Instead, he walked forward until he was two paces in front of me. Then he lifted his hands. "Lift yours as I am lifting mine."

I followed suit, holding them before me, elbows bent so I could gaze at the palms.

"Summon your magic."

I closed my eyes a moment as I let wild emotions course through me. I had to admit I was getting better at this part. I could merely remember the vacant look in Finn's eyes and my power leapt to the surface. I had done it so many times I no longer felt the burn of tears.

"Good," Manelesi murmured. "That was faster. Now think of me as the person who hurt him."

My eyes opened. "Who?" I asked automatically, even as my brain knew exactly what Manelesi referred to.

"Must I answer that?"

I shook my head. *Finn.*

I took a breath and focused on the pale face of the Master before me—the Master who was also Manelesi. I willed myself to imagine he was the figure behind the voice that haunted my dreams, that urged the creatures on, that sliced Finn down.

My palms blazed brighter.

"Good," Manelesi repeated, quieter this time as if his raised voice would scare my power back inside me. "Now throw it at me."

I startled. "I could hurt you," I murmured. The look of charred ash that had once been bodies flashed across my memory.

But Manelesi merely laughed. It was a harsh sound, a grating sound like glass scratching against glass. I forced myself not to cringe at the violence of it. "Even you, Daughter, would not be able to do that."

I bristled but did not say anything. I merely looked at my palms once more and watched the silver glow shine brighter. It hurt my eyes to look directly at it so I looked back at Manelesi.

"Are you sure?"

Manelesi merely smiled. "Give it your best shot."

It was silly of me to even ask the question. I knew I could not send my power out on will. Finn and I had worked for a year to even bring my power to the surface. How was I supposed to master the direction of that power in only a few weeks?

Yet even as I thought that, a voice that sounded like Finn's admonished me. *You have proof of your power now, Sahle*, it said. He said. *Use it. Use it for me.*

I closed my eyes against the twin emotions of devastation and anger that flowed through me. And when I looked at Manelesi again, I did not see Manelesi. Instead, I saw the first creature that materialized out of the purple-tinged darkness. I overlaid Manelesi's face with that creature's and replayed the moment when the half of his head fell back, when that terrible voice spoke like a sick game of telephone.

I thought I heard myself whimper but could not be sure. All I knew was that Manelesi was standing there, looking back at me in one moment. And in the next, white light was all around me, all around us.

For a split second, I was alone in that brightness. I blinked my eyes against the luminescence of it, the way it almost sparkled like blue and pink and green glints of diamonds.

When I blinked again, Manelesi was seated. And he was laughing.

He tipped his head back, letting that strange laugh travel up and over the walls of the roofless arena. "That was surprisingly good," he said once his chuckling had stopped. He pulled himself to his feet and only then did I notice the singe mark on the right portion of his Masters' robes.

"Did I do that?" I breathed out. I scanned him over quickly. "Did I do that?"

He smiled at me, and for the first time, I saw pride in those strange eyes. "You did. Well done."

I gaped at him. "Are you injured?"

Manelesi looked down as if he had only just thought to consider it. I supposed when one did not have a corporeal form for hundreds of years, it was not something that factored in.

He poked at the burnt portion, finding soot and untouched skin beneath. "I am hard to hurt," he said finally, factually.

"And the Master's body you're currently residing in?" I asked. Manelesi conveniently seemed to be forgetting that young man.

He shrugged. "He and I are one at the moment. If I am hard to hurt, so is he. Do not fret so much, Daughter."

"Hmph," was all I said before Manelesi smiled. For once he seemed delighted by me and he stepped back, raising his arms towards the sky.

"Do it again," he commanded.

So I did. I blocked out Manelesi's happiness, even my own mingled dread and curiosity. I focused once again on need and fear and anger. And I let that flow through me as I stared with narrowed eyes at Manelesi.

This time, I knew what to expect. The white light flashed. It moved out of my palms and I had the wherewithal to see that now. I did not blink at the brightness of starlight. No, I stared into it as it shot in that same veining structure I had seen when Eliza and Roland and I traveled to the Alterealm the night of my twentieth birthday.

I watched it wind out, snapping at Manelesi. And I watched as it hit him square in the chest, pushing him to the ground once more.

Regardless of what Manelesi had told me, I did fret then. I closed my palms and distantly, I was aware of that veining presence reeling back into me. But I was already moving forward, sinking to my knees in the red dirt beside Manelesi.

Before I could say anything, Manelesi cackled again. He wiped a hand across his cheek, obviously so moved in his humor he was crying. He looked down at his chest this time and the burn mark in the fabric there, and then his laughing fit began all over again.

"I'm glad someone finds humor in this," I muttered as I looped my arm under Manelesi's elbow and helped haul him to his feet.

"Oh, this is fantastic," he said. He doubled over in laughter as soon as he was standing. I waited patiently for the chuckling to subside and, slowly, he straightened fully. "I never expected to be knocked to my feet once, let alone twice by another's magic."

I raised my brow in surprise. "What do you mean?"

Manelesi dusted a mixture of ash and red dust off of his worse-for-wear clothes. Then he focused his gaze on me. "It means you're the most powerful being I have ever encountered—besides myself of course."

He smiled again and one more little derisive chuckle snuck loose.

I did not see what was so funny.

Manelesi had me try again to hit him, this time with particular goals in mind: a shoulder, a knee. I hit his targets directly and he laughed over and over.

But I could feel my body beginning to sag. The exhaustion was setting in and—I realized with a quick glance to the sweltering sun still directly overhead—it was not yet afternoon. Manelesi seemed to sense my waning strength, and he wrapped up our session.

As we both stepped out of the arena's unobtrusive doorway, he said to me simply, "We'll make a god out of you yet."

I looked at him in surprise, but before I could ask whether he was kidding or not, he walked away.

I did not have the guts to follow him. And I was not sure I wanted clarity into what he meant.

Over the melodic trilling of a marching tune, the buzz of hundreds of bodies pressed into the cobbled city street, Joachim said, "Tell me more about you."

We were standing on a tall, erected platform but even from our position above the crowd, we were immersed in the feeling of activity, the sounds of excited voices, the stomping of booted feet. Red dust rose in the air from the commotion, mingling with the heat of the afternoon.

This was a military parade in honor of Izwe's strength, and of course, Prince Joachim and his attendees were all *invited* to attend.

My eyes rolled involuntarily at the thought. I had seen the invitation. I was there at the picnic lunch when two Vikela delivered the folded note. I shook my head then as he read the missive aloud, and I shook my head now.

It was no more than a pissing match, a flagrant show of Izwe's might meant to impress the foreign guests. But it was also a warning. I saw that clearly. Each synchronized step, each swing of a Vikela's spear, each laughing call of a zebra signaled to Joachim and his four companions that Izwe was strong.

Izwe was fierce.

Foreign.

Deadly.

Different.

And it truly was all of those things, I noted, as I tore my eyes away from a company of Vikela in their dress uniforms marching in formation. Each soldier held an instrument and the mingled beat of carved flutes, *djembe* drums, and malleted marimbas built louder and louder in the air.

I turned to Joachim, where he stood on my left. My voice rose high in an attempt to cut through the notes of the thumping music. "I'm sorry. What did you say?"

Joachim glanced between me and the veritable marching band. When the group had passed our platform, he finally repeated, "Tell me more about you."

"You've heard nearly all there is to know," I replied, confused. We had talked about my time in the Alterealm, my journey here, my challenges as a ruler. He had met Eliza and Roland, and he had asked plenty of questions to and about them.

But Joachim shook his head. He angled his shoulders more squarely in my direction, the parade all but forgotten. "I've heard about your last year, but you have a tendency to not dwell on anything before that. You lived twenty years before you returned to Izwe."

I took in the sweep of his dishwater blonde hair, the earnestness in his hazel eyes before I shrugged. He was right. I did avoid speaking about that period of my life. "I guess it's because I think it has no relevance here. It's a different world, a different *realm*. Everything that I did, everything I knew, everyone I knew…it's all irrelevant now."

"That's where you're wrong," Joachim replied. That kind look was in his eyes again. "All of those things might not fit into your life now but they created the woman you are today. That matters."

My eyes shifted away from him, suddenly uncomfortable by the caring his words implied.

When I made no move to respond, he continued. "Perhaps my question was too much. How about this? Tell me about your favorite food in the Humanrealm."

A surprised little laugh slipped out. "I'm not sure what I expected you to ask but it certainly wasn't that!"

"Why not?" he replied with his own amused chuckle.

"It's just a very random thing to want to know," I answered. But then I thought. I asked myself what I had missed, and I knew instantly. My lips curved in delicious memory before I said, "Root beer floats, without a doubt."

"You'll have to explain it to me…" he prompted gently.

And so I did. As the residents of Izwe cheered for a group of Vikela mounted on nimble zebra, each holding a waving red and gold standard, I thought back to my childhood in another world.

"It's a dessert made of two parts: ice cream and soda. Ice cream is a frozen dish made of sugared cream. You scoop spoonfuls of it into a glass and then top it with a sweet drink—something we called soda—that was fizzy and effervescent. It sounds strange but the two together made the best combination.

"The outside of the ice cream where it touched the root beer would harden almost like an icy shell, but the inside would stay soft. I'd eat it on hot summer afternoons in my backyard as I waited for fireflies to come out. It was my favorite thing as a child."

As I explained the treat, I could almost taste it again. I could see my suburban home and feel the warmth of the humid afternoon, the condensation of the iced glass in my hand.

"It sounds delightful," Joachim said simply.

I nodded. "It was. If I could figure out what root beer was made out of, I would try to recreate it here. Even if I could teach the palace kitchen how to make ice cream, I would. That would be enough in itself."

"Perhaps one day."

"Maybe," I answered with a genuine smile of my own.

A movement behind Joachim caught my eye.

Lord Anson.

My eyes narrowed as I watched his retreating dark form. He walked to the end of the platform and quickly took the steps down without a backward glance.

He and the other Lords had accompanied us onto the platform, but just like when Joachim and I sat at the head table in the Great Hall, they gave us room. Oh, they kept an eye on us. It was like having twenty stifling chaperones, but none of them came within hearing distance unless they had something pressing to bring to my attention.

But now Anson was leaving. As Lord of War, perhaps he had duties to attend to during this military parade. Frankly, I was surprised he wasn't down there marching, dressed in soldier brown.

I smirked at that—at the image of the oh-so-fearsome Anson lowering himself to the level of a common soldier. He would never. And I would have paid handsomely to see it, to see any instance where he was made to get off his figurative high horse.

"What in the..." Joachim explained, pulling my attention back to him. But he was not speaking to me, not really. He pointed down at the next group in the parade, and my own eyes popped wide. My lips parted in surprise.

Coming our way was a small group of Vikela. They were dressed like any other Izweian soldiers with their double-breasted formal tunics and their horned helmets. The only difference was that each of them had a beige band on their arms. In each hand, they held a leash.

And on the end of each leash was a lion.

I leaned over the railing as the lions prowled our way. Their bodies moved with smooth grace, each paw eating up the ground in confident, powerful strides. Their thin pelts rippled over strong muscles, and three of the six lions had wide, proud manes framing their faces.

"Oh my," I breathed.

I could feel the crowd still as the lions came to a stop just before the platform. A hush fell over the people as the three Vikela controlling the lions turned to face us—to face me.

I was high above but I, too, froze as the beasts fixed their eyes on the people below me, on the elevated group of nobles and royals.

Nothing happened for the space of a moment. The crowd held its breath. The lions shifted on their tethers. My heartbeat thudded in my ears with a potent mix of excitement and fear at seeing these great creatures.

Then Anson appeared.

He was not marching in formation. No, he did something altogether more shocking.

He walked right up to the lions, their low guffaws seeming to greet him. He turned his back to them. And then he bowed my way.

As he bent, the lions opened their great maws. Each of the six roared.

I gasped at the booming sound, hand flying inadvertently to my throat in surprise.

Mid-roar, Anson righted himself. He stood tall as the lions continued their growls, the sound seeming to flow from and through him. And even from my position high on the platform, I could see that infuriating man smirk up at me.

As his lions—the Ingonyame lions—roared around him. Roared at me.

I stared down at him, all excited thoughts clearing away.

I was no longer impressed. I was annoyed. I felt a scowl carve itself across my face at the display of sheer power, of fearlessness, of stupidity.

But the sound of clapping made me turn in surprise. Joachim was beating his hands enthusiastically, his companions quickly following suit. Moments later, the Lords and the crowd below joined in. Hoops and hollers mingled in the air.

All the while Anson remained standing there, back turned to the lions, gaze trained on me. I forced my lips out of the scowl and into a semblance of my queenly smile. I clapped my hands together lightly, politely.

And from below, I could have sworn Anson's eyes gleamed with mirth. He bowed once more, signaling the close of the military parade amid more shouts, more applause, more adoration.

"What a sight!" Joachim exclaimed from my left.

"Yes," I replied, my voice flat. "Quite."

A KNOCK SOUNDED AT MY DOOR AND THE BRUSH combing through my hair halted abruptly. I met Mara's eye in the mirror where I could see her standing over my right shoulder.

"Shall I answer that, Your Majesty?" Kaiht called as she materialized from my bathing room.

"Yes, thank you," I replied. I was about to ask Mara to please continue with my hair when a jovial voice—one I was growing to know—sounded from the doorway.

I spun in my seat in surprise. "Prince Joachim, I didn't expect you."

It had been just over twenty-four hours since I had seen him last, at the military parade where Anson had put on his show. Joachim had been impressed and had complimented me on *my* lions. I had taken the compliment with a grimace, thinking about how cocky and arrogant Anson's display was. I was seemingly the only one not in awe of the stunt.

Now, Joachim looked from me, seated before my dressing table, to Mara with the brush, and then back to Kaiht with whom he had been speaking. "My apologies, Your Majesty. I was hoping to escort you to dinner but perhaps I am too early. I did not mean to interrupt."

"Not at all," I said. I made to stand but then caught a glimpse of my hair, the left half curled up into an elegant style and the other half frizzed out from dry brushing.

I waved my hand towards the chairs before the fireplace. "Please join us. Mara is just finishing up," I said nonchalantly, even though I felt the prickling of embarrassment at not being put together. At least I had already dressed.

Joachim bowed before making his way to the chairs. He turned one so that he was facing me as he sat. He wore his own crown tonight. "I've never seen hair like yours. It's beautiful."

I turned my head slightly to catch his eye. The earnestness in his smile lit some part of me and I felt the corners of my lips rise in response. "Thank you. It's a handful, but it's mine. I guess I have to like it."

"It's unique."

"Not so much in Izwe, of course," I replied. "Many before had hair like mine."

"Many royals," he countered. "So not only is it unique, but it's a mark of nobility. It's a crown in its own right."

I blushed at that, forcibly pushing past all of the memories of the Humanrealm life where my hair had marked me as *other*— and not necessarily in a good way. "Thank you," I said again.

Joachim looked around the room, scanning past my enormous four-poster bed, the framed maps, the leafy plants, the wall of windows. "And this room, it's glorious in its own right."

"I believe all of the rulers of Izwe have had this room. My mother certainly did before me."

"Queen Bekha," he stated. "I have always heard remarkable things about your mother. She was well-respected across the Alterealm. Sadly, I have no memories of her. I was just ten when she died and, of course, I never traveled outside of Niel."

"I'm told she was formidable, a force to be reckoned with."

"As are you," Joachim replied.

"Please, your flattery is too much," I said with a chuckle.

I felt Mara's fingers pinning up the last section of my hair and then Kaiht stepped forward with two boxes. She placed both before me so I could pick my crown.

As usual, my gown was a rich nearly-charcoal gray and I had no desire to wear a crown that was more ornate than that. I glanced between the two options—one the plain platinum forehead band and the other a more traditional crown in a dark metal that almost looked like iron. I chose the iron.

"Do you normally dress so severely?" Joachim asked, watching as Kaiht secured the crown into my updo.

"Yes," I replied simply. I did not want to explain why. I did not think I had words to express the pain and guilt and regret that walked beside me, the nearly tangible ghost of Finn that haunted me. Nor did I *want* to open that topic now, with Joachim.

Something shuttered in his eyes, as if he could sense, despite the relative openness with which I had always spoken with him, that this was not a topic I wished to broach. "Everyone in your Court seems to favor such vibrant colors. It struck me as curious that you did not share their tastes."

"I do not, nor have I ever," I answered. I could hear the note of finality in my tone and I did not try to hide or make apologies for it. I surveyed the crown in the mirror for a moment more. Then I stood.

Turning to Joachim, I asked, "Are you ready?"

Joachim unfolded himself from his chair, his usual tan pants topped tonight by a deep blue brocade formal jacket. "Certainly, Your Majesty."

Taking my arm and looping it through his, Prince Joachim escorted me through the halls of my palace. My guards flocked behind us. Courtiers greeted us as we passed. They too were on their way to the special dinner being held this evening.

While an ornate dinner took place every night in the Great Hall, this evening would be what Grimly had called a state dinner, held in honor of Prince Joachim's continued presence in the palace. He had been here for two weeks already, surprising though it was. It did not seem that much time had passed.

Music ushered us as we neared the Great Hall, and as we stepped through the doors to the grand ballroom, the musicians paused. Each member of the Court turned to us and bowed.

Joachim leaned in to whisper, "Do you ever get tired of that?"

I knew his question was rhetorical. Every ruler was bowed to. But still I replied honestly, "Yes, very tired of it actually."

He chuckled quietly. "You actually mean that."

"I do," I replied, smiling. We moved into the Hall, arm in arm. And I admitted, "What I wouldn't do to enter a room and have everyone go about their business as usual."

Joachim shook his head as if I were truly a mystery. Maybe I was: a Queen who, despite swearing an oath to herself to become the best Queen she could be, did not want to be monarch.

As the courtiers rose, the music began again. Notes from drums, marimbas, and *mbiras* mingled with the renewed chatter of those packing the hall. And it was packed. It seemed each and every member of the Court was here to partake in the state dinner and witness the foreign prince and me.

Joachim and I made our way to the head table, alternately approached by Lords and Ladies as we went.

"Lady Eliza, Lord Roland, Lady Sybil," I said warmly as I approached the three. They all gave another bow, strange and too-formal though it was coming from this group—my parents and their closest friend.

All eyes turned to Joachim.

"Prince Joachim, none of us can believe it has been two weeks since your arrival in Izwe," Sybil began. "How are you finding it?"

Joachim smiled kindly. "I am consistently delighted by it, Lady Sybil. As I told the Queen, I've never seen anything like it. The plants, the animals, the architecture—it's very different from Niel."

"And our Queen?" Sybil continued with a sly grin. "How are you finding her?"

My eyes widened at the impertinent question even as I watched Eliza battle to keep her smile in check. Roland looked like he wanted to be anywhere other than here.

To Joachim's credit, he was not one to be easily flustered. Rather, he took my hand in his and brought my fingers to his lips with the lightest of kisses. "A finer woman and ruler the Alterealm has never known."

My cheeks burned with embarrassment, and for the millionth time, I was grateful that my dusky complexion did not allow me to shine bright, lobster red. Gently, I loosened my fingers from Joachim's teasing grip.

"What flowery words from you, Prince Joachim," someone called from behind me. I turned to find Lord Anson, dressed in his usual dark, muted colors, his usual smirk pasted across his face. Beside him, Lord Silas quietly stood in a vibrant green suit that landed somewhere between neon and pastel.

The two Lords bowed before adjusting their stance to join Eliza, Roland, and Sybil in the small group.

My cheeks still aflame, I met Anson's gaze head on. His green eyes seemed to flash as he tracked them over my burning cheeks and neck. Then he shifted his attention to the Prince.

Joachim responded first. "What you call flowery, I call earnest, Lord Anson."

Anson watched the Prince another moment before inclining his head.

Silas took the opportunity to add, "We can only be so lucky for the Queen to find not just an ally but a doting companion."

I looked back and forth between the two men, between Eliza, Roland, and Sybil. My brow rose in confusion. Not only was everyone speaking as if I were not here, but the topic of conversation made me want to run and hide.

While Joachim and I had spent the last two weeks getting to know each other, we had carefully avoided any direct questions on the state of our relationship. We had avoided any certainties, erring instead on vague niceties and polite possibilities.

I had no idea what we were doing, and here these Lords and Ladies were being so overt in their questions and comments.

I cleared my throat. "If you'll all excuse me, I must greet the rest of my Court."

"Certainly, my Queen," Anson said with a too-pointed smile. The look in his eye told me he well knew the last thing I would ever *want* to do was engage with the members of the Court for any real amount of time.

"Of course, Queen Sahle," Silas replied with his own bow. Eliza, Roland, and Sybil echoed his words.

I mentally shook myself as Joachim and I carried on our walk towards the head table. Each conversation followed a similar line to what had happened with Eliza, Roland, Anson, Sybil, and Silas. It was as if the entire court was somehow celebrating my marriage but I had missed the ceremony.

As usual, Joachim pulled my seat out for me at the high table. As usual, the members of the Senior Council were noticeably absent—scattered in other seats around the room in order to give Joachim and me space. I took a sip of my *konstans*, willing my confusion and budding annoyance to remain in check.

"You're quiet," Joachim said from my left. "Did I do something to offend you?"

I did not know whether to say yes or no. But I realized that none of my annoyance was his fault. My court was asking pointed questions and he had simply attempted to be accommodating.

"No," I finally replied with a soft huff. "It's not you. It's everyone else. They ask too many questions."

I watched Joachim give an approximation of a princely shrug, his brocade-clad shoulders rising towards his neatly coiffed hair. "You are their Queen. They care about you and, therefore, want the best for you when it comes to choosing a Consort."

"Yes, but they speak as if the matter were settled," I replied sharply.

And I was not prepared for when Joachim asked, "Is it not?"

I turned in my seat, wine glass frozen on its journey towards my mouth. "Excuse me?"

Joachim took a drink of his own wine before standing. "Perhaps we should move somewhere more private for this conversation," he suggested.

He offered me his hand. I glanced from it to the court now watching us curiously from their groups around the room.

"The meal is about to begin," I said quietly. Already, servants had begun bringing wide platters and deep tureens to the tables running lengthwise down the hall. One servant was making their way towards us at the high table.

But Joachim merely asked, "Are you not the Queen?"

I knew no one would sit. No one would eat. Nothing would happen until I was seated once more at the high table. I hated letting the food get cold because I was having a chat. Still, to my ears, his words sounded almost like a dare. I looked again between him and the court before reluctantly grasping his fingers.

Glass in hand, I guided him to the wall of French doors and then out onto the long balcony. Miraculously, it had not been damaged in the explosion.

Several Courtiers were on the balcony but, as if they sensed our need for privacy, they melted back into the Great Hall. And then we were alone.

I could not help myself. Not caring whether I looked petulant or not, I crossed my arms across my chest. "What do you mean by 'Isn't it?'"

Despite my souring attitude, Joachim did not seem fazed. He met my gaze earnestly and said, "It is what's implied by my continued presence here. If you did not like me, if we did not get along, you would have sent me back to Niel by now. Having a foreign suitor in residence is rare, but when it does occur…well, any longer than a few days is all but an acceptance of the suit."

My mouth dropped open. "Says who?"

Joachim shrugged again. "Everyone in your kingdom and mine."

I shook my head, suddenly seeing Joachim and not seeing Joachim. In my mind, I sped through all of the smiles, all of the eager faces, all of the high-pitched voices over the last few days in preparation for tonight.

All of them thought I knew what I was doing by keeping Joachim here. All of them were probably holding their breath, waiting for me to make the announcement in mere minutes. When, in actuality, the entire court—no, the entire Alterealm— had simply overlooked explaining this small detail to me.

Or perhaps they had. Somewhere at the back of my mind, a niggling voice told me Grimly had mentioned something along these lines. He had said something about the length of time. I just had not paid close enough attention, and my Humanrealm mind had filled in the gaps.

It would be laughable if it were not so horrifying. This was simply a case of miscommunication, a subtle nuance of manners and customs lost in translation.

An ironic laugh slipped past my lips and I took another sip of *konstans* to calm myself. "So, we're basically engaged. This is an engagement party."

Joachim crossed the distance between us, shaking his head. "No, Your Majesty. Nothing is final until you say it is. But this event is seen as you *tentatively* saying yes."

"Simply because I haven't kicked you out of the palace yet?"

"Well, yes," he replied with a sardonic quirk of his lips.

I laughed again but the sound was brittle. "Oh, this is… incredible, ridiculous. I don't even have words to explain this."

But if I thought this grand miscommunication was funny, Joachim did not see the humor. I watched him take in my laughter, my derision. And then he asked gently. "Is there someone?"

That stopped me.

My face stilled. All traces of the giddy, anxious, disbelieving laughter evaporated.

"What?" I asked.

"Is there someone else? Is that why you're hesitating now?"

I looked at Joachim, or as much as I could see of him in the part-shadow that was the darkened balcony. So many times over the past weeks, I had purposefully steered the conversation away from any topic that might bring us to Finn. If Joachim knew, as the Lords surely feared, he had never mentioned it.

Yet here the question was, unavoidable and simple and there. Was there someone else?

I debated denying it. But I had tried to be as honest with Joachim as I could be these last weeks. If he was to marry me, he deserved to have this truth, too.

Looking out over the balcony's edge, out past the darkened mass that was the silver tree forest surrounding the palace, I said quietly, "There was someone. He's…gone now."

"Hence the gray gowns? They're to mourn him, I would assume."

Perceptive as he was, it should not have surprised me when he guessed it. Still, I looked back at Joachim with startled eyes. "You see everything, don't you?"

He shrugged, looking down at his feet. "Not everything, but I do see more than most." Then, as if he could sense, too, that I did not want to discuss Finn, he added, "For instance, I know without a doubt that I am not your only admirer here."

"Excuse me?" I must have heard him wrong.

"It's true. It would be indelicate of me to name names, but let's just say there is someone who cares a great deal about you even if they would never dare act on it."

My mind flipped through the faces of all the people Joachim had interacted with in my presence. Lord after Lord, Lady after Lady passed my mind's eye. I considered the soldiers, the servants. And I came up with nothing.

Everyone treated me with cool respect or barely contained disdain. I could not imagine any of them harboring some secret love for me.

"You really won't tell me, will you?" I finally asked.

Joachim shook his princely head. His own state crown glinted in the shadows as he moved. "Sadly no. It would not help my suit to name a competitor."

I scoffed. "And your suit…You say I must state our engagement if it's to be final, but what of you? After getting to know me these last weeks, are you still interested?"

Joachim smiled. It was a gentle thing, a kind thing. Slowly, he reached out and took my hand in his. The skin of his palm was warm and dry and pleasant. It felt comfortable.

"Yes, I am still interested. Whether you speak of it or not, I understand you have been hurt and that your heart is healing. I can respect that and still want whatever part of you is available to give—and more whenever you are ready to give your heart fully." Then he leaned in conspiratorially. "That is, if *you'll* still consider it."

I looked at him in surprise. His thoughtfulness endeared him to me in a way that had been growing, burgeoning these past weeks. And there it was, in all of its glory and fullness. He *was* kind. He was understanding. He was my friend.

"Yes," I replied, giving his hand a little squeeze. "I'll consider it."

We reentered the Great Hall soon after. I noticed the dishes of food had been covered, but seeing my return, servants rushed forward to resume the service.

As we took our places at the high table, the musicians' tune shifted and dancers took to the empty spaces between the long court tables.

In companionable silence, Joachim and I ate our meals of roasted *insephe*. Trays of dressed salad were placed before us, as were loaves of crusty bread, and slices of passion fruit, papaya, and mango.

I watched the male and female dancers, clad in ostrich feathers, giraffe pelts, and kudu horns jump and twirl and oscillate across the floor of the Great Hall. Several times, I glanced over at

Joachim, taking in how effortless his back seemed to rest in the stately chair, a near-mirror of my own throne. I watched how his eyes crinkled good-naturedly as he clapped for a particularly gifted set of male acrobats in zebra skins, as he accepted another glass of wine with a smile to the servant.

Joachim was a *good* man.

There was nothing to be said for attraction between us, let alone love. Each time he complimented me, it felt as if Roland were singing my praises. Each time Joachim took my hand, it felt like a theoretical brother was assisting me to my seat.

Despite that, I had to admit there was a certain ease that had bloomed. And when I considered having to marry to ensure my kingdom's safety and security, there would certainly be much worse options than a *friendly* marriage.

My eyes skipped unbidden to where, many seats down one of the long tables, Anson's dark head turned towards the dancers. There could just as easily and swiftly be a marriage of animosity, a marriage that was as abhorrent as being trapped in hell with the person you hated.

I turned back towards Joachim. This time he felt my gaze. "Your Majesty?"

"Don't mind me," I replied. I placed my hand on his forearm where it rested on the table between us. "I'm just watching you enjoy the festivities."

I TURNED OVER THE NEXT MORNING AND, EVEN BEFORE my eyes opened, my mind began to race.

Was this it? Was I really about to accept Prince Joachim as my Consort?

I had considered the question a dozen, no, a hundred times last night. I asked myself it while I sat beside Joachim. I asked myself it as we drank glass after glass of *konstans* and laughed. I asked myself it as we—in a very un-Sahle-like move—strolled from group to group of courtiers in the Great Hall and mingled.

Joachim had kept his hand at the small of my back the entire time. The sensation was comfortable and safe, but there was nothing else there.

As he escorted me back to my chambers at the end of the evening, as he once again brought my fingers to his lips in a chaste goodbye kiss, I could not force my heart to flutter. There were decidedly no butterflies in my stomach.

But that was good. I surprised myself in liking that I felt nothing more.

Even though I never loved Finn, I had fallen deeply into caring for him. I had opened myself up to the tumbling velocity of *what if.* I had risked my emotions once and if I were being honest with myself, I was still reeling from it. The proof was in the gray of each gown I donned, the little voice in the back of my head that had taken on the timbre of Finn's voice.

No, to love—even to care—was risky. This was not.

Especially when it would secure my kingdom.

I threw back the down blanket and climbed from my bed. I had not seen Kaiht or Mara yet this morning but that was not surprising; it was still early and the light was a gray glow where the sun was trying to push past the horizon.

I padded to my desk in bare feet, my nightdress brushing softly against my legs. I unearthed a sheet of paper and had just touched the nib of a pen to its surface when a soft knock sounded at my door.

My head turned to the pre-dawn sky before looking back at the door. It was early, much too early for visitors. If someone were knocking, it must be urgent.

I moved to the door and pulled it open abruptly. To my surprise, Lord Robert stood with my guards to either side of him.

"Your Majesty," Robert said with a deep bow. His eyes tracked over my nightdress in discomfort and I crossed my arms over my chest.

"Lord Robert, what a surprise."

"My apologies, Majesty, I did not mean to wake you…"

"No, no, don't worry. I was already up," I said reassuringly.

He bowed again. "I won't keep you long. I came to deliver a message. Prince Joachim kindly asks if you would speak with him at your earliest convenience."

My brow crinkled. Joachim, as he had shown last night, had no qualms with coming to my door on his own. Possibilities flitted across my mind as to why he had sent Lord Robert in his stead.

"Is anything the matter? Is Joachim alright?" I asked.

But Lord Robert would do nothing but give a noncommittal bow. "It is best if you speak to the Prince directly."

Confused though I was, I nodded. "Thank you, Lord Robert. You can tell him I'll see him as soon as possible."

Lord Robert bowed again before disappearing down the shadowy hallways. My guards closed in once more as I shut the door.

I knocked on Joachim's door. Anxious moths flitted around my stomach. Two Vikela stood behind each of my shoulders.

I knew I was the Queen. I could open this door and walk in if I wanted, but something about that felt wrong. I did not presume to think I could encroach on Joachim's space, or any other person's in this palace. Yet another way in which I was still just Sahle…

Lord Robert opened the door moments later and I froze at the sight before me. The three soldiers who had come to Izwe with Joachim and Robert were all present. Each of them were busy packing items into trunks. A palace servant assisted, as was—surprisingly—Prince Joachim.

He folded a shirt into one trunk before turning to the noise in his doorway. His eyes lit in surprise. "Your Majesty, I did not expect you so soon."

It was fair enough. I had waited all of two minutes after Lord Robert left my chambers. Then I had sent for Kaiht and Mara. I had dressed in a hurry, donning a casual gray gown. Mara had pulled my hair back into a simple bun before placing a low tiara on my head. Needless to say, I had been eager and antsy to find out why Prince Joachim was sending for me so suddenly.

Looking at Joachim now, a pit in my stomach opened. His hair—usually so coiffed and polished—was messily tousled as if he had just risen from bed or had never made it there in the first place. His long-sleeved shirt was casually open from throat to chest and his sleeves were rolled up to his elbows.

He approached me with a hesitant look in his hazel eyes, and I felt all the hours of envisioning him as Consort blow away like dust in the breeze. I knew nothing good was about to happen.

"Everyone out," he called over his shoulder. The soldiers and Lord Robert and the palace servant halted their packing immediately and hurried from the room.

The sudden quiet was deafening and strangely at odds with the disarray on every surface around us. Books littered the floor. Clothes were strewn across the bed and draped over the backs of chairs. A small pile of leather books stood sentry near the entrance of the bathing chamber.

Joachim's voice called my attention back to him. "Queen Sahle, I must speak with you. Please." He motioned to the single uncluttered chair. He waited for me to sit before continuing. "I don't know how to tell you this. Believe me, I wish I could say anything else but this now. But alas, I have no choice."

"Joachim—" I stopped him. He was rambling. "Just tell me."

He took a deep breath and faced me head on. He rubbed his chin roughly, scratching against the stubble sprouting there. "I must leave, Your Majesty. Today."

"Leave the palace?" I asked, despite the clear evidence of the departure all around me. Still, as if my brain could not put two and two together, I needed to confirm it.

Joachim looked down. "Yes."

I waited all of three heartbeats. I hoped he would continue. I wanted him to give some explanation but his lips were unmoving. His eyes remained glued to the floor.

"I thought everything was going well. The last weeks, everything we said last night…"

Really, it felt like whiplash. In the space of twelve hours, I had gone from not realizing we were all but engaged to understanding that—even accepting that. And now this.

I shook my head as if I could physically clear away the abrupt, world-altering changes that were coming too fast these days.

"They were, Your Majesty," Joachim replied. He met my eyes

and I could see the truth in his words. He looked physically pained. "Please believe me when I say that there's nothing I'd like more than to stay and continue my suit. But last night, almost as soon as I returned here after dinner, I received a note from my father."

A sense of dread had me whispering, "And?"

"And he has summoned me back to Niel with the utmost urgency."

My mind conjured a hundred possible explanations. Perhaps a family member was ill. Perhaps his father needed him for another diplomatic trip. Perhaps, perhaps. Perhaps anything but the words Joachim said next.

"Several days ago, my father received a missive urging him in the strongest possible terms to end this particular allegiance with Izwe."

Joachim was always the diplomat, even in this moment. I met his eyes, begging him silently to be blunt. "Joachim, tell me what that really means."

He swiveled his gaze to the ceiling as if he would find encouragement there. Or maybe strength. "To put it plainly, the body of a man with my same build and hair was dumped in my father's chamber. The note was pinned to his chest and signed in blood."

My eyes widened in horror, imagining that scene—the mingled shock and fear and relief that must have gone through the King's mind as he thought and then unthought his favorite child was dead.

But there was one last question, the most important one. "Who signed the letter?"

Joachim looked at me then. Sadness and pity warred in his kind eyes. "The last line said 'Falin, leader of Trina Cheile.'"

All of these years, we had never known the name of Trina Cheile's leader. Oh, we knew he was out there. We knew he was powerful and scheming and strategizing. But we did not have a single person to assign the blame, only some grandiose idea of a country that hated us. Now we knew who was in charge: Falin.

Ice ran through my veins and my heartbeat picked up, double-time. With wide eyes, I stared back at Joachim.

"I'm sorry, Queen Sahle, but you must understand that I have no choice. My father is distraught. He thought he was prepared to formalize our allegiance through this marriage but he did not believe Trina Cheile, this Falin would go this far to put an end to it.

"The message was clear: if I go through with this suit, it won't be a random man next time. It will be my body delivered to my father. And my father, politics or not, will not accept that possibility. I am sorry."

Shocked as I was, his apology seemed to shake my words loose. "You're sorry? There is nothing you need to apologize for, Joachim." I rose from the chair and approached him where he stood. "It's me who should apologize. I'm the reason you and your family have been dragged into this insanity. If you weren't here for me, none of this would have happened."

Joachim being the safe, sweet Joachim he always was took my hands in his. "Still, I'm sorry for it. In the last weeks, I've grown quite fond of Izwe and the idea of a life here. I've grown quite fond of you."

Despite everything, I gave him a sad little smile. "You said in our first meeting that you'd see if you liked my personality. Did you ever get around to deciding?"

"Of course," he said. "I decided that first morning in the garden. And if not for this, I would hope to have many years enjoying it."

I nodded. "It would have been nice, you and me. We get along. Dare I say we've become friends?"

It was his turn to smile, the corners of his eyes crinkling. "Yes, that's a fair assertion. I hope to consider you a friend for a long time still, even if only as an ally from Niel. Would you accept that, Your Majesty?"

"I'd be honored," I replied. And I *was* honored—shocked but honored. I struggled to understand how I had awoken so certain that I was about to take a husband and, in the space of an hour, had lost him.

Yet there was nothing to be done. Joachim's father had made his decision, and I could not fault him for it. Any parent would make the same choice rather than risk the life of their child.

Joachim was leaving.

I squeezed Joachim's hands once more and then sighed. "I guess that means I must start my search for a Consort again."

He tipped his head forward as if he would tell me a secret. "I don't think you'll have any problem finding one, Your Majesty."

"So you think," I scoffed. "See, even you won't take the job."

That made him laugh and I appreciated the normalcy in the sound. "I told you before but I'll tell you again, as your friend. You are a beautiful woman, Queen Sahle. You are a competent leader, despite your newness to the role. You will do great things for Izwe and, I hope, the entire Alterealm. And you will find your Consort. Of that, I'm certain."

"You make it sound like men are lining up to marry me."

"Aren't they?" he said, a teasing glint in his eye.

"Hardly."

"We'll see. I expect you to write and tell me all about it."

I nodded in agreement as Joachim smiled at me once more. And as he let my hands fall from his, I knew I would miss his jovial spirit in the palace.

There was not much to say after that. I said my goodbyes with well wishes for his journey. Then I left him to finish packing.

PART 2

13
drawing board

PRINCE JOACHIM AND HIS CONTINGENT LEFT THE CASTLE before the sun was high in the sky. I was not there to see them ride out, but Kaiht and Mara whispered to me later that courtiers had lined the windows overlooking the palace yard. All speculated on the Prince of Niel's abrupt departure. The Queen and Prince had looked so cozy last night, they sighed. Perhaps she said something to upset him, they guessed. Perhaps he tried something on her, they whispered.

Fortunately or unfortunately—I was not sure which yet—no one had guessed at the true cause of Joachim's departure. I was still trying to wrap my head around it. But I needed help.

Not ready to confront the entire Council of twenty Lords, I sent my guards to fetch the five Lords of the Senior Council. I sat on one of the wingback chairs in my chambers and wrung my fingers while I waited. Luckily it did not take them long to appear.

Lords Grimly of House Kubuga, Anson of House Ingonyame, Lucas of House Nkwe, Marcus of House Inyathi, and Ivan of House Ndlovu entered my chambers as a group. They bowed in unison, and when they rose, Anson was the first to speak.

"What happened?"

"Excuse me?" I bit out. It was the question we were all here to discuss, of course. I just was not ready for his abruptness, not to mention the overt accusation in his tone.

"I asked what happened, Your Majesty?" he repeated.

"I heard you the first time, Lord Anson. But I struggle to take the question seriously when there is so much blame attached to your words. Why do you assume that I did something?"

His eyes seemed to snap. "I never said *you* did something."

"But it's certainly what you're implying, is it not?"

"Your Majesty," Lord Grimly jumped in. He took a step forward, all but blocking my direct view to Anson. That was probably for the best. I did not need to see that man. "What Anson is attempting to ascertain is what occurred between last night and this morning. Prince Joachim and you looked to be quite happy together last night. It is at odds with his abrupt departure today."

I sighed and told them everything about my decision to name Joachim as Consort this morning, Lord Robert's arrival, my trip to Joachim's room, and Falin's message tacked to a dead man's chest. I even explained my lack of understanding the subtext of last night's state dinner—to which I thought I saw Anson look at me like I was a clueless child. His usual smirking mask was back so quick I could not be sure I had seen the incredulous look, but I was fairly certain it had been there.

Anson never failed to be shocked by my ignorance.

Marcus cleared his throat. "Your Majesty, I believe I speak for the entire Senior Council when I extend my condolences to you. I can only imagine how difficult it must be to have selected a Consort only to have them decline for reasons beyond their control."

I nodded. "Thank you, Lord Marcus."

"Yet, Your Majesty, I must also urge you not to allow this blow to affect you," Marcus continued. "The safety of your nation is more at risk than ever. It may seem like a small thing but Falin revealing his name, when he has kept it secret for so many years, is a calculated act. It shows that he is watching and that we are making him anxious. We must continue the course. We should move on to another suitor, and quickly."

I looked from Marcus to the other Lords with a sinking sensation in my stomach. "Joachim has only just left."

"We understand, Queen Sahle, but this is important. Trina Cheile has shown how far they will go to prevent us making a powerful allegiance with your marriage. If we are to have any hope in it, we must act before word can travel across the Alterealm."

It made sense in a cold, detached sort of way. I needed to marry someone and cement an allegiance before the nations could know what was truly at stake. It reeked of trickery. I did not like the idea of pulling the wool over a potential husband's eyes but there did not look to be another choice.

I met the Lords' gazes one by one. "I don't like it but I admit you're right. So we're back to the drawing board then?"

"Yes, Your Majesty," Grimly confirmed. "In a usual circumstance, this matter would be something to bring to the entire Council. However, we need to act with the utmost urgency so I suggest we have messengers sent to each of the kingdoms who answered our initial queries for suits. If any of those suitors remain interested, they can accompany the messenger back to Izwe to meet you. Would that be amenable?"

I was surprised to feel myself nod. It was not that I was past caring, but my nerves were shot. My mind seemed to have divorced itself from my own emotions until all I was considering were logistics.

There really was no choice but to nod in acquiescence. If I wanted a foreign allegiance, I had to act. And whenever a suitor arrived, I had to accept him. I was past the point of being picky.

I nodded again. "Yes. Do it. Send the messengers today. You can alert the Council of our decision."

"It will be done, Queen Sahle," Grimly said.

I looked between these advisors, exhaustion curling around me. "Thank you for answering my summons so quickly, Lord Grimly, Lord Marcus, Lord Lucas, Lord Ivan, Lord Anson. Now we wait."

14

too late

The days ticked by slowly as we waited for word to come from the other suitors. I had turned them all down when I had selected Joachim as a potential Consort. I knew that and I was sure they knew that, too.

Still, I hoped that we were quick enough with our messengers, or that one of the suitors simply did not care. The latter seemed more probable. Despite our discretion, everyone in the palace was whispering about Joachim's abrupt departure. I turned corners and courtiers immediately quieted. Their watchful, curious, cautious stares told me all I needed to know about the subject of their conversation. I felt their hushed words like cotton balls around me, solidly there but soft and almost forgettable.

Almost.

The whisperings were not contained to the palace. No, that would be too simple. Eliza and Roland had returned home soon after Joachim's departure. They had stayed in the palace nearly the full two weeks Joachim was in residence, and for almost all of the time since my ill-fated birthday. Their leaving was long overdue.

I was surprised, therefore, when I received a note from them less than a day after their goodbyes. The missive was brief, just two short lines scrawled out in Roland's matter-of-fact handwriting:

The servants at Chez Eliza were already talking when we returned. News of Joachim's departure has traveled fast. - R & E

I was not sure what to make of the message. I folded it back in half, tucking it into the pocket of my skirt. Over dinner, seated with the Senior Council Lords, I pulled it back out and passed it around.

Grimly, Marcus, and Anson all looked at me with carefully veiled concern. Ivan and Lucas would not meet my eye.

"That bad, huh?" I asked them quietly. I smiled absently out over the room of courtiers, even though my face wanted to drop into a scowl.

"It is not ideal," Lucas replied. "The problem is not that Lord Roland and Lady Eliza's servants are chatty. The issue is that they knew before the Lord and Lady's return."

"And if word has traveled that far that quickly—" I began.

Anson finished my thought. "Then our messengers to the suitors may have been too late."

I was too concerned to be annoyed at his interjection.

Yet this realization changed our waiting. Gone now was the impatient waiting. In its place was the anxious waiting, the heart-in-throat pacing before the window in an effort to spot a contingent of Lords galloping out of the forest towards the palace.

I began to worry each evening as I let Kaiht and Mara tuck me into bed without any word. There were two other suitors. Surely, surely one of them still had to be interested in me—or at least interested in wielding the power of Consort of Izwe— regardless of what had happened with Joachim.

Still they did not come. Still they kept their distance.

I channeled my worry, my nervous energy into my training with Manelesi. The strong emotions only seemed to heighten the fear and desperation I already summoned each day in the arena. And in this heightened sense of despair, I found a strange silver lining.

I was improving, being able to spool out my magic in increasingly difficult tasks: knocking down the rock cairn, hitting targeted spots on Manelesi's body, and even blocking a blast from Manelesi himself.

That last task was treacherous, to say the least. I had balked when Manelesi suggested we try it. It was one thing for me to shoot magic at a divine being. But I was no such thing. I could feel my blood in my veins, the spot where the back of my boot was rubbing the skin into a blister. I was very much alive and human and non-divine. And I did not feel like dying just this moment.

Still, I nodded my agreement, letting the nerves guide me to a reckless, wild place. And when Manelesi sent forth his own blast of white light, mine jumped out to meet it. Like a shield, it wrapped around me, deflecting Manelesi's hit.

And when the light faded, when our hands returned to their normal shades of beige and cream, Manelesi smiled that pleased Cheshire cat smile reserved for when I did something particularly delightful.

"Good, Daughter. Very good," was all he said.

THE DAYS PASSED AND WITH EACH ONE, MY BELIEF THAT
I would find a new Consort slipped further away. Then, one day,
I returned from my training to find a sealed note on my desk.

I sighed out a mingled sound of relief and anxious nerves. We
had waited long enough for word and now I would learn which
suitor would be next in my path towards marriage.

I cracked the seal—Grimly's—immediately and scanned the
words.

Your Majesty,
The Council kindly requests your presence this afternoon for an
important matter. We will commence the meeting at two o'clock, as
long as it suits Your Majesty's schedule.
Grimly

I steeled myself as I called Kaiht and Mara to help me bathe
and change into appropriate attire for the Council Meeting.
When I emerged from my bath, a bowl of golden pureed soup
and a chunk of crusty bread sat before the fireplace. I let myself

enjoy the balanced salt and sweet of the butternut squash, the crunch and softness of the bread. And I braced myself for what was about to occur.

Whenever I was summoned, it always seemed to be for something unpleasant, something heavy. The times where I went willingly to the Council Meetings, those were the lighter meetings. Those were the meetings where the Councilors discussed routine palace business or the needs of certain Masters or Courtiers. And if it was really good news, Grimly would often just include it in his letter. No, I was asked to appear in the Council Chamber when serious, unpleasant business needed to be dealt with.

I finished my soup, checked that my crown stood straight on my head, and then headed to that dreaded chamber.

When I entered the room, the Lords were milling about, chatting in small groups. Seeing me, they immediately quieted and dropped into low bows.

"Rise," I called as I walked the distance to my seat at the opposite end of the room. The stiff material of the formal gray gown rustled as I strode forward, stepped up onto the dais, and settled in the ornate chair.

Grimly was the only Lord who remained standing, all others having taken their seats. "Thank you for joining us, Your Majesty. We called this meeting today to discuss a delicate matter—"

I braced myself for whatever words would come next.

"—We received word from each of the potential suitors. With their utmost respect, they send their regrets and retract their offers of marriage."

I sat there, stone faced.

It had been too long. I knew that instinctively. If one had wanted to be my Consort, he would have clamored to this palace as soon as news of Joachim's departure reached him.

Neither man had done that. There was no clamoring. And Grimly's words sealed it. I was suddenly stripped of suitors.

I blinked as I accepted the reality I had contemplated for days. "I feared as much."

"Yes, well," Grimly began reluctantly. "Unfortunately, that is not all. As you know, Your Majesty, rumors have been circling as to why Prince Joachim departed so suddenly. We feared it had spread across Izwe, and perhaps abroad. We were correct. Our sources tell us that the people are implying less than savory things about you, Your Majesty."

My brow rose. "Less than savory? What exactly do you mean by that?"

Grimly looked uncomfortable and swallowed once before he continued. "One rumor is that Prince Joachim came to the castle and was so displeased by you that he left as fast as possible."

"Alright," I said slowly. I bristled at the implication, at the blatant lie, but worked to remain calm. This was not Grimly's doing; he was merely reporting. "Is that the worst of it?"

"Not quite, Your Majesty. The people have been saying that no foreign Princes will consider you, that they actively want nothing to do with you as a bride or an ally."

This was not the most comfortable of conversations, but I squared my shoulders and tried to be impartial. "It's not entirely untrue. You yourself just told me the suitors retracted their offers."

"Yes, Your Majesty," Grimly replied. "However, rescinding an offer of marriage does not mean that their kingdoms are now hostile to us. That is what the people are implying by these whispers. And, more crucially, the people are also saying that none of the Lords will have you either?"

"The Lords?" I questioned. I scanned my eyes around the room.

These Lords?

If these men were an option for me, this was the first time I was hearing anything about it.

"Yes, Your Majesty. Lord Silas, your informants brought news of this. Perhaps you would like to explain?"

"Certainly," Lord Silas said as he rose from his seat. He smiled apologetically at me before he continued. "My intelligencers tell me that traditionalists across the nation—

as well as their sympathizers in other kingdoms—are using the fallout from Prince Joachim's suit as an example that our allies are beginning to reject us and even Izwe's Lords are reluctant to show fealty.

"Majesty, they are impressing upon your subjects that the Royal House is losing its hold on Izwe. They insist that it is clear now that Izwe is alone in the Alterealm and destined to fall to Trina Cheile. Internally, it shows the crown is losing the ability to keep the kingdom unified. As you will well know, Majesty, the traditionalists have long argued that the descendants of Warbeck are the rightful rulers and should retake the throne—"

My eyes flicked to Anson at the mention of Warbeck, his family's House before it was renamed Ingonyame after Manelesi's arrival. It may have been my imagination but it felt like Anson pointedly avoided my gaze.

"The traditionalists are gaining momentum with this now. Your perceived weakness gives credibility to their cause. Unfortunately, the rumors, and the potential for internal unrest, are spreading," Silas concluded before retaking his seat.

I took a breath, training my gaze back on Grimly. "I take it this is not good?"

Mouth grim, the Chief Advisor shook his head. "No, it is not. In fact, each day that you go unmarried, the possibility of these whispers materializing as a real internal conflict grows."

Even I did not need him to state that we could not weather an internal threat, as well as the external one we were already facing.

"So what do we do about it?" I asked the assembled Lords.

Silence was my answer and I looked closer at the men. They suddenly looked uncomfortable and I braced myself for the response to my question.

"Your Majesty, the Senior Council met this morning to discuss this," Grimly continued after a moment. "While we had hoped to secure external allies through your marriage, it is clear now—given Trina Cheile's involvement with Niel—that this is not possible.

"Given that, we feel we must focus our attention domestically to shore up our internal strength. It is in your best interest, as well as the kingdom's best interest, if you were to pick a Lord to wed with the utmost haste."

My brows rose of their own accord. "Choose a Lord…one of you? Just like that?"

"Well, yes, Your Majesty. While it will not settle the talk of failed allegiances, it will put to rest the idea that the Houses have abandoned the Crown."

I could not help but picture a rowboat leaking water. Apparently my move now was about trying to plug the holes in this leaking, creaky vessel.

With a short pause, Grimly added, "Of course, we do have a recommendation as to who we feel would be the most suitable candidate."

I wanted to laugh at the absurdity of this, at what the search for my Consort had come down to. I looked around the room once more and felt the Lords were about to pick straws. The one with the shortest would win the bad, horrific, no-good prize of being married to me.

It would be funny if it were not so humiliating. At the back of my mind, I wondered how we had gotten to this place. Mere days ago, I had been drinking wine with Joachim and marveling at the ease in which we interacted, at which we could interact for the rest of our lives.

At the forefront of my mind, I focused on keeping my face void of all emotion. I inclined my head in a Queenly fashion and bit out the words necessary for my kingdom. "Yes, Lord Grimly. I will consider your recommendation. Who is it?"

"Lord Anson."

My breath hitched. The air stilled.

If I thought the room had been quiet before, I was wrong. No, this was quiet. All eyes turned to me. All breathing stopped.

All shuffling feet and repositioning of bottoms on chairs ceased. Everyone wanted to see what I would think of Lord Anson of Ingonyame being proposed as a potential Consort.

"Lord Anson?" I croaked, hoping to the God and gods I had misheard.

"Yes, Your Majesty. The Senior Council felt that he was the strongest candidate for several reasons—"

"And they are?" I asked shortly. My eyes moved back to Anson and I willed him to look up. Why was he just sitting there like a stone when he was being discussed with such consequence?

Grimly responded, "Lord Anson would have the power alone, as the leader of House Ingonyame, to squash the dissent regarding Warbeck's desire for the throne. He is also one of the few magic wielding Lords left. And he is a member of the Senior Council so he is already committed to the betterment of this kingdom. He is no stranger to service to the crown."

Service to the crown.

I mused over that phrase, bitterness seeping into the edges of each word, each letter.

Service to the crown.

That is what marrying me would be for a man like Anson.

I looked at him once more. And his lack of action, his unwillingness to engage in this conversation at all sent me over the edge. "And Lord Anson? Have you nothing to say about this? It seems your fate is being decided right in front of you, yet you could not be more disinterested."

At this, Lord Anson finally met my eye. There was a defiance in that gaze that both put me at ease and made me brace for his words. He opened his mouth. "I can only tell you what I told the Senior Council this morning. I will not marry you, Your Majesty."

My mouth gaped open. I knew I did not look dignified and I tried to will the muscles along my cheeks and jaw to respond. Yet, try as I might, my shock was too great.

"Excuse me?" I finally bit out. I felt the skin of my forehead stretch as my eyes widened in both anger and shock.

"I said I would not marry you," Anson repeated, standing from his chair. When I made to speak, he held up a hand. "If you'll allow me, Your Majesty, I do not mean any offense. I state this not from a place of preference but merely one of logic and fact—"

"And which facts are those?" I cut in. I knew I should be relieved that Anson was pushing back on this match, for I could not imagine a world in which I was married to…*Anson.* But my pride rankled. A new voice that screamed *I am the Queen!* echoed in my head. It seemed there were some ways I had grown into this role, after all.

Anson leveled his gaze at me from where he stood. "If you'd let me speak, Your Majesty, I'll tell you." He waited to see if I would reply and when I bit my lip—to physically stop myself from responding—he continued, "Your Majesty, I do not consider myself a worthy Consort for the following reasons. First, I do not have enough magical power to meaningfully contribute to your line—"

"You have as much as any of the Lords," Grimly countered.

"—Second, I have spent too long as a soldier, as your Lord of War. I can advise you on the machinations of battle, but I would be ill-suited to the finesse that is the strategy of a Consort."

"Yet you have experience on the Senior Council. Everything else can be learned with time," Grimly again added.

Anson continued to ignore the Chief Advisor. His gaze remained locked on mine and mine alone. "Third, I am too old for you, Your Majesty. You would be better suited marrying a Lord closer to your own age." He leaned forward, placing his hands on the table in front of him. "And finally, perhaps the most important point is this. You and I do not suit, Majesty. What you would like to see happen in Izwe would always be at odds with what I would like. Even in matters of a more personal nature, you and I would never see eye to eye. Warring with one's Consort is not the right battle—not when we have traditionalists attempting to fracture the kingdom from within and enemies knocking at our gates from without. No, Your Majesty, you are much better suited with another Lord as Consort."

"Lord Anson," Grimly started to say but it was my turn to cut him off.

I stood from my chair, my own hands planted on the table before me. And I stared at Anson as if we were the only two souls in this Council Chamber. "You put that in such a diplomatic way, Anson. But you don't have the guts to simply say you don't like me."

Anson closed his eyes and took a deep breath in an exaggerated show of patience. "Please, Your Majesty, when have I ever said that?"

"You didn't have to say it," I spit out. "You have never liked me, and you have taken every opportunity to cut me down and belittle me since I arrived here in the Alterealm. And that's fine. You don't have to like me. But let's not kid ourselves into thinking that your stated reasons are the real opposition to this. You don't *want* to be married to me."

Anson shook his head, a look of incredulity cut into every line and angle of his face. "And you want to be married to me?"

"I would *never* marry you, Lord Anson," I seethed from my spot at the head of the table.

My chest rose and fell in quick succession. And as Anson and I continued to glare at each other with open aggression, I slowly, slowly began to notice my surroundings once more. As my tunnel vision cleared, I realized each of the Lords were still sitting in their chairs. Each whipped their heads from me to Anson as if they were observing a Humanrealm tennis match, and it was the most fascinating thing they had ever seen.

I cleared my throat in sudden embarrassment. I knew I had a temper. I knew it could spark to anger quickly, but I never thought I would make a scene such as this.

I refocused my gaze back on Anson and my eyes narrowed. Of course, he was the cause of this. He always seemed to be key in my deepest shame and humiliation.

From the far end of the Council Chamber, Lord Marcus rose to his feet. Apparently he was the bravest of the Lords, the only one who dared get in the line of fire. "Queen Sahle, Lord Anson. I believe the Lords have heard enough on this particular topic. If neither party will entertain it—no matter how much the Council may believe in its merits—then we will move on. Lord Grimly?"

"Certainly," Grimly called from his spot nearer to me. He rose to his feet. "There are twenty Lords on this Council. I move to adjourn this meeting for today. Let us all consider possibilities and perhaps we can present new candidates to Your Majesty the day after tomorrow?"

I took a deep breath, pulling my hands away from the table as I drew myself up to my full height. "I would appreciate that. I look forward to hearing the names of *suitable* candidates."

"Of course, Your Majesty," Grimly said with a bow.

I nodded stiffly before I stepped down from my dais. I left the chamber without another look behind me.

Only when I returned to my chamber, shutting the door firmly, did my hands stop shaking.

16
sacrifice

I LAID IN BED, STARING UP AT THE WISPY CANOPY OVER my head and thinking what a little shit Lord Anson was.

His words in the Council Chamber echoed in my mind. He did not want to be my Consort and had, in fact, brought up every argument conceivable for why he was the least suitable person.

And he was right. We were not suited—not at all. While he might be powerful, in whatever limited magical way as well as his influence at court, he had entirely the wrong personality for me. We would not complement each other but instead be locked into a never-ending battle of wills.

Instead of affection, we would verbally spar. Instead of gazing into each other's eyes, we would glare. We would be the most ill-suited couple in all of history.

I turned in my bed so that I could look out the wall of windows. It was just past dawn and the angle of the sun was severe; its rays hit me directly. I closed my eyes to feel the warmth radiate across my cheeks.

Even knowing that Anson and I could never work, his rejection stung. Of course, I had no interest in the Lord. I hated him and he hated me. But an ugly part of me realized that my pride was wounded.

I had suspected that his ambition would outweigh any personal dislike he felt for me. I knew there was a kind bone somewhere in his body. He had sided with me about Finn once, so long ago. He had checked in on me in the library after tough Council sessions. He had brought me Finn's battered gift. But a part of me had always assumed that any kindness served a purpose for him. It bought him favor in some way.

Anson seemed like a man who did nothing without careful calculation. That was why I was so shocked to hear he would not marry me, should I consent to the match. His marriage to me would lift him above all men and women in Izwe, except for me. He would become Consort, nearly all powerful.

I would have thought any man with his ambition would jump at the possibility. I expected ten of the largest bouquets of flowers from him. I expected him to be waiting outside of my chamber doors, ready to say and do anything he needed to win my affection.

Yet Anson had had the opposite reaction.

I closed my eyes. None of this mattered anyway, for Anson and I would each choose death before marriage to each other.

Eventually I pulled myself from bed, dressed, ate, and went about my usual routine. I trained with a too-quiet Manelesi. I ran until my lungs felt ready to burst. I read over a few reports Grimly sent me. And when the sinking sun began casting a red glow through my room, I began to prepare for dinner.

Kaiht and Mara had just finished lacing me into a gray formal gown when a knock sounded at the door.

I nodded at Kaiht over my right shoulder. Then I refocused on the floor-length mirror before me, pulling the hem of my right sleeve over Finn's bracelet. In the reflection, I saw a familiar blonde head and another one with close-cropped hair the same texture as mine.

I spun on bare feet and was in their arms in two seconds.

"Hi, Sahl," Roland said into my hair.

"What a welcome!" Eliza chimed in. "We only saw you a few days ago."

"It feels like so much longer," I replied, detangling my arms from theirs. "What's the occasion? Or did you two just want to say hello?"

Mara snagged my attention as she bid me to sit and let her work on my hair. I complied, signaling to Eliza and Roland to take a seat, as well.

"Well, sweetheart, we actually wanted to speak to you about something…"

"About what?" I asked, distracted by the feeling of the brush passing through my curls.

There was silence behind me where my parents sat. Loaded silence.

I turned slowly towards them, giving Mara enough time to follow my movement. "About what?" I repeated, louder this time.

Eliza and Roland looked at each other. Then Roland spoke. "Better just to get it out, isn't it?"

"Yes," I replied hesitantly, not liking at all where this was going.

Roland continued, "Eliza and I heard about Anson being nominated by Grimly as a suitor—"

"A reluctant suitor," I added, butting in.

Roland raised his eyebrows but did not comment on that point. "The long and the short of it is that Eliza and I agree with Grimly. Anson would be the ideal Consort."

I felt my jaw drop as I whipped my head between Roland and Eliza. "I'm sorry, what?"

"I know it's a shock," Eliza said. She stood from her wingback chair and came towards me, reaching for my hand. I pulled it away, tucking it under my thigh. It was a rude thing to do to the woman who had raised me, but a sickening sense of betrayal bubbled in my blood.

"A shock?" I said, standing abruptly. Mara took two steps away as if I might turn on her next.

In a quiet voice that broached no argument, even now with me as Queen, Roland replied, "Sit down, Sahle, and let Mara finish your hair."

And I sat, dammit. I had spent many years of my life listening to him use that quietly stern voice to reprimand me. Suddenly, I felt twelve years old again and my limbs moved of their own volition.

I felt the brush land in my hair once more.

"Now," Roland carried on. "Hear us out—"

"You both know exactly how I feel about him. He hates me, and the feeling is mutual."

Roland just looked at me. "You're not listening."

"Fine," I grumbled, more for Mara's sake than my own. I crossed my arms over my chest and sat back.

"We both know that you and Anson have not gotten off to a good start," Roland explained. "But you have to realize that Anson is the second-most senior Lord. Only Grimly is more influential and powerful in Izwe but he is already married, not to mention he is quite a bit older than you."

"Anson is almost sixty," I reminded them.

Eliza merely shook her head as if I was being silly. "That's more like thirty in Humanrealm years. Our physical aging slows dramatically after the age of twenty in the Alterealm."

"Yes," Roland took up the baton. "Anson is a more suitable age. He is powerful. He is ambitious. He is loyal to the crown. He is a member of the Council and the Senior Council, and has served as Lord of War for two decades. He is unmarried. He carries some magic, though nothing compared to your abilities. Any children the two of you had would be powerful. And he is the sole heir of Ingonyame, of Warbeck, which would silence the traditionalists kicking up a fuss in the first place. I know you don't want to hear this, Sahl, but logically there isn't a better match than Anson."

I felt Mara finish securing my hair with pins and then I started shaking my head, back and forth, back and forth. Maybe

I could shake what they were saying out of reality.

"Sahle?" one of my parents asked. I was not sure which.

Kaiht approached with a small wooden box. I saw the simple golden circlet earlier so I was not surprised when she placed it low on my head so that it sat across my forehead.

"I…" I began. I was so overwhelmed by what they were saying, I could hardly organize my thoughts. "I…Are you both crazy? Anson and I would kill each other. We can hardly be in the same room together without one of us jabbing at the other one. And now you think I'd marry that bully of a man? That I'd *have children* with him?"

I stood abruptly. I needed to move. I needed to pace. And I let my bare feet wear a soft path into the floor before the wing-back chairs from which Eliza and Roland watched.

I continued, "There is nothing in this realm or the next that would make me pick him as Consort. Oh, everyone says he is so dedicated, so loyal—a model Lord of the realm. But did you know that he argued for me to be left in the Humanrealm *for years?*

"I don't think that's loyal or dedicated, especially when there has been a faction of Izweians who believe he and his House should still be rulers. Apparently they believe Manelesi should never have taken power to begin with. And now, Anson handily would take the crown. That's not loyal, that's careful planning."

I had expected Roland to be shocked at Anson's behavior, at the possibility of his treason. Instead, Roland's eyes were trained on me patiently. "I knew about that. There were many Lords, myself included, who argued to leave you in the Humanrealm. We wanted you to be safe. Would you say I'm not loyal?"

"Of course not," I sputtered

"Then why do you hold Anson to a different standard?"

I threw my hands up. "Because he hates me! He is not you, Dad. He did not argue for me to be left alone because he *cared*. He argued that because, with me gone, he would have a better claim to power—"

"Has he told you this?" Eliza cut in, her eyes quickly flitting to Roland's before settling back on me.

"No," I said with a dismissive gesture. "We don't talk except to be rude to each other."

"Then how can you claim to know his motivation, Sahl," Roland asked softly, stilling my pacing with a hand on my shoulder.

I shrugged. "I just know. Call it gut instinct. From the moment I met him, I *knew* he had it out for me. He did not like me and he's taken every opportunity to embarrass me, make me feel stupid, talk down to me.

"Even if you were right—that everything he's done has been for the kingdom, that he really is this amazingly faithful servant to Izwe—it doesn't change the fact that we do not like each other."

"No," Roland agreed. "It doesn't. But you can learn to like someone in time."

I laughed, a noise without humor. I did not like how empty it sounded even to my own ears. "Do you hear yourself?"

I spun to Eliza, finding her now standing as well, watching Roland try to reason with me. "And you?" I asked her. "You were so taken with Joachim, but it seems he's long forgotten now."

Eliza's eyes would not meet mine, and a part of me felt bad. I did not want to see my mother look down in shame. I did not want her to fear my retribution. She said, "I'm sorry, Sahl. I was excited for the possibility of the Prince of Niel being Consort, but that's over. The reality is that you need to safeguard your crown and your kingdom by marriage *now*. You're out of time."

Hard as it was to hear, I knew she was right. Marriage was a card I had to play, and I did need to play it now, not later, in order to safeguard Izwe. I was fine with that, in a purely logical part of my mind. I had come close to marrying Joachim out of duty, after all. I was sure I could muster that same level of patience and acceptance for marriage once more.

But it would not be a marriage to *Anson*. I knew this because I was sure, deep in my bones, that he would never, ever consider accepting me as his bride.

"This conversation is moot," I said with finality as I spied my shoes sitting by the door, ready for me to head to dinner. "Even if I would consider Anson as Consort—and I'm not saying I would—he would never agree to it. You said you saw the report from the Council? Grimly brought up the idea and Anson was as appalled as I was. He argued every point—very convincingly, I might add. By the end of it, *I* didn't even want to marry me."

I expected Roland and Eliza to roll their eyes, maybe even give a little chuckle. Instead, their gazes met in a pregnant pause.

"Mom? Dad?"

The silence lengthened. Roland turned to me, and I knew what he was going to say a moment before he opened his mouth.

"Eliza and I just came from his rooms. We spoke to him. We explained the benefits of this marriage and why it would ensure the security of the kingdom. Anson has agreed."

It was my turn to stare and stare I did. I must have misheard. "I'm sorry?"

Eliza approached, slowly, as if she would frighten me away if she moved too quickly. "Sahl, Anson has agreed to become Consort if you will have him. He understands what's at risk for Izwe, and he is willing to put aside any ill-will—which I think you're overexaggerating, by the way—to protect this kingdom."

"Can you say the same?" Roland asked.

It was a challenge. I saw it in his eyes. There was a somberness swimming in them for what was being asked of me, but also a deep understanding.

He was daring me to be brave, to think about the objective logic of Lord Anson as a suitor; not the needling, cocky, little shit that was Anson the man. And if I allowed my mind to go there, I could see the reasoning behind this choice of Consort. I knew it was sound. It was a good pick.

But it was *Anson*.

I shuddered involuntarily, seeing his green gaze cheekily glinting at me as he strode into the Council Chamber on that first day, winking at me in Ukuwela, taking over my field of vision when he pulled me from Finn.

The objective and subjective warred between my ears. And I had no answer. I was not sure if there would ever be an answer for this.

"I don't know," I finally said. I walked to the door, suddenly exhausted by this conversation. "I need to think about it. I'll consider your points and then decide. It won't be now."

Eliza took my hand as I tried to balance on one foot to slip a shoe onto my foot. "That's fine. Just think about it," she urged.

I met her gaze straight on. "I will. I'll consider it."

"Good," Roland said from my other side. He took my arm in his as he reached for the door. "Shall we head to dinner then?"

I picked at the plate in front of me, much too distracted to taste the food. I was sure every dish was delicious. It always was. Steam curled from a mound of baked yams on a tray to the right of me. The sound of an *umtshingozi* flute floated through the air, the notes weaving into some sort of excited beat.

I was half tempted to ask the *umtshingozi* to play something sad and mournful. I felt like I was heading to a funeral for my own soul.

"More kudu, Your Majesty?" a servant asked as he extended a plate of venison to me.

"No, thank you," I said with a smile—fake though it was. At least I had enough wits to be courteous to the servants.

As the server ambled off, occasionally dishing out slices to hungry courtiers, Eliza leaned in from where she was seated on my left. "You're spinning out," she said quietly into my ear.

And I was. From the moment I entered the hall, I had been. A half dozen Lords and Ladies all headed in my direction as soon as I stepped into the room but Eliza and Roland saved me. They each took one of my arms, effectively blocking me from the courtiers, and quickly escorted me to my seat.

I was grateful for that. I was in no mood to be nice, nor was

I in a mood to disappoint my parents when they witnessed my inevitable rudeness to one of their friends.

As Eliza had put it so well, I was spinning out.

"I'm just processing," I replied. I reached for my wine, taking my first sip of the evening. I had been too distracted to even notice the glass sitting full before me.

"It's the same thing. I know how much this bothers you, and you do need to think about it. But you have a few days. Relax, eat your meal, drink your wine, and sleep on our suggestion."

I turned to her, and knew it was a mistake instantly. Facing Eliza put Anson right into my line of sight, seated as he was just three seats down the head table.

Seated there because of his immense influence in this court.

"I…" I tried to say, but my gaze was caught on Anson over Eliza's shoulder.

He had not tried to speak to me once since I arrived at dinner. He had not even made eye contact with me, and that confused me, as well. Surely if he had agreed to marry me mere hours before, he would at least say hello? Perhaps a quick, "Hey there, looks like we'll be sharing a bed in the near future."

Assuming I agreed, of course.

But nothing—he did not spare a word or a glance. He merely sat beside Lord Marcus, chatting away. I watched as he chuckled at something Marcus said. Then, as if he felt my gaze, he looked my way.

Those knowing green eyes locked on mine and I knew the music was playing but I could not hear it. I knew the smell of food wafted all around me but I could no longer smell it, nor could I feel the cool kiss of the gold circlet on my forehead or the balanced weight of the silver fork in my hand.

I stared at him and he did not look away. There was nothing in those eyes—maybe boredom at yet another court dinner, maybe his usual sour humor. But he did not look at me with desire, with love, with interest. He did not look at me as if I were a woman he would marry.

And then he looked down, took a drink of his *konstans* and said something to Marcus. They chuckled again, seemingly unaware of the tempest brewing several feet away.

But I did not look down. I kept staring at his profile, boring my own gaze into his cheekbone, the knife edge of his jaw. My vision narrowed, my heartbeat picked up, my breath grew tight in my chest, and my palms became suddenly clammy.

A clattering sound drew my eyes finally from Anson. I had dropped my fork onto the fine porcelain plate.

"Queen Sahle?"

"Your Majesty, are you alright?"

Several voices—Eliza, Roland, a passing server—said the same thing but I could not focus on their words. My dress suddenly felt too tight. I could not seem to breathe in enough air.

I needed to get out of this room. Immediately.

A small voice in my head that sounded like Finn whispered, *Don't do this.* Once, long ago, he had called me out for running when something got hard. I had tried to break that habit. I even think I was successful for most of a year. I had been able to put aside my own fears and worries and be a Queen.

But now, the prospect of marriage to the one man I hated was different. It was more than acting brave in front of a crowd. It was more than saying the right thing in Council or studying enough to understand the political ramifications of a decision.

Those things were all public, temporary, and external. I could do all of those activities, make all of those decisions, and then return to my bedroom to cry or rage or shake with self-pity. And I realized there was a part of myself—some little inner sanctum— where I was still free to be *just* Sahle and not Queen Sahle.

Marrying would change that. My marriage would certainly be public and external and for the people, but it would be equally private and *internal.* I could not leave my marriage, my husband, at the door to my chambers. When I crossed that threshold where I could pretend to be *just* Sahle, I would no longer be able to do that.

My marriage would be with me always, when I was sitting in Council and when I was curled into my bed. And the thought of being bound to a man I hated, who I was convinced would rather see me dead than on my throne, broke a part of me I did not think could break.

It is what made my vision blacken at the edges, my pulse race, and my breath shorten. It is what made me shove Finn's voice from my mind and do what I promised him I would not do.

I stood from my throne, pushing it back in what I was sure was an undignified way. And then I was rushing from the Great Hall.

The weight of every pair of eyes turned to me. The *umtshingozi* quieted. I heard the scraping of chairs and benches as the courtiers hurried to stand and bow.

I did not care. I said a quick apology to the ghost of Finn, and then I hurried my step.

I passed several courtiers in the halls, late stragglers heading into dinner, but none tried to speak to me. No Lords offered me their hand.

As soon as I burst through my chamber doors, I began pulling at the laces of my dress—as many of them as I could reach with my arms straining behind my back.

"Your Majesty!" Mara exclaimed, hurrying through the servants' entrance. "Let me help you."

"No! No, I'm fine," I replied through pinched lips. I tugged at the laces again, growing more frantic with my motions. I needed to get this dress off or at least loosened if I were to get a full breath.

My vision seemed to narrow even more and I realized I was having a fully-fledged panic attack. Light sparked from nearby— a candle being lit or maybe my power jumping at the emotion coursing through my trembling limbs. I was not sure which.

Distantly, I heard Kaiht enter and exchange a few words with Mara. I sunk down into the wingback chair closest to me, leaning forward and wedging my head between my knees. I did not care that they were here. I barely cared that I was here. I just needed to breathe. I needed to calm down. I needed to not panic.

I knew panic. It had been years since I had had a proper panic attack, but I was no stranger to it. In truth, I was surprised I had not had one when I first came to Izwe over a year ago. I certainly was stressed enough, with the rug pulled out from under me as if the normal, everyday life I had lived for twenty years was somehow a fantasy.

Yet the panic never found me. Somehow, I had coped, and I wondered if it was because of that realization I had at the dinner table—I had somehow always been able to act the role of Queen while being truly me the moment I was alone. I could keep that distinction, that balance. And with it, I could control the idea that I was losing myself and who I always knew to be me.

But now, I felt like I was finally breaking.

Taking Anson out of duty would be a sacrifice. It was, in a way, the ultimate sacrifice. I would be physically giving my body to a man I did not care for. I would be sharing my crown and my power with someone with his own selfish ambitions. I would not be able to close off the flood gates of what was public Queen Sahle and private *just* Sahle because that man would follow me through both circumstances.

And though it made me sound like a hopeless romantic, I would also be giving up any hope of finding true, abiding love.

During my weeks and months with Finn, we understood we would one day go our separate ways when we found people who were more than companions, when our duties demanded it. I had been fine with that because Finn was what I needed him to be at the time: freedom and choice.

Even in that briefest of moments where I had come to pick Joachim, I had reconciled myself to the idea that at least there would be tenderness and respect locking us together. Perhaps that could fill the void. Perhaps that would allow some space for me to still be *just* Sahle.

But this, the stark reality of Anson, blew apart even that possibility. There would be no separation anymore. Queen Sahle would take over *just* Sahle; the public would become the private. And me, true me, would cease to exist.

My chest ached again as I tried to get a deeper breath, and then I felt nimble fingers flitting over my back. Kaiht or Mara began untying my laces as I remained bent forward.

"Your Majesty, can we get you anything?" Mara's soft voice called from above me.

I was not sure if she could hear me, my voice muffled in the thick folds of my gray skirts, when I replied. "Whiskey, please."

I heard a door open and shut, then a moment later, the clink of a bottle and glass as it was placed on a side table next to me.

"Thank you," I murmured.

The dress loosened, falling away as the bodice slipped open over my back and shoulders. The air felt refreshing on my bare skin, and I willed myself to take a fuller breath. In and out. In and out. In and out.

"Majesty, let's get you into something more comfortable," Kaiht called. I felt her fingers grip my knees, and I took one more deep breath before sitting up to see her crouched before me.

Her face searched mine, all traces of her usual joking gone. But she did not ask me what was wrong. After a year of knowing me, a year of being my friend, she sensed I did not want to talk about it.

I shook my head. "I'm fine. Really, please just let me sit here."

Kaiht thought about that. I saw it in the set of her mouth, the tilt of her head. Her Queen was asking her to do something, but she did not agree—not in the slightest. "With all due respect, Queen Sahle, I insist. At least let us help you into your dressing gown."

I looked from her to Mara, remembering to breathe slowly, in and out. Then I nodded.

Kaiht did not waste any time. She jumped to her feet, taking my hands to pull me up with her. Someone pulled the circlet from my head, the shoes from my feet, the dress from my arms. Someone slipped the dressing gown around me. Someone opened the bottle and poured a glass of the amber whiskey.

And then Kaiht and Mara stood side by side in front of the fire. Kaiht seemed to see right through me, seemed to understand that I needed to be alone with my thoughts now. And so, dressed and comfortable as she had insisted, she now accepted that it was time to leave me be.

"If there's nothing else, Your Majesty…" Kaiht said.

Mara merely watched me with too-observant eyes.

I shook my head. "That's all. Thank you."

"No need to thank us," Mara replied softly. "We're happy to help you, always."

It was said so simply, so softly, so truthfully that the back of my eyes suddenly burned. I waved the two women off, back out the servants' entrance and to whatever their evening entailed. I wiped at the tears that threatened to fall.

These two sisters had been with me here since day one. They knew me better than anyone, save for Eliza and Roland. They had become my friends, part of my little band of servant-soldier confidantes when Finn, Kaiht, Mara, and I used to sit up late into the night drinking *konstans* and laughing.

And they were just two of the people I was responsible for, now that I was Queen.

Roland had dared me to put aside my own wants, my own likes and dislikes for the sake of my crown. But it was not about the *crown*. It was about all of the people that crown represented: Kaiht and Mara and the many more Kaihts and Maras out there, spread across the kingdom, who would live or die depending on the decisions I was willing to make.

The sacrifices I was willing to make in order to ensure strength and stability.

Marriage to anyone I did not love would be a sacrifice, but marriage to Anson would test me as nothing else here had. To marry the man I despised, who had taken joy in my failures, who had sought to minimize me…

I paced back and forth before the fireplace where I had paced earlier. I tossed back my glass of whiskey, barely aware of the bite. Then I poured another.

And I focused on what Roland was asking me to do. He was challenging me to be brave, to face this head on, to decide that my people were worth more than my happiness. He knew I hated Anson, but he was asking me to say yes to this union despite that because it was what Izwe needed.

I would have to crown Anson as Consort, allow him to weigh in on my decisions. I would have to take him to my bed; there would need to be children one day in order to secure my line. My life would irrevocably change if I agreed to marry this man, and change for the worse.

The slights, the jabs, the humiliation would be continuous. Because Anson would not change. Anson was Anson—confident and arrogant and slick. *I* would have to accept that treatment and learn to live with it.

I poured another glass of liquor and suddenly stopped pacing. Finn's words came back to me—the ones he had spoken moments before explosions sent us reeling. He had urged me to make Anson an ally. He had insisted Anson was a good man, a loyal man.

I shook my head, taking a sip and thinking about what Finn would say now that I was considering taking Anson to my bed.

My mind spun in a dozen directions. But, as I stared at the fire, I asked myself the only question that really mattered.

I would always hate Anson, and he would always hate me. We would be miserable together. He would humiliate me, mock me, and insult me. I would seek to belittle him, put him in his place, and discredit him. It would be a terrible life.

But was my own happiness more important than the millions of lives spread across my kingdom?

I swallowed, the harsh alcohol scorching my throat. I knew the answer. There was never any other one, not really.

I would do this.

I knew the Council was right that Anson was the most powerful, the most influential Lord available. He could strengthen this kingdom as no one else could. He could even, possibly, ensure the line had magic running through its veins.

And he had agreed to put aside his personal dislike. He had agreed to sacrifice his own wishes, as well.

All that was left was for me to do the same.

I thought of Anson's eyes at dinner, the way they had stared back at me blankly, almost as if I were not even there. Those would be the eyes I would begin and end each day looking into.

I shivered, suddenly cold despite the roaring fire. I downed my drink. I sat at my desk and, before I could change my mind, I took out a pen and a piece of paper.

The letter was simple. There was no need for flowery language, for professions of love. This was not a matter of the heart. No, this was a matter of necessity, of urgency, of sacrifice. This was me doing what it took to secure my kingdom.

With a steady hand, I addressed the note to Grimly and then I wrote out simply:

You can tell Lord Anson that I'll have him as Consort. Please begin making the necessary arrangements.

-Q.S.I.

I did not bother to seal the note. This would not be a secret for long. Instead, I immediately walked to the door of my chamber, afraid that if I delayed, I would chuck the missive into the fire.

I said to the first Vikela I saw, "Please take this to Lord Grimly immediately."

Then I sat down heavily in my chair and stared at the fire.

I could feel in my bones that this moment was a cliff side. The chasm before me yawned wide and beckoning. And I had hurled myself into it.

I was doing what was necessary, and I would never, ever be the same.

I ATE MY BREAKFAST OF WARM *PAP* MECHANICALLY, mulling over what felt like a terrible dream. Terrible though it was, I also knew it was right. It was what needed to be done to save this kingdom.

But honestly, selfishly, I was sad for myself. It felt like an entirely new mourning period as I dressed in my usual gray gown, formal this time as I was expected at the Council Chamber momentarily. I watched my reflection as Kaiht laced me into this gown that had become like a second skin. I picked out a crown and Mara nestled it into my lushly braided hair. The crown was heavy, stately, and solid in an almost masculine way—a crown fit for a king…or a consort.

I knew I had picked this crown on purpose, even if it had been a subconscious decision. I knew exactly who I would see at Council, who had suddenly transformed from enemy to soon-to-be-spouse. I would have to engage with and speak to Anson, and I was just petty enough to want to remind him who wore the crown—the king's and the queen's.

Despite whatever games he was playing, strategies he had mastered, schemes he had devised, *I* was and would always be the ruler. I wanted him to realize that when he looked me, his future bride, in the eyes today.

I scoffed at myself. I was being silly and morose. Yet with the faintly dusky bruises under my eyes—the marks of my lack of sleep—I looked the part. Today was not a joyous day. I felt like death, and I looked like death. And I had no desire to try to be anything else. I was no blushing bride promised to Anson. I was a Queen, a foreigner, even the tiniest bit of a rebel—or fool, depending on one's prerogative. And I accepted this moment reluctantly but purposefully. I would do nothing but be entirely me.

Absently, I spun Finn's bracelet around and around my wrist. I marched from my room, a purposeful surrendering army. I made my way down the staircases and along the passageways that led to the Council Chamber, and I was surprised at the chatter. There was a sense of normalcy that juxtaposed the dreariness of my own mind.

I had expected Grimly to have shouted the news from the rafters already, from the towering jacarandas and silver trees that ringed the palace. Yet it seemed the man could keep a secret after all. Whispers did not float in my wake; the Courtiers had no idea the storm that had raged within me last night or what had driven me from the Great Hall at dinner. They were blissfully ignorant and I—

I was standing face to face with Lord Anson.

In fact, nose to nose was a more accurate description. I had turned a corner just as he had, and the speed at which I was moving, not to mention my general distraction today, nearly pitched me into him before I could stop myself.

Strong hands—hands I seemed to instinctually remember at my cheeks, my back *that* night—grasped my upper arms as I tottered. Even through the thick fabric of my dress, I could feel the heat radiating from his palms. I did not remember that from my recent birthday, but I had been overwhelmed by shock then and sheer animalistic desperation.

Quick as his hands had found my arms, they dropped away as if I was a hot tray straight from the oven, scalding and blistering his flesh. I had to abruptly alter my stance to keep upright.

Yet if my body burned him, my gaze certainly did not. His eyes locked on mine as he crossed his arms over his chest. He did not say a word.

And for some reason, that irritated me.

"Lord Anson," I said by way of a greeting. I remembered the crown I had selected today, and I did not shy away. "No bow for your Queen this morning?"

One corner of Anson's mouth twitched, the barest hint of a smirk. I wondered whether anything could be funny on a day like today.

"Good morning, Your Majesty. I trust you slept well," he said, bending slightly at the waist. His voice was too sweet, like cotton candy at a balmy county fair.

"Never better," I replied.

He knew it was a lie. I could see it on his face as his gaze dropped from mine to skate over the shadows under my eyes, the sag of my shoulders. "Same for me."

His smirk dropped then. His gaze honed in, that green so vivid it looked lit from within. "In truth, Your Majesty, I did not sleep much at all."

I willed my face to remain impassive as I took that in. What was he trying to do? Sympathize with me? Oh, he had voiced his displeasure at the idea of our marriage, but I also had my doubts. I was sure the reluctant leader act was part of his angle. He must have spent significant time last night patting himself on the back for a game well-played.

"And why is that?" I bit out. The muscles of my face felt frozen, stiff.

Anson did not reply for a moment. He simply watched me, his gaze boring into mine as if the longer he looked, the deeper he could see, the more secrets he could puzzle out. "Queen Sahle..." he replied admonishingly.

I did not respond. I did not blink. I simply waited.

"I received your letter."

"You mean Lord Grimly's letter," I corrected. Here I was being petty again.

If it annoyed Anson, he did not let on. He merely nodded, his face uncharacteristically serious. "Grimly's letter."

I could not bear to look at him suddenly. I could not bear to stare into his eyes as I said the next words, too scared he would see through the carefully resolved decision I had come to. "Then you've been informed that I'll have you as Consort."

He did not speak for a moment, a heartbeat. My eyes remained trained on a painting of a wildebeest on the far wall— seeing and yet unseeing all at the same time.

"Yes."

It was a simple word, yet I felt as if the axis of the universe had realigned. And I had to ask the next question. I had to confirm that this new reality was real. "And you accept?"

"Yes."

I forced my eyes back to his, and for a fraction of a second, I could almost imagine I saw *wonder*.

Yet my eyes fooled me. There was no wonder, no joy. There was only me nodding although I desperately wanted to shake my head no, no. There was the echo of a door slamming shut, and I knew it to be the sound of my fate being sealed, my path being chosen.

Still, my lips moved robotically. "Very well." When he did not say anything, I added. "I've tasked Grimly and the Lords with making the arrangements."

"Of course, Your Majesty," was all he said.

And for the first time I doubted my demonization of this man.

I had been so convinced that despite his outward complaints, he would inwardly be quite pleased to hold the power of Consort. But this did not seem like a man who had just won the power jackpot. This did not seem like a man who had schemed his way to the top and made it. His eyes looked flat, all traces of humor gone, as if this was as unthinkable to him as it was to me. As if duty alone compelled him to agree to this ridiculous marriage.

I must be losing it if I had started sympathizing with Anson.

I shook my head sharply, hoping to clear that pesky line of thought. The other Lords had begun streaming past us, filling the hallway as they spoke and moved as one clamoring wave to the Council Chamber.

"Good day, Lord Anson," I said formally, too formally for a man I had just agreed to marry. And then I let the Lords sweep me away.

It felt like a secret.

That was the thought that stuck with me as I took my seat in the Council Chamber, spreading my charcoal gown carefully around me. Grimly kept looking my way, as did Eliza and Roland who had remained at the palace after yesterday's late arrival. I had the distinct impression all three of them were waiting for me to combust in a show of tears and flame.

And in my case, literal flame.

I could physically feel their glances sliding sideways to me and then away. But I was not going to throw a fit. Instead, I smiled. It was a small thing, a cold thing, but it was there nonetheless.

For possibly the first time since I arrived in the Alterealm, I was going to shock these assembled Lords. I was going to announce a consort that none of them would expect. And I would shock Eliza, Roland, and Grimly because I was about to do it with dignity and grace.

In fact, I wanted to get it out of the way. I stood.

"My Lords," I called, pitching my voice above the din of twenty-odd voices that bounced off the Council Chamber walls. I turned to Eliza with an added, "My Lady." When I had the room's attention, I said, "I have an announcement to make."

Grimly rose from his seat. "Perhaps you'd allow me, Majesty."

I shook my head without giving it a moment's thought. "No, thank you. I am perfectly capable." I considered holding out my hand to Anson, seated several places down the table. I considered asking him to come and stand by my side.

No, this was for me to do. Me alone.

"My Lords," I said again. "As you well know, the question of Consort has been on all of our minds these last weeks. I was disappointed at Joachim's abrupt departure but, in light of that, and the need to firm up our internal strength, I've been urged to accept an Izweian Lord instead."

I paused momentarily to take a breath, to clasp my hands behind my back—a posture that exemplified strength yet also kept my hands from shaking. "I thank you for your patience and your thoughts on the matter as I've considered both what I'd like and what our kingdom needs. It is with this appreciation that I announce I have selected a Consort: Lord Anson of Ingonyame."

The quiet that had descended upon the room as soon as I stood stretched out. Not a Lord made a sound. Rather, they all stared back at me as if I had just spoken gibberish to them, some far-flung language of the Humanrealm that sounded entirely foreign to their ears.

Of their own volition, my gaze met Anson's and a blankness stared back. He did not stand, not as all eyes swung from me to him, not as the Lord next to him clapped him on the back.

Again, I was stumped. I had expected him to stand and bow, make some elaborate speech in which his barely veiled arrogance all but suffocated me and made me instantly regret this choice I had made.

Yet he looked stricken, just as he had in the hallway. He met my gaze and held it, but it was like looking into a deep, dark, empty well. All I could see was stillness, silence. Not even a single lap of water against the stone walls.

Grimly had settled in his chair when I dismissed him, but seeing that I took my seat once more, he rose.

"Your Majesty, I know I speak for every Lord in this chamber when I say we wish you a heartfelt congratulations."

I shifted my gaze to his, too confused and concerned by the nothingness in Anson's eyes. Where was the cockiness I had grown to know? Where was the strutting, impossible Lord?

If even Anson looked as shaken as I felt, this must really be an abominable choice we had made.

Grimly continued. "We wish you nothing but a lifetime of prosperity and strength together. While we had alternative business to discuss today, I would suggest a change of agenda given this momentous news."

I nodded my head absently.

"Your Majesty will not be aware of the nuances of a royal wedding, so perhaps the Lords and I may take over the planning? You would, of course, have as much say as you would like…" Grimly led off.

But here I had already decided, as well. I meant what I said to Anson in the hall—I would let these Lords make the arrangements. I was not some eager bride who had dreamed of this day since childhood. I was a reluctant Queen who merely did what was required. No amount of mulling over dresses, glassware, and flowers would change that.

I waved my hand dismissively. "No, Lord Grimly, I trust your and the Lords' judgment. I do not need to be involved in the planning. I only have two requests.

"The first is that the festivities—or at least a portion of it—be accessible to the people for it is their day as much as anyone's. Second, I ask that you do not delay. This wedding should take place as soon as possible."

If the Lords had been silent, this last statement shook their voices loose. I distinctly heard one Lord ask with hushed—but not hushed enough—words, "Do you think she's pregnant?" Another whispered something about me being eager to *have* Anson—whatever that meant.

I held up a single hand as I stood once more. "To answer your whispered questions, no, I am not pregnant. No, I am not anxious to be married. No, I am not a soft-hearted bride who can think of nothing besides the day.

"What I am is your Queen. What this is is a duty to you, and to the people of Izwe. You know the threat we face as well as I do. I seek to empower us as a nation, and I believe the best way to do that is to have this marriage take place as quickly as possible.

"Now, if there are no further questions, I will leave you to it. I would appreciate a full plan for the wedding formulated by tomorrow."

I did not wait for them to respond. I told them what they needed to know, and I did not care about any of the particulars besides what I had laid out. Let the Lords create me a royal wedding that was as traditional as possible. Let the Lords create me a royal wedding as modern as possible.

I did not care. All I wanted, now that the decision was made and the announcement had been shared, was to have the ordeal over with.

I descended my dais. I placed one foot in front of the other as I made my way to the door of the Council Chamber. I did not meet Anson's gaze or any other's.

18
wedding gift

THE DAYS AFTER I ANNOUNCED ANSON AS INCOMING Consort were some of the longest of my life. It was a horrific juxtaposition—my dread and reluctant acceptance set against the Court's overwhelming elation.

Wherever I went, the Courtiers approached me. They bowed and scraped, and the few daring ones kissed my hands. Some even wept. It was all out of joy. I heard more versions of congratulations than I had ever heard before. It was as if I had graduated high school all over again or landed the job of the century.

Or perhaps like I was getting married.

I had to remind myself that was exactly what was happening. I had chosen a Consort, and in a matter of days, I would be marrying him before the entire court and the people of Izwe. The Courtiers were not odd; rather, I was odd. I was the reluctant bride, the woman who had no interest in the marriage or the man.

In fact, I hated them both.

And so, time and time again, I smiled in what I hoped was an approximation of graciousness. I pasted that wooden, queenly smile across my face, and I begged life to show in my eyes rather than the dead, fished-eyed stare I saw looking back at me in the mirror.

I would soon be a bride. I could be happy about that.

Right?

Yet as I stared at myself in the mirror, all I could see were the permanent circles under my eyes from the sleepless nights, the tossing and turning, the fussing over this decision. I had made the correct choice, but it did not make it any easier to accept the sort of life waiting for me—the sort of life that would bind me to Anson until the end of time.

But the decision was larger than me. I had made this choice for my people and for the security of my kingdom. I had decided on Anson because it was the logical decision. It was the right one.

My personal opinion on the matter was immaterial.

Despite it all, it was hard to take the congratulations that greeted me around every hallway's turn, every new door's opening. It was hard to sit at the high table in the Great Hall each evening, mere seats from the man I would marry, and pretend to be happy with him. It was hard to *perform*, even if I had become more adept at it over the last year in the Alterealm.

But this too was a duty. This, too, I could do.

What I could not do was care about the trivial details that somehow landed on my desk each day. I had told the Lords that they could take care of all the planning for a royal wedding befitting a queen. Perhaps even they could not believe I truly meant that. Surely a young woman must care about the flowers, the candles, the dress. Surely a young woman must want to select the music and the food.

Surely, surely.

But with each choice brought before me, I lost more and more patience. With each question about the seating arrangements in the Great Hall and the speed of the processional, I was beginning to regret my decision.

And when a knock sounded at my door one morning and a messenger left a note about the exact shape of the wine glasses, I snapped.

"What is this?" I exclaimed, waving the note around in the air before me.

Kaiht and Mara's barely contained giggles sounded from the other side of the room, and I looked at them with a scowl. "Who cares about the wine glasses?"

Kaiht aimed a sympathetic expression my way, but it was Mara who responded. "If you don't mind me saying, Your Majesty, most brides would care."

I stared back at her for a moment. "You're kidding?"

But she shook her head. The earnestness on her face spoke all too clearly. "No, Your Majesty. Most brides want the day to be exactly as they have always dreamed, down to the very last detail."

I huffed. I knew she was right. In fact, I had been that girl once, long ago and in a different world. I used to imagine my puffy white dress, the exact shade of cream roses I would carry. I knew which aria from *Carmen* would play as I walked down the aisle. Yet, I never knew what the groom's face looked like. For some reason, my imagination never filled in that too-important detail.

Maybe my subconscious, fate, or the strings that made up the universe knew the face of the groom would never be of my choosing. Maybe Manelesi was, even then, meddling with me.

I sighed in resignation and frustration both. "I know you're right," I said to Mara and Kaiht as I laid the paper down on the desk before me. I futilely tried to smooth the wrinkled edges under my palm. "I just can't bring myself to care about the details when this wedding is not what I chose."

"We understand," Kaiht replied. She approached on sure feet and held out her hand. I took it without hesitation. "If I may speak plainly, it's alright to feel discombobulated in a situation like this, Your Majesty. No one would judge you for being anxious."

I squeezed her hand before letting go. "Everyone will judge me. That's the problem."

I left the note behind me on the desk as I stood from my chair, my charcoal skirt sweeping the floor. "I'm going to the library," I continued. "Could you please respond to that note?"

"What would you have us tell them?" Mara asked demurely.

I took in the soft brown hair that was tied in a bun at the nape of her neck. Her usually pale cheeks were rosy. "I don't care. Pick whatever you would choose for your wedding, Mara."

Excitement lit Mara's face as I turned to the door. At least I could make someone in this palace happy.

It did not take me long to make it to the library, not now that I knew the way like the back of my hand. Although, I had to admit it had been some time since I had visited.

Since *that* night, I had tried my best to avoid this space. The silence seemed to reverberate too loudly, too brightly. That did not mean I had stopped my studies. No, Ruth being Ruth made sure I still had whatever books I needed and wanted. She sent letters with recommendations for deeper dives into the history of the kingdom, Izweian classic novels, even a biography of my mother, Bekha.

As the first female ruler of Izwe, her reign was notable even in its brevity. Yet, I had avoided that book. As if the pages were laced with poison, I had tiptoed around where it had sat on a shelf in my chambers. Eventually, after weeks of staring at the cover—the same state portrait of my mother which hung in the palace—I sent it back.

I still wondered after that book. Even more so, I wondered why I could not bring myself to pick it up. Surely I wanted to know everything about Bekha? I only knew what was written about her in historical and political accounts, and those were more about her impact on Izwe than her actual life.

As for my father, I knew next to nothing about him besides his name, Otto.

Yet that was comfortable to me. I had had parents in Eliza and Roland and something about the idea of giving my biological parents flesh and blood and dreams seemed like a betrayal to the two people who had raised me.

It was simpler to let the dead lie.

I walked through the tall stacks lined with leather-bound tomes and I let my fingers run along the spines like the keys of a grand piano. All of the worlds, all of the knowledge under my fingers. It spoke to me in a way so few other things did.

I sighed.

"Your Majesty," a soft voice called from beside me.

I spun, my hand coming instinctively to my neck. I felt my quickened pulse beat under my fingers.

Ruth bowed low, an apologetic smile on her lined matronly face. "My apologies. I did not mean to startle you."

"That's alright," I replied, taking a moment to drag in a deep breath. When my pulse and my breathing had settled, I continued, "I'm on edge these days. It's not your fault."

Ruth nodded thoughtfully. Her long servant-brown gown was the same as always. Her gray hair wound in a series of braids that wrapped around her head. "Regardless, I am sorry to be the one to set you off."

I waved away her words. "No need."

"Would you walk with me, Your Majesty?" Ruth asked, motioning before her. "That is, unless you came here for a specific purpose. In that case, I would be more than happy to help you find whatever it is you are looking for."

"I'm happy to walk," I answered. I was not sure why but I did not want to tell Ruth I had fled here to escape my wedding. It seemed sad suddenly. It seemed unqueenly.

We set off, winding ourselves through stacks that had once been more familiar to me than the rest of the palace. At each turn, each new room, I marveled how this library had become a sanctuary during my last year in the Alterealm. And then one day, I had just quit coming here. I had walled myself off from what made me happy. It was all I could do in the wake of every-thing.

It had not been the right thing to withdraw from the life I was building here, but I had had little choice.

"You're deep in thought today, Majesty," Ruth said softly as she led us to a table she often sat at. A pitcher and two glasses sat on the surface. She poured me a glass of water without asking whether I wanted any.

"Please sit," she nodded to one of several chairs as she handed me the glass.

I did what I was told. Ruth had that effect on people, queens and servants alike. "Thank you."

She settled into her own seat before fixing me with her assessing gaze. "Of course, Your Majesty. I hear congratulations are in order."

My fingers tightened around my glass, but I pasted a practiced smile on my lips. I wished I could blush on command. Perhaps that would sell the excitedly nervous bride act more. "Yes. Thank you for your kind words."

Ruth's gaze narrowed at me infinitesimally. Then she dropped her gaze to her own water glass as she took a sip. "You are not happy about this turn of events?"

For a split second, I debated denying it. But there had always been something about Ruth that made me feel safe and vulnerable, like I could bear all of my truths to her and she would never use them against me.

Through pinched lips, I replied, "That is one way to put it."

"What is another?"

My lips curled up in a small smile—a real one. I always appreciated Ruth's sharp wit. "That Lord Anson and I are not suited. That I chose him as Consort because it is what duty commands."

Ruth sat still for a moment. Then she nodded thoughtfully. "I suppose that is the burden of a monarch, to marry for duty rather than love."

I crossed my legs under my charcoal gown. "Unfortunately."

"You do not like the man then?"

My brows rose. She was the first person who had asked me that outright. I should say something noncommittal. I should say something diplomatic. He would be her Consort, after all. But I had already admitted how I really felt. What was more truth to one of the only people I considered a friend in the palace?

"No," I admitted.

"That's a pity," Ruth replied simply.

I took a sip from my glass and let the cool liquid skate across my tongue. "It is."

"And so you came here to get away from it all?"

"Is it that obvious?"

She shrugged and the gesture seemed oddly casual on such an elegant woman. "You have not frequented the library these past weeks."

I moved my gaze to take in the relatively open room we sat in now. It was hard to meet Ruth's eyes when I felt I had abandoned the relationship we had built. "That was not my intention."

She shook her head. "Oh, I do not pass judgment, Your Majesty. I know it has been difficult since the attack. I would be more concerned had you lived through that and been entirely unaffected."

I had never thought about it like that, but I let her words surround me like a warm cloak. I had changed for good and bad. I had become colder and harsher since Finn's death. I smiled less and was less forgiving.

But I had never thought to see those changes as natural, as proof that my heart was still there, still beating.

Or that it alone should be celebrated.

Unbidden, tears filled my eyes. I blinked them away quickly but Ruth saw. As is the way of all grandmotherly types, Ruth saw everything.

She took another patient sip from her glass. "And so you come here now to get away from it all," she repeated.

I cleared the tightness from my throat. "Yes. If I have to decide on one more piece of music or one more shape of a wine glass for the reception, I'll scream."

Ruth laughed. "I imagine it is hard to care about the details when the event itself is not to your liking."

"Most definitely," I replied with a sad smile.

"Yet the groom…"

My brows rose. "Lord Anson?"

"Yes, Lord Anson. You say he is not your choice, but in my experience with him, he is a good man."

I watched Ruth. I waited for her face to break into laughter as the joke landed. But a few heartbeats later, I realized she was not kidding.

She meant her words.

I put the water down on the table before me. "You're serious."

Ruth nodded. "Of course, Your Majesty. I've known Anson for decades, since he was a young Lord sent to the palace as a representative of Ingonyame. I worked alongside him during your mother's reign. He is thoughtful and loyal, if a little direct. He is learned and accomplished. I cannot imagine a more suitable Consort."

My chin would have been on the floor had I not forcibly clamped my jaw together.

"You're speechless," Ruth said with amusement in her voice.

I blinked at her in genuine confusion. "Are we talking about the same man?"

But Ruth just chuckled again. "Of course we are. Lord Anson with the dark hair and broody face. Lord Anson who commands Her Majesty's army of soldiers and sits on the Council for Ingonyame."

"I'm not disputing any of those facts," I agreed. "But it seems you and I have had a very different experience of the same person."

Yet Ruth shook her head once more. "Anything Anson does, he does with purpose. He is not cruel or heartless or offhanded."

I stared at her as I attempted to reconcile all of the humiliation and anger and sheer horribleness I had faced because of Anson. I shook my head. "Then perhaps he has changed over the years."

"With all due respect, Your Majesty, he is the same man I have always known. The heart of a child does not change even once it lives within the body of an adult."

All I could do was shake my head.

But Ruth was not done. No, she had one last thought for me. "Give him time. He will show you who he really is. Promise me that. As a wedding gift."

I picked up my glass again and finished the remaining water in one gulp. "I think it is *you* who is supposed to give *me* a wedding gift—not the other way around."

Ruth smiled at me, a smile as deep and bottomless and mystical as the sea. "It is for you, Your Majesty. And I have one more: the biography of your mother."

I stared back at her blankly. Then all at once, the knowledge of which book she meant snapped back. "The one I never finished."

"The very one," Ruth replied. As if she knew I would come here today, she pulled the concise tome from one of her deep pockets. She set it on the table before us. "Take it, Majesty. I urge you to read it."

I looked between her and the book, afraid to touch those pages, afraid to uncover more about the woman I looked so much like. But something in Ruth's gaze told me this was not a pointless request. There was a purpose here.

And so I picked up the book with a nod. "Thank you."

19
consort

I AWOKE THE MORNING OF MY WEDDING WITH A NECK kink, and realized there was nothing more fitting than being in physical pain today.

I was supposed to be happy. Was this not the day that little girls dreamed about, that women looked forward to since the moment they fell in love?

The problem was that I was not in love. I could never be in love with a man like Anson. His green eyes popped into my mind as I lay in bed, staring up at the gauzy fabric that blocked out my view of the thatch roof overhead. I sighed, thinking about how I would be stuck with those green eyes until I died—or at least until he did, being older than me by a good forty years.

I had to admit that the eyes, the chiseled jaw, the dark tumbling hair, none of his features were unpleasant. In fact, I reminded myself, I had once thought him the most handsome man I had ever seen. But thinking about that now made me shudder. He might be beautiful but his harshness effectively veiled that from me.

No, I would have to make do with my lot in this life. I would have to make do with the fact that Lord Anson was to become my husband and the Consort of Izwe today.

I was sure he was thrilled. A Lord such as he—who had worked all the years of his life for power and prestige in the realm—would no doubt be waking up today with stars in his eyes and a spring in his step.

As I pulled myself from bed, I willed the bile that rose in my throat to stay down. This was all but a done deal. All I could do now was follow the plan, marry this man, and do my damnedest to maintain control.

Because that was what this was really about. For all of his protests and complaints that he did not wish to marry me, I was sure he was playing the reluctant leader. He said no and looked modest and humble, which only made the Lords want him as Consort more.

Today, he would gain the ultimate power. He would become second only to the Queen, above all the Lords including even his own Senior Council. Anson was not just taking a wife today; he was taking a kingdom.

I paced to the wall of windows, letting the morning sun stream across the skin exposed at my throat and along my bare arms. I shook my head, trying to still my spinning thoughts. I could think and wallow and bemoan all I wanted, but this was happening.

In a few short hours, I would be married to Lord Anson.

I heard the servants' entrance to my chamber open and Kaiht and Mara bustled in. "Good morning, Your Majesty," they sang in nearly a sing-song. They made it sound like today was a *good* day, a happy day.

"Morning," I responded, too engrossed in the way the *hadedas* and sugarbirds winged above the trees outside to turn my full attention to them.

"Your Majesty?" Mara asked as she approached me. She held out a cup of *rooibos* tea. "Is everything alright? Are you not excited for your wedding day?"

I thought I heard Kaiht softly snort from where she was fluffing the pillows and making the bed. "I'm resigned to it," I told Mara with a little smile. I hoped it looked happier than I felt.

"Resigned," she repeated, as if she had to sound out the word, test it on her tongue until it would make sense.

"I'm not exactly in love with Lord Anson," I explained. That was an understatement if ever there was one.

The snort from the bed was louder this time and I turned to face Kaiht. "Do you have something to add?"

"Apologies, Your Majesty. It's just that we know how you really feel about the situation. Mara, of course she's not excited. Why keep asking her?"

With both of them in my line of vision, I watched as Mara squared her shoulders defensively. "It's just…surely there is excitement in the importance of the day, even if one is less than enthusiastic about the bridegroom?"

I thought about that for a moment. Perhaps Mara was right. Even if I did not love Anson, this was still an *occasion*, an important milestone in anyone's life, not to mention an historical moment for the entire country of Izwe.

This was a royal wedding, and its importance dwarfed me or my own feelings on the man who would meet me at the altar.

I took a sip of my tea. "You're right, Mara. Maybe I need to look at it that way rather than dwell on my own personal feelings about Lord Anson."

"It's for the best, Queen Sahle."

I sighed again, and feared I would continue sighing all day. "Right. Well, let's get on with it," I called to both women. "What do I have to do to prepare for the day?"

Taking my words as an acquiescence, Mara and Kaiht began pulling me in myriad directions. They brought a large meal of *pap*, eggs, mushrooms, and tomatoes. A small bowl of mango and passion fruit sat to the side. I ate without tasting, my mind too preoccupied to enjoy the steaming warmth of the vegetables and eggs or the lush pulpiness of the fruit.

When I was done with my meal, Kaiht and Mara prepared a bath scented with jasmine. I let my head fall back into the oiled water as my eyelids slid shut. I felt the gentle pressure of fingers in my hair—either Kaiht or Mara shampooing and detangling my mass of curls.

I rinsed and toweled off and then pulled my dressing gown over my naked body. Kaiht and Mara told me I would put on my wedding gown last and the dressing gown would be the simplest to get off, tying as it did in the front with a single sash. I followed their advice and let them pull me to a chair where they combed through my curls and began an elaborate series of braids.

At some point, Eliza bustled in. She merely glanced at me before rushing to my side with a murmured, "Whatever is wrong, Sahle?"

I shrugged. "Nothing."

"She's resigned," Kaiht said from behind my head. I scowled at her in the mirror.

"Ah," Eliza replied, her gaze never leaving mine as if she was reading all of my thoughts and the asterisked fine print that went with it. "I know that Lord Anson is not your dream, but he is the finest choice for Consort. He will serve you well."

I nodded. I could find nothing wrong with her assessment. It was pure logic. "You're right."

"But you wished today had turned out differently," Eliza continued.

"I wished that we did not hate each other," I replied bluntly. In the mirror's reflection, I saw Kaiht and Mara meet each other's eyes.

"He does not hate you," Eliza admonished but I could hear the hopefulness in her words. She was trying to convince herself of that as much as she was trying to convince me.

I shrugged again, suddenly tired of rehashing the same point over and over again with myself, my attendants, and now Eliza. "It's kind of a moot point at this stage. Where's Roland?"

Eliza understood. She knew I was finished with that line of conversation and allowed me to pull it in another direction. "Just like when you were officially crowned, he'll join us to travel to the ceremony. But he wanted to give you time and space to get ready."

"Sure," I said, focusing once more on the braids that Kaiht was deftly plaiting.

A knock sounded on my door and I saw more familiar faces. The jeweler from my coronation curtsied as she entered, boxes of the God and gods knew what in tow. And then the dress designer arrived with four servants in his wake. Between them, they held what looked like a large dress bag.

I shook off Kaiht, not caring that my hair was half plaited, and approached that bag. "Is this the dress?" I asked.

I had not cared about it before. Not as Eliza had asked me my preference in material, cut, or color. Not as the designer had droned on about what was traditional for a Queen to marry in. Not as an advisor had explained what my mother had worn on her wedding day.

I simply had not cared. This was not *my* day but the people's day. As such, I would wear whatever the experts advised.

But now, seeing the large bag, the many people it took to carry it, I was intrigued. I made my way over to it but Eliza's hand on my arm stilled me. "Later," she said. "Let's finish your hair."

I allowed myself to be led back to the dressing table but my eyes stayed glued on the dress bag. I wanted to know what was in it. For the first time today, I was excited about something.

The realization surprised me.

Kaiht spent what felt like an eternity on my hair, weaving the coiled strands around and around themselves. Then suddenly she was done and I turned my head to see the intricate pattern. The braids wove and crossed around my crown in geometric patterns but the ends, which I had felt her braid into long straight plaits down my back, had been twisted into a crown of braids that was then wrapped back up and around my head. All I needed were some wildflowers and I thought I would look like a futuristic Germanic princess—albeit one with more melanin.

I felt my lips lift at that thought.

Then hands tugged at me to rise from my seat, and I was sorry to see the mirror go. The jeweler who had also covered me in paints before my coronation a year ago approached with her wares. She opened the many boxes before her and I was surprised to see white metal instead of the gold I was expecting.

The bracelets were the same, as was the signet ring etched with the letter "I." The thick manacle of a necklace was the same. Even the wide disk of a headdress that Kaiht and Mara pinned to my hair looked nearly identical to the one I had worn for my coronation. The only difference was the color of the metal.

"Platinum," Eliza provided the answer to my unspoken question. "It's mined here, as is the gold that you wore for the coronation. But for a wedding, this color is more appropriate."

"It's beautiful," I said, running my fingers over the cold metal, nearly creamy in its sheen.

"Beautiful and rare. Like you." Her lips titled up into a proud, wistful smile. And I felt my own smile answer hers as the jeweler began to adorn me with pieces.

Given the color of the jewelry, I was not surprised when she approached me with silver paint and began to paint the same markings as before: a fine mist in a band from ear to ear and eyebrow to nose; larger dots along my cheekbones, the bridge of my nose, and my chin. But she did not add the silver paint to my lips as I expected. I blinked my eyes open at the different consistency and brush, only to see a deep scarlet paint being applied there.

I glanced at the windows as the jeweler put on the final touches of paint, and I was surprised to see that the light was bright above the trees outside. It must be past noon.

"How are we on time?" I asked the room. I figured someone present must know the plan, even if I did not.

"We're fine," Eliza replied from a seat she had recently occupied. "We need to be leaving in an hour for the ceremony. Let's get you dressed."

I nodded, the excitement of the gown coming back to me once more. I approached the dress bag where it rested on my bed. With surprisingly unsteady fingers, I reached for the silver fabric that just barely dangled from the open bottom.

"Allow me, Your Majesty," the dressmaker said with a bow. And then he and the servants removed the bag and hung the gown on the framing of my four-poster bed.

I felt my eyes grow large as they swept over what looked like miles of silvery-white fabric. It was sewn into a wide, cascading skirt that fell in a graceful bell shape. Some type of white embroidery ran from waist to hem in a vining pattern that looked like proteas. A structured bodice, boned and lined with the same white seaming, sat above the skirt and I could see the sweetheart neckline in the cut of the bodice's top. But where I expected there to be sleeves there were none.

Then movement to my left caught my attention and I watched as the dressmaker hung a second piece of fabric. It was an overcape of sorts, billowing equally long and wide as the dress; however, there was only a single panel of material. That panel would cover the back of the dress. Long structured sleeves that fit over the arms and shoulders were all that would be visible from the front. It seemed a series of platinum buttons would hold the overcape closed at the neck in an inverted V-shape so that the entire front of the dress—and its low neckline—would be visible.

"It's not what I was expecting," I whispered, awestruck by the beauty.

"What were you expecting, Your Majesty?" the dressmaker asked. He did not sound panicked, though. Perhaps he heard the amazement in my voice, rather than any displeasure.

"I don't know. Something from the Humanrealm, I guess. Some lacey or gauzy prom dress."

"A 'prom' dress?" he asked, unsure of the term.

I laughed to myself. "It's a type of formal dress for young people in the Humanrealm. Never mind. This…this is magnificent."

And it was. It truly was. I ran my fingers over the thick satin and felt a lightness in my heart I had not felt in days. Maybe Mara had been onto something. It was possible to marvel in the moment even though the circumstances that led me here were not perfect.

"If you're ready, Queen Sahle, we'll dress you now."

I let Kaiht and Mara remove the dressing gown as the dressmaker approached with material I had yet to see. There were four pieces, lacy in the extreme, and I raised my eyebrows at Eliza as if to say "Really?"

But Eliza had averted her gaze when my clothing had been peeled from me, so I merely rolled my eyes and let the comment go unspoken. I moved as prompted, lifting my leg here and there to shimmy into a risqué pair of panties with an attached belt. I raised my arms as a long-lined contraption somewhere between a bra and a corset molded to my chest. I stood still as stockings were rolled up and then secured by little buckles that dangled from the panties.

From there, the dressmaker took the gown off the hanger, unlaced the back, and helped me navigate the opening as Kaiht and Mara tugged it up. Someone laced the back closed and then the dressmaker returned with the overcape. He tugged the sleeves up each arm and the long cut of them fit as if a second skin. The three platinum buttons in the front closed at my throat. And then Kaiht and Mara helped me balance as the dressmaker slipped two matching satin slippers onto my stockinged feet.

I smiled when they spun me around to see the finished product.

Where I had been a golden goddess before, a creature of the sun, I was now a daughter of the moon, the stars. My blue-gray eyes shone out of a sea of silver mist. The constellation pattern on the platinum headpiece framed the otherworldly makeup.

And the gown was regal, all long-lines and subtle silvery-white patterning.

I could not have dreamed of a better dress for my wedding day. And even if I did not relish marrying this particular man, I had to admit I took pleasure in this version of myself that stared back at me.

I spun back to the waiting helpers and smiled at them too. "Thank you all. This is beyond what I could ever have imagined."

"It's what we're here for," Eliza replied, dabbing her eyes with a handkerchief.

"It's my pleasure," the dressmaker said solemnly as if this was not just a job but a vocation.

"Of course, Your Majesty," Kaiht and Mara both replied, genuine pride shining in their eyes.

I was proud to see it—the blooming joy there as they looked at their Queen. This was what today needed to be. This occasion was for Izwe, not for me. And I was pleased to see that maybe, just maybe, in this I would be enough.

The ride to the ceremony was much like the one to the coronation. Roland, Eliza, and I sat together in a yellow and ebony wood carriage pulled by numerous zebras. My parents looked at me with adoring eyes and I could tell Eliza was trying to hold back her sniffles.

But unlike during the coronation, I was calm enough this time to feel the anticipation throbbing in the air around me. I could feel it vibrating off every servant we encountered, the stablemen, the carriage drivers, even the Vikela who walked two steps behind me as I left my chambers. I could feel it hanging like a cloud over the city as we drove through the streets. The sound of cheering, of whistles, of music being pounded out on *djembe* drums gave the excitement a palpable edge. It was a heartbeat and it beat in time with my own as if my heart, the heart of a queen, was truly the heart of this land.

The people were happy. They were excited to see their Queen wed, to welcome their Consort, and maybe, just maybe, one day a new heir to the kingdom.

I stopped that thought from progressing as I focused on the people outside of the carriage. I waved to them as we passed and the roar grew.

It was not long before the carriage pulled to a halt before the Ceremony Hall, its white roof sailing over the glass walls and making me think anew of seafoam. I did not hesitate this time as the carriage door opened. I willingly allowed Roland to hand me from the carriage and I moved with purpose past the pressing crowd and towards the building.

I looked at the glass doors that were thrown open to welcome me, and then glanced back at the crowd held at bay by a barricade and a line of Vikela.

"How much time until the ceremony begins?" I asked Eliza, who walked at my right.

"Whenever you want it to, Queen Sahle."

I nodded and looked again at the crowd. And then I slipped my hand from Roland's arm and started towards them.

"Sahle?" Roland asked, following in my wake.

"I'll be just one moment."

Out of the corner of my eye, I saw Roland signal to the Vikela to come in closer. He wanted me to be safe, but to his credit he did not try to stop me. I did not want him to. This day was for the people and I wanted them to have the opportunity to see me.

As I approached, I held out my hands—Lords be damned. I allowed those close to stroke their fingers over my fingers, to shake my hand, to touch my cheek. An older woman whispered a prayer as she held her hand to the top of my head. A child reached his arms up and I allowed him to wrap them around my neck in a warm hug.

I was not Sahle. I was the Queen, their Queen. In a part of my mind I knew my focus on that was a sort of disassociation. If Sahle were not marrying but *Queen* Sahle, then there was less fear. There was less pressure on this day and on the choice I was making.

And so I laughed as a group of young men bowed and blushed at me. I smiled as a young woman handed me a single thickly-petaled pink protea. I thanked everyone I could for coming to greet me.

Then I turned, my guards melting back into position along the barricade, and I took a decided step towards the Ceremony Hall. But that step very nearly faltered as I saw what was before me.

Or rather, who was before me.

Beside the glass door to the ceremony space was the man I was to marry.

There Anson was, standing tall and straight. And for the first time he was dressed not in dark colors but in matching silver and white. Only his hair, long and tousled, was dark against the tableau that was his beauty.

And he *was* beautiful.

I could admit it. Even if I did not like him, did not think the soul that lived within was gorgeous, I still saw how strong and honed and beautiful he was. There was no other word to describe him.

His eyes shone a green that nearly glowed in intensity. His jaw, the planes of his face were chiseled as if whatever maker in heaven had carved these features with the utmost care.

He was perfect. And I could see clearly why he had been selected. Why he was to be Consort. Why I would marry him.

Eliza had explained to me days before what would happen in the ceremony, how it differed from what I was used to in the Humanrealm, so I knew Anson would accompany me down the aisle. He would not be waiting at the altar, staring adoringly. He would be right there, by the door, waiting for me whenever I was ready.

And so I walked towards him with my head up, with my shoulders set, with resolve deep in my bones. I would marry this man because it was what my kingdom needed. And I would worry about the rest—about me—later.

But strangely enough, I realized I had stopped worrying about myself the moment I looked at Anson.

Even across the empty space between the barricade and the entrance to the Ceremony Hall, I could feel his gaze. I felt it track over my face and my gown. I felt it take in every inch of me from the arc of my headpiece to the points of the satin shoes that just barely slipped past the hem of my gown with each step.

I stopped in front of him, quietly, solemnly, and he gave me a great bow, one that was deeper and more serious than any he had given before. When he rose, there was no mocking in his eyes, no pride in his own accomplishments. That glinting cheekiness I had come to associate with him was gone. In its place was a severity, a gravity that made my heart soften just a little.

I knew he did not want to marry *me*, even if the very shiny silver lining was power. I knew I was the last person he hoped to spend his days and nights with. But above all of the warped scheming, the anger at each other, I could not help but think he understood, as I understood, that today was about more than us and our wishes as individuals. We were servants to the crown, and if we did not love each other, we loved Izwe.

I wrapped that understanding around me as I offered my hand to him. "It's a fine day for a wedding, don't you think?"

The ghost of a smile graced his lips. "It is indeed."

He reached out and took my hand, and I was startled to feel myself startle at the contact. Where his skin touched mine, it tingled. I looked at him in confusion and he looked back at me, but I could not tell if I alone had felt it. If he had, he did not let on.

And I realized I had never once shaken this man's hand. I had never brushed his skin against mine. I had never come as close to him—except for the night he carried me from Finn—and now he would become my husband. This was the first time I had willingly touched him.

The crowd roared behind us as Anson tucked my hand into the crook of his elbow. "Are you ready, Your Majesty?"

I took a deep breath. "I am. Are you ready, Lord Anson?"

I could have sworn the breath he exhaled wavered. "I am."

And so I took the first step forward, him moving a fraction of a second after I did. "Then let's do this."

Over the years, many brides have told me they remember nothing of their wedding day. The nerves take hold. The weight of the decision presses in. The sensation of too many eyes overwhelms. And at the end of the celebration, they are left with nothing but the sense of happiness, relief, and a slight surprise that they said the right words, knelt at the correct times, and kissed their new spouse with joy when the moment came.

I was not one of those brides. My emotions did not swell. I did not blush with joy. I walked sedately, seriously, arm-in-arm with Anson down the long raised aisle. I listened to the individual notes of the drums beating out around me. The moments did not rush by, they did not linger. They moved as they always moved, as if this moment was like any other moment in my life.

And perhaps it was.

Since I arrived in the Alterealm a year ago, the entirety of my life had reoriented around this kingdom as if it was a new planet and I, just its moon falling into the correct gravitational pull. Here I was making another orbit. I was glad to do it. I was *proud* to do it.

Looking back now, I am grateful I can remember every moment of the ceremony.

How the Courtiers smiled up at me and Anson for the first time in my recollection.

How Anson helped me up onto the raised dais, paying care to position my substantial dress' train.

How Anson's face looked somber as if he were attending a funeral rather than a wedding.

How the Masters prayed over our heads and then over a thin golden thread that shone like woven metal.

How that golden strand was wrapped around Anson's wrist and mine and then sank, disappearing under our skin and binding us together.

How Anson's green eyes locked on mine as we turned towards each other, as we were pronounced husband and wife.

How the Courtiers cheered, a cheer distantly echoed outside by the people, as we turned to face the assembled Lords and Ladies once more.

I smiled at the crowd, more interested in them than my husband. But I could feel his gaze on me, on the lips that curved up in secondhand pleasure, on the silver paint that hid half of my face like a veil. He looked at me as if he could not believe what had just occurred. And perhaps he could not, for he was about to become Consort. He was about to be anointed as the second-most powerful person in Izwe.

Two thrones were set up further along the dais and I took a seat upon the more ornate of the two. Anson followed, sitting on his own, as the Master carried on.

Two other Masters approached, holding the bowl of blood that had anointed me. I watched as they took Anson's hands and began the painting. They whispered over the bowl in prayers I still did not understand, and I could almost feel their fingers on my skin as they drew over Anson's exposed flesh.

His eyes were the last to receive the paint, and he looked at me before closing them to allow the Masters to paint his eyelids. I did not love this man. I did not even *like* this man. But I respected him in that instant. I could see the weight of the burden he was taking on shining in those green eyes. There was no happiness in them, not the shimmer of self-satisfaction I had expected to see. No, there was nothing but reverence.

He closed his eyes and the Masters continued painting. And when they were done, a Master approached with a simple platinum crown. It was a band more than a crown, and it was fitted low on his head so that it partially covered his forehead. When the Masters backed away from the throne upon which he sat, they said the words that would seal this ceremony.

"Rise, Anson of Izwe. Rise as chosen Consort to Queen Sahle."

He opened his eyes, the green contrasting with the red that surrounded them, and rose. As he stood, the crowd bowed. And I watched in fascination as the red markings flared as mine had flared, faded as mine had faded, until his tan skin was once more devoid of all paint.

Anson of Izwe—no longer Anson of Ingonyame—turned to me and extended his hand. I took it without hesitation, and I stepped up to his side.

We looked out at the crowd and they looked back. They roared and roared.

The crowd continued to cheer as we headed back to the palace. I had no clue where Eliza or Roland went. I did not see them after Anson took my arm to walk into the Ceremony Hall. They did not approach after the ceremony ended either, Anson instead occupying their place in the carriage we both sat in now.

I alternated between looking out of the window, waving at the crowd, and glancing at Anson. The crowd was calling my name, wishing us well. Anson did not speak, and I did not try to pull words from him.

What was there to say to Anson? There was nothing between us apart from duty. A part of my mind whispered, telling me to think of the tingle of our skin touching, the way the platinum of his crown contrasted so well with the silken strands of his nearly-black hair. But I was very good at quieting that little voice.

As the city faded behind us, as we bumped over the cobbled yard before the palace, I met Anson's gaze. I smiled awkwardly.

He gave a slight, wary smile back.

And I wanted to sigh as I had sighed this morning.

I was not sure what was more infuriating: his needling or his silence. I abruptly broke the gaze and focused on the commotion outside, the footmen descending the large staircase, the carriage drivers alighting, a servant opening the carriage door from the outside.

"Allow me, Your Majesty," Anson murmured before quickly hopping out of the carriage in order to better help me descend the few steps in my gown.

I placed my hand in his offered one, feeling the tingle that sparked in my fingers once more, and allowed him to carry some of my weight. As soon as I was once again on stable ground, he dropped my hand as if it would burn him. I smirked to myself at that.

We moved in tense silence up the grand staircase to the palace doors, through the checkered halls and into the Great Hall where the courtiers were waiting. Again, I wondered how I was always the last to arrive at these post-ceremony banquets. And I sighed in relief as Eliza and Roland accosted me.

Their presence forced me away from Anson. Courtiers swept him up into conversation as I turned to my parents, and I was grateful for the reprieve. "There you two are," I muttered.

Eliza clasped my hands in hers, tears filling her blue eyes anew. "Oh, Queen Sahle. We are so proud of you."

I forced my eyes from rolling. What were they proud of—the fact that I had not run off before doing my duty, or the fact that I was now paired up with an acceptable match?

Before I could say anything along those lines, Roland added, "Congratulations, Your Majesty."

I did snort at that, though it was quiet and ladylike enough that only Eliza and Roland noticed. Roland narrowed his eyes. "Queen Sahle," he warned, barely lifting his voice above a whisper. "Please try to be serious. Many of these courtiers are about to wish you congratulations. I hope you plan a more dignified response than that."

I took a slow, deep breath before pasting a stiff smile on my face that I hoped was convincing. "Thank you for your well wishes, Lord Roland."

"Much better," he replied past a small smile of his own.

I rolled my eyes again before giving Eliza's hands a final squeeze and then making my way towards my usual seat. Many courtiers came up to me, bowing and saying their own "Congratulations." From behind me, I thought I heard the mirrored sentiment and assumed Anson was following in my wake.

At last, I made it to the main banquet table. A Vikela stepped forward to pull out my chair but Anson was suddenly there. "Your Majesty," he said, offering me the seat.

I looked at him with a raised brow. "You don't have to pretend to be nice to me, you know."

He stared back at me, as if trying to read the thoughts swirling in my head. Finally, he bit out, "I'm not."

"Sure," I replied, dropping into the seat and rearranging the long silver skirt around me.

Anson took the seat on my right, and I opened my mouth to tell him that Eliza and Roland typically sat on either side of me. Then I saw that they had taken seats further down the table.

Of course my new *husband* would now be seated in this position of honor. I sighed again, and I wondered what other changes were heading our way.

One being would know—Manelesi—not that he would tell me what to expect. I thought of him off in the Yesonto, perched on its highest floor. He had not wanted to attend the festivities though I had extended an invitation, though he would have blended into the drove of Masters who had been in the Ceremony Hall. No, he had merely smile and shaken his head in refusal.

"I'm not pretending to be nice to you," Anson repeated. "I merely seek to treat you with the respect you deserve as Queen."

I thought my jaw would fall open. "Since when?" I quipped back, pitching my voice low. "You have never sought to treat me with respect before. This marriage is not about us but about the duty we must do for Izwe. Let's not pretend it's something it's not."

His green gaze swept over my face, my hair, the exposed skin above the bodice of my gown. And then he smiled, a simple cheeky smirk that brought some of the life back to his eyes. "As you wish."

Servants filled the flutes before us with sparkling *konstans* and I took a sip as he continued. "This gown doesn't suit you."

I nearly spit out my wine. "Excuse me?"

Anson shrugged, taking a sip from his own glass as he turned to survey the Lords and Ladies taking their seats in the hall. "It's fine. The style is suitable for the occasion. But I preferred you in the gold you wore for the coronation. It complemented your skin."

"I'll be sure to wear more silver and white," I muttered.

"Pardon?" Anson asked, but I knew he heard me. I saw the way his eyes glowed with mirth.

I set my glass down, smiling out at the courtiers even as I said through gritted teeth, "I'll be sure to wear more silver and white then, as I do not need you admiring my skin or anything else."

Anson's laugh brought my gaze back to him. And I was once again reminded of the time in the library where that laugh had filled the quiet space. I was shocked that such a warm sound could come from such a cold man.

"Don't worry, Your Majesty. I will keep my eyes to myself regardless of what you are wearing."

"Perfect."

Platters of food began to arrive. The beat of drums thrummed in the air, and I let the music fill the silence between us. Anson spoke to Grimly who sat on his opposite side. I spoke to Eliza, who had moved nearer in case I needed anything.

We ate. We drank. I chatted with to Eliza. I ignored Anson. And when the meal was over, I stood. My face had begun to ache from all of the smiling—forced and real—I had done today. I was tired from the continuous attempt to separate Sahle from Queen Sahle. All I wanted to do was sit in my room alone.

I knew the etiquette of these banquets. I knew I had only to stay until the meal was finished, and it was. While Roland had announced my departure at my coronation banquet, I figured that duty now fell to me. I was about to open my mouth when I felt a hand upon my lower back.

The feeling was gentle but insistent and I turned towards its owner in resignation. "Yes?"

Anson looked up at me from his seat, his arm still outstretched, his hand still planted on my spine. "Had enough of me, have you?" he asked quietly.

"Had enough of the whole day, actually," I replied truthfully. I did not savor my time with him but he also was not to blame for my imminent departure.

Anson nodded thoughtfully, his gaze holding mine as if he wanted to say something but then thought better of it. He rose from his seat, turning to the crowd. "My Lords and Ladies. The Queen will take her leave and wishes that you continue your revelry in her absence. Thank you, from the both of us, for your congratulations on our marriage."

The courtiers clapped and smiled. I could feel the heat from Anson's hand even through the layers of my gown, and I stepped out of his reach the moment the clapping had quieted.

"Enjoy the festivities," I said quietly, dismissively, before getting as far away from the banquet as I could.

BACK IN MY CHAMBERS, I ITCHED TO SHAKE THE SILVER-white gown from my shoulders. It was suddenly far too big, far too heavy, as if the weight of the hollow vows I had uttered pulled on the cloth pooling at my feet.

Eliza had followed me out of the Great Hall despite my protests that she stay and enjoy the evening. But she had shaken her head. She wanted to be wherever I needed her.

It was how she ended up behind me, assisting Kaiht and Mara in unlacing the back of the gown and pulling the sleeved overcape away. The three of them helped me out of the little slippers and removed the wide headpiece from my hair. And when all that was left were my structured underclothes, I waved them off.

"I can manage the rest. I need to get this paint off," I said, angling away from them in my stockings and long-lined bra. I took a step towards the bathing chamber, but someone grabbed my elbow.

"Sweetheart, Mara will grab you a cloth. Come sit beside me for a moment while she does," Eliza said. There was an insistence in her words that made me turn my full attention to her.

I let her pull me towards the chairs before the fireplace. "What is it?"

For all of Eliza's patience and kindness, it was a rare moment that she looked nervous. Yet here she was, fidgeting with the hem of her sleeve rather than meeting my eye.

"Mom?"

That caught her attention, and she looked up at me with a smile. It was rare that I still referred to her as such, after all this time in the Alterealm, but I knew she liked it. I knew she still felt as if she was my mother regardless of the fact that I had had a mother, albeit a dead one. And I liked it too—the nostalgia of the days when Eliza and Roland and I had lived as a carefree, happy family in the Humanrealm.

The Humanrealm where there was not the press of violence hanging over our heads, a marriage of necessity stifling the air around us, death and destruction at every turn.

I watched as Eliza swallowed once more. "Sahle, I know you've had boyfriends before. I know you and Finn…were close—"

"Were lovers, you mean," I corrected. I did not like the bitterness in my voice, and I took a breath to calm myself against the torrent of emotions that rose in me.

"Yes, of course," Eliza replied with a small nod. "What I mean is…I do not believe I have to explain what happens between a man and a woman."

I felt my cheeks heat instantly. "No, you certainly do not."

"I know we've discussed it before, years ago. And you had sex education at school. So you know how it works…"

I could tell Eliza was floundering, circling an awkward conversation instead of getting on with it. I wished she would spit out whatever it was she had to say. I was sure whatever made her this uncomfortable was better dealt with quickly.

"Where are you going with this?" I finally asked her.

She glanced at the fire and then back at me. "What I'm trying to say is that you and Anson will be expected to consummate this marriage."

And there it was. The thought I had been trying to avoid since the moment I agreed to this ill-fated wedding.

Anson was not an unattractive man. In fact, I remembered thinking he was the *most* attractive man I had ever laid eyes on when I first met him. But that was then.

This was now—after all of the harshness, the bullying, the slight remarks. The simple fact of the matter was that we did not hold any fondness for each other. I certainly could not see either of us enjoying the other in the way Eliza was implying.

And yet it was expected. As Queen, I would be expected to produce an heir which necessarily meant taking Anson to my bed. I shuddered at the thought of those smirking lips caressing me.

Still, I nodded at Eliza. She was right even if I could not imagine any circumstance where Anson and I would fall into bed willingly. "I know."

Eliza let out a long relieved exhale. "Good. I just wanted to make sure we were on the same page."

"We are," I confirmed.

Eliza seemed happy with my response and she smiled. "I'd imagine he'll be here momentarily. While it's customary for royals to maintain separate chambers throughout their marriage, it is tradition for the Consort—male or female—to visit the monarch's room on the wedding night."

Ah, so that was why she brought up the topic—it was not a future possibility but the fact that Anson could come strolling through the door any second.

"I didn't realize you meant I should consummate the marriage *tonight*," I said lamely.

"Better to just get it over and done with."

I shut my eyes at that. *Get it over and done with.* What a way to contemplate sleeping with one's husband. As much as I wanted to rebel against it, push back on the idea of going to any man's bed I was not personally interested in, I could not feel that rebellion within me.

I did not feel much of anything these days, besides a determination to do everything I could to be a good Queen. I had pushed back. I had cajoled. I had forged my own way for a year here, and I could not help but think Finn might be alive today if I had tried harder to adapt to this world from the get-go. Maybe then I would have had control of my magic before a sword went through his stomach, not after.

Of course there were things that I would always insist upon—like showing respect to servants and offering kindness and compassion when I could—but I understood now what me refusing to be a Queen cost.

I would do anything to ensure the safety of my people. Including falling into bed with someone I despised.

"I agree," I said as Mara returned with a damp rag and a small bowl of water. I thanked her as I scrubbed at the silver paint. The water in the bowl turned progressively more and more gray with each dip of the cloth.

"Kaiht," I called through pouted lips as I wiped off the lipstick. "Could you please pour me a glass of *konstans*?"

Kaiht took no time in pouring me a glass and placing it on a low table near my seat. When I had sufficiently scrubbed my face, I lifted the glass and gulped it down in three long swallows.

"Sahle," Eliza said admonishingly from her seat.

I leveled my cool gray eyes on her. "Please stay out of it. In fact, don't you think you should be on your way? As you said, Anson could be here any moment."

I rose from my seat, my stockinged feet slipping softly along the polished wooden floor. I padded towards the door but Eliza beat me there, turning to block me from opening it just yet.

She reached out her hand and cupped the damp skin of my cheek. "I hate seeing you like this."

"Like what?"

"Cold, calculated, resigned."

I mulled over her description of me, aware that I was certainly all of those things now. I had worked hard to be those things ever since Anson had dragged me away from Finn's lifeless body a mere weeks ago.

A part of me wanted to deny her words, tell her she was being silly and that everything was fine as always. But that would be a lie, and I did not see any good in denying what was plain to everyone. "It's what I have to be right now."

Her eyes shone as she looked at me. "I know, sweetheart. In time, I hope you can find happiness."

The best I could do for her was smile, and so I did that. I do not know if the gesture made it to my eyes. I do not even know if my lips cooperated as I wanted them to. But whatever Eliza saw on my face was good enough. She turned and grasped the door handle as I stepped out of view of anyone who might be in the hallway—no need to give my guards a show of me in my lingerie.

"Good night, Eliza," I said gently.

"Good night, Your Majesty," she replied. Just before she closed the door behind her, she added, "Everything will be fine. I promise."

I smiled once more and nodded.

I had heard that all before, from her and Roland.

And as I turned back to my chamber—Mara and Kaiht occupied with hanging the giant dress and tidying up in expectation of my husband—I could not help but hope things turned out better this time around.

I considered sitting in my lingerie to wait for Anson, but I did not think he deserved a show. We were not interested in each other, so why pretend to be a seductress intensely interested in pleasing him or, worse yet, some sort of present for him to unwrap? I was not and I never would be.

Instead, Kaiht and Mara helped me out of the lacey undergarments and into my usual white nightdress. I wrapped a white dressing gown on top of that and then dragged a comb once more through my curls in an effort to make the coils release the shape of the braids they had been forced into earlier.

And then I waited. I poured another glass of *konstans* and sipped it as I sat before the fire. I picked up a novel I started two days prior, but my eyes could not focus on the words. They ran over the same three sentences time and time again, and I realized my concentration was outside my chamber door. My ears were tuned for the scuff of boots on the stone hallway, the murmuring of "Consort" or "My Lord" by the guards.

I was waiting for Anson.

In a huff, I put the book back down. What time was it anyway? I was sure I had been in this chamber for an hour or two, and still he had not arrived.

I knew I heard Eliza correctly when she said a consort would come to the monarch's chambers on the wedding night. Anson was a stickler for tradition so I was sure he was aware of that.

But then where was he?

Annoyed, I leaped to my feet. Kaiht was stirring the fire and I turned to her. "Do you know where Lord Anson's chambers are?"

She blinked at me and then straightened, almost as if she was shocked I would ever willingly go see that man. "Excuse me, Your Majesty?"

I sighed deeply. "I'm going to see Anson. Do you know where his chambers are?"

Now she looked even more shocked. "But why, Your Majesty, if you don't mind me asking? He's supposed to come to you, and if he hasn't then all the better for it, right? If you don't mind me saying…"

I sighed again. I loved Kaiht and appreciated her frankness on most days, but I did not need her logical mind working right now. "I don't mind you asking or saying. But I do need for you to tell me where to find him. He obviously isn't here so I'll go to him."

"Of course, Your Majesty," Kaiht replied with a curtsy. "His chambers are one floor down. Turn right at the bottom of the main staircase, and at the end of the hallway, you'll find the Ingonyame crest. That's his room."

"Thank you," I said quickly before marching out the door. If he would not come to me, then I would go to him.

Vaguely, I noticed the Vikela straighten and bow as I passed them in the hallway. I knew two fell in line behind me as soon as I heard their clink of boots over my shoulder. Only then did I realize I was not wearing shoes of my own, my bare feet landing softly over the cold polished floor with each step.

In mere moments, I was down the main staircase and to the next landing. It was a rarity that I came to this part of the palace. It was no surprise, therefore, to see the courtiers stare at me with curious eyes. There were not many about—not when a marriage banquet still carried on floors below—but just the handful I saw would surely have the palace talking by daybreak. The Queen in her nightgown, traipsing to the Consort's chamber on their wedding night! The scandal!

I preemptively rolled my eyes, annoyed anew at Anson. Not only was I married to a man I hated and who hated me, but now he would make me the laughing stock of the palace by not coming to my chambers.

But then again, what was new? Embarrassing me seemed to be Anson's favorite pastime.

I did not stop to knock when I saw the crest of the lion painted on the door at the far end of the corridor. I simply turned the handle, vaguely surprised that it was not locked, and pushed my way into the room.

I was not sure what I expected—perhaps for him to be passed out, having stayed behind to drink more after I left the banquet. Perhaps I expected him to be entertaining another lady. I *had* never thought to ask if he had a mistress…

Whatever I thought to find behind that lion-crested door was not Anson sitting demurely in bed, reading a book.

I took half a heartbeat to scan my surroundings. I told myself it was to make sure we were truly alone, no servants or mistresses about to witness what I had to say. But really, I was curious about the sparsely decorated room. No art hung on the wall except for the same lion crest above his bed. A single chair sat before a desk that faced a window, smaller than my own wall of windows one floor up. A wooden wardrobe sat along one wall, next to a door to what I assumed was a bathing chamber. And then there was the bed, nearly as tall and stately as my own except it did not have any wispy fabric hanging from the posts.

No, nothing as soft and floating could exist in this cold, almost sterile domain.

Sitting in the bed, Anson raised one eyebrow at me. I noticed he was shirtless although I could see the waistband of some sort of pants just above where the blankets were pulled over his lap. The pop of an ember cracking in the fireplace was the only sound.

"Well?" I demanded.

He held my gaze a moment before slowly marking his page and setting down the book. "Well what?"

"Were you even going to come to me tonight?"

"No."

That was all, as if that word held the entire explanation I needed. That was all, as if I were crazy to have thought anything else.

Maybe I was. But I was also angry and bewildered and increasingly embarrassed to be standing here before him, essentially asking why he would not fuck me.

In the time it took for me to consider these emotions, Anson threw back the covers and climbed from the bed. My eyes were drawn to his tan chest even as I urged myself to avert my gaze. But my eyes would not listen. They tracked across his muscled form, the leanly strong lines of his pectorals, the hard planes of his stomach, the rise and falls of his arms, and the dusting of hair that all but pointed to worlds unknown beneath the waistband of his pants.

Anson spared me any further moments of staring. He wrapped a robe around his own shoulders and tied the sash at his waist. Then he moved my way, slipping past me to close the door at my back. I shivered at the sound of the latch sealing me in.

"What?" I finally said, my gaze tracking him as he came back to stand near the bed. I shook my head slightly, puzzled by my visceral reaction to seeing him half naked now that the display of skin was safely covered.

But Anson did not seem nearly as affected by me, standing before him with my hair unbound, my feet bare. "I said, 'No.'"

I shook my head again. "I—I don't understand. Everyone told me that the Consort was supposed to come to the Monarch's room on their wedding night. It's tradition."

"Your Majesty—"

"You should probably call me Sahle now that we're married," I interjected.

He leveled his cool gaze at me and calmly ignored my words. "*Your Majesty*, as I was saying, I was not planning on visiting your rooms tonight."

I felt an angry and embarrassed blush begin to seep across my skin. I had expected it to be me who would turn him away, if anyone would. I never expected that it would be *him* who would say no. And even when I hated him, even when I did not want him in my bed, the rejection still stung. "Why not?"

Anson being Anson did not seem fazed by my growing discomfort. I wondered if he even noticed it. "Did you want me to?"

"No, but—"

"Exactly," he broke in. "I know you do not like me, Queen, and that you only allowed the marriage cord to sink into your skin today because it was expected of you. I have never been accused of being a kind man, but even I cannot countenance forcing myself on a woman who does not want me."

"Oh," I whispered, unsure of what else to say.

But Anson knew. "I know you do not like me but I'd hoped you thought better of me than that."

"I do…I just assumed that consummating the marriage was part of our duty."

He shrugged, as if we were discussing the weather rather than his lifelong pursuit to serve Izwe. "Perhaps and perhaps not. What happens between us stays between us, my Queen."

He leaned in as if to whisper a scandalous secret. But only his piercing gaze moved for a moment. It raked across my body slowly, as if he were only now taking in my state of undress. "And one day, should we consummate this marriage, it will be by choice. I will never touch you, not until you ask me to."

Until.

I wanted to scoff, but the air got caught in my throat. It seemed there was no air at all in the room, such was the tension that locked us together.

I put all my effort into my best haughty expression, but I was not sure I could truly look down my nose at him when he towered above me. "What makes you think I will ever ask you?"

"A man can dream, can't he?"

And I could finally scoff. I did so loudly.

Anson chuckled, the sound seeming to light up his eyes with mirth. "It was good of you to come by, though."

I lifted my eyebrows in question. "Why is that?"

"You may be right—people will expect this marriage to be consummated. You traipsing down the halls in your nightdress will certainly take care of any questions there."

I scoffed again, pulling my robe tighter around my body.

But Anson was done. He turned back to his bed, sank into the blankets, and picked up his book. Only when it was open before him did his gaze meet mine again. "Now, if you'll excuse me, I was getting to a good part."

I stared, my mouth veritably falling open in surprise. "Are you dismissing me?"

"I rather think I am," Anson said thoughtfully. Only the glint in his green eyes told me how much he was enjoying this.

"Hmph," I grumbled as I turned my back on him. I was halfway out of the door before his next words sounded.

"Perhaps next week, I'll come by your chambers for a nice cup of *rooibos*. Keep the courtiers talking and all."

I did not dignify that with a response. Instead, I slammed the door behind me and began my walk of shame back to my rooms. Even with the door shut, I could make out Anson's laughter. I was sure the lion painted on his door laughed, too, as it watched me retreat.

I BATTED MY EYES OPEN EQUALLY HORRIFIED AND settled. The weight of my actions yesterday pressed in on me yet where I thought I would find panic, I only felt cold, calm resolve.

I threw back the covers on my bed and climbed out into the day. From the corner of my eye, I caught my reflection in the mirror. I shuddered involuntarily. I was still dressed in the same nightgown in which I had traipsed down the hallway to Anson's room.

My cheeks burned in shame and embarrassment. Of course, I was happy nothing occurred. I had not wanted anything to happen, even as I made that walk. It had been borne out of duty, and duty alone.

But it still stung to be sent packing.

I wondered at my hatred of rejection for what felt like the millionth time in a matter of weeks, even as I warred with relief at not having to go through *that* part of this marriage. Still, a little voice in my head whispered, "That's how much he hates you." He could not even fulfill the full obligation to the crown.

The thought made me physically ill, putting sex and obligation together. But this was my new reality. Eventually we would have to go through with it. And then it would be all too real.

That day was not today, though.

No, today I was a new bride. I chuckled to myself in a resigned, humorless sort of way as Kaiht and Mara bustled in from the servants' entrance.

"Good morning, Your Majesty," Kaiht said as she set out a pot of steaming *rooibos* and a tray of crunchy rusks.

"You must be exhausted after such a day!" Mara exclaimed.

"It was perfectly fine," I said as I sat down at a wingback chair. I took a cup of *rooibos* from Kaiht's outstretched hand.

Mara blinked at me. "Was it not exhilarating, Your Majesty?"

I took a bite of rusk before settling back in the chair. I shrugged. "It was what it needed to be."

Mara's mouth popped open in surprise, maybe a little disbelieving pity. But before she could say more, Kaiht scolded, "Leave Her Majesty alone." She elbowed Mara gently out of the way as she folded a napkin into my lap.

I waved my thanks at her as a smattering of crumbs fell from the rusk.

"Mara," I eventually replied after swallowing the mouthful. "I do appreciate your attempt to make me see this as something larger than just a wedding. But the fact remains that neither Anson nor I wanted this, and neither of us are particularly happy about it."

Mara looked at me as if I had spoken a foreign language. I turned to look at Kaiht, hoping she could explain. But Kaiht just rolled her eyes at Mara's back.

"But you're married," Mara answered quietly. I could see the wheels turning behind her eyes. She was struggling to reconcile her vision of being a bride with the reality of my marriage. And for her sake, I hoped she never had to travel the path I just had.

Mara stood still, close to me. I reached out and took her hand. "Thank you for your excitement," I told her, and I meant it. "But you saw what I was like the days before the wedding. I did not want it and having the ceremony done does not change it. I'm resigned to this marriage and that's as far as my feelings go."

She blinked at me before nodding quickly. I could almost hear every romantic notion of hers shattering.

I squeezed her hand again. Then I looked at both of the women. "Really, thank you for all you did the last few days. I wouldn't have gotten through it without you both. You've been my rocks."

"You're welcome, Your Majesty," Kaiht replied. Mara echoed it, just softer.

Then Kaiht turned curious eyes on me. "May we inquire as to how the rest of the night went?"

I nearly choked on my rusk.

I gulped down a sip of tea before responding. "You may not."

From anyone else, it would seem inappropriate. But I had long come to see Kaiht and Mara as my friends, and friends could tease each other. Kaiht laughed with good humor now.

I did not have it in me to laugh, not after the horror of being turned out of Anson's rooms. But I did roll my eyes, just slightly.

For a split second, I considered telling Kaiht and Mara everything. I relished in the idea of confiding in them just how mortifying it was to stand before Anson in my nightgown, how terrible it was for him to give me the cold shoulder whether I wanted it or not.

But I thought better of it. Anson had mentioned that people would assume we had consummated the marriage last night. And if this marriage was to be seen as legitimate—and it needed to be for the security of my kingdom—then everyone must think it was a proper union in every way possible.

I shuddered at the thought.

I did not think Kaiht and Mara would talk, but I could not risk it. If Anson and I were playing a game of marriage then I had to do my best to uphold my part of the act. It was the only thing keeping Izwe together. It was my duty.

So I kept my confession to myself. I swallowed back the memory of Anson telling me to leave. And I vowed to never speak of it to anyone—not these two women before me, not Eliza, not anyone.

The only person who could be party to this secret was Anson, the one in cahoots with me in this fib. It was ironic that after everything, Anson and I would be united in something. But here we were bound in the same charade that was a union.

He was my Consort. And I was his Queen in more ways than one.

I downed my cup of tea and held up the empty cup for more.

Kaiht refilled it without question.

Kaiht and Mara bustled out of the room soon after, heeding my request to give me some privacy. There was something I had to do. On quiet, tentative feet, I walked over to my wardrobe and I began to rearrange it.

The last weeks, months, I had worn the charcoal gray dresses I had commissioned upon Finn's death. Even though Kaiht and Mara offered other gowns each morning, I refused them. Even though Eliza looked at me with a quietly disapproving gaze whenever she took in the dark color, I kept wearing it. The gowns had been my silent protest to the Council's attempt to stop me mourning a servant to the crown, a good man, and an even better friend. The whole Council knew I wore the gowns in rebellion. I was sure most of the courtiers realized it, as well.

Yet now, the act of wearing them felt wrong. While I knew my marriage was nothing more than a political decision, I could not square the idea of being married with openly mourning a past lover.

The two concepts were incompatible in my mind.

I pulled the heavy gowns from their hangers in my dressing room and gingerly, reverently folded the yards of satin, cotton, and brocade. There was a large wooden trunk in the corner of the closet and I pulled the lid open, relieved to find it nearly empty. I placed each of the three gowns inside.

As I shut the wide lid, a glint of metal caught my eye and my gaze shifted to the bracelet on my left wrist. I paused.

My right hand moved to the thin band, ready to put it aside. It too was an object of memory, infused with the spirit and caring of Finn. Yet, I could not seem to pull it from my wrist. The thought of doing so made me instantly cringe away like it was something sharp as thorns or deadly as venom.

My fingers skated over the three simple twists, the only adornment on the piece. And I knew I could not take this bracelet off. My heart would not allow it to be discarded like the gowns.

But perhaps that was alright. My mind spun a tale of rationalization, telling me there was a difference between a dress and a bracelet. One was a loud proclaiming. One was a small thing, something I could quietly hide.

Besides, it was not like Anson would ever know that this simple bracelet had come from Finn, nor would he care. We may be married but neither of us expected a depth of emotion to accompany our vows.

I hesitated a moment longer, fingers shaking, before I let my right hand drop away from the only thing Finn ever gave me. I stood from my crouched place in the dressing room. I turned to the many colorful dresses around me.

Today I was a married woman. What color did a newly married woman wear?

If I thought it would be hard to live the lie, I was wrong. Most of the courtiers I bumped into were too busy complimenting my wedding gown, the ceremony, my choice in spouse. All I had to do was nod and thank them. Really, they all seemed too busy speaking about my wedding day to ask me questions about how it felt to be married—or where my new husband was. I had not seen him since that moment in his room.

No, my new husband had left the castle first thing the day after our wedding. Something about necessary training for some of Izwe's troops. I had been too distracted by my relief at not having to face Anson to take in the particulars after that.

He would be gone for four days, and that was OK with me. It was ideal actually. I smiled and nodded and asked the courtiers to tell me more about what they liked about the floral arrangements, the music. I figured letting them show their interest could be the easiest way to make them believe in my interest in the topic when really I had none.

With each discussion on my platinum gown and headpiece, I itched to get to the training ground. The harsh reality of the marriage—not to mention the lie by omission that it was consummated—felt like ants crawling under my skin. I needed to run. I needed to swing a sword and summon my magic. I needed to sweat.

I needed anything that would allow me to drop the plastic blushing bride smile off my face.

And so I dutifully trained each day with Manelesi. In between bouts of blasting white light, I bit back my tongue from asking questions. I suspected my inner monologue rang loud and clear for him. I was sure he heard all of my tortured thoughts about my husband, about the futility yet usefulness of this match.

He watched me sometimes when he did not think I was looking. From the corner of my eye, I noticed his stare. Yet, Manelesi did not voice his thoughts on the matter. I did not ask. I had learned better in my weeks with him.

On the fourth day, I donned my soldier browns and strode into the training ring. My favorite sword, heavy with a fine, worn leather hilt, rested in my hand.

Across from me stood Caleb. I had picked Caleb weeks ago because he reminded me exactly nothing of Finn. And it was for the best. I could not afford to be reminded of him now, while I swung a sharp object at my sparring partner or while I defended blows to my own chest. Caleb was good at fighting but that was where the similarities ended.

"Congratulations on your Marriage, Your Majesty," Caleb said with a shy bow. His brown eyes shone with genuine warmth.

"Thank you," I replied shortly. I was in no mood for talking. "Shall we?"

Caleb nodded. "On your mark."

Best practice surely would tell me to drop into a fighting stance, to circle my partner, to trick them into guessing from which angle I would attack. I had patience for none of that.

I struck, simply and quickly.

My blade flew with a year's worth of practiced blows and weeks' worth of anxious energy. Caleb matched every one. He spun when I spun. He blocked when I lunged. He attacked when he saw a weak spot.

He did not make it easy for me. He did not cow because I was Queen. He challenged me, and it was exactly what I needed.

Who knew how long we sparred. It could have been seconds. It could have been hours. There is a place the mind goes when it is so deep into the focus required in a fight. And in that place, time is an illusion. There is only your feet under you and the sword in your hand, the breath heaving in and out of your lungs.

It is a place of silence and simplicity where only one rule reigns: strike or be struck.

I relished that place. I needed that place. It was a balm to my senses after the last weeks, the last days.

And so when Caleb slowly let up, when the illusion of that focused solitude began to fade, I let out an angry wail. I lunged and struck two final blows, which Caleb blocked with quick efficiency.

Then he dropped his sword to his side and bowed.

I let my mind sink back into my body before acknowledging him. Between heavy breaths, sweat streaming into my eyes, I said, "Thank you, Caleb."

As he stood, I noticed a few strands of his auburn hair had swung forward. "Anytime, Your Majesty."

I smiled genuinely, and for the first time in days. It felt good. "I may take you up on that."

His answering smile was brief. There was too much awe in it to be anything genuine. And for the millionth time I wondered what I had done to earn such awe and reverence. Oh, everyone knew about my power—barely controlled though it was. Everyone knew who my mother, and grandfather, and great-grandfather were.

Yet a part of me would always wonder why those things alone earned me the respect and fear I seemed to wield. I did not feel special. I did not feel out of the ordinary. I was just Sahle.

I vowed to keep telling myself that.

I returned my sword to the training shed where all weapons were kept. When I stepped back out onto the red dirt of the training ring, Lord Grimly was waiting.

He dropped into a bow automatically. "Your Majesty, I wonder if I could have a word…"

I nodded as I looped my arm around to loosen my shoulder. Already, I could feel the muscles tightening. "Of course, Lord Grimly. Would you walk with me?"

"Certainly, Your Majesty."

My Vikela fell in silently as Grimly and I made our way up the stone stairs that led from the training grounds and to the palace. Grimly, too, was silent at my side.

I glanced at him from the corner of my eye. "What is it, Lord Grimly? What did you want to speak to me about?"

"It's more of a musing than anything, Your Majesty…"

"Yes?"

He seemed to hesitate again before speaking. "I thought to call a Council Meeting to discuss this but I am not sure there is enough to warrant bringing everyone to the table. Yet, I did want to bring it to you."

We climbed the steps slowly, my pace measured so that Grimly could keep up easily. But the pace of this conversation was making me wish otherwise.

"Grimly, please just say whatever it is that's on your mind," I said. I hope it sounded kinder to his ears than it did to mine.

He twisted his hands together in a show of nerves. "We know, of course, that Trina Cheile scared Niel away from its suit."

"Interesting choice of words," I muttered under my breath. I would call leaving a dead look-alike to one's son something more than scaring away.

"But after that, we've heard nothing. Our spies report quiet—too much quiet—from our borders. It's as if Trina Cheile has given up or has gone underground in their hatred for Izwe."

"Well, I don't think they gave up," I said. I nodded to the two Vikela who opened the door to the palace for our small group.

"No, neither do I. Granted, Trina Cheile did have its way in pressuring you out of a foreign match—"

"And you think that's the only thing they wanted?"

Grimly shook his head. "Well, no, Your Majesty. We also know they want you dead."

I swallowed. "Pleasant." It was nothing new to me, but it was unsettling to hear it spoken so matter-of-factly nonetheless.

Grimly did not seem to notice my discomfort. "They have been so singular in the past, and they have made pointed attempts recently yet now they are silent? There must be some explanation."

"Perhaps they have taken a break to allow me to enjoy my honeymoon."

"Your what?" Grimly asked. We made our way up one of the polished staircases and to the checkerboard floors that marked the true court space of the palace. My training boots clicked on the marble with each step.

I waved off the idea. "Never mind. It's a Humanrealm tradition. But genuinely, if Trina Cheile has gone quiet, that's a good thing, right?"

"Not necessarily," Grimly countered. "Our spies need to know their every move so that we can anticipate when they will strike next and where. They would not give up this easily, regardless of your new marriage to the Consort. So the question really is what does Trina Cheile mean to do next?"

I sighed, keeping my pace. As we strode through the hallway, I unwound the piece of cloth I had wrapped around my wrist for training. I probably should stop, I mused. I probably should take Lord Grimly and have a proper conversation about this in the Council Chamber, but I did not want to. Not when I had promised Ruth I would come to the library this afternoon. Not when I had promised Kaiht and Mara that I would be back early for dinner so that they could fit me in some new gown they had devised.

Glancing down at my wrist as I was, I did not notice the small contingent of Lords and Ladies coming in the opposite direction. That is, I did not notice them until I almost ran into the Vikela before me as my contingent stopped abruptly.

My eyes rose with impatience. But any annoyance died the moment I saw who it was that rose from the bow before me.

"My Queen," Lord Anson said as he righted himself. With him was Lady Madeline, Lord Silas, Lord Marcus, and a smattering of younger courtiers whose names I still struggled to remember.

But now was not the time to try to remember them, not when Anson was standing before me: my new Consort here for the first time since our wedding.

I instinctively went to greet him with "Lord Anson" but I had to hold the words back. No, he was not just Lord Anson anymore. With the slightest irritation and regret and self-pity, I said through tight lips, "Consort."

Anson being Anson seemed to see all that. If he had looked solemn on our wedding day, that momentary lapse in usual behavior was gone. Back was the twinkling-eyed, smirking man I had come to know *so* well in the last year.

And he did smirk, brow raised in expectation like I was supposed to say more than his title.

Perhaps I was. I had no idea what to say. In fact, I stared dumbly back at him, all too aware of the eyes of my contingent and Anson's watching our every move.

And damn him to hell, Anson did not seem to mind any of it. My eyes flicked to his fingers where they tapped a spot on his thigh as if he was impatient with me, as if he had better things to do than stand here and greet his Queen.

His new wife.

I swallowed at the thought, even as I forced myself to bring my gaze back to his.

We stared at each other. We did not speak. And everyone watched.

I could feel the tension in the air like a palpable force, like the air itself had ossified into a thick gelatinous sludge made up of the animosity and anger and resentment that Anson and I felt for each other.

I wanted to storm off. I wanted to say something haughty. I wanted to do anything but stand here staring at him.

But of course I could not.

When it came to Anson, it seemed there was nothing but humiliation and anger that could result from our interactions.

Just as I felt that familiar itch of shame and embarrassment begin to climb up my neck and chest, Grimly bowed to Anson and said, "Consort, a pleasant morning, I take it?"

Anson watched me a moment longer, one brow quirked. Then he shifted his attention to Grimly. "Quite. We were just taking in the air in the gardens. We watched the Queen train."

He what?

I knew there were parts of the training grounds visible from the gardens but never in a million years did I think Anson would take interest enough to watch.

"You are very talented, Your Majesty," Lady Madeline added.

My gaze swiveled between her and Anson, between the men behind them. "Is it a usual pastime of yours—to watch me train with the Vikela?"

Lord Silas edged his way closer to the front until he was shoulder to shoulder with Anson. "No, Your Majesty. We joined the Consort on a congratulatory picnic. The spot happened to overlook part of the training ground you were in."

"Hmm," I grumbled—a very un-Queenlike sound. It was petty of me to think they were spying on me. I was being childish. Yet I viewed anything Anson did with suspicion. And how could I not—him being him, him sending me out into the garden that fateful night, him being Warbeck and somehow ending up on an Izweian throne.

I squared my shoulders. I forced myself to lift my head higher, all too aware that I was still in soldier brown and that everyone around me was dressed in the fine clothes of the court.

I refocused on Anson, hoping I could find something Queenly to say. But nothing came, not as Anson looked back at me with haughty expectation, not as his brow rose even higher as if it alone were mocking me.

"Good day, Lords, Lady, Consort," I bit out. And without waiting for anyone to follow me, I moved past Lord Grimly and the guards who seemed to be stuck in the same gelatinous air.

A moment later, I heard their footsteps behind me.

I did not wait up, all too eager to put as much distance between Anson and myself.

IT WAS STRANGE TO SIT UP ON THE DAIS WITH ANYONE, but especially Anson. I had grown accustomed to being the lone head raised, the center of attention. Yet here I sat now with… my husband.

Even stranger, Anson had summoned us. I had not even summoned the full Council before, and here Anson was merely a week crowned and already holding court.

I tried not to let that thought rub me the wrong way. It was entirely in his right to call the Council to order—or so I had been told when Grimly briefed me on a Consort's various duties. Still, a niggling voice in my head told me to watch, to be careful. It whispered that if I blinked just long enough, Anson could snatch this throne out from under me.

"My Queen. My Lords," Anson finally called as he stood from his seat. It was nearly as ornate as mine yet I noticed, with a little smirk, that it did not shine as brightly—as if the palace cleaners purposefully only polished it every once in a while. "Thank you for attending my summons. As my first act as Consort, I'd like to put forward a motion that the Queen take courtiers as ladies in waiting."

I did not know what I expected Anson to say but it certainly was not that. Cool shock washed over my head followed immediately by a wave of outrage that heated my skin. I turned in my seat to look at the Consort.

"Ladies?" I whispered, futilely. No matter how quietly I spoke, the acoustics of this chamber would transport my words down the long table to each seated Lord. "Ladies? You didn't think this was something we could have discussed privately?"

I tried to control my face but I was not sure I was doing a good job. My smile felt pasted on and my words slipped past teeth gritted too tight. My irritation rolled off of me in pulses.

Yet, if Anson felt any of this directed at him, he paid it no mind. "Ladies," he answered at full volume, turning his eyes from mine and back to the Council. "It's a matter for the Lords to weigh in on, so it was only fitting that I brought up the topic here."

"Quite right, Consort," a voice called and I was forced to tear my disbelieving gaze from Anson and to the speaker, Lord Grimly. "Since you arrived in Izwe, Majesty, we have wanted to appoint Ladies-in-Waiting to attend you. One thing or another always got in the way of that. But our Consort is correct, you do need Ladies and now is as good a time as any to decide."

Of course Lord Grimly would support this. My mind skipped back to a particular conversation his daughter, Lady Lisideria, and I had some months ago when she was first appointed as my etiquette tutor. Even then, she had angled to become one of my Ladies. If her calculated hints taught me anything, it was that the conversation we were about to have would be fraught, prideful, and vitally important for the power rankings of the Lords seated around this table.

But it was true that I had wondered why a Queen would not have more attendants. I was happy, so happy with Kaiht and Mara as my helpers. They had grown to be friends since my arrival in the Alterealm, but knowing the Council as I now did, Kaiht and Mara would not be seen as worthy companions for a queen.

The Lords stared up at me from their seats, and with a measured exhale, I said, "Very well. Lord Grimly, how many Ladies does a queen typically have?"

"Five, Your Majesty."

I nodded. "And I'm sure each of my Lords has someone to put forward. Let's hear it."

As if I had fired the starting gun at a horse race, voices exploded across the Council Chamber. Nearly half the Lords spoke at once, a chorus of "Your Majesty," "If you will, Queen Sahle," "A suggestion for you, my Queen."

I angled one eyebrow up and glanced sideways at Anson as if to ask, *Is this what you were after?*

But he kept his gaze cast far down the Council table. If he was avoiding my gaze on purpose, he was doing a good job of it.

"Quiet!" Lord Grimly called over the hubbub. "In the interest of hearing everyone, we'll go around the table and give each Lord a chance to voice a Lady of his choosing for Her Majesty's consideration. Consort, would you like to begin?"

Curiosity and wariness interlocked as I braced myself for the name of whichever Lady he favored. To my surprise, Anson shook his head. "I have none to put forward."

I knew Anson did nothing out of the goodness of his heart, and thus I expected him to name a family member, perhaps a romantic partner, someone who would personally benefit him to be close to me. But now, I was confused. There had to be some other reason for him pushing Ladies-in-Waiting on me.

Before I could consider further, the Lords began putting forward their choices.

"Lady Ava"

"Lady Irene, Your Majesty."

"Lady Lillian, if it pleases the Queen."

I was not surprised at the picks; each man named a woman from their own House. Some were daughters, or wives, or sisters. Others were particularly vivacious cousins—someone who would benefit from being near the Queen, either for marriage prospects or the hope that their vivaciousness would lead to a friendship with me that could influence court politics in a House's favor.

When each Lord had named a Lady for consideration, all eyes turned to me once more.

"Thank you for sharing your picks," I said into the eager silence. "I am not prepared to make any decisions now, but I will take your recommendations into consideration."

With that I stood. I could see on several faces the barely constrained impulse to call out, to urge me to pick my Ladies. But my Lords were too well behaved.

I stepped from the dais, pulling the train of my deep green gown into place. "Consort, I'd appreciate a moment of your time," I said without looking back.

I heard his footsteps echo behind me even over the scuffle of twenty chairs being pushed back so the Lords could stand and bow.

Anson continued to follow even after we exited the Council chamber. That was fine. I did not need us to speak until we got somewhere private. I weighed out going to the expansive gardens, but there was no promise of privacy there. I considered the bowels of the palace, but I did not trust myself to hold my temper in the quiet confines of the library.

It left only my chambers as an option. For a split second I was reluctant to lead him there, but if I needed to have a private conversation with Anson, I might as well kill two birds with one stone—believing as people would that we were doing other things in the recesses of my rooms.

I hurried down the halls and up the stairways, past bowing courtiers and servants carrying trays of refreshments and piles of fresh, scented laundry.

Guards opened my chamber door as I approached, and I heard Anson enter behind me before it clicked shut.

Kaiht and Mara were making the bed, and they turned from their work at the sound of my entry. They took in my face, the form of Anson lingering behind me, and only their slightly widened eyes gave away their surprise as they sank into their own bows. "Your Majesty. Consort."

"Kaiht, Mara, if you would be kind enough to excuse us," I said with the smallest of smiles.

"Of course," Kaiht replied. I watched as she tugged on Mara's hand as if to pull her sister back to attention, and then the two of them slipped quietly away.

I turned to Anson, opening my mouth in preparation for the words I wanted to shout at him.

"You speak with such care to those servants. You do realize you are Queen, correct?" he said before I could get a word out.

My jaw dropped and I felt my hands open in a gesture of exasperation. "What is your problem?" I yelled.

"My problem?" he replied with a steady voice, the slightest quirk of a smile. "I have no problem, my Queen. I only seek to serve."

I could feel my heartbeat in my ear, a metronome of my rage. "You spew such bullshit sometimes. Do you know that?"

Anson shrugged. Of course he shrugged.

"First of all, how I speak to my servants—who, by the way, I consider *friends*—is none of your concern." When he opened his mouth to reply, I quickly continued. "No, don't speak. I don't care what you have to say to that, and I'm not done talking.

"Second, that stunt you pulled in the Council Chamber was ridiculous. I do not appreciate you making me look like a fool. You've done enough of that the past year. In fact, I'm fairly certain you take a sick delight from making me look and feel stupid. But you're my Consort now. I am your Queen. And regardless of the new power you possess, I will not have you undermine me, especially in front of the Lords. Do I make myself clear?"

Anson looked down at me, and only then did I realize that I had stepped closer to him as I vented out my anger. I abruptly stepped back, setting a more comfortable distance between us.

He blinked, as if waiting for me to continue. I merely stared back at him. It was his turn to talk, to answer for whatever performance today had been.

"My Queen," he began.

"Stop calling me that," I replied sharply.

"My Queen," he repeated, pointedly. My anger simmered but I wanted an answer so I forcibly bit my tongue to keep quiet as he spoke. "By all means, consider and speak to your servants however you see fit. I was simply remarking that it was most unusual."

At the risk of looking like a petulant child, I crossed my arms over my chest and stared at Anson. He knew he was talking around the most important part of this conversation—I could see the glimmer in his eye at how it set me on edge.

I waited, displeasure and impatience signaling from every angle of my body.

"As for calling the Council together to discuss naming Ladies-in-Waiting, I see no problem with that."

"You don't?" I asked rhetorically.

"No, Your Majesty. As Consort, it is within my power to summon the Council for matters of state. This is such an instance."

I shook my head. "I disagree. You may be Consort and it may be within your right to call the Council, but as my husband, you and I are meant to be a team. Regardless of the sham that is this marriage in private, we can at least project a dignified, unified front publicly."

"Dignified?" Anson asked with a raised brow. A quiet chuckle slipped past his lips. "You wouldn't know what dignity looked like if it smacked you in the face, Your Majesty. Your conduct was anything but."

"*My* conduct?" I said incredulously. "How dare you speak about my conduct! You were the one who started this."

"That may be so, but a *dignified* head of state would have taken it in good stride. You all but had a meltdown in front of the Council. Then again, that seems to be your usual course of action, is it not?"

My mouth was hanging open in earnest now. I tried to close it and only succeeded on the third try.

Anson was right, of course. I had reacted badly. And I was prone to do that when the weight of the crown grew too heavy on my shoulders in a given moment. But it burned to have him see it so clearly…just as Finn had seen my running so clearly.

The thought of Finn, at what he had seen in me, at what I had promised him and yet still failed to accomplish time and time again, overwhelmed me.

As quick as the spark of rage lit within me, it went out. I tore my gaze from Anson, speechless and careening.

The chamber was silent around us, the only sound the pop and hiss of a released ember in the fireplace. Even the usually chatty *hadedas* in the trees outside the windows seemed to hold their breath.

"Queen Sahle," Anson finally said. It was a cautious pairing of words, spoken with a hesitancy as if the all-knowing Anson was finally uncertain.

Without looking at him, I shook my head and turned away. The wooden box my crown had come out of this morning sat at a nearby table and I approached it as I tugged pins from my hair. I pulled the crown from my head and laid it on top of the box, and then I headed to the bottle of *konstans* that sat at the table near the fireplace.

"Get out," I said quietly as I unstoppered the decanter and poured a short glass.

"Your Majesty—"

"I said 'Get out," I repeated. This time I looked up at Anson, and whatever he saw on my face must have convinced him, for he said no more.

With only the slightest hesitation, he bowed and made his way to the door. I took a sip of the wine once I heard the latch click shut and then I sat heavily in the chair.

Abruptly, without thinking, I threw the glass into the fireplace and watched as the wine alighted. The flying shards illuminated the flames like the glint of a thousand diamonds.

Fuck that insufferable, arrogant man, I seethed. Fuck that man.

But quietly, somewhere deeper in my mind, a little voice that sounded like Finn replied, *And if he's right?*

I sat in that chair for God and the gods knew how many hours before I finally fell into bed. When morning came, I pulled myself together enough to don soldier-browns and head to the arena. I could have gone to the training grounds or the library, but something in my skin itched. My magic stirred and it begged to be released.

Or maybe that was Manelesi summoning me, I mused, as I found the arena door wide open. Manelesi stood within, an expectant look on his face. "Thank you for joining me."

I raised my brow in question, even as I rotated my arms and cracked the knuckles of my hands. The magic buzzed in me.

"I would ask how you knew I would come, but I've learned to stop expecting normalcy from you," I said bluntly. I also had no filter when it came to the Father, it seemed.

But Manelesi simply smiled. "Normalcy is relative. You should know this, magic-wielder. How you move through the world is infinitely different from non-wielders."

"I wouldn't say so."

"And that is only true because you choose to exist in it as they do. But I digress. You did not come to discuss the philosophy of power. You came because your magic wants free."

I nodded, stretching my neck to the side. It did little to settle the screaming in my veins, and so I let it out. It was not a conscious thought. It was a half-thought. I merely thought *let it out* and it erupted out of me. Each pore seemed to leak light as my magic moved out in all directions.

I had no desire to rein it in. I had already shown that I could not hurt Manelesi, and so I let it consume me and shimmer out of me and drain me of the frustration and anger that coursed within me.

After several moments, a voice that sounded like a whisper called, "That's enough, my daughter."

I was loath to pull the power back but I obeyed. My magic told me to. It listened to Manelesi's whispered command and responded because it was *of* him.

Like slinking tendrils, the light reeled back into me. I was left panting, staring back at an untouched Manelesi.

"Feel better?" he asked, as if I was a child and had just had a temper tantrum. In many ways, I guessed that was exactly what happened. And like a patient parent, he looked at me with wary, reproachful eyes.

I nodded but this time did not feel the need to circle my shoulder or bounce my leg. My restless energy had settled somewhat. "Yes, thank you."

"Would you like to tell me why your husband irritates you so?"

I looked back at him incredulously, feeling stunning anger rise up in me in a flash. "Why don't you tell me!" I yelled. I stalked up to Manelesi, heedless of the threat, blinded by my emotions. "You're the one who started this whole marriage thing and now I'm stuck living a nightmare!"

But he merely blinked slowly at me. He looked down at my seething form with impatient eyes and through tight lips, he warned, "Step away, Daughter. Compose yourself and speak to me like an adult."

My anger rose higher and I felt my magic stir, but something in me said, *Be careful.* Something told me to listen, to hold my tongue. This was not my friend. This was an infinite being, and it would be nothing to him to silence me for less than what I had already done.

I stepped back. I bowed low. "My apologies, Father. I am not myself today."

"That goes without saying," I heard him mutter. "Rise."

I straightened, feeling my cheeks burn with an ashamed blush. "I apologize," I repeated. Then I met Manelesi's gaze.

He surveyed me with cool indifference. A slight breeze moved the Masters' robes he wore. The skin around his bright eyes remained tight. But then he nodded imperceptibly. "I accept your apology. As to your accusations, I accept those, too."

My lips parted but I did not dare react further. "Excuse me?"

Manelesi surveyed me skeptically. "You accused me of engineering your life. I admit to it. I am the Father, God, the Great One. What I will into being becomes. That includes your mere existence, and that of everyone you know. It includes the fact that you are Queen and alone the most powerful person in the kingdom. And it includes your marriage."

"But why?" I whispered. "Why *him*?" My voice broke on the last word and I swallowed against the raw emotions there.

"What I can tell you is this: trust that all is as it should be."

With that, Manelesi stepped around me. He turned to the door of the arena, but I could not comprehend that was all, that he would leave with only those words between us.

Just before he stepped through, he turned to look at my stricken face. "Trust, Daughter. And come back to the arena when your mind is at peace."

Trust, Manelesi said. *Trust.* I used that word as a scourge. I let it whip my skin and open old wounds. I let it scrape over the argument Anson and I had had, and the image of Joachim's kind face. I let it chase me to the library.

I sat amongst the quiet books and the even quieter librarians and I let the word exist in my mind. I could not take in a single page of the books open before me. Each printed word said *trust* no matter how many times I reread the lines.

And so, I decided to try. I decided to suspend my disbelief and try to trust. I did not know what that truly looked or felt like. But I used the word like a meditation. I let it settle my unsettled mind.

By the time the sun set, I felt prepared to face the Lords and Anson again over dinner. I dressed with quiet determination; a gown of gold and red, a low-profiled crown, little burgundy satin slippers. Then I made my descent into the Great Hall.

The bustle of a full room of courtiers accosted me but I pulled back my shoulders, determined to face the Court and the one person I dreaded seeing most.

Anson.

My husband.

The sound of an *umtshingozi* mingled with the many Lords' and Ladies' voices as I made my way through the sea of faces. I spied Eliza and Roland to one corner. They bowed with the rest and I made a mental note to seek them out before the end of the night. In many ways, I suspected my marriage had been the final nail in the coffin in terms of how close they could be to me. Granted, it had been mere days since my wedding yet I already felt a greater distance between us, as if their absence alone would provide space for Anson and me to strengthen and deepen our bond.

Oh, if only they knew how wrong that assumption was…

I tipped my head in acknowledgement of them as I carried on. My eyes moved of their own accord to the head table where my usual seat was located. There, sitting quietly and watchfully was Anson.

I was so used to him being late to attend any gathering that I had not expected to see him. My step hesitated only an instant before I held my head higher and made my way to the chair besides his. Although it was not strictly required for him to stand and bow now that he was Consort, he stood and bowed deeply. Then he righted himself and angled my ornate seat to better allow me access.

"Thank you," I said reluctantly, smoothing my gown over my bended knees.

"No thanks necessary, Queen Sahle," he replied. There was something in his voice, some quality that made me seek out his gaze.

His eyes met mine and before I could say anything else, he leaned forward. He placed a single hand on the carved arm of my chair, bringing his face mere inches from mine.

I froze. My eyes shifted down to study the long fingers, the strong wrist that dared move into my space.

"I am sorry."

My gaze snapped to his and my lips parted slightly. Surprise was a mild way to describe the shock at ever hearing those words pass Anson's lips.

"I'm sorry," he repeated when I did not acknowledge his declaration. "I misspoke earlier, in your chambers. What I said was unconscionable, and I hope Your Majesty will forgive me."

I blinked, suddenly aware of the numerous eyes trained on us. I ran my hands along my skirt once more before turning full to the table.

Anson sat back as food was set before us. I took a tentative bite of dressed greens, a welcome moment to collect my thoughts. "Let me get this straight," I finally said. "You're apologizing for what exactly? For essentially calling me a brat or for going around my back to create the situation in the first place?"

Anson's jaw hardened as he looked at me. I could almost see his struggle with whatever quip he would have naturally thrown out. But whatever it was, he swallowed it back. "Both, Your Majesty."

"Hmm," I replied noncommittally around another bite. I savored the dollop of golden butter that so nicely sank into the bread roll I was working on.

He looked at me a moment longer before picking up his own fork and taking a bite of the roasted meat on his plate. "You are correct that we are supposed to be a team now. I failed to act as such when I summoned the Council without your knowledge." Then, after the briefest of pauses, he added under his breath, "Much as it pains me to admit it."

I laughed at that, at the obvious discomfort Anson was in apologizing to me of all people. It was a cruel thing to do, but I could not help myself. This man had treated me terribly for over a year. Was it so awful that I wanted to revel in his humility, just for a moment?

"Thank you," I eventually said. "I know how hard it is for you to be nice."

He looked at me quickly and away, and for the briefest of moments, I wondered if I had hurt his feelings.

But this was Anson. He had no feelings. All he had was sheer pride and arrogance to offend. I had to remember that.

He smirked, and his face set into his usual cocky smile once more. "You know me well, Your Majesty."

"Hardly," I muttered.

"In any case," he continued. "While I could have handled the situation with more finesse, the fact remains that you need Ladies…"

I sighed but this was an unavoidable conversation. "I'm listening."

"You taking Ladies-in-Waiting, quite frankly, is something you should have done months ago. It is the way of the court in Izwe and seeing you carry on the tradition is vital for the Lords. With much upheaval both here and throughout the Alterealm, some sense of order, of tradition will go a long way to assuage their worries."

"And that's accomplished as easily as naming five Ladies of the court?"

Anson's eyes twinkled. "Ah, but not just any Ladies. The right Ladies."

"I assume you alone hold the answers to who those women are."

"Certainly, Your Majesty."

I scoffed. I polished off the fluffy roll and reached for my glass of wine. In the distance, some Lady's laughter sounded light, like the twinkle of fairy bells.

"You also need to start making friends," Anson added.

I looked over at him sharply. Friends, or lack thereof, was a touchy subject. "I have friends."

"Your servants don't count."

"And why not?" I shot back.

He sighed, placing his fork down loudly as if it were as heavy as the world. "You misunderstand me, my Queen. They can be your friends. They can be whatever you want them to be. But for the purpose of this conversation, we're talking about your court. For too long, you've been allowed to keep your distance from the courtiers. But this disadvantages you.

"A strong queen only grows as such with allies. Formidable ones. Regardless of how close you are with the staff, they can never protect you in the way that carefully chosen court allies can. This is where your Ladies come in. Pick them well and their influence can ensure the stability of your reign. Pick them wrong or, as you're currently doing, don't pick them at all, and you open yourself up to greater vulnerability."

I watched him warily, taking in the fine bones of his face, the green of his eyes, and the dark tousles of his stupid hair. It pained me to admit it but he was making sense.

I needed Ladies.

"What if I told you that you're right," I finally bit out.

It was his turn to scoff. "Of course I'm right. I always am."

"I wouldn't go that far," I quipped back.

He laughed, that surprisingly light sound. "No, perhaps not always. But in this I am. I've been around this court for decades, Majesty. I knew your mother and her father before her. I know what works within these walls, and what does not. Let me help you."

It was rare that he spoke of anything regarding his past. I knew he was old, at least for Humanrealm time, and I had done the math readily enough to know he would have seen the last several rulers before their untimely deaths. But never had he mentioned my mother or my grandfather. Never had he alluded to any kinship we might share on that account.

I stared at him, confused at this sudden openness and willingness to help. It did not seem merely a duty but more— as if he was truly vested in my reign.

It had to be an act. I could not forget the fact that his line had reigned before mine, or that there was a faction somewhere out there that believed that Warbeck was the true royal house still.

Yet even with that knowledge, there was bound to be something I could glean from his advice—even taken, as it was, with a grain of salt.

He was as slippery as a shining black snake, as quick to strike and as daring in his demeanor. And I had to keep a careful eye on him. Reluctantly, slowly, watchfully, I nodded. "Fine. If you are so keen to help, then tell me the ladies you consider the correct ones."

Anson took a sip of *konstans* before responding. "That's easy. Each Lord will name a Lady from his own House, since a position in your household is a prestigious appointment. But you can discount the fifteen houses in the regular Council. The Ladies that make up the five houses of the Senior Council are the only ones you should consider."

I mulled that over as I took a bite of what looked like venison. "And within those five houses? There is more than one Lady per house. I suppose you also have suggestions there."

"Certainly. Ladies Genevieve, Zara, Mona, Lillian. And let's not forget Lady Madeline."

"Of course. Can't forget your own house there," I said, thinking of the dark haired, red-lipped woman I had often seen Anson speaking to.

"Never. Although technically, Ingonyame is no longer my house. When I became Consort, I joined the Royal House of Izwe."

"Sure," I said, thinking of the way that woman always seemed to have a glowing smile for Anson. "Still, I'm sure you'd like to keep your girlfriend close."

Anson lifted one brow. "Lady Madeline?" He laughed again, though the sound was harsh this time and nothing like the lilting laughter from before. "Hardly."

"She seems fond enough of you," I said around the meat I was chewing. I was surprised to feel a touch of embarrassment in going down this line of conversation, and I studiously did not meet Anson's eye.

"Trust me. She's not," Anson replied. "But even if she was, would it make a difference to you?"

"Of course not," I replied quickly, perhaps too quickly. I cursed myself for not being a better actor. It did not matter. Of course it did not matter. Anson and I were anything but lovers; I would not even say we were friends. We could hardly stand each other.

I certainly held no claim on him, apart from some ceremonial oaths that bound us publicly. I did not care.

"Good," Anson said simply, tidily putting an end to that line of conversation. "Will you consider the Ladies I mentioned?"

"Yes. Thank you for the recommendation," I said formally.

"Once you've considered it and realized I'm right, I'll be ready with an 'I told you so,'" he replied with a glint in his eye.

I rolled my eyes, too wary of his hot and cold to have more reaction than that. "Don't push it. You're on thin ice, Consort."

"Noted, my Queen."

AS MUCH AS IT IRKED ME, I HAD TO ADMIT THE CONSORT had been right. His stunt had not been about Ladies at all, but about trying to shore up my reign internally. And despite my arguing and storming, despite his chastising and belittling, I could also admit it had been *good*.

Oh, I still hated my husband. His stupid smirking mouth and those mirth-filled eyes seemed to mock me daily, but a reluctant partnership had formed between us. We were on the same page now that we had to be a team, regardless of our personal feelings for each other.

I never thought it possible. Never in my wildest dreams did I think that the sauntering Lord I had met the first day in the Council Chamber would become my ally. But here it was.

Anson, the Consort.

Anson, the reluctant ally.

Still, that did not mean I was choosing Ladies. At least not anytime soon. There was too much to do.

My mind careened between conversations in Council—where Anson always let me take the lead now—about Trina

Cheile's movements and traditionalists' whispers. The autumn high holiday was approaching and the Lords were split between wanting Anson and me front and center as a show of solidarity to our internal threat, and wanting to keep me tucked away in the palace so as to not tempt our external one.

Anson and I looked at each other, up on the dais. I expected him to speak, to answer for us both. But instead he inclined his head in a peace offering. *Go ahead*, that gesture seemed to say.

And so I told the Lords that I wanted to be out there, that I needed to be out there. To me, a strong show of internal strength could only be a deterrent to Trina Cheile. We could kill two birds with one stone.

Anson's eyes had shone in the barest hint of pride, but then he blinked and it was gone.

I was imagining things.

When I was not in Council, I moved through my usual routine. I visited the Yesonto to pray, trying my best to forget of the otherworldly being just above the ring of candles. I willingly and unwillingly visited the arena and wielded white light under the ever-watchful eye of my Father. I tried hesitant little magic tricks squirreled away in my room. I trained with Caleb, using the beating of swords and fists to push away my worries about my kingdom.

I even cracked open the book on Bekha once more.

I had come to the library and pushed the ghosts away as I settled into my study spot. I pulled the book from a pocket of my dress and reluctantly peeled open the first page.

I had read this far already—my grandparents' marriage, Bekha's birth, her mother's inability to have another child. I knew all about how the Lords had deliberated for days, after Bekha's father's death, about whether a queen could be anointed.

What I was not prepared for was the intimate depictions of each Lord of the Council and their specific objections. All objections at first, save one.

And the one? Anson.

I stared at the name in surprise. But then my eyes ran over the words in a hurry, as if they would disappear from the page if I did not consume them all in a rush.

Nearly thirty years ago, Anson had been the one Lord who had lobbied for my mother's right to the throne. The book detailed how he had waged a campaign both in Council and without, single-handedly convincing a majority of the Lords that Bekha was fit to rule, that a *woman* was fit to rule.

I turned the page, looking for more about what he had done. But the chapter ended with a final note that Bekha had been deemed worthy.

I flipped through more pages, looking for my husband's name. And though *that* chapter ended, I saw his name pop out here and there—everywhere.

I sat back in my chair heavily. I blew out a breath I did not know I was holding, and I realized exactly what Ruth had done in giving me this book. The subject might have been my mother, but Ruth wanted me to read through the lines about someone else entirely.

I shook my head, trying to knock the surprise loose. Apparently there were things about Anson and my mother that I should know.

24
umlilo

"YOUR MAJESTY," A VOICE CALLED.

I blinked surprised eyes towards the sound and watched as Lord Wiley came into focus.

Lost in thought as I was, I had not noticed Wiley approaching the high table. His footsteps had blended into the sound of stomping and drum beats and background chatter of the Great Hall. His shape had been camouflaged behind the scenes running through my head, playing like a movie as I gave form to the words I had read just hours before.

I had spent the afternoon sitting in the library, deep in Bekha's book. I was intrigued now and was taking my time, reading between the lines. I was guessing at what Ruth wanted me to know.

I thought about asking her directly but I had not seen her since the day she handed the book to me. Perhaps she was avoiding me. Perhaps she wanted me to focus.

And so I did just that. I read page after page about my mother's coronation and her first years as Queen. This tale was supposed to be about her yet time and again Anson's name popped up.

He was already an important Lord, I told myself. He was already on the Senior Council, I reasoned. Of course he would be featured.

Yet Grimly, Marcus, or any of the other Senior Council Lords were not discussed nearly as often. It could only mean one thing—Anson was important to this story.

My answer appeared in a single line that made my eyes freeze, my breath hitch in my chest.

It was assumed that Queen Bekha would marry Lord Anson.

I ran my eyes over the words again. I read them a third time, a fourth.

Anson and my mother?

But then I hurried past and breathed the barest sigh of relief—and surprise—when the next chapter explained how the two were close friends. She chose to marry Otto and Anson remained her supportive Lord.

Sure, I knew Lord Anson had served my mother. But I could never imagine them existing in the same space, try as I might. And I certainly could not imagine the mirror image of me being *close friends* with the man I had reluctantly, begrudgingly married.

The thought occupied my mind as Kaiht and Mara helped me dress for dinner. I was distracted as I picked at my food, too uncertain to broach the topic with the mysterious Anson seated silently at my side.

I blinked now, trying to bring my attention back to Wiley.

For so long he had been my least favorite Lord on the Council—apart from my husband, of course. He was always the one to say something impulsive. He was the first to take a question or topic too far. He was the one to break tradition and approach me at the head table where, technically, no one was supposed to interrupt me unless it was for a formal purpose such as planned gift-giving or oath-swearing.

I forcibly stopped myself from sighing warily. I plastered the Queen's smile across my face. "My Lord. Thank you for gracing us with your presence."

"Of course, Your Majesty," he replied with an exaggerated bow. "As one of Her Majesty's most loyal Lords, I would not miss a festive occasion like tonight."

I smiled again, wondering why this evening was any different than all of the others. Sure, some people had started dancing but not for any particular reason.

From the chair beside me, Anson snickered softly under his breath.

But Wiley did not notice, not as he righted himself and extended his hand. "Would Her Majesty do me the honor of a dance?"

My brows lifted. And from the corner of my eye, I could have sworn Anson's glass paused as he raised it to his mouth.

I glanced around the room once more and watched as the couples began breaking apart. It looked like they were preparing for a circle dance.

Refocusing back on Wiley, I nodded. "Of course, Lord Wiley. I would love to join you."

I made my way from the table and applause began as the courtiers saw that I was joining the dance. I took the hands of both people on either side of me in the circle—Wiley and a woman I had never met. Then the music began and the dancers set into motion.

The tune started off slow before winding into a quicker jaunt. As it hit a furious pace, the dancer broke out of the circle to grab their partner's hands and spin around and around. I held on to Wiley's hands and let him guide me in circles, and I struggled not to find a little joy in the movement.

I had never been a dancer. As a child, I held no interest in ballet or tap or whatever else my little friends had been into. Equally so, I had never been the one to spend time in clubs as a college student. I had never learned the latest dance moves or the viral steps.

Yet something about the dances in the Alterealm were different. I enjoyed them and so when I laughed, when Wiley

266

spun me here and there, it was a real laugh. And the feel of it, the shape of it on my tongue, felt good after so long frowning.

As the music wound back to its soft, slower tempo, I clapped my hands and spun to acknowledge all of the courtiers around me.

"Thank you for joining us, Majesty," one called.

"You dance beautifully, Queen Sahle," another said.

I nodded at each of them, and then I turned back to Wiley. "Thank you for asking me to dance."

He bowed. "Of course, Majesty. You looked like you could use some cheering up."

My brow rose at that comment as we wandered away from the main dancing area where another set of courtiers were preparing for the next turn. "What does that mean?"

A servant approached with glasses of *konstans* and Wiley offered one to me before taking a glass for himself.

"Just that it must be hard being married to a man like the Consort."

My jaw fairly dropped. I might not like Anson but that did not mean I expected one of my Lords to say it. "Excuse me?"

Wiley took a sip of his wine, unconcerned. "You both made your thoughts on the matter plain that day in the Council Chamber when he was proposed, Your Majesty."

My jaw snapped shut. I had. Anson had. We had nearly ripped each other's throats out right there. But that was then. This was now, and whether we liked each other or not was no longer the question. Somehow Anson and I had become a team. And no one would challenge that.

"Regardless of what you thought you saw," I replied with a haughty tilt of my head that I hoped conveyed confidence, "Anson and I are happily married. We had our differences early on but that's behind us now."

The words felt fluffy on my teeth, like the feeling of eating spinach raw. I fought past the discomfort of the boldfaced lie. I added, "I trust him."

And to my surprise, Wiley scoffed into his cup.

"Do you have something to add, Lord Wiley?"

Wiley lifted knowing eyes to mine and I felt my heart skip a beat—and not in a good way. "With all do respect, Majesty, I would merely caution that you might not know your husband as well as you suspect."

"Meaning?" I said through gritted teeth. But it was a show. In reality, my pulse thudded in my veins. Despite our reluctant partnership, our tentative agreement after our argument about Ladies-in-Waiting, I realized I had no idea who I had married. It became clearer each time I cracked open Bekha's book.

Wiley tilted his head back as he drained his cup. He reached the empty vessel out and a servant materialized to take it away. "I fear I've already said too much."

My fingers pressed into the glass in my own hand. He could not start this conversation, poke at this topic, and then retreat. "No, you haven't said enough," I bit out. "Please tell me what you're implying."

Wiley sighed and, glancing around to make sure we were alone, leaned towards me. He whispered. "I'm talking about the second part of your prophecy."

The room stilled. My vision both narrowed and expanded until I saw nothing and everything. Such was the nature of shock.

"The second part?" I repeated, barely louder than a whisper.

Wiley nodded solemnly, though some glint in his eyes told me he was enjoying seeing me thrown for a loop. "Yes."

"What is it?"

I had never heard that there could be a second part of the prophecy. It was not recorded on that ornate scroll, deep in the library with the rest of the prophecies. And the idea that it existed, that people knew it besides me, set my blood on fire.

Of course, Wiley shook his head at that. "You need to ask Anson."

"Wiley!" I demanded. It came out nearly as a shriek and I quickly scanned the crowd to see if anyone else was watching this interaction.

"No, I'm sorry, Queen Sahle. It's not my story to tell."

"But you know it, obviously."

I could see my continued pestering was useless. Wiley was digging in his heels. "I may have heard it, but I cannot say."

My eyes moved to Anson. At some point while I danced, he had left the high table. Now he half leaned against a window ledge, speaking to a small group of courtiers.

His crown, that low metal band that had been placed on his head during the coronation, glinted in the candlelight bathing the Great Hall. Much to my surprise, he had not requested another crown since that day. I had expected him to immediately order a whole suite of them, one for every day of the week, in order to peacock to the fullest extent.

But no, he had not ordered crowns or ornate outfits. He wore his usual clothes and that simple headpiece.

Anson sipped at his drink and laughed at whatever a Lord said. Then, as if he could feel the weight of my gaze, his eyes shifted to me.

I debated leaving this discussion for later, but a little voice in my head said, *Go, go.* It wanted answers. I wanted answers. Bekha's book had highlighted all too clearly that there was a side of Anson, a history, that I had never seen. Wiley's words merely confirmed my suspicions. I needed to know what my husband was keeping from me.

"Thank you, Lord Wiley. That'll be all," I said, my eyes still locked on Anson's. Wiley melted away into the crowd, as if he was more water than man.

I inclined my head to the side—a subtle gesture that I wanted to speak to Anson. I watched as his mouth moved in the shape of "Her Majesty beckons." My eyes rolled of their own accord.

Then Anson was strolling my way. "My Queen."

"My Consort," I replied ironically, warily. Yes, I was right to do this now. I needed answers and quickly. "If you're done here for the evening, perhaps you'll walk with me?"

Anson's eyes glimmered. "When have you ever asked me something so nicely?"

But my eyes did not glimmer in surprise or mirth or whatever humor Anson's did. No, my eyes flashed a warning even as my smile stayed glued on my face—a public mask with which to fool the court into thinking all was fine. "Don't push me," I whispered past my teeth.

And because I could not keep my face placid for much longer, I spun on my heel and marched towards the door. A moment later, I heard Anson's leather boots follow along.

I made it out of the Great Hall with a sedate, easy smile on my face but I let it fall as soon as the guards closed the doors behind us.

"My Queen?" Anson called from over my right shoulder.

"Not here," I replied. I bundled my skirt in my hands and took to the stairs that led to the upper floors and my chambers.

One floor up, I realized that Kaiht and Mara would likely both be there, preparing for my return. But, even trusting them as I did, I did not want them to witness this conversation. I quickly changed course.

"Is your room unoccupied?" I questioned, even as I began the walk down the hallway that led to his lion-crested door.

"I'm here, aren't I? Who else would I keep there?"

"That's your business. I'm merely asking if the room is free."

"Of course."

"Good," I replied shortly. The great lion head came into view and I reached for the polished handle. Before my fingers could grasp it, Anson's hand was there.

"Allow me," he said quietly. Then he pushed open the chamber door to a room as quiet and unassuming as I remember it to be.

I strode in, past Anson, and then spun to face him as he shut us into the quiet space. "I need answers."

Anson's face did not give anything away. He was too good of a politician, a statesman. "Answers to what, Your Majesty?"

I watched him settle on a corner of the foot of his bed. He motioned to me to take the other corner. I promptly walked over to the lone chair before his desk and sat. Being anywhere close to his bed sent a strange pang of nervous adrenaline through me.

"Wiley told me something just now." I thought I saw a muscle in Anson's jaw tick but I could have been mistaken. It could have been just shadows dancing from the light of the fireplace. "He told me that you heard a part of my prophecy that no one else did. Is that true?"

This time, I did not imagine Anson's discomfort. He resettled on the bed before stroking a hand through his hair. "Yes."

I stared at him a moment, both relieved that he would admit it and shaken that he could confess it that easily. "Yes what?" I bit out. I took a deep breath, willing myself to be calm, to hear him out.

"Yes, Wiley is correct. I did hear another part of your prophecy, but I haven't told a single soul of it for 21 years."

"A single soul," I repeated. "Including me."

He closed his eyes momentarily. When he opened them, a steeliness shone past the green. "Including you."

Anson was not being the most forthcoming and my patience was close to snapping. I dug my fingers into the arms of the chair. "And you didn't see a problem with that? You didn't think I had a right to know?"

"Not particularly, my Queen. It didn't have much to do with you," he replied flippantly.

I did not know why anything Anson said still shocked me. But it did, even after all my time knowing him. For the millionth time, my mouth threatened to gape open. I held it shut, barely.

"It—my own prophecy—doesn't have anything to do with me." I tried the words on for size, feeling them out across my tongue and around the shape of my teeth.

"No," he replied resolutely. I watched as he squared his shoulders and stared back at me.

But I was done playing games. I wanted answers and I stood from the chair. I marched towards him, a defiant, seething Queen. I stopped only when my skirt almost brushed the knees of his pants. Almost.

"Tell me," I whispered. The firelight around us flickered. "You'll tell me now. That is a command from your Queen."

Anson held my gaze, staring deep into my eyes a moment, a second moment. I wondered what he saw there—my mother or myself. Then he let out a long breath as if he was about to give up this battle of wills.

I hoped he was.

"Fine, my Queen. If you command it, I'll tell you."

My only reply was to lift an eyebrow in anticipation.

Anson cleared his throat. "I was there with the Council for the reading of your prophecy. You must have been weeks old at the time, sitting on your mother's lap and playing with some toy—"

"My mother who you were *friends* with," I interjected.

Anson's eyes narrowed but he did not acknowledge the statement. He continued, "You know everything that was told to the Council and transcribed for perpetuity on record. What you do not know, what the rest of the Council does not know, is what the prophet told me after.

"The other Lords had left the chamber and your mother sent me back to retrieve something. I thought the prophet was through and maybe she was. But then she opened her eyes and looked at me with that clear-as-ice gaze and she started speaking again."

Despite my best efforts, I had leaned in, riveted by the story, the image of a younger Anson alone in that chamber. "What did she say?"

"Nothing long-winded, I assure you," he replied, looking up at me from his seated position. I stepped back, putting three paces of distance between us.

"She said, 'Anson of Ingonyame, of Warbeck, there are things even you cannot change. She will be your leader, your *umlilo*, as you will be hers. You will burn for her.'"

I stared at him. Surely there had to be more. "What does that even mean?"

Anson shrugged. "Your guess is as good as mine, Your Majesty. I've wondered for over two decades and I'll keep wondering for much longer—until one day I won't."

"*Umlilo*" I mused, trying the sound of the word on my tongue. "Does that mean fire?"

He nodded. "Yes."

But that did not make sense. Me being his leader—that was me being Queen, of course. Him being mine probably referred to him being Consort. But the fire? And him burning for me?

There had to be more. There had to be further explanation. "That's all she said? You're sure?"

His eyes flashed. "Why would I lie to you now? I've already told you this much."

That was too good. I could not help but laugh with a dirty, conniving chuckle as that question sat between us. "Oh, I don't know. Only because you've been keeping it a secret for two decades. There's a reason for that but I'm sure you won't tell me now. Why would you? I'm only your wife and Queen. We're only bound to each other."

His eyes narrowed at me but he did not speak. Not for several heartbeats.

"Like I said, it had little to do with you. From where I'm standing, it has everything to do with my fate, with my service to you."

"Hmph," I scoffed. "Still, you should not have omitted something like that. Why didn't you at least tell my mother?"

His eyes flickered but he did not avoid the reference this time. "As you've apparently learned, your mother and I were friends. I would have told her if I thought it had any relevance. Despite whatever it is you think of me privately, my Queen, I am a loyal servant to Izwe."

"But it held relevance to her daughter. To me," I replied pointedly.

It was not a direct question and so he did not reply. But that was fine. My mind had drifted to another thought, perhaps a more important thought in the present moment. "If it means nothing, why would Wiley imply otherwise?"

"What Wiley does is a mystery. You know that, even after knowing the man for just a year."

I nodded. "True. But how he put it…he felt it meant something. Burning…burning could be bad—"

"You could say that," Anson muttered under his breath.

"Like burned in a flame. Dead." My mind jumped to the image of Trina Cheile's creatures as piles of ash. I flinched internally at the idea of anyone, even Anson, being subject to my power in that way. "It could also be meant like sickness, like fever."

"That interpretation might be a stretch."

I ignored his comment. "Or it could mean romantically—to burn passionately?"

Anson broke his gaze away from mine as he fully doubled over in laughter. The sound filled the chamber and I could almost admire the richness had the purpose of it been less insulting.

A full minute later, he righted himself, wiping at an eye as if the force of such mirth had roused tears. "You're too much, Your Majesty."

"And you're rude. You don't have to laugh that hard at the idea."

He just smiled that infuriating grin. "Let's stick with the fever option."

"Whatever," I huffed. "But in any case, it doesn't seem great for you."

Anson shook his head. "No, it does not. Lucky for you, I made up my mind a long time ago. I'm a servant to the crown and now I'm your Consort. If I wanted to run away from this, I would have. Yet, I'm here."

"Shall I admire you for that?" I bit out because I could not imagine a moment where I would praise Anson.

"No," he replied. "I'm simply stating."

"And Wiley—if you never told anyone then how does he know?"

Anson sighed. "Wiley was in the hallway, outside of the prophecy chamber, when the prophet spoke. I swore him to secrecy on the spot."

I crossed my arms. "He thinks it means something."

"He's welcome to think whatever. We know otherwise."

I leveled my gaze at him. I drank in the easy way his limbs rested on the edge of the bed, how he looked at me with such a cool detachment—too cool of a detachment. Something niggled at me, as if there was more to be said, as if Anson knew or suspected more than he was confessing.

But I was slowly coming to know Anson. If he had not told me his suspicions, he never would. And reluctant team or not, for now there was no point in pushing it.

I let my arms relax at my sides. "Very well. Thank you for telling me the second part."

Anson inclined his head. "Of course, my Queen."

25

festival

Regardless of my resolve to leave the puzzle of Anson's prophecy alone, the thought of *burning* plagued me for the next days. I considered it as I magically heated my tepid bathwater to near-boiling again and again. I thought of it as I pummeled Caleb with a series of swords and fists. I played our interaction over as I wandered the library, letting the feel of the worn leather spines skate across the pads of my fingers.

The only two times when I did not think about the implicit secretiveness—and implied meaning—in Anson's prophecy was when I was training with Manelesi or paging through the book on Bekha. As I lit my magic around me in white domes or threw it in sharper and sharper spears of light at the Father, my focus physically could not contemplate my husband and his veiled history. I would too easily get myself hurt, if so.

And so I trained. I studied every line and word of Bekha's book. I watched Anson warily as we sat in Council and discussed the latest intelligence on Trina Cheile. And the days passed. The year of the wheel kept turning.

All too quickly, fall was upon us and the Masters were summoning me to the autumn high holiday. After participating in several, I knew what to expect. The only difference was that this time I would have a Consort with me.

This time, my Consort and I were on display.

Grimly had explained this pointedly the night before, as he sat beside Anson and me at the high table in the Great Hall. "Your Majesty, Consort, tomorrow's festival is the perfect opportunity for us to show the world that you are a true and united front. The people know you are married, and Lord Silas ensures me that this has helped squash rumors of a Warbeck resurgence.

"However, whispers still abound. Anything we can do to put Your Majesty and Lord Anson out in front of the people will hammer this point home. As such, I have taken the liberty of discussing the proceedings for tomorrow with Master Edgar. Your Majesty will, of course, open the festivities with the letting—of which, Lord Anson, you need not take part. It would be beneficial, though, to have Lord Anson stand beside Your Majesty on the dais."

"And afterward?" Lord Anson had asked from my other side.

Lord Grimly had leaned a little closer. "The Lords humbly ask you two to…act the part of newlyweds."

I had felt a scoff build in the back of my throat but washed it down with a hearty gulp of *konstans*. "What does that mean?"

Anson was the one to answer. "It means we should act like we like each other."

"Do we not already?" I had replied. It was a rhetorical question; I knew the truth of it all too well.

Lord Grimly had cleared his throat uncomfortably. "Your Majesty and Lord Anson could perhaps be kinder to one another?"

I had laughed then, the sound surprisingly loud even amongst the nightly revelry of the Great Hall. "Good one, Lord Grimly." Anson had not joined me in my humor.

Hours later, standing in front of the palace doors at the start of a new day, I thought about the horrified look that had swirled in Lord Grimly's eyes. It was not necessarily a secret that Anson and I shared a difficult relationship. I was unsure what Anson had told his friends or the other Lords. He certainly seemed happy to let the entire palace believe that this marriage was consummated.

Even if Anson and I had forged a begrudging team after our argument about Ladies, it was exactly that—begrudging. There was no mistaking the veiled hatred with which Anson and I regularly interacted.

"Your Majesty," the man in question spoke now from behind me as he traipsed down the steps of the palace. A nearly black cloak fanned out around him as he moved. His crown sat nestled in his tousled hair, and below, his usual dark clothes were punctuated by a dark brown waistcoat.

"Late as usual," I muttered under my breath.

"How would you know it was me if I was not tardy?"

I rolled my eyes before turning to face him. Distantly, I heard the clinking of the carriage approaching. "I thought you were all in agreement that this day needed to be perfect in the eyes of the citizens. Surely that starts with being on time."

"I thought it only started when we were in front of the people," he replied smoothly. Then, looking around him with a mock-squint, "Or do my eyes deceive me? Are the people here already?"

The carriage stopped in front of us and a servant opened the door for me. "No, Consort, your eyes do not deceive you," I sighed.

"Very well, Your Majesty. Then let us be ourselves for these last minutes."

Anson approached the carriage before turning back to offer me a hand up. "Your Majesty, may I?"

The slightest chill was in the air, so Kaiht and Mara had dressed me in a weighty gown of burnished gold *chitenge* cloth. Dark leather boots covered my feet and ankles. A low crown, pinned to my curls, sat atop my head. A beige cloak draped over my shoulders and thin, tan leather gloves covered my hands.

I was grateful for those gloves as I placed my hand in Anson's, as he boosted me up into the carriage. Still, through the leather I could feel the heat of his fingers.

We sat in silence as we journeyed out of the palace walls and to the central city square where all festivals took place. I fidgeted with the skirt of my gown. I circled Finn's bracelet around and around my wrist.

But if I thought Anson did not notice all of these little movements, I was mistaken. As the carriage came to a stop in the heart of the city, Anson leaned forward.

I started in surprise, immediately snapping to attention as I pulled an inch away from him.

"Take a deep breath," his voice said softly. My eyes met his green gaze questioningly. Somehow, those eyes of his shone even in the dim light of the carriage.

I wanted to tell him to mind his own business. I wanted to yell at him to lean back, away from me. But those words did not come out. Instead, I obeyed.

I took a deep breath, as if hypnotized by his gaze. As if some part of me wanted to listen to him.

"That's right," he said softly. "This will all be fine. We'll climb out of this carriage and go through the motions and smile at each other. And then we'll go back to the palace and continue our bickering. Everything is fine."

I nodded at him.

"Do you trust me?" he asked.

Regardless of how softly he spoke or how lulled I was by his words, that question shocked me out of whatever fleeting hypnotization I was in. I thought of the prophecy he had kept to himself for years, the fact that he and my mother had been friends, the reality that there were a band of traditionalists out there that wanted him King. I thought it all, but I merely answered, "No."

I do not know how I expected him to react to that but I certainly did not expect him to laugh. But laugh he did.

"Fair enough, my Queen. But still, *try* and trust me today. The aim is to make the people believe that you and I are in love, that our marriage is true. Follow my lead. I promise I will not lead you astray."

My brows squeezed together as I studied his face. I did not like the idea of trusting Anson. It was something as foreign to me as the Alterealm had been upon landing here on my twentieth birthday.

Yet Manelesi had told me to trust. Something in me said, "Fine." Something in me told me to nod. Only then did Anson lean back against his seat.

"Are you ready?" he asked as he checked the buckle on his own dark cloak.

I swallowed. "Yes."

And then Anson opened the carriage door and the roar of the city greeted us.

Just as before, Anson handed me down from the carriage. But unlike before, Anson held my hand tightly in his once my two feet were firmly planted on the ground.

I looked at him questioningly, but he only leaned towards me and winked. Then he turned that smirk of a smile, that glinting of green eyes on the crowd and the cheering rose again.

I tried to shake myself. I tried to focus on the crowd of people before us. Bells tolled somewhere and voices shouted, "Majesty! Consort!" Flowers in shades of red and orange and yellow seemed to fill the space. Fallen leaves were strewn across the ground like a carpet. Gourds and squash and corn cobs were placed in strategic places like a Thanksgiving cornucopia. The scent of spiced apples wafted in the air. A scythe leaned against a building.

But all I could focus on was the feel of Anson's hand wrapped around mine.

A figure approached, and I turned my wooden smile towards it. Master Edgar.

"Your Majesties," he said as he bowed deeply. His burgundy and yellow robes swept the ground before him. "Fall tidings to you. The wheel turns and is honored to have you acknowledge it."

"We are pleased to be here," I answered, pulling my attention fully to something other than my too-warm hand.

Edgar motioned towards the raised dais in the center of the city square where the wide vat of water sat. "If you will come with me."

"Of course."

Anson and I followed along behind Edgar as the crowd drew in. Unlike past festivals, I noticed Vikela in the audience. They drew tight around the dais as if forming a barrier between me and the people.

I did not like it. I did not like feeling as if my people were a threat to me.

But before I could dwell on it, Edgar's voice pitched high above the drone of the crowd. He was calling the ceremony to begin.

The crowd hushed as Edgar intoned, "Majesties, Lords, Ladies, and people of Izwe, we come together on this high holiday to celebrate the turning of the wheel from summer to fall. We take this moment to thank God and the gods for their bounty, for the fruits of the year which have been sown and which we harvest today.

"We ask that in this season of abundance, you bless us and keep us. We ask that you provide us with health and good fortune. We pray that you provide safety and strength as we face foes known and unknown to us.

"In the letting of the blood, we pray you will share these blessings with the people."

As Edgar finished, I knew my cue. Two Masters moved closer, and I noticed one held my least favorite knife.

I tugged my hand from Anson's slightly, needing it to remove the glove from the other. But Anson would not let go.

"If you'll allow me, my Queen," he said quietly. Then, slowly, he pulled the tan glove from my hand, finger by finger.

I wanted to roll my eyes at the show. And he was putting on a show—it was exactly what this was. He wanted each and every man, woman, and child present to see him remove my glove with such adoring, delicate care.

Then, he raised my bare hand to his lips and kissed the back of it. His eyes met mine.

I do not know what he saw reflecting back in my gaze.

I was not sure what I felt in my own heart. There was horror. There was heat. There was softness for a gesture so far removed from the Anson I knew. And there was malice that this was all just part of the act.

I forced my brow to not rise in surprise. I forced my lips to curl in a soft adoring smile, the sort of smile one would expect of a blushing bride.

Anson smiled back at me as he passed my hand to Edgar, who spun it so that the palm faced up. Then, with a quick slash, he cut through my skin in a heated sting.

I had been through this enough times to know the feel of the knife opening my palm, but the knowledge did not stop the pain. I let out a quiet hiss, even as I turned my hand and let the blood trickle into the water.

Willing and unwilling—that was how I bled each time into this vat.

Anson kept his face trained on mine. I could feel his look like a brand across my skin but I did not meet his gaze. No, I watched my blood continue to trickle into the vat. I watched the clear water turn a murky pink with each passing second.

Moments later, Edgar approached again, this time with the small handkerchief that would stop the bleeding. To my surprise, he did not hand it to me but rather to Anson. I watched as Anson took my hand back in his reverently and held pressure to the wound.

"Thank you," I said reflexively.

Anson was focused on his task and did not raise his head even as he replied, "You are most welcome, my Queen. Are you alright?"

"It's not my first rodeo," I said to him.

I could see people beginning to form a line before the vat, and as usual, I had no interest in watching the people drink. I motioned to Anson that we should move aside.

We found a secluded corner away from the dais before he asked, "What's a rodeo?"

"What?"

His green eyes looked back at me in confusion, even as his warm fingers maintained pressure on my palm. "You said, 'It's not my first rodeo.' I do not know what a rodeo is."

A genuine smile spread across my lips. "I'm sorry. Of course you wouldn't," I laughed. "It's a competition, of sorts, where you try to wrangle cows. But what I said, that's a Humanrealm saying for when you've done something before so it's not new to you."

Anson nodded seriously. "Does that mean you're OK?"

I glanced around us. We were out of direct sight of most citizens yet Anson still held my bleeding hand and asked if I was fine.

I looked back at him, tugging my hand more forcefully from his. There was no use pretending without an audience.

Where his fingers had been, I pushed my own fingers into the handkerchief. "Yes, it means I'm fine. It's never *fun* to have your palm cut open but I know what to expect now."

"I can imagine," Anson replied, rocking back on his heels slightly. He, too, looked around us. "We should join the festivities."

I lifted the handkerchief. The blood had all but stopped flowing so I folded the cloth and tucked it into a pocket in my gown. "Yes. Let's."

With the letting done, the musicians were free to begin their playing. The sound of marimbas filled the square and a general feeling of excitement stole across the gathered guests.

I wove through the crowd, studiously keeping my eye away from the dais and the vat. Anson followed closely at my side. But instead of reaching for my hand as he had before, he placed a firm palm along my lower back.

I forced myself not to pull away from the pressure of that hand, from the heat of it. I forced myself to smile at the gathered people who bowed as we drew near.

I spied Eliza and Roland speaking with a small group of courtiers. I headed in that direction.

"Lord Roland, Lady Eliza," I said in greeting as we neared them. Eliza and Roland dropped into their usual low bows but rose with wide smiles on their faces. It had been several weeks since I had last seen them.

In fact, I had not seen them since my wedding. They had supported me then. Their eyes had shone with pride as I accepted the Consort beside me, but despite their presence then and now, I could not deny there was a tension that hung over the three of us.

These were my parents in every way that counted. These were the people who knew me best in the world, yet in a small, loud part of my being, I felt they had betrayed me when they had convinced Anson to become Consort without my knowledge.

Rationally, I knew all of the arguments. I understood that from an outside perspective Anson was ideally suited to the role. But as the people who loved me for me, who had soothed my toddler tantrums and dried my tears over my first ill-fated junior high crush, I expected more from them. I had expected them to do what was best for me—Sahle, not Queen Sahle.

Eliza's voice tugged me from my stormy mind. "Your Majesty, it is a pleasure to see you today." She ran her eyes over me in that appraising way of mothers. Then she turned her attention to Anson. "Consort. Are you looking forward to the festivities?"

From my side, Anson nodded. "Certainly. It is my honor to support the Queen today."

As he said this, his hand moved from my lower back to rest along my waist. I felt my body freeze in automatic response.

But as quickly as I froze, I forced myself to relax. I widened my smile as I took a deep breath and looked at Anson. "And I'm so glad he's here to do it."

If my too-sweet smiles were fooling onlookers, they were not fooling Eliza. She glanced between Anson and me, her brow lowering.

"Queen Sahle," Eliza started hesitantly. "Would you mind if we had a private word?"

I knew what Eliza would ask. But explaining to Eliza that Anson and I had agreed to perform the role of doting newlyweds was not on the agenda for today. I had too many people to greet, and too many people to impress the strength of this match upon. A little part of me also whispered that she and Roland did not deserve an explanation. They had washed their hands of my feelings weeks ago.

"Perhaps another time," I said coolly. "Are you staying at the palace?"

"For a day or two," Roland answered from alongside Eliza. While Eliza's eyes kept darting between me and Anson, Roland's gaze seemed glued to the hand planted along my waist.

"Lovely," I replied with more enthusiasm than I truly felt. "Perhaps I'll see you. Now, if you'll excuse us."

If either of them wanted to say more, they held their tongues. They bowed in farewell as Anson and I turned away.

A moment later, Anson leaned in to whisper in my ear. "That was a strange interaction."

I smiled up at him as I replied back, "What do you mean?"

"You brushed them off. Why?"

I sighed, though I hoped any onlookers would see it as a loving exhale rather than a sign of exasperation. Unwillingly to go into details, I merely said, "They know me too well. I could tell Eliza read right through our act. That's what she wanted to speak to me about. She probably thought I was being held hostage."

Anson chuckled as I felt his hand fall back in place on my lower back. "By me?"

"Who else?" I said sweetly.

A servant holding mugs of steaming spiced cider approached. Anson handed me one before taking another for himself.

"Is it so strange to think that perhaps you and I could be genuinely enjoying ourselves?" he asked softly.

It was my turn to chuckle. "Are you trying to make me laugh? They know exactly what I think of you."

"And what's that?" Anson asked.

For a split second, I second guessed myself. I questioned why I had said that. I worried about hurting his feelings. I considered lying.

And then all too quickly, I made up my mind that honesty was the best policy with this man.

I blew on the surface of my cider before responding. "I don't like you."

Anson watched me over the rim of his mug as he took a sip. He took another and looked away at the revelry.

I was not sure if he would respond to that.

But just as I was about to change the subject, walk off to another group, or go see what the crowd was so interested in at the center of the square, Anson sighed.

"You say that so simply."

I shook my head. "Should I not speak the truth?"

"Always," he replied as he refocused on me.

There was something in his eyes that made me pause— a certain somberness or sadness that had not been there before. I watched it fade away.

"There's no use in lying. You and I have never liked each other. Being married doesn't change that. Some part-prophecy linking us together doesn't change that. I'd think you'd agree. Do you not?"

I expected him to assent as quickly as I had. But he did not.

He watched me a moment longer before his lips drew up in a smile. But for the first time, I recognized the veil. That cocky smile was *his* mask as much as the wooden grin on my face was mine.

286

"Being married to one another changes nothing," he replied.

I nodded. "I'm glad we're on the same page." Then, scanning the crowd, I spotted Lord Silas, Lord Marcus, and a handful of other Courtiers. "Shall we say hello to some Lords?"

"After you," was all Anson said.

An hour later, Anson and I had mingled through the crowd. Each time we stopped, Anson's hand moved to my waist. Each time we walked through the crowd, Anson's hand found its place on my lower back.

It had become such a fixture that I had nearly become used to it, to him. I had nearly stopped caring at the closeness with which Anson and I moved.

The heat of the day rose up around us and I gratefully shed my cloak and gloves. Anson handed these, as well as his own cloak, to a servant. When he spun back towards me, his eyes moved slowly over me from head to toe.

"Could you not do that?" I whispered to him, out of earshot of anyone else.

"Do what?" he replied with an innocent smile. The glint in his green eyes belied his words.

"You know what. I don't appreciate being ogled."

He held out open, supplicating hands. "I was merely admiring your gown."

"Sure," I scoffed.

"It is so rare you wear gold," Anson replied. He opened his mouth as if to add something else but was interrupted by a group of revelers hesitantly approaching.

I pasted a smile on my face as I turned to them.

"Your Majesties," one of the city dwellers, a middle-aged man with hair the color of milk chocolate, said in greeting as he bowed. "Would you honor us with a first dance?"

I blinked at them, turning my head to assess the space. All eyes were on us. The musicians held their marimba mallets as if waiting to strike another note only once they knew the recipients of their tune.

"We would love to. Thank you," I said to the man and his friends. Wide smiles greeted me in return.

The marimba musicians, seeing our approach, struck the first notes of a slow song—an achingly slow song.

I paled.

I had assumed this dance would be much like festival dances I had participated in before, the dance with Wiley in the Great Hall not long ago. Those had always been fast-paced, breathless near-runs that left me doubled over both panting and laughing after.

That was what I had agreed to.

Yet as Anson and I came to a halt in the center of the town square, I realized no other dancers filled the dance space. It was just Anson and me.

He turned to face me before dropping into a low bow of his own. When he rose, a soft smile graced his lips. The autumn breeze's fingers picked up strands of his dark hair.

But I did not know how to move. I did not know what this was and so I stood there motionless as a statue.

Anson was not fazed. No, he stepped into me, took one of my hands in his and placed another on my back. "Put your other hand on my shoulder."

And I did, because it was the only thing to do.

"That's it," he said softly. As close as he was in this position, I felt the brush of his words across my cheek. "Just follow my lead."

"Alright," I breathed out.

Then the music swelled and we started to dance.

There was not much to it. In fact, it reminded me of a waltz I had once learned at a high school summer camp back in the Humanrealm. With a slight pressure at my back or a pull at my hand, I allowed myself to be guided in a box step.

We moved with careful, slow steps at first. As I became more comfortable with the movements, our steps became wider. We covered more distance.

But if I thought focusing less on the steps would be a good thing, I was entirely mistaken. Without that concentration, my mind was freed up to think about Anson.

Anson so close I could feel the heat of his body thrumming alongside mine.

Anson so close that when he took a step towards me on the one-beat, the line of his thigh brushed along my skirts.

I forced myself not to shudder. I ran a mantra in my head: *This is the man I love. This is the man I love. This is the man I love.*

I forced myself to believe that, if even for a few moments. I had a duty to believe that, or at least pretend convincingly.

My eyes turned to the assembled crowd around us, watching their Queen and Consort dance. Their faces were both stagnant and blurred as we moved one-two-three-four, one-two-three-four. I thought I spotted Eliza and Roland in the crowd, but by the time we turned, by the time I had a chance to look back, I could not find them again.

But as I watched the crowd, the weight of their gazes began to grow heavy. The need to impress upon them the performance of my marriage suddenly seemed too large, too hard.

On the two-beat of the box step, my footing faltered.

Anson corrected as effortlessly as if it had not happened, but the motion brought his undivided attention back to me. He caught my gaze with his own as he looked down. "Focus on me," he said quietly.

I nodded, again unable to do anything but obey. And I both hated that I needed to obey in this moment and was grateful that he was here to lead me.

I took a deep breath. "Sorry."

Anson swept us around and around as the music's tempo picked up slightly. "There's nothing to apologize for. People miss dance steps."

"I was getting in my head," I replied past teeth gritted in the shape of a lover's smile.

Anson's own answering smile was less forced. "I know. Also no reason to apologize. Just focus on us. It's just you and me here."

"That's not particularly relieving."

A knowing glint lit up Anson's eyes so that when he smiled this time, it was genuine. "Fair enough."

I did not know how long this song could go on but it seemed to be never-ending. With each second, I could feel my resolve faltering. I wanted off this stage. The weight of pretending began to feel like a claw squeezing at my throat.

"Distract me," I said to Anson. It was not a question, but rather a command.

If he was insulted by being told what to do, he did not act it. He immediately said, "Before we were asked to dance, I was going to tell you that gold suits you."

"What?" I said in surprise. He had told me before, of course, but I was not prepared for that line of conversation to surface now. I angled my head back to see his face more clearly.

"Your gold gown. You tend to wear darker colors, but the gold lights up your face. It's like the shade itself was made for you."

My brows lifted in surprise.

Anson leaned forward and whispered into my ear. "Don't forget to smile."

I pulled the smile back onto my surprised face. "You like the gown then?"

Anson spun us towards one side of the dance floor. "Yes. It is regal."

"Ah," I replied. "So it's not that it looks good on me, or that it highlights any particular assets. Just that the color is what a Queen should wear."

But this time Anson's gaze bore into mine. "Something like that."

"You're an interesting man," I said through my smile.

"How so?"

"Just when I think you're complimenting me, you say something that could be construed in ten different ways."

"You don't want my compliments, Your Majesty," he said softly.

I opened my mouth to quip back…something. I was not sure what exactly. Because he was right. He was the last person I wanted compliments from.

But the music was fading out. The tempo was slowing back to its original pace. Anson was turning us in smaller circles.

We came to a stop as the music ended. And we stood looking at each other for a moment before the crowd around the dance floor began clapping enthusiastically.

But Anson did not drop my hand. He did not step away. His arms continued to cage me in towards his chest as if he would rather I stayed close by his heart.

Why that thought popped into my mind, I had no idea. It was a silly thought. This man wanted nothing from me, and I wanted nothing from him.

My heartrate had picked up at some point and my chest rose and fell with my quickened breath. I stared up at Anson as he stared down at me. And then slowly, so slowly that I could have stepped away if I wanted to, he brought one hand up to cup my face.

I did not step away. I was not sure if I could. I was both horrified and curious at what he would do next.

He leaned towards me, and for a split second, I thought he would kiss me. But then he pressed his lips into the skin of my cheek softly, for only a moment.

My heart skipped faster at the contact. My skin tingled where his lips touched. A low, taunting ache pulled deep in my stomach.

As he drew back, his eyes locked on mine. I stared back in confusion and dread and the barest hint of…longing.

And the idea only horrified me more.

"Smile," he reminded me in a whisper.

I smiled, the biggest lie of a smile yet.

Then Anson, for the first time since we arrived in the city square, let me go. He turned and walked away, leaving me alone in the center of the dance floor.

I stared at his retreating form with that stupid smile still plastered across my face.

I realized with dismay that my cheeks were hot in a furious blush. And I hoped for my sake that it had everything to do with dancing and nothing to do with the man I had been dancing with.

I was not alone in the center of the dance floor for long. The moment Anson left the floor, a set of drums joined the marimbas and a louder, more boisterous beat filled the air. The revelers rushed towards me, calling vague approximations of "Dance with us, Majesty!"

I was only happy to agree.

Anything to remove those thoughts from my mind—the horror that was the feeling of longing that clanged through my veins a moment before.

As I spun around in a familiar dance, hands linked with hands that formed a large communal circle, I told myself that it was fine. It was natural to react when another's body was so near. I was a woman after all and he was a man. And no matter how much I hated him, no matter how much he hated me, it was natural to feel some animal instinct, some heat kick in when in such close proximity.

Yes, that was it. That was all.

I smiled to myself and laughed as one of the revelers whooped and jumped and threw a pile of orange leaves into the air. They rained down on my head like a blessing of autumn.

Yes, that was all. My body was still a body. I was not a corpse. It was OK to react as any normal body would.

That was all it was, I repeated to myself.

And I let myself believe that as I laughed again with the revelers.

I let myself believe that as I continued dancing and tried to forget everything about the feel of Anson's hands on me.

I did not see Anson for several songs after he left the dance floor. Only when I finished dancing did he reappear, standing stoically on the edge of the dance floor with a hand outstretched to me.

Reluctantly, yet with that patented smile, I took his hand.

The dancing would continue for hours but I was tired. I said as much, and soon, Anson was handing me back up into the carriage.

We did not speak on the ride back. I was grateful for that. I was not sure what I would say to him, not when my own body betrayed me, not when I worried that he had seen that truth in the blush on my cheeks and the look in my eye.

Not when I wondered if that was why he left me on that dance floor the moment the music had ended.

As my mind turned, I grew more and more annoyed at him. I grew more and more annoyed at myself for being a weak body, swayed by a strong man standing too close.

I was only too happy to sit in silence as we wound through the streets of the city and returned to the palace. I was only too happy to allow my embarrassment to turn to annoyance, the annoyance to morph into anger. It built a protective wall around me.

When the carriage drew to a stop before the palace, a servant opened the door from the outside and I hopped out without waiting for Anson to hand me down. Kaiht and Mara would be waiting for me with a bath and a plate of food and a warm fire, and perhaps all of those things would help me put this day behind me.

I started up the staircase without waiting for Anson.

"Good evening, my Queen," Anson called from the base of the stairs just as I made it to the top, just as guards opened the doors of the palace wide for me.

I spared him only one glance, my eyes narrowing in dismay.

Then I slipped through the doorway without a word.

It was not long before Eliza's note arrived at my chambers. I thought I would write to her tomorrow morning, long after I washed the dancing from my skin and let sleep soften the memories.

But her letter arrived as I was getting ready for bed. I read the words reluctantly.

If Her Majesty pleases, would she join me for lunch tomorrow?
Yours,
Lady Eliza

I shuddered at the formality of the note. Equally, I dreaded the conversation I knew only too well that we would have. I did not bother writing out my reply. Rather, I opened my chamber door and asked a guard to send word to Lady Eliza to meet me at noon the next day.

That time came all too quickly. Dressed in a gown of plum *chitenge* cloth and a simple gold crown, I entered the solarium. It was the same space that Lisideria and I used to meet at before I had canceled those sessions and Lisideria had retired to the country.

It had been months since I set foot in the rectangular room. Like my own chambers, an entire wall was made of windows. The black and white checkerboard floor contrasted with the wicker tables and chairs set periodically down the room. Wispy ferns sat in every corner.

I immediately spied Eliza, standing along the windowed wall. She turned at the sound of my heeled footsteps on the stone floor.

"Your Majesty," she said as she curtsied low.

I turned my head to look for an audience. Eliza only was this formal when we were in front of others, when the reality that she was the only mother I knew had to be downplayed.

But there was no one there besides the small contingent of Vikela who followed me wherever I went.

I raised my brow but did not address it. Rather, I motioned to the nearest brown wicker table. "Shall we?"

"Of course."

As I settled into my chair, a servant came forward with glasses of lemonade. I took one with a quiet, "Thank you."

"Where's Roland?" I asked Eliza after I took a sip of the tart drink.

"Unfortunately, he had pressing business to attend to. He asked me to give you his love."

I nodded, not quite able to meet Eliza's clear blue eyes.

That same strangeness sat heavy between us, a hesitation, a certain awkwardness that belied the deep history that bound us. But while I wished it were not there, I could not deny it. I had been too distracted by the very prospect of my marriage and the rationality of the choice to have dwelt on the feelings of my parents' involvement.

But my hurt was there all the same.

I had expected Eliza and Roland to champion me, to tell me I could marry anyone I wanted, to believe that my marriage was the one place I should have happiness. That was not what occurred.

No, they had gone to Anson behind my back. They implored him to accept the role of Consort, wrangled his agreement, and then used that agreement to convince me of the match. It was not technically betrayal, but knowing what they knew about my feelings towards Anson, it damn well felt like it some days.

Since then, Eliza and Roland had been noticeably absent from the palace. The three of us had not talked—not really— since that night they had come to my chambers and told me to accept Anson.

I leveled my gaze at Eliza now. I willed myself to take a deep breath. "That is unfortunate. I've seen so little of you both since my wedding."

"We know. And we miss you, Sahl, but we thought it was best to give you and your Consort space in this new phase of your marriage."

My brows rose. "Why?"

Her brows rose in equal surprise. "What do you mean why? So that you two could become acquainted, of course."

I scoffed at that. "If there's anyone who knows the ridiculousness of that happening, it's you."

"That's what I want to speak to you about," Eliza started. She had leaned forward in her chair, as if pulled towards me subconsciously. She sat back now as the servant returned with plates of fluffy rice topped with grilled fish. The scent of lemon rose from our plates in wafts of steam.

But Eliza ignored the food. She watched the servant retreat before she continued. "What is going on with you and Anson, Sahle? What was that yesterday at the festival?"

I studiously dropped my gaze to the plate in front of me and picked up my fork. I took a bite of the fish and let myself savor the delicate flakes of meat before answering. "I don't know what you mean."

"Sahl, your performance yesterday may have fooled the people and the courtiers. But I am your mother. I know you better than you know yourself. Don't do me the disservice of lying to me."

I sighed. And I told her everything: how Grimly and the Senior Council wanted to take every opportunity to parade Anson and me out in public in order to squash the rumors that Warbeck was against us, how Anson and I agreed to play the role of newlyweds, how our relationship was nothing like that in reality.

When I finished, it was Eliza's turn to sigh. "Is it really so bad? Your marriage?" she asked as she reached her hand out to grasp mine from across the table.

I looked at her as if she had asked if the ferns along the wall were purple, if spring came before winter.

"Of course it's bad," I bit out. I pulled my hand away from her. "What did you think it would be when you schemed for this marriage to come about?"

A pained look crossed her face and she sat back in her chair, her food forgotten. "You know I want nothing but your happiness."

I scoffed. "Getting me to marry someone I hate isn't really compatible with that sentiment, Lady Eliza."

If my use of her formal title even registered with Eliza, she did not let on. She merely shook her head and leaned forward again. Her voice pitched low, she said, "Has something happened? Has he hurt you?"

For some reason I thought that was funny. I laughed humorlessly as I watched her concerned eyes widen. "No, of course not. He wouldn't dare."

"Then tell me what's the matter?" she implored.

But there was a wide chasm between physical violence and kind, welcomed affection. "It's not as black and white as does he hurt me or is our marriage wonderful. It's just bad, filled with animosity and a year's worth of resentment and anger."

"Perhaps there's hope that it can change?" Eliza asked.

I shook my head. I took a few more bites of food I barely tasted. And then I pushed the plate away. "Never. Anson and I are a match made in hell. I just have to accept and deal with that."

Sadness filled her eyes. "For my part in this, I am sorry, Sahle."

I did not know what to say to that. Her apologies changed nothing.

And so I stood quickly, setting my napkin down on the table beside my half eaten food. "I have training to get to," I announced stiffly. "Thank you for joining me for lunch."

Eliza looked up at me from her chair with both hurt and sorrow in her eyes. But I watched her take a breath, swallow back any words she would say, and rise to bow to me. "I'll tell Roland you send your love."

"Please do," I replied shortly. "Good day, Lady Eliza."
With unspoken words hanging in the air, I left the lunch room.

26
little lion

APPARENTLY, MY BIRTH HAD BEEN ACCOMPANIED BY the most spectacular fanfare. Or so the biography of Bekha explained.

Rulers came from across the Alterealm to pay their respects to the newest crown princess. Days of feasting and dancing and music lit up the palace and the city of Izwe. All were overjoyed to have a new heir to the kingdom, even if it was a little princess rather than a little prince.

I read all of this, curled up before my fireplace late one evening. The night sky was dark and star-filled outside my windows. Shadows danced in the corners, cavorting with the fronds of the ferns. A steaming mug of rooibos was my only companion.

It was the day after my conversation with Eliza, two days after the festival, and I had been holed up in my room since I returned from my discussion with Eliza. It had all been too much—the feeling of my body betraying my mind as I danced with Anson, the bitter words spoken in the solarium. I had needed some time to myself to put distance between it all.

And so I had not gone to train with Manelesi. I had not sat amongst the candles in the Yesonto. I had not even attended the Great Hall for dinner. Rather, I begged out sick and stayed cooped up in my room.

Kaiht and Mara kept me company. They had helped me bathe and comb through my curls. We had reordered my wardrobe and discussed whether I needed any new pieces. We had sat and drunk *konstans* and chuckled like the old days.

After a shared dinner in the fire-warmed peace of my chambers, Kaiht and Mara had left me for the night, and I had settled into one of the wingback chairs with Bekha's book.

Now, minutes or hours later, I was oblivious to the world around me. I was lost in the pages of the biography. The more I read, the more I learned of my mother and Anson, the more I wondered. Several times, I contemplated getting up and going to Anson. Perhaps he would explain everything.

I laughed to myself each time I had that thought. Who was I kidding? Anytime I hinted at the knowledge of Anson and my mother's closeness, he clammed up. It was not a topic he seemed eager to discuss.

And so I had to puzzle it out on my own.

I flipped to the next page and read through a passage on my *presentation*, a sort of public showing-off of a new royal before his or her court:

Seated at the head table, Queen Bekha and Consort Otto welcomed the foreign guests and local nobles alike. Princess Sahle laid in her mother's lap though her yellow-wood crib sat nearby. The child fussed and Queen Bekha soothed her in between the formal offering of gifts…

I knew that offering. I had experienced a version of that during my twenty-first birthday when courtiers lined up and brought presents before my seat in the Great Hall. I could see the same occurrence play out, just with my mother and father and a tiny, gray-eyed version of myself.

I read on.

The gifts were lavish, even for the standards of Izwe which boasted the largest natural metal and mineral mines of any nation in the Alterealm. A plethora of wealth was offered: gold pressed into the shape of chalices, tapestries woven with the finest and most exotic dyes, enormous gems faceted and set into pendants.

Each gift was more extravagant than the next. The baby fussed. Queen Bekha soothed. Consort Otto smiled patiently.

Then one Lord brought the most peculiar item forward. Lord Anson of Ingonyame made his presentation. He walked up to the high table and set a tiny, carved lion down before the restless baby.

Those present recall how the child instantly stopped fussing. The Princess seemed to train her infant eyes on the wooden lion, and she reached out a small hand in its direction. Queen Bekha smiled first at the child and then to Anson where he remained bowed before them.

"Rise, Anson," she called. Anson stood. "You seem to have captured the Princess' attention with this. Thank you. Tell me, where did you get it?"

"I carved it myself, Your Majesty," he replied.

The Queen's smile widened. She gestured to the stack of gifts behind her. "Then it is worth more than all of these treasures combined. It is special indeed."

The passage went on to detail how a minor uproar amongst the nobles came about because of the statement that a little piece of wood was more important than a pile of precious metal and gems. But my eyes moved over the words without taking them in.

Something niggled at the back of my mind, some half-memory.

It was not that I recalled the moment; I had been much too young. It was not that I wondered at Anson carving anything—

though that was a surprise to imagine Anson the smirking Lord as a humble, quiet carver.

No, the back of my mind tingled with the knowledge that I knew this somehow.

And suddenly I had it.

I was up and moving before I consciously decided to rise from my cocoon of blankets. On bare feet, I tore through the palace hallways and hurried down staircases. This late in the night, no one was about except for my ever-vigilant Vikela.

I turned down one echoing hallway, then another. I scanned the paintings and maps hung along the walls.

I had *seen* that moment before. I just knew it.

I rounded a corner that led to the solarium. And there it was.

Hung on the wall was a portrait of myself as a baby. Even in the dim light, I could make out my face clearly. Two little arms looked chubby even hidden as they were under sleeves of an ornate, miniature, green *chitenge* cloth dress. I was sure a child of this age could not sit up on its own, but I was certainly posed seated. I wore a dainty gold crown over springing curls that shot up and out in every direction.

And clutched in my little hand was a tiny wooden lion.

I blinked at the carving a time or two, as if my mind was playing tricks on me.

But I knew it was not. I had seen this painting before. I had once stopped to shake my head at how funny it was to see a baby *painting* rather than a baby *picture*.

Now, it took on a new light. Now, my vision narrowed in on the carving that, even in a painting's rendering, looked like finely grained and polished ebony.

I knew that every stroke a painter made held purpose. I was sure the green color of my little gown was symbolic. I was sure my seated make-believe posture was a show of strength. What I did not know was why they would have me hold that lion, why it seemed to be positioned prominently in the portrait.

What significance did it have? Had I refused to give it up and the painter begrudgingly accepted? Had my mother placed it there since, according to the biography, she thought highly of it?

I stared at the painting of baby Sahle and shook my head. Every time I picked up that book, I had more questions than answers. That little lion was just one more.

IN JUST THE TWO WEEKS SINCE THE FESTIVAL, LORD SILAS had reported less and less whispers from traditionalists saying my Lords were leaving me, that I had no control over Izwe, that Warbeck would rise up the moment it had a chance. Apparently, it was one thing to marry the Warbeck heir. Seeing him lay the gentlest of kisses on my cheek was something else entirely.

I was chuffed with myself. We had achieved something. *I* had achieved something, even if it was solving the most minor of our problems. Trina Cheile was still looming out and above us but at least we were shoring up our people inside the borders.

At least that.

Then there were our allies.

One evening at dinner, a letter was set before me. I opened it without looking closely at the seal, concerned as ever that this could be word of foreign aggression. My eyes tracked the short note and then I laughed with true delight.

"Your Majesty?" Anson asked from my right, his brow quirked in question. Several Senior Council Lords craned their necks to try to make out the scrawled text.

But a wide smile stretched across my face as I watched brown-clad servants melt in from the edges of the room with covered metal dishes. One young man set a dish before me, and as he lifted the lid, swirling cold air visibly rose from the off-white mounds.

Ice cream.

Prince Joachim's note explained that he had arrived back to Niel and tasked his cooks to recreate the favorite Humanrealm treat I had once told him about. Having perfected some semblance of what he thought ice cream would look and taste like, he had corresponded with my own kitchen and shared the recipe as a late wedding present.

He apologized for his tardiness. But tardiness be damned, I thought, as I sunk my spoon into the first ice cream I had had in over a year. My eyes drifted shut as I savored the icy, sweet cream. The tiniest contented sigh slipped from my lungs.

I was pleased these days. The court seemed pleased. I was achieving stability. And there was also the question of Manelesi.

Despite the progress I was making, I knew that my time with him was quickly drawing to a close. It had been nearly four months—just a few weeks shy of the time stamp we had set on his channeling. I kicked myself daily and asked why, oh why had I agreed to such a short period of time.

I had come to depend on Manelesi as not just a trainer but, in a way, a friend. He knew me as he knew everything and everyone. Plus, he was my family in a very odd and unsettling way. He was important to me. I could admit it, even if he was challenging and much too know-it-all for my personal taste.

I liked him—if one could use such relaxed terms in the context of an all-powerful being.

But I was not the only one watching the calendar, it seemed.

Sweaty and panting, I came back from training late one morning to find a letter sitting on the desk in my chambers. It was from Grimly, asking for a private meeting this afternoon with the members of the Senior Council.

I did not think much of it until I read the location: my chambers. That caught my attention. Except for my arrival in the Alterealm and that unfortunate morning with Finn, Roland, and Grimly, I had never had the members of the Senior Council here in any great number.

There was a reason for the location, and I would bet the very palace I stood in that it was about Manelesi. What better way to not be overheard than to have the discussion in the Queen's chambers?

Sighing, I pushed a curl away from my damp neck and sat heavily in one of the wingback chairs.

Mara had noticed my return and she hurried to my side, duster in hand. "Can I fetch you something, Your Majesty?" Her eyes glanced at the crumpled note now in my lap.

"Erm, yes," I finally said. I turned a weary smile on her. "Can you please tell one of my guards to deliver a message?"

"Of course, Majesty," Mara replied with a bow.

Hours later, the clock chimed four o'clock and a prompt knock sounded on my door.

I put aside Bekha's biography. Then I stood, smoothing the deep burgundy of my silken skirts, as Kaiht opened the door.

Lords Grimly, Lucas, Ivan, Marcus, and Anson all stood staring back at me. They dropped into a synchronous bow.

Grimly was the first to step through the doorway. "Good afternoon, Your Majesty. Thank you for agreeing to see us so promptly."

I inclined my head. My loosely bound curls stroked across the back of my neck with the motion. "Of course. Thank you all for coming. I can guess at the importance of this meeting."

"Certainly, Your Majesty," Lord Marcus agreed with a knowing expression on his lined face. I felt he communicated the world in every look he bestowed.

Yet, it was Anson who my gaze flickered to.

Dressed in a deep green that was almost black, he stood stiffly and quietly beside the door. The latch snicked shut softly as the Vikela on guard pulled the door closed.

"Consort," I nodded at him, somehow fascinated at the discomfort that radiated from him.

I had not spent much time alone with him since the festival. I had seen him around court, of course. But that quiet tension I had felt in the carriage ride back to the palace still sat between us. We addressed each other only when necessary. We did not linger near each other.

That was most assuredly for the best. I could not seem to shake the memory of Anson's and my dance at the festival. I shivered every time I remembered the feel of Anson's lips on my cheek, the way his breath had caressed my skin.

I did not want to question why that was. I had absolutely zero interest in reliving the moment that my body betrayed me, when for a split second my mind and my body moved out of sequence and I was lost in the feeling of a certain man's arms.

Before I realized that man was Anson and came back to my horrified senses.

It was unnerving, to admit that my body reacted in a way so far removed from my mind. I willfully put it from my thoughts. I did not want to dwell on it, or ask why it could be, or let myself consider the possibilities.

There were no possibilities. There was Anson and me. There was our reluctant marriage, and there was our tense allyship.

There was nothing else to consider.

Anson's gaze turned to me and it was as if a switch flipped. With a blink of his eye, the discomfort was gone. In its place was the cool, collected arrogance I had long come to associate with my husband.

"My Queen," he said as he bowed low—almost mockingly so—a second time.

When he righted himself, the usual humorous gleaming shone in his green gaze. He glanced around himself once more, then strode towards me with sure feet.

And just as I realized his own mask while we were at the festival, I knew he was performing now, too. Not for me, of course. Oh, no. He was putting on a show for the Lords around him. He was trying to make them believe that he was comfortable here despite what I had initially seen when no one else was looking.

He was showing them the confident, comfortable Consort they would expect him to be in my chambers, not the uncomfortable husband who was not really a husband and never, ever came here.

I nodded at him, surprised to find that I respected the performance even if it was a depressing reflection on the true nature of our relationship. And if he could put on such a good act, so could I.

I smiled at him in my best approximation of an approving, sweet wife's smile. I reached my hand out to him.

In the hours since I sent the messenger and when these Lords arrived, I had tasked servants with setting up enough chairs to seat us all. The two usual wingback chairs had been subsequently turned and placed like thrones at the far side of the circle. Other plain, wooden chairs formed the rest of the circle.

Standing where I was before my wingback chair, I braced myself for Anson to take my hand. He came forward. He inclined his head once more.

He looked down at the hand held out to him.

And he walked around it and sat in the other wingback chair beside me.

I let my hand drop, carefully keeping my face neutral. Lord Grimly and the other Lords were busy chatting amongst themselves so I doubt they even noticed the strange exchange. But I glanced down at Anson with a raised eyebrow.

I sat in a flurry of burgundy *chitenge* cloth. "So much for a princely Consort," I grumbled.

"You mean consortly Consort," Anson said in a voice so low I thought, for one moment, I was imagining things.

I angled my knees towards him and leaned in so that we would not be overheard. "I'm sorry. What?"

He glanced at me before refocusing on the Lords now taking their seats. Kaiht and Mara passed out glasses of what looked to be iced *rooibos*. Delicate lemon slices bobbed amongst ice cubes in each tall glass.

He replied, "I'm not your son or your brother. I'm your husband. So what you meant to say is 'consortly' and not 'princely.'"

I forced my brows from rising in indignation. "That's not even a word."

"It is if you say it is," Anson replied. He flashed me a mocking smile before turning to the men. Then he abruptly changed the subject. "My Lords. Shall we begin?"

I shook my head at him, then slowly pulled my gaze away from Anson's stupid, mocking face. The Lords looked back at me. Several nodded.

I cleared my throat. "Thank you all for coming."

All the men looked back at me expectantly, and I had to bite my tongue from snapping, "Weren't you the ones who called this meeting?"

Instead, I smiled and added, "I assume the reason why you wanted to speak urgently, as well as why you chose this location, is because it is about Manelesi."

Five sets of heads nodded at me enthusiastically, yet it was Lord Marcus who answered. "Yes, Your Majesty. We were remarking earlier today that time is nearly up on the channeling. He will be returning to the plane of the dead in a matter of weeks.

"Considering that, we wanted to discuss several matters with you. The first is whether you feel prepared from your time with him, or whether we must speak to the Masters about a way to keep Manelesi here on this plane for longer…"

When Marcus trailed off, I looked between the men for only a moment. Then I lifted my hands. Five sets of wide eyes stared as I spooled out the light in the palm of my hands. I let it curl up, wrapping in on itself over and over until twin domes rested in each hand. Just as quickly, I closed my palms. The light dispersed, and I lowered my hands back to my lap.

I cleared my throat again. "No. That is, I do not think I need Manelesi to remain here any longer. With his tutelage, I have much more confidence and control of my magic, though it is untested—"

"Apart from your abduction," Anson interjected.

My lips tightened. As if I could ever forget the night of my twenty-first birthday, the night I realized the depth of my powers.

The night Finn died.

Without looking at him, I responded, "Yes, apart from that evening. Through that, we know that I can access my magic when in a panic. And because of the training with Manelesi, we now know that I can control it in practice. But I still hope I never need to put my skills to the test again, even after all of these weeks of learning the nuances of my power."

"Unfortunately, I fear it is only a matter of time, Your Majesty," Lord Lucas added sadly.

"I'm sure you're right," I lamented. Just the thought of that white light whipping out in blind panic and terror was enough to raise goosebumps on my skin. I could feel them press against the underside of my thick sleeves.

"Then overall, Manelesi has been a helpful teacher?" Lord Ivan asked.

I thought about that a moment before responding. "Yes, I would say so. Of course, it is strange having a being such as him channeled into a living man. It's even stranger when the being is my many times great-grandfather and insists I call him Father."

"Really?" Anson asked with genuine curiosity in his voice.

I glanced to my side at him before responding. "Yes, he does. It's strange. But it is endearing in a way. I'm still trying to work out whether he genuinely wishes me well or if the endearment is simply a statement of fact about our familial connection."

"I would take it as the latter, lest you get too carried away with ideas of your own importance," Anson replied. Then he added, "Comparatively."

I cleared my throat at that, rather than acknowledge those words.

"And speaking of importance," Marcus added. "I am very glad to hear that Your Majesty has been successful in mastering her power, of course. I do not mean to change the topic but this question is vitally important. In your opinion, after spending much time with Manelesi, do you believe he will leave?"

I stared at Marcus, letting his words sink in. "Does he have a choice?"

Marcus shrugged, a gesture that was so far removed from the gravity of the question. I nearly laughed at the juxtaposition. "He is God. I would never presume to believe that we have trapped him in this form. All of the Masters and all of the power in the world would not make me believe we had him caged."

"Then you believe he is here willingly, that he could leave his host anytime?" I asked. My eyes widened at the idea.

Marcus nodded solemnly. "That is my assumption. I, as many of my fellow Lords here, believe he stays caged—for lack of a better word—because he wishes to help you. If that is indeed the case, it means he could decide to break free of the channeling at any point. It also means he could choose to not leave at the end of his fourth month."

"And that's why you're asking about our relationship," I reasoned aloud. That was what the Lords ultimately wanted to know—whether Manelesi respected me enough to willingly relinquish his corporal form and kingdom once again and let another rule.

"Yes," Grimly answered. "This is a blunt question, Your Majesty, and I beg your forgiveness ahead of time for asking it. But in your opinion, do you think he believes in your capability to rule?"

My eyes widened. The Lords silenced. Only the creak of the wingback chair Anson sat in echoed around the too-quiet room.

"I believe so," I said finally. And I did believe that. In all of the sessions we had had, there was nothing that made me believe Manelesi planned to bide his time and wait to wrest control from me. If he had wanted to do that, he could have done so anytime in the last three months—assuming the Lords were right about him willingly staying within his host.

A collective sigh of relief released around the circle. "Very good, Your Majesty," Lord Grimly said.

I nodded but my mind was elsewhere, turning. The thought had not occurred to me that Manelesi could, at any moment, explode from his earthly shell and take control of Izwe as he had once before. Perhaps that made me naïve and foolish. Perhaps I was too trusting.

My eyes glanced back at Anson.

Well, perhaps I was not *that* trusting.

Anson met my gaze, and for only a moment, we stayed looking at each other. His stupid smirk was there, plastered across the too-slick planes of his face. His green eyes glinted even in the seriousness of the moment.

Perhaps you'll keep your throne after all, those mocking lips seemed to say.

But of course they did not open. Of course Anson did not say that.

And even as I thought the words, they felt hollow in the make-believe of my mind. These were old words, words he might have said to me before we married. Somehow in the weeks since our wedding, we had brokered one begrudging truce after the other. I would not go as far to say that I trusted him—how could you trust a person who had lied by omission for twenty years? Yet I realized as I stared at him that I no longer believed he wanted the worst for me.

Maybe just maybe, he did want me to succeed.

I spun Finn's bracelet around my wrist nervously as I tore my gaze from my husband's. "Is there anything else, my Lords? Or was that all?"

Lord Ivan tilted his head in my direction. "I believe that is it, Your Majesty. We merely wished to ascertain whether or not Manelesi would come and go as we all imagined. Or if his channeling would be more complicated. If there is nothing else to tell…"

Without another word, the Lords began to rise to their feet. I followed suit out of instinct, out of too many years of Human-realm manners that dictated one stood when others stood.

Some things would never change.

The Lords bowed again and began making their way to the door, chattering quietly amongst themselves. But there was one person I wanted to speak to.

"Consort," I called over the soft chatter filling my chambers.

All eyes turned to look from Anson to me.

The weight of those green eyes fixed on me. "Yes, my Queen?"

"Would you mind staying back?"

Perhaps I was imagining it, but I could have sworn his eyes widened in genuine surprise. But only for a moment. Then he smiled wide and bowed with a flourish. "Of course, my Queen."

I did not like the look on his face. I did not like the stupid smirk and the raised brows that hinted at too much, that *acted* out an idea of what he and I would be doing once the doors closed.

Just as I knew it was a performance for the Lords when he arrived, so I knew it now. I tried to control my scowl as the Lords made their exit. The door shut resolutely behind them.

And then there was only me and Anson. He dropped his suave performance.

I looked around for Mara and Kaiht, suddenly wishing they were here dusting or folding or doing any manner of busy work—anything to distract from the fact of us two alone in our terrible game.

As if Anson could see my sudden hesitation, his brow rose. "You asked me to stay behind?"

"Erm yes, would you like to sit?" I motioned to the wingback chairs we had just risen from.

But Anson settled further back on his heels. He crossed his arms over his chest. "I'll stand."

I looked at the cross of his forearms, the way his dark emerald jacket pulled across his shoulders. Then I shrugged, "Suit yourself."

He nodded before rephrasing his first question. "You asked to speak to me?"

He was right, I had. But suddenly, I could not remember why I had asked him to stay behind. It certainly was not because I liked his scowling company.

I crossed my arms in front of my own chest, a mirror to his stance. His eyes flickered as he took in the pose but he did not comment.

And because I could not handle any more of his silent assessing, I said the first thing that came to mind. "Why are you acting for the Lords?"

His brows rose in surprise. "Acting? What do you mean?"

I leveled a look at him with more confidence than I felt. "Oh, come on. You know what I mean. You came in here all arrogance and swagger, like you owned the place. Then when I asked you to stay behind, you all but winked in suggestion about what we might be doing."

As if it were a brilliant thought, Anson said, "And what could we be doing, my Queen?" Then he gave the wink in question.

I scoffed. "You're ridiculous. You know that?"

But if he did, he did not say. He merely tipped his head back and laughed. "Any performing was done in your benefit."

One of my hands rose to my collar bone. "Mine?"

"Certainly. I thought we were married. Is spending time in each other's chambers not what married people do?"

I looked away in embarrassment. I felt the start of a blush burn across my cheeks, and I willfully did not think about the last time he made me blush. "Well, yes, I suppose."

Anson shrugged. "Then I don't see the problem."

"I just…"

He leaned in, as if to hear me better by bringing his body an inch closer. "Yes, Your Majesty?"

I dropped my arms and turned towards the fireplace where embers barely smoldered on the grate—an afternoon fire, as Mara called it. It was not dead, just waiting its turn to light again and burn as fiercely as it had the night before.

Staring at the embers, I finally said, "I thought we were only acting for the crowds, for the people. I thought the plan was to make everyone believe that this was a legitimate marriage in order to secure my reign."

"Are the Lords not everyone?" he countered.

I swiveled my head back in his direction. "I mean, yes. But I thought they all knew the truth of this." I motioned at the empty space between us.

Anson's gaze did not track my hand. Instead, he kept those green eyes trained on my face as if there was a secret there he could read, some puzzle he could work out. "They might have known that was how it began, but it's important that even they begin to believe this marriage is true."

"But it's not," I said simply, factually.

Anson shrugged noncommittally as if we were talking about something as straightforward as the way the strong Izweian wind kicked up red dust at midafternoon. "And that is between us."

I nodded, assessing him in a new light. This game of ours was changing and I wanted more information. "Are you concerned about them?" It was the only reason I could think of to try and trick even the Senior Council.

He stared at me a moment. With each breath he did not speak, I felt the start of a skittering up my spine. "I have no reason to be, necessarily."

I turned to face him head on. Instinctively, my voice dropped lower. "But you are, despite that?"

Anson nodded once. "Yes. And keep that to yourself."

I took a step closer. He could not stop there, not now. I needed more information. "What are you concerned about exactly?"

He sighed as he reached a hand up to run through his dark hair. "Just that the rumors floating around about internal fractures are being fed by someone. They are too pointed, too sure to be something created out of thin air. And there are several Lords who would benefit from those whispers."

"Like you?" I said without thinking.

His eyes flashed. "I'll pretend you did not say that."

I swallowed at the way his voice lowered and took on a gravelly tone. It was almost as if I had truly offended him. "I just mean that you're Warbeck. If my rule was overturned in favor of the traditionalists, you would be the natural choice. So the question must be who wants you to rule, if you think it really is a Lord behind the uproar?"

"There are many who would benefit from that."

"And were you ever planning to tell me of your suspicions?" I asked.

His gaze met mine once more. "Not unless I had to."

"Hmph," I mused. My mind considered prophecies. It conjured up secrets hid for decades. "I wonder what else you're keeping from me."

Anson did not respond to that. He made a sound somewhere between a laugh and a scoff as he turned towards the door. "Are we done here?" he asked, even as he reached for the door handle.

"Yes, yes," I called to his retreating back. I could not help myself from adding, "Not that I dismissed you…"

He turned to throw a cheeky smile over his shoulder as he dipped out of the room. "Good evening, Your Majesty."

THE SENIOR COUNCIL'S WORDS PLAYED IN MY HEAD consistently over the next days. I continued my routine of going to the Yesonto and the arena in the morning, dealing with Council business at midday, paging through notes about my mother, and heading to the Great Hall for dinner. And repeat.

Yet each day, I was more and more aware that it could be the last day with Manelesi. I did not know exactly when he would leave. I had not marked his arrival on my calendar and, besides, I certainly was not sure how stringent the four-month time frame was.

I also was not brave enough to broach the topic with him, especially in light of what the Senior Council Lords had mentioned.

I was sure he would leave when his time was up. Why would he not?

Why would he not?

I entered the arena this morning with these thoughts in my mind.

Manelesi was reclining against one of the rounded stone walls, his face tipped up to the sky.

I hesitated, unwilling to disturb him, but my schedule rattled through my head. It listed itself like a to-do list, urging me to get busy.

I cleared my throat. "Good morning, Father."

Without opening his eyes, he replied. "Good morning, Daughter. Did you sleep well?"

His question threw me off. "Umm, yes. Thank you. I would ask you the same, though I am not sure you sleep…"

He chuckled at that. "I have no need to sleep but this human form I inhabit does. It starts to wear down if I do not allow it time to rest."

In the months Manelesi had been on this plane, the separation between Manelesi and the Master he inhabited still boggled the mind. I opened my mouth to remark on it but shook my head at the last moment. "Okay," I began. "Anyway, are you ready to train?"

He cracked his eyes open then, looking at me down the line of his nose. "Of course. I am always ready. Are you?"

The slight jab in his voice made my mouth quirk up. The day before, I had been testy during our training. My magic had seemed to sense it, or perhaps being part of me, it merely was one with what I was. In either case, we had gotten very little done.

"Yes, I am," I replied simply. I was more than happy to let yesterday's session be forgotten.

"Good," he replied. He stood then, pulling himself away from the wall. As usual, he was dressed in the yellow robes of the Masters. His hair was shorn close to his fair head. Only those blue-gray eyes that told of too many years gave away his other worldliness.

"Come to me," he ordered.

The command in his voice brooked no hesitation, no discussion. I moved closer as I was told.

He motioned to a spot before him. "Stand here and hold up your palms."

I did as he ordered. I turned my palms to the sky, looking at the creases that always looked like the veining of my magic when I could see past the white glaring.

"Bring your magic to your hands."

My palms lit as if lightbulbs glowed cool and silver from within.

"Now throw it at me."

I did not hesitate as I had hesitated so many times before. In one moment, I was standing still. And in the next, my eyes narrowed in on the center of Manelesi's chest. My fingers twitched as if feeling the physical power move through them. The white glow I had come to know so well shone out. And when I blinked again, Manelesi was sprawled out, several paces back from where he had been.

He wiped dirt off the seat of his pants as he stood again. "Very good, Daughter."

I nodded at him, trying not to look at the singe mark on the center of his chest. He had told me over and over again that the singe did not hurt him, that there was no permanent damage, even when I allowed my magic to flow at full force. Still, I always hesitated when I saw the hurt I could inflict. It reminded me of other damage I had caused, white ash and broken bodies that had not come soon enough.

I was curious why we were back to this, back to me throwing magic at him. "We've done this many times. It is nothing new."

"It is not," he replied. "Though I wanted us to start here, I have other plans for today."

"And what are they?"

"I would like to test you," he replied.

"Test me?" I asked hesitantly. Little warning bells began tolling in my head but I pushed them aside. This was Manelesi, Father, Grandfather. I had nothing to fear.

Yet something deep in those boundless eyes twinkled. "Yes. I would like to see what happens when we spar."

"Spar, like how the Vikela and I spar?"

"Yes, something like that. You've become adept at blocking but I would like to see how far I can push you."

My stomach dropped. All of the times before when we had hurled magic at each other, I had somehow been able to pull out enough white light to block Manelesi's magic. Yet I always knew he was holding back.

I did not fool myself into thinking that he actively liked me as a person, or that he cared about the pain he might inflict on me. But I was sure that he needed me. I was his pony in this living race. I was a continuation of his line and rule in Izwe.

I was fairly sure he would not kill me.

Still, the voices of the Lords came back to my mind—their questions about whether or not I thought Manelesi would go willingly. It had seemed ridiculous to me at the time but now I could see it. This was the moment the Lords had warned me about. This was the moment that, if Manelesi wanted, he could destroy me in one fell swoop and take the kingdom for himself.

Despite the tolling in my head, I kept my face neutral as I inclined my head. I forced my voice not to shake as I replied, "Alright. How shall we begin?"

I expected Manelesi to explain, to give some indication of whether he would throw his magic at me or whether I should begin. Neither of those things occurred.

No, on my assent, Manelesi threw a beam of light so hard and so suddenly that I had to jump into a fighting stance as I physically worked to block it. My magic shone out like that veined white dome, arcing around me. I gritted my teeth as I pushed back against Manelesi's magic.

I felt my heart pick up in tempo as my mind struggled to comprehend what was happening. But I knew I had no time to think. There was only time to react, to move my body in pure feeling and instinct.

Thinking could get me killed.

Something told me I should wrap my magic around myself, that I should wear that white light like a cloak. And, to my surprise, I felt a wisp of magic suck in and move around each contour of my body.

Manelesi's magic continued to pelt towards me in a relentless stream, but I pushed back on it. Now that I felt protected, armored, I could focus on going on the offensive.

And I did just that.

Gritting my teeth, I pushed back on his magic with my own. I felt my magical self separate into two. One stayed wrapped around me while the other lashed out at Manelesi.

As he was not concerned for me, I was not concerned for him. No, I had hit him one too many times with my magic and watched him bounce back. I was sure he had long ago mastered this magical cloak around his form—and that of the Master's—and so I threw that half side of me at Manelesi as hard as I could.

It was enough. I watched as my silver light mingled with Manelesi's, as it pushed back on his until it was his time to brace his feet with the onslaught.

I had never seen him show any sort of exertion yet I saw it now. His face was cut into a mask of concentration, his brow crinkling with the force of his focus. His eyes were trained on me but I had the sense that they saw through me and within me. They were visualizing the shape of my magic, the exact spots it wrapped around me.

He was looking for weak spots.

I was sure of it.

My heart picked up, and for the first time, I felt genuine fear here in the arena.

I could die. He was powerful enough to do it. And that would be it. There was no one that could stop him and nothing that could be done to recriminate him for it. He was Manelesi, God, the Great One. We were all just his subjects.

I had always known that on a theoretical level, but for the first time, I felt real fear. For the first time, I regretted what the Lords and I had done in bringing Manelesi back.

Seeming to gather himself and his power, he pushed back in one forceful burst of light. I blocked as long as I could but there was only so much I could do. Like a tidal wave, I felt it rise over me. I thought I could hold it back yet suddenly I knew. Suddenly, there was a point where the wave should have broken, where the tide should have begun to ebb. Instead, it rose and fear spiked hot and ragged in my body.

Instinctually, I knew I would die if I stayed in the path of the onslaught. I had never faced this amount of power but I knew. My body screamed it at me. My magic screamed it at me.

I threw myself to the side. The force of my movement made me fall to the floor of the arena.

Perhaps I had been a fool before—believing in his goodness inherently—but I was not a fool now. I did not hope for a reprieve now that I was sprawled in the red dirt of Izwe. I knew Manelesi would not let up, not on a good day. And definitely not in whatever *test* this was.

Instead, I spun so I could still see him. I hugged that portion of my magic that was a cloak around me tighter and I pulled my focus inward.

We had been trading magical barbs but that would not stop this test. I needed to do something that would break this up. I needed to do something that was big enough, bold enough to throw Manelesi and his onslaught off of me.

I thought for two seconds, still pushing back on the white light that pushed inward. I could feel tendrils of his magic moving around my shield, checking for the cracks, even as the majority of it felt like a gust of wind, pushing everywhere.

And then I had it. I knew.

With the smallest of prayers for my own cleverness, I let my offensive half-magic fall. In the same moment, I willed the cloak to move in, to weave into my pores, glide under my skin.

The abrupt pulling back of my magic shocked Manelesi and I felt his magic shudder in the sudden absence of resistance.

My skin burned as his magic slammed into me. I smelled smoke and in the corner of my vision saw flames. But I could not let that distract me. Life was more important than any vanity I had.

The surprise at pulling my magic back had bought me a moment and I used it. I considered rising to my feet but I did not have time, not as I felt, more than saw, my soldier browns disintegrate on my body. No, I had to act. And act I did.

I glanced away from Manelesi's entranced face to look at the stone walls of the arena, the blue sky above. I blinked and the stones were rising above us. The stones were old, older than Manelesi and his reign in Izwe. Their rounded, uneven surfaces twirled around us like a tornado of rock.

Manelesi was still trained on me and that was fine. I struggled to my feet, pushing past the heat of the last of my clothes burning. I felt hot rubber under my feet where the soles of my boots had once been. Then, naked and unashamed, I raised my arms to the stones. I willed the exoskeleton tendril of my magic to hold. And then I slammed the stones down on us.

29
dare

THERE WAS BLACKNESS THEN. UNDER THE PILE OF RUBBLE, I breathed in a mouthful of dust and coughed violently. I closed my eyes, or at least I thought I did. There was no difference in the quality of light between my eyes open or closed. But the burning was gone. The onslaught on my magic was gone.

And somehow I was still alive.

A tomb of stones rested above me. I could feel their shape, their weight. Yet, the magic woven around my body and threaded through each pore supported them. It held the weight up so that my physical form was as sturdy as those stones—so that I was not crushed.

Crushed.

That thought jarred me. A pang of panic raced through my veins, and instinctually, I began clawing at the stones that entombed me. But then I stopped. I willed myself to breathe in. I willed myself to take a moment and think.

I had brought these stones down. I could lift them back up.

I focused my magic on the stones that piled around and above me. And on my next inhale, I told them to rise.

They rose.

I breathed a cool breath in as the weight lifted from my chest. The dust swirled around me, muting the light from the sun and impeding my view of Manelesi. I spotted him a few paces away, also laying on the ground.

I tamped down my urge to run to him. No, he did not need my concern. I looked back above me at the suspended rocks still spinning. They looked caught in a web of silver light, like they moved viscously through gelatin as they swirled.

I breathed in again and on my exhale, I *wanted* them to go back to their places in the arena wall. And they went.

Each stone fit itself back into its place as if none of this had ever happened, as if I had not ripped every one of them from the stacked order in which they had existed for hundreds of years.

Then, a cleared throat sounded behind me.

I spun, my hands held up defensively. My magic glowed at my fingertips, ready to spark.

But Manelesi merely clapped.

"Very well done, Daughter," he said simply.

My brow rose in sparking anger. My palms glowed brighter. "How dare you? You tried to kill me?"

"If you had not been able to best me in that test, you would have had no right to live."

My eyes grew wider, more uncertain. "You meant to kill me," I murmured.

But Manelesi shook his head. Even in the dusty yellow light of afternoon, I could see the tatters that were his clothes. "No, I did not mean to. But I would have if you had not proved yourself capable."

Each word he said was like a pin stuck into me. Each one was a realization of what could have so easily happened had I not acted and reacted as I had.

I hugged my arms around myself and only then did I realize fully that I was naked.

I looked down at my body. Where there had once been soldier browns, there was just skin. Charred marks and remnants of ash marred my skin but I could see no wounds. I cast furtive, uncertain eyes at Manelesi again.

"Here," he said as he held his shredded red and yellow robe out to me. His pale chest was visible over the long pants the Masters apparently wore under their robes. Despite my anger, I snatched the robe from his hands.

I shrugged it over my upper body and let it hang limply. My eyes narrowed further at Manelesi. "How dare you?" was all I seemed capable of saying.

I backed away a step but Manelesi moved forward by two. He stepped into me, reaching his fingers under my chin and tilting my face up to his.

I balked under the feel of his hands, the intensity at which his gaze bore into mine. And I was afraid. I felt myself shake, and I tried to stop the tremor, but I could not. I was past having control of my body.

"You can say that all you like but it does not change the fact that I do dare. I did dare. And you succeeded in spite of it."

I sent a spark of magic through my skin and to the place he held my chin. It shocked him and he hissed softly as he dropped his hand, shaking it at his side.

"You are more powerful than we could have hoped," he said quietly. He looked at me, but I had the distinct impression he was speaking to himself. His eyes did not focus on mine but took on the look of one here yet at the same time eons away. "It is good."

I looked back at him with wide eyes but I had no words. Instead, he said once more, "It is good."

But I was shaking my head. I would have fled from the arena but I was too frightened to turn my back to him. Instead, I backed away several paces.

Manelesi watched me with curious eyes. "You do not have to fear. I will not challenge you again."

"How do I know?" I whispered.

Manelesi had the gall to shrug. The motion pulled taught the pale skin of the Master's slim chest. "I told you. You passed the test. You would not be here if you had not."

I shook my head again, incapable of wrapping my mind around that. "I…I have to go."

As I backed towards the door of the arena, he inclined his head lower than he ever had before. I paused at the deference, the bow given to me by one so powerful. "That is fine. But Sahle, thank you."

"For what?" I bit out, past frozen lips.

"For besting me. I am proud of you. You have learned well. You have done more than most could ever dream."

I shook my head again but Manelesi did not seem to see my struggle.

"Goodbye, Queen of Izwe," he said.

My back hit the arena door and I yanked it open. I turned and ran.

I did not say anything to anyone. Even had I wanted to, I do not think I was capable of it. No, in the way of shock, my body did not want to move. It did not want to speak.

Somehow I made it back to my rooms, clad in the long Masters' robes. I did not recall seeing any of the courtiers or Lords upon my return from the arena, but the trancelike state I was in could have deceived me.

Only Kaiht and Mara looked at me with surprise as I stumbled back into my chambers. They looked at my clothes, at my loose, knotted hair with concern, but something in my eyes must have told them not to ask. The only thing voiced was by Mara, a quiet "Do you need anything, Majesty?"

The smell of burning was caught in my nose. It clung to my hair and seeped out of every pore. I shuddered involuntarily as I replied, "A bath. Just a bath."

With the women's help, I bathed and dressed. My hair was redone. A crown was placed upon my head and then my body moved automatically towards the door. It was time for Council.

Walking through the halls of the palace, my Vikela as my shadows, I was sure none had seen my return to the palace. No one approached me and no whispers about Masters' robes followed me.

Not that I cared—not truly.

I sat through a session of Council, listening yet not listening. Only Anson's voice calling me turned my attention to him briefly.

He leaned over the arm of his chair towards me. I turned my head in his direction, trying to focus my eyes on his suddenly too-near face.

Green eyes narrowed in curiosity, as if he were trying to puzzle out what thoughts turned in my mind. "Your Majesty?"

"I'm sorry?" I asked quietly. I forced my thoughts to focus, to narrow back into the moment, this room, the Lords before us.

All I could see were Manelesi's fathomless eyes as he mercilessly pelted me with light.

"I asked if everything is alright, Your Majesty?" Anson asked. I opened my mouth to reply, but he added, "Or perhaps Her Majesty has more important things to think about than a possible war with Trina Cheile."

Any other day, my blood would have boiled. My hackles would have risen. But today, I could only look back at Anson and blink.

"No," I said quietly to him. I turned to glance at the room around me but the Lords were in a period of private conversation. "Nothing is more important."

Anson's brow lifted as if he was shocked I had not lashed out at his words. Yet I did not have it in me to revel in the fact that something I did surprised him. I could be dead. I *would* be dead had Manelesi's test taken place earlier.

The thought even made Anson's needling pale.

"Are you alright?" he asked this time. There was a rare worrying tone in his voice, a concern in his eyes I had not seen since that night when he pulled me from Finn.

But I could not think about that now. I nodded my head sharply as I sat up an inch taller. "I'm fine. Just tired."

I turned back to the Lords but Anson did not. I could feel the weight of his gaze on my profile, skating over the arch of my cheekbone, the shell of my ear.

Then he sighed. In my peripheral vision, I watched him sit back in his own chair. "At least try to pay attention, my Queen."

I merely nodded, happy I could still nod.

Hours later, I moved from the Council Chamber to my rooms to dress for dinner, and then to the Great Hall. I went through the motions but could not focus. I did not register the concerned looks that Kaiht and Mara still shared. I did not acknowledge the courtiers when they bowed and greeted me.

And as I fell into my bed, pulling the covers up over my head as if it would protect me from the power Manelesi wielded, I only had one thought: the Lords had both been right and wrong.

Regardless of what I once believed of Manelesi, he would not allow his kingdom to be ruled by one less than him. He *had* considered taking my crown for himself and he would have had I not passed his test.

I had proved myself worthy.

Yet, it could have so easily gone another way.

I shivered into the sheets, even though they were warm and fuggy, pulled over my head as they were.

And as I fell into starlit-tinged sleep, a little voice asked whether I really believed this was the end of it. I wondered whether Manelesi would challenge me again. Perhaps this time, I would not win.

Rising from my bed the next day, I knew there was only one way to put my fear to rest. I had to face Manelesi and challenge him again, if need be. I swallowed the rush of panic that bloomed in my chest.

This was necessary. I had run from Manelesi so quickly yesterday, I had not stopped to ask what happened next. I had not thought to wonder what else he planned or what he had in store.

Not that he would tell me directly.

Still, I had to try to find out. And, should he want to wrest power from me or anyone else in the Alterealm, I had to try and stop him. I was the only one able to—he had made that quite clear with his test.

It was early in the morning, well before dawn. I knew the Masters in the Yesonto would be preparing for their daily prayers, even if most of those in the palace were still fast asleep. I dressed in a spare set of soldier-browns before pulling a cloak over my shoulders.

Then I raced through the halls of the palace on silent feet.

I let my fear and determination propel me forward, through the winding garden paths that led to the Yesonto and through the sanctuary's doors. A few Masters milled about and they turned to me with questioning eyes as I hurried past.

I moved up the stairs, taking the steps two at a time. And then I was pushing open Manelesi's door without a knock, with no hesitation.

He and I needed to speak. We needed to fight. Now was not the time for niceties.

Yet for all of my bravado, all of my furious footsteps, I was not prepared for what met me on the other side of the door.

Over the past months, Manelesi's rooms had always been sparse yet the bed had been made up with sheets and blankets. A pitcher of water had always sat on the small table below the window. An extra change of robes had always been folded on one of the Yesonto's simple chairs.

Now, the bed was stripped. The pitcher was gone. No clothes were folded. The room was empty of Manelesi and any of the earthly things he used.

I spun in the center of the room as if he might be hiding behind me, ready to strike. But there was no one there. I cast my eyes around the bare space once more before turning on my heel.

I had to find Master Edgar and, if need be, rouse the Lords.

Manelesi could be anywhere. He could be about to take control of the palace. He could be preparing to conquer a neighboring nation—all because the Senior Council and I had been stupid enough to believe we could control a God, all because we had *needed* his help.

The thought seemed almost laughable to me now. And perhaps I would have laughed at my own arrogance and ignorance had a voice not pulled me from my thoughts.

"He's gone," Master Edgar's voice called out.

My heart shuddered as I turned quickly towards him. "Where?" I asked simply.

But Master Edgar knew what I was asking. "Back to his home. Back to the plane where God and gods exist."

My breath caught. I stared. "What?"

Master Edgar stepped over the threshold, moving towards me as if proximity could help me understand. "Manelesi has left this plane and returned to his own, that of the gods. He is with us no longer. His time was up."

I knew my eyes were wide. I could feel the skin of my face stretch, and I willed myself to settle, to ask what needed to be asked. "How do you know?"

"We felt it last night. We Masters are always aware of God. It is the way of it for those who dedicate our lives to him, even from afar. We felt the shift when he came to this plane, and we could feel his distance when he moved back to his own."

"You're sure?" I breathed. My heart thumped with adrenaline now more so than dread. I wanted to believe Edgar but I had to be certain. I had to know that the potential threat was truly gone.

Edgar merely bowed towards me as if this were any other day, as if this were any other moment. "Of course, Your Majesty. Here. Come with me."

Edgar motioned for me to follow him and I went willingly. I wanted to see whatever he had to show me. I needed to see it.

Adrenaline warred with hope, with the initial feelings of overwhelming relief. But I had to hold on. I could not allow myself to be lulled by false ideas of safety if Edgar was mistaken.

I followed Edgar back down the stairs. Side by side, we walked across the main floor of the Yesonto. The eternal candles cast moving shadows around us.

To the far wall, a small cluster of Masters stood. Each had a set of candles in their hands. Each trimmed wicks to prepare to add to the central floor's vast sea of light.

As we drew near, one looked up at me.

I froze mid-step.

It was Manelesi. But it was not Manelesi.

No, it was the Master who had volunteered as the host to Manelesi. He met my gaze with curious, deferential eyes before he dropped into a low bow.

Everything was different: the way each muscle moved, the slight hunch, the tilt of the head. It was the same man and yet an entirely different one.

And when Master Gilman rose from his bow, when his eyes met mine, the gaze that stared back at me was brown. It was not blue-gray. No otherworldly glimmer swirled there.

It was just the Master—just a brave young man who had served as a vessel despite not knowing what would happen to him.

I blinked at those brown eyes and then turned his direction.

"Your Majesty?" Edgar called but I was walking away. I moved quickly through the sea of candles, past the concentric circles of chairs.

Gilman's eyes widened with each step I neared, and when I stopped before him, he bowed hurriedly once more.

"Master Gilman," I breathed. My gaze tracked over every inch of him, looking for some outward sign of inward harm. "How are you?"

Gilman struggled to meet my eye. His shy gaze flickered to mine and then away. His knees continuously bent as if he thought I required constant bowing. Finally he murmured, "I am well, Your Majesty."

I stepped an inch closer, reaching out to grasp one of his hands where it held a pale candle. He flinched at my touch but I squeezed his fingers lightly. "Are you sure? I…your sacrifice for the crown has been great. I'd like to make sure you're well."

Gilman's eyes shifted to something over my shoulder and I dropped my hand as I turned. Edgar stood behind me, scowling slightly.

"It was my honor to serve as vessel, Your Majesty," Gilman said quietly.

My eyes turned back to him, my brows pulling close. He said he was well but I wanted to know if he felt in control of his body, if Manelesi's inhabitance had altered him in some way. Yet he held his tongue and I was not sure what made him do so—the fact that he was truly alright, his sense of duty, or Edgar's cloud of a presence.

I watched Gilman a moment longer, watched as his throat bobbed and his knees bent once more. Then I nodded in acceptance. I knew he would say no more.

"Thank you. I am forever in your debt," I finally replied before turning back to Edgar.

For all of my worry, the lead Master merely smiled. "Be at ease, Majesty. All is well, and God has returned to the gods."

I nodded at him, too, mingled relief and disbelief warring in my mind

Manelesi had gone.

He had truly gone.

PART 3

I WAS SEATED AT THE HEAD TABLE WHEN THE SOLDIER barged into the Great Hall.

The musicians had been strumming out their usual jaunty dinner tunes. The scents of roasted meat and sugared stone fruits floated in the air. Laughter sounded from all corners. It was a good night, a happy night.

Even Anson and I, seated beside each other on our respective thrones, did not insult each other. Anson did not take every opportunity to highlight my flaws. I did not roll my eyes or call him ridiculous. It was as if all of the courtiers and Ladies and Lords and even the servants had been fed a steady diet of laughing gas.

There was peace and joy, and for the first time in a long time—possibly ever—I felt comfortable and warm and safe looking out over my court.

I can remember smiling genuinely as I tapped my foot to the beat of a marimba.

Then the towering door at the opposite end of the Great Hall opened, and I watched as a man tumbled through.

No one tumbled through these doors.

No one stumbled and fell.

And they certainly were not smeared in blood and clothed in ripped soldier-browns.

I stood from my seat abruptly as the musicians cut off their tune.

"Your Majesty," Anson called from my side, but I was already moving. Vikela flocked around the soldier who had fallen. They helped him stand, and I watched as he struggled forward on their supportive arms.

I walked quickly, navigating around the high table and down the long aisles between the suddenly quiet courtiers' tables.

"Your Majesty," Anson called again. I did not turn towards his voice but I knew he was a step behind me. In the abrupt silence of the room, I could hear his footsteps moving in time with my own. Further back, the scuffle of boots told me other Lords followed.

As we neared, the man dropped once more to his knees. At this proximity, I could see the tears to his clothes did not stop there; bloody cuts and scratches were clear under each rend.

"Queen Sahle," the man wheezed past cracked lips. "I came as soon as I could...I had to tell you..."

Each breath seemed to strain him. He forced out each word as if pushing them the distance from his mouth to my ear was a monumental task. And so I dropped to my knees and took the man's hands in my own in an effort to steady him.

Hushed whispers sounded behind me but I paid them no mind, not as I felt the tremble that vibrated through the soldier's hands. I said softly to him, "Yes, soldier? You made it. You can tell me now."

The tremble increased as he focused his eyes on me, as he said with an edge of panic in his voice, "They're coming."

It was said quietly, but the silence of the room made it so the words traveled further than they should have.

"Who?" someone asked from behind me.

"Who's coming?" another called.

My pulse thudded in my ears but I forced my face to remain calm. I forced my own hands to remain steady as I squeezed the bloodied soldier's hands. "Soldier, can you tell me who is coming?"

If I had a million dollars to bet on his answer, it would not have been enough for I knew the words on his tongue even before he spoke them.

"Trina Cheile."

Gasps sounded behind me and the silence broke suddenly. Bodies moved, and as if Trina Cheile were right at the palace walls, courtiers began rushing from their seats and to windows and out of the door to the Great Hall.

"Your Majesty," Anson said for the third time. But this time, I felt his hand under my elbow. I waved it off, annoyed.

Instead, I held onto the soldier, and I focused on him over the buzz of movement around us. "Can you tell us where they are? How much time do we have?"

The man took a deep breath but the pained look on his face had me glancing down. Blood dripped from his brown tunic and had smeared across the floor. He needed a doctor.

I looked up at the guards now standing in a circle around us, boxing us in from the commotion. "Get me a healer," I said to one and all of them. Distantly, I registered that one of the guards took off at a run, but I had refocused on the man in front of me.

"A healer will be here soon. If you can, please tell me where they are."

The injured man took another ragged voice. He gently pulled one hand from mine and pushed it into a cut on his abdomen. "The last I saw, they were past the border."

"Which border?" Anson asked. I glanced up at him but he was focused on the man, as if he could read every clue in the man's head.

"The southern one," he replied with a grimace. The movement pulled at a tear on his lower lip and I winced in sympathy. "We were on patrol…and we saw a large army. It seemed to be on the move. We were spotted…and attacked. No one else made it."

An image of an army, grandiose and expansive and deadly, flitted through my mind. My pulse skittered and I swallowed past my suddenly dry throat even as I nodded encouragingly at the soldier. "Thank you," I said to him. "Thank you for making it here and warning us."

"Anything for you, Your Majesty," the man bit out. He tried to bow forward but the motion sent him reeling. He fell in a crumpled heap before me.

"Oh," I exclaimed as both I and the guards moved forward to help right him once more. But then the healer, clad in the burgundy-brown robes of his profession, was pushing through the circle of guards and I realized I was useless here. I was in the way.

I scrambled back on hands and knees, my palms suddenly slick as they moved through a patch of blood.

"Here," Anson said, and this time, I did not push him away as he grasped my elbow and helped me to my feet.

I looked down at my bloodied hands. Then I fisted them in balls, the blood squishing past the seams of my fingers. I raised my eyes and found Anson and a handful of Lords before me.

"The Council Chamber. Now, please," I bit out as I relaxed my fingers.

They did not need any prompting. As one, we moved from the Great Hall and to the Council Chamber steps away. Courtiers still milled around, the air suddenly charged with a frantic, worried kind of excitement rather than the go-lucky giddiness of mere moments before.

The Vikela pulled in tighter around us and stood watch at the door after we shut it on the Council Chamber. And then we sat, and a servant came forward to me with a bowl of water and a towel.

"Your Majesty," the servant said with a bow. He held the bowl towards me, and for the briefest of moments, I was unsure what he was doing.

But then I felt the slickness like oil in the crevices between each finger. I pointedly tried to not look at the blood as I dipped my hands into the lukewarm water.

"My Lords," I called as much to distract myself as to get this discussion going. "Thank you for coming so quickly."

Silence fell in the room as the men turned to me.

I took the towel that the servant offered me and patted my hands as I continued. "Most of you would have been too far away to have heard what the soldier said. I'll tell you."

I explained word-for-word what the injured man had told me, and when I quieted, the Lords looked between themselves.

"Any thoughts?" I asked. It was rare of these men to keep their opinions and wishes to themselves.

"We need more information, my Queen," Anson called from the seat closest to me. He reached out and took the towel from my hands. Only then did I realize I had been worrying a corner of it, twisting it around and around in my restless but now clean fingers.

"I agree," Lord Silas called from further down the table. "It is odd that Trina Cheile would approach from the south since their recent focus has been on our western border, as you saw recently in Ukuwela, Your Majesty. Still, it is a small mercy that the army is near the southern border. That means it is nearly a week away. We have time to assess the threat, and to plan our response."

Lord Marcus stood, a strand of hair sticking up on end the only sign of his discomposure. "I endorse this, as well, Majesty. I would advise you in the strongest possible way to send out a Vikela battalion now to scout and send word back. Even to engage immediately, if need be. In the meantime, it would be wise to also begin amassing our troops."

That pulled me from the daze that was descending. "Amassing the troops?" I repeated numbly.

Lord Marcus bowed in assent. "Yes, Queen Sahle."

"All of the troops?" I replied.

A sort of shocked hush was falling over me. I could feel it like a numb blanket being draped over my head and shoulders.

I knew Trina Cheile was a threat. I had lived through their attack once before. I had planned for the day when they would no longer send explosives and magic and trickery to whisk me away.

I had planned for this moment. Yet now that it was here, I felt robbed of time. I could not believe it was really happening.

It had to be a joke. This had to be a misunderstanding. There had to be more ti—

"My Queen," Anson called from my right.

I turned unseeing eyes to him.

He took in my face, and his mouth set firmly in a line. "What Lord Marcus says is wise. I recognize that you may have another opinion, but I urge you to trust his advice. As the leader of soldiers for decades, as your Lord of War, I agree that this is the right move.

"We should send out a battalion now. And a team should leave at once to amass as many of our soldiers as possible. We must meet Trina Cheile at the border. We cannot let them gain ground in Izwe."

I blinked at him. I turned my eyes to the long Council Chamber and took in the faces of all twenty Lords before me.

This was it.

For decades, this conflict with Trina Cheile had loomed raw and sharp and at times deadly. My mother had been killed. My father had been killed. They had tried to kill me. But never before had they brought an army to our border.

This was it.

My gaze came full circle, back to Anson. I took in the seriousness in his green eyes, the way the space between his brow crinkled in concentration. And then I nodded.

"Yes," I said finally. I cleared my throat and spoke again, louder. "Yes, I agree. Send a battalion now. We will follow after. How soon can we move?"

From my left, Lord Grimly replied, "With tomorrow to prepare, the team could be on the move the following morning. Dawn."

I nodded thoughtfully. Dawn the following day was so soon. "And we would all go?"

Grimly replied, "It would be unwise to take the entire Council but a contingent of us should travel. You could decide whether you would like to go or whether you would like to stay behind."

"I'm going," I spit out without a second thought. There was no world in which I could imagine myself staying behind for a fight that was, at heart, mine and mine alone.

Grimly gave me an approving look. "Very good, Your Majesty. Your powers would be beneficial if it comes to a fight."

"Lord Grimly," Anson bit out. The tone of his voice had me swiveling my gaze to him instantly. "Is that wise? Would it not be best if the Queen stayed here, at least until we know more?"

But even as Grimly opened his mouth to counter Anson's words, I shook my head and said with finality, "It's out of the question. I don't care if it's safer. I'm going, and I won't hear another word about it."

Anson's gaze crackled as he narrowed his eyes at me. I stared back at him, daring him to counter me here before the Lords, daring him to try and tell his Queen what to do.

But then he set his mouth firmer. "Fine. Then I will request the best of the Vikela to travel with us as guards."

"Done, Consort," Lord Grimly replied. "I will have a special contingent held back from the battalion leaving tonight."

Anson nodded but his gaze never left mine.

I broke away first.

"Which Lords will travel with us," I asked the table of men.

"It is traditional for all five members of the Senior Council to travel with the monarch," Lord Silas replied. "Then any volunteers from the larger Council will be admitted, as well. Do we have volunteers?"

I watched as a smattering of Lords rose to their feet. I counted six in total, most of them younger, most of them ready for adventure and war and glory. I nodded at them as one.

"Thank you," I called down the length of the Council table.

"It is our pleasure," one of the volunteers, Lord Isaac, replied.

I nodded at them once more. And then I turned back to Grimly.

"I believe that is all for now, Your Majesty," Grimly said. "I will ensure we are ready to march the day after tomorrow."

But it could not be all—not when the world was crashing down, not when a man came bleeding to dinner, not when our enemy was at our gates.

I opened my mouth to say that, or something, anything, but Anson beat me to words. "Thank you, Lord Grimly, my Lords. If that is all, I will escort the Queen back to her chambers."

Normally I would have found Anson's heavy handedness insulting. Yet the press of the endeavor before us pushed in on me more and more every second.

I rose to my feet on instinct and the Lords before me rose and bowed.

"Thank you, all," I said once more.

I left my throne and walked the length of the table. And when I made it to the door, the guard who manned it reached out to open the latch with hands bloodied as mine had been bloodied.

The injured soldier's face flashed before my eyes.

"Vikela," I said to him. He looked back at me in surprise; it was rare anyone addressed the servants and guards directly. "Will you have the healer send word as to how the soldier is? I would like to know."

The guard blinked once at me and then bowed. He spoke in a deep, sure voice. "Certainly, Your Majesty."

I nodded at him and stepped through the doorway. Anson followed on my heel, and though he walked one step behind me the entire way back to my chambers, he did not say anything else.

It was as if he knew I was past the point of talking. Reality swirled with my darkest, most terrifying fears. My unhinged mind conjured the image of a soft serve ice cream cone from childhood beach days in the Humanrealm.

But instead of the chocolate and vanilla swirl I had loved so much, there was the cool blue of reality and the dark burgundy of my most fearsome nightmares. They blended together, swirling around and around each other until it was impossible to tell them apart. It was impossible to tease out reality from horrific make-believe.

The Vikela standing guard outside my chambers opened my door as I approached. Anson did not step in. No, he let them shut me inside, quiet and confused.

And I was grateful for that.

Kaiht and Mara greeted me at the door the moment I returned. They did not seem surprised to see my blood-smeared dress or my dazed face. Word had whipped around the palace, it seemed.

"We leave the day after tomorrow," I told them numbly as they undid the laces of my gown.

From over my left shoulder, Mara softly replied, "Yes. A note arrived just before you did. It told us to pack your clothes."

I nodded. "I don't know what would be proper to bring."

Kaiht pulled the gown away from me and slipped my nightdress over my shoulders. "Don't worry about that now, Majesty. We'll take care of it in the morning."

I let them gently pull me towards my bed and drape the downy covers over my too-still body.

I realized I was in a sort of shock. I had been here before.

But this time was different. This time all-out war was before me.

I squeezed my eyes shut. Like a child, I wished I could make the monsters go away. Yet when I opened my eyes once more into the darkness of my room, I knew with the mind of an adult that the monsters were not under my bed but out there in the night. Out there on the southern border. And daylight would only bring them closer.

I spent the next day in a blur of movement and boxes.

I was not sure if I slept a wink in the night. My mind raced somewhere in that in-between state of dreams and deep thought. I was not sure whether I dreamed of the soldier's blood again or merely thought of it. I was not sure whether I felt my fear as part of a nightmare or whether the numbness had begun to give way as I laid there, wrapped in my blankets.

Either way, I rose before the dawn. I wrapped myself in my widest and warmest cloak, and I tiptoed in quiet shoes out of my rooms and to the Yesonto.

Vikela fell in beside me as I moved through the palace. I nodded at them but paid them no other mind. And when I moved down the garden path that led to the sanctuary, as the *hadedas* sang overhead and the wind whipped through the violet jacarandas, I felt that the beauty of this world could not exist in a world at war.

Horror could not live where soft grace lay. It did not seem right. I ran my hand over the head of a protea and I could not reconcile that something so marvelous could coexist with something so hideous.

I stepped into the Yesonto and felt all eyes turn to me. A heartbeat passed and then Master Edgar came to my side.

"Your Majesty, how are you this morning?"

I took in his tired red and cream robes, the creases at the knees. It seemed I was not the only one who passed a sleepless night. "Concerned."

Edgar assessed me frankly. "Concerned is an appropriate word," he replied. "We've heard that tomorrow you march. We have spent the night praying for you, and for Izwe."

Tears blurred my vision but I blinked them away. "Thank you. I fear I will need it."

Edgar motioned to the candles on the floor, the simple chairs that ringed them. "Won't you enter the circle, Majesty?"

I nodded as I stepped forward. I chose a seat. I dropped my head into my hands. I thought of Manelesi, Father, God,

346

somewhere back in his own plane. He had told me I was capable and powerful. He had shown me in no uncertain terms that I could survive and fight for what I needed. And so I prayed to him for guidance and strength. I prayed for success. I prayed that no other lives would be lost.

Yet even as I silently begged for that last one, I knew there was no way to achieve it.

Already, we had lost a contingent of men. And, as is the way of war, the only way to end it was to lose more. My eyes pinched tighter at the thought.

I arrived back at my chambers to a flurry of trunks and gowns. Grimly stood beside Anson, pointing and directing the packing.

I pulled my cloak tighter around me. "Good morning, Lord Grimly, Consort."

"Good morning, Your Majesty," Grimly replied. Anson merely nodded in my direction, his face tight, his eyes gleaming with unspoken words.

It seems he was still unhappy I wanted to go with the army.

Lord Grimly continued. "We came to give direction to your servants as to what to bring. I also wanted to give you this."

He snapped his fingers at a servant who waited near the door and the man brought forth a box. With a bow, he pulled back the lid. I was unsure what I was looking at for a moment, but then the hunk of metal took form.

As did the reason for it.

It was a steel helmet, what I imagined to be a piece that matched a wider suit of armor. On top of the helmet was an attached gold crown.

My lips clamped together, and I let my eyes shut briefly.

I would wear this piece as I rode into battle. With the physical item before me, the crush and cries of war became more of an inevitable than a possibility.

I lifted resolved eyes to Lord Grimly and Anson. "Thank you for bringing it."

"It was your mother's. It matches her larger suit of armor, which we are having polished for you," Anson replied.

I nodded. Of course it was Bekha's. It seemed fitting to don her armor and wear her battle crown as I avenged her death two decades later.

"Thank you," I said again. I turned my attention to Kaiht and Mara. I watched as they folded sets of soldier-browns and came back from the closet with my navy riding suit.

There would not be a time for flowing, ornate gowns anytime soon.

I could feel Anson's eyes on me and I brought my gaze to his. He seemed to take in my every truth this morning: the cloak I refused to take off with them in the room, my curls that had turned to frizz in the night, my unwashed face.

I did not like the assessment. And it felt worse coming from him, as if I needed to be the polished Queen before his eyes, as if I could show no weakness. Perhaps I had once thought that. Perhaps I had once been resolved to show Anson that I was a capable Queen, to prove he was wrong all of the times he had humiliated and teased and bullied me.

Now, I did not care.

I met Anson's gaze straight on. I blinked at him in honest, truthful despair. "I'm sure Kaiht and Mara can take it from here. If you gentlemen would excuse me, I'd like to dress."

Only then did Grimly seem to take in my lack of gown, my reluctance to remove my cloak. He nodded hurriedly. "Of course, Your Majesty. I will send word of any other details throughout the day."

I nodded and watched as the two men left the room. Then I turned to Kaiht and Mara. "How can I help?"

They looked between each other. "We've drawn you a bath, Your Majesty. Take it. Relax."

"Isn't there something I can do?"

"No," Kaiht said more firmly. Then she tacked on, "Your Majesty."

I exhaled in a huff. "Fine. But when I get out of the bath, you have to let me help pack something."

"We'll see," Kaiht said with a twinkle in her eye. If I had been less stressed, less frazzled from the weight of tomorrow, I would have laughed at her impertinence.

But right now, I just nodded as I made my way to the bathing chamber.

Mara and Kaiht being Mara and Kaiht knew I needed the input. They brought me each outfit they were packing and asked for my approval. I felt stupid sitting in this bathtub, letting the warm, scented water lap at my skin as they ran around and put items into my trunks.

Eventually, when the water had cooled and I felt more like a human, I climbed out of the tub and let them dress me in a soft, cream-colored gown. It was casual, what I imagined a Queen staying in to knit would wear.

And then I did help them pack. I insisted on it, and Kaiht put a stopper in her refusals. I folded nightdresses. I picked out my sturdiest boots. I placed one simple crown onto the pile of clothes in the trunk. I would need no more. I already had the war crown sitting ominously on the small table between the wingback chairs.

I let the flurry of the packing wrap around me, the specificity of the task soothing my tumbling mind.

Throughout the day, guards arrived carrying missives for me. It should not have surprised me that the first letter was from Eliza even though she and Roland were away at their estate. Her handwriting was lopsided and smudged, as if she had penned and sent her note in a hurry. I read over her pleading words, the urgings to be safe and smart. I held the letter for a few moments after I finished reading, but I did not have it in me to worry about the state of our relationship or revel in the love that fairly poured from the pages. I set aside the note.

Grimly's letters came next. He wrote to tell me the first battalion of soldiers had left the palace. He wrote and said the carriages had been packed. He told me word had gone out to each of the bands of soldiers controlled by the Lords to be ready to meet us in the south. His last missive explained that Anson had hand selected the Vikela who would accompany our contingent, and those who would remain behind to protect the palace in my absence.

I rolled my eyes at that. Of course Anson had personally seen to it.

Yet for the second time in two days, I was again grateful for him. He was overbearing and ridiculous and teasing and stupid, but I could almost imagine—once in a while—that he really did care.

I knew it was not about me. It was about the crown or maybe even my mother. If not for that, he would let my head fall from my neck. He would have no problem sending me into battle armorless.

But the crown and I were the same, and Anson was loyal, and Anson would fight for Izwe. All of those things combined into an irrefutable truth that he cared.

I scoffed at myself.

I was truly losing it if I started believing that.

So I refocused on my packing. I wrote back my approval to each letter Grimly sent. And I waited for the next dawn to arrive.

I did not have to wait long.

DRESSED IN MY NAVY RIDING HABIT AND A PLAIN, low crown, I walked out of the palace doors and to the awaiting carriages.

There was motion everywhere: soldiers rushing to and fro, Lords donned in their own traveling clothes directing zebras, servants lifting final trunks onto the carriages and carts.

But all motion stopped when I appeared on the landing above the palace courtyard.

As one, my court, my people, my soldiers bowed. I nodded back at them stiffly as I folded my cloak over my forearm and tugged a set of rough leather gloves over my hands. My fingers trembled slightly and I balled them so no one else would see.

From below, I spied Anson's dark head. His green eyes seemed brighter today, shining in the way of those fevered or sleepless. He bounded up the stairs to me.

"My Queen," he said with a bow of his own.

"Consort," I replied.

"We're putting the final touches on our convoy. We should be ready to depart momentarily."

I nodded at that, even as trepidation strummed through my veins. I turned my head to take in the palace grounds once more, the white plaster walls of the towering residence, the jacaranda and silver trees and proteas threaded through it all.

Something whispered, *Take a good look. You may not be back.* But I knew that was just my nerves talking. A louder, stronger voice—one I had not heard in a while—said, *You'll be back, Sahle, and you will come back victorious. Believe that.*

The back of my eyes burned and I blinked away the sensation. Yes, he would say that if he were here. I knew that. And I needed to believe it.

"Your Majesty?" Grimly called from several steps below. "Your carriage awaits."

I would have laughed at the turn of phrase, the relative jauntiness of the words, had I not been trying to master my fear. Instead, I nodded and moved with purpose down the steps. Anson followed at my side.

Our departure from Izwe was a quiet affair. Perhaps the people were aware of our purpose. Perhaps they had heard all about the soldier smeared in blood, the news of Trina Cheile's approach. There was no fanfare as our carriages moved through the city and beyond its bounds.

Around me, all five Lords of the Senior Council sat. The carriage was barely big enough for the six of us but the discussions were too vital to miss. They pondered where to camp. They considered how many days it would take to get to the border, and which factions of troops would join us on the way. They argued over Trina Cheile's motives and what battle strategy would be most effective.

I contributed what I could to the conversation. I knew the men around me had decades of experience and knowledge. They turned to me for final approval on any decisions and I was happy to give it. I needed them in this moment, and I would freely admit it.

At some point, the Lords' words fell away. Enough had been decided for now, and the six of us sat hip-to-hip in companionable silence. I tugged Bekha's book out of my skirt pocket and picked up where I left off.

I was up to the fateful final weeks of Bekha's life, and I read the paragraphs anxiously. They told of a Council Lord who passed away suddenly. He had been a bull of a man, it seemed to me. Giant and up-front and charismatic, if the text could be believed. He was also the Lord of War. He oversaw the Queen's armies and commanded them in battle.

With his death, a vacancy opened. The next section of the book explained:

Much jockeying took place throughout the palace, for the Lord of War was second only to the Chief Advisor in importance to the crown. It was a difficult and deadly job. Still, it came with an inordinate amount of prestige. Many Lords vied for the position.

Queen Bekha held an open forum. Each interested Lord came before her to make the case for why he should be the next Lord of War. When all had been heard, she sat back. She contemplated for a matter of minutes. Then she announced that none of the candidates would do.

The Court was shocked. The Consort approached and began whispering in her ear, but she shook her head and shooed him away. Her eyes scanned the crowd before settling on Lord Anson.

"Anson," she called. She motioned to a spot on the floor before her throne. "If you would, please."

Lord Anson approached. He sank into a bow. "Yes, Your Majesty?"

"You did not make a case to the crown."

"No, Your Majesty, I did not."

The Queen's brow rose. "And why is this?"

"Because I have no interest in leading armies, Your Majesty."

Hushed whispers broke out among the crowd. It was unheard of to speak in this manor to a monarch. No one dared upset them.

Yet Queen Bekha smiled. From somewhere behind her, the infant Princess began crying. The Queen held out her arms for the child and the Consort set Princess Sahle down on her mother's knee.

Once the child quieted, Queen Bekha turned her attention back to Anson. "Would you leave this child undefended?"

"Of course not, Your Majesty," Anson replied immediately.

"I thought not," the Queen said, bouncing one leg. She and the child fixed matching blue-gray eyes on the Lord before them. "Then I accept you as Lord of War, effective immediately."

"Your Majesty, I am not the right choice," Lord Anson countered. More whispers and even a few gasps sounded at this show of defiance.

Queen Bekha paid it no mind. She toyed with the Princess' curls. "Your reluctance is why I choose you, Lord Anson. I do not need another peacock pretending to be a soldier. You have always been skilled and loyal. You are meant for great things, even if you fight against it."

The Court held its breath. Finally, Lord Anson nodded. "If you command it, Your Majesty."

"I do. I will take no refusal."

My foot tapped within my boot as I finished the passage. Distantly, the impression of someone watching tickled my mind. I looked up over the edge of the book to find Anson, emerald eyes fixed on me.

Seated on the plush bench opposite me, he held my gaze for only a moment before breaking away. He turned to look out the window, to survey the passing acacia trees, but I did not mistake the wariness in his look.

This book made him *nervous*, I realized with a start.

And I wondered why.

I had picked up this book to learn more about my mother, but each chapter seemed to illuminate something else about my husband: the friendship between Bekha and Anson, the man who would carve a toy for a baby Princess, a leader who served not for power's sake but for duty alone.

It was at odds with the man I met all of those months ago. And, as I skated my gaze over Anson's profile, I wondered for the millionth time whether I knew my husband at all. Had he changed so much in the twenty years I was away? Or was there merely a side of him I was perpetually unable to see?

At some point, I slipped the book back into my pocket. There was only so much wondering that my mind could take, taxed as it was by the omnipresent idea of battle looming before us. I watched the countryside pass outside of the window beside me. I let my head tip back and my eyes close. I did not sleep, but the gentle rocking of the carriage wheels on the packed dirt path lolled me into a sort of gentle drowsiness. It felt good. It felt safe, like a mother's arms rocking back and forth.

That thought made me think of Eliza and Roland. With the speed at which news traveled in Izwe, I had not been surprised to receive their letter the day before. I was sure they knew all about my plans to march on the southern border.

Still, I had not glimpsed them in the crowd as we left Izwe. That fact did not rankle; rather, it filled me with relief. I hoped they would remain at Chez Eliza. I wished them peace for as long as peace would last. War was upon us and, I feared, peace would be a long time coming. The battle ahead served as the culmination of decades of strife. It would not be simple or easy, and I would bet every man, woman, and child in my kingdom that it would not be the only one in this war.

I knotted my hands together in my lap and I hoped and I prayed I was wrong.

At some point, I opened my eyes to a gleaming red and gold sky. I blinked at the beauty of the sunset, stark against the tilted acacia trees this far out into the countryside. Here, like at the palace, *hadedas* winged past. Their silhouettes looked painted on the luminescent sky like black brush strokes on a red canvas.

It was so beautiful it ached. I blinked against the swell of emotions, the deep love that rose in me for this land and this kingdom. It was mine, and now more than ever, I realized it was me who would determine its fate. For this beautiful place, I would do anything. There were no limits to what I would sacrifice.

And that thought terrified me.

"Your Majesty," Anson called from his place across from me in the carriage.

I pulled my gaze from the window. "Yes?"

"We will be arriving soon at the camp. At midday, a small contingent of soldiers and servants left to travel ahead of us and set up before our arrival. Everything should be ready when we arrive."

I nodded. "Great."

Within minutes I felt the carriage slowing. It pulled to a stop and I quickly accepted a hand from a servant.

My eyes widened at what rose around me.

Where I thought there would be a few simple campfires and tents, a small village of what looked almost like beige circus tents stood in a line. Soldiers' smaller a-framed tents surrounded these larger ones. The smell of roasting meat wafted in columns of smoke from a large fire at the center of it all.

"Wow," I said, more a breath than an actual word.

Grimly stepped up beside me. "It's quite something, is it not, Your Majesty?"

I nodded wordlessly.

"If you'll follow me, Your Majesties, I'll show you to the Great Tent."

I looked to my other side and only then noticed Anson had come up beside me. We followed after Grimly.

"The Great Tent like the Great Hall?" I asked them both as we made our way to the largest tent before the fireplace.

"Yes, my Queen," Anson responded from my side. "When on campaign, there will always be a Great Tent for meals and meetings. It functions as a gathering place just as the Great Hall does."

"I see," I replied. And I did see as we stepped through tent flaps that led into a wide space. In an approximation of the Great Hall, a long table was set at the far side of the space—a variation of the high table I always sat at. Smaller tables were placed strategically where the traveling courtiers could sit. An open space was left at the center.

From one edge, I watched a smattering of musicians with *umtshingozi* flutes and *djembe* drums bow to me. Lords and Ladies poured into the space a moment later, and the musicians took up a jaunty tune. I guessed there were no false walls to hide behind this far from the palace.

"Musicians, too?" I asked Anson and Grimly as they led me to the makeshift head table. Anson pulled my chair out for me and I sat. It may have been my imagination but I felt like a cloud of red road dust puffed from my skirts as I settled into the chair.

Grimly sat in his own chair to my left. "Certainly, Your Majesty. It is the way of the court."

"Alright," I said on an exhale. I was too tired to ask why that was necessary. I just accepted, like so many other oddities in the Alterealm. Perhaps it would one day make sense. Perhaps it never would. Regardless, I did not have the energy to contemplate it.

"Your silence speaks as loudly as your words, my Queen," Anson called from his seat to my right.

I shrugged. "Then there's no need to talk."

He let out a noise halfway between a snort and a scoff. But then the servants were entering the tent with trays of roasted meat and root vegetables. The mass of Lords and Ladies who traveled with us took their seats, and dinner began.

"*Konstans*, Your Majesty," a servant asked, holding out a silver pitcher.

"Yes, thank you," I replied around a mouthful of yams.

Though the Lords and Ladies at the other tables spoke and laughed and generally conducted themselves like they did every night back in the palace, the members of the Senior Council and I sat silently. We had done our talking today in the carriage and now the weight of the day set in.

I let the beat of the music wrap around me. I drank the sweet *konstans* and let its pleasant buzz steal over my senses. I let the warm fullness of the roasted meat and yams settle in my stomach.

It was all too comfortable and too familiar and too much like being back in the palace. I looked out at the Courtiers. Their wide smiles and loud laughter made my brow crinkle in confusion.

Did they not understand that we were marching to war? Did they not understand that in a matter of days, the Vikela who lined the tent edges could be dead? That they themselves could be dead or injured?

I shook my head to myself.

When plates began to clear and glasses of wine emptied, I felt myself yawn.

Lord Grimly leaned in from my left. "There is nothing left for us to discuss, Your Majesty, if you would like to retire for the evening."

I cast one more glance around the wide tent, taking in the wooden furniture, the glowing candelabras, the detailed burgundy carpeting that made up the makeshift floor. There was even a pair of ferns set up on each side of the tent opening. Then I nodded. "I think I'll do that, Lord Grimly."

Grimly raised one hand and snapped his fingers. Two Vikela pulled away from the wall and approached the high table. "They will lead you to your tent," Grimly explained.

"Thank you," I said softly. "Good night."

I rose to my feet and, with a start, noticed Anson doing the same. My brow threatened to rise in confusion but I clamped it down. I wanted to ask him where he thought he was going, but I could not do that here before the court.

Lords and Ladies rose and bowed as Anson and I made our way out of the tent. We followed at the heels of the Vikela and they led us to a structure set up mere steps away from the Great Tent.

358

They pushed the tent flaps open for us. "We will be stationed outside, Your Majesties. Let us know if we can be of service," they said as they bowed.

I slipped inside with Anson on my heel. Then I turned. "You didn't have to leave the Great Tent."

His brow rose. "Of course I did. It would not be seemly for me to let you go to bed on your own."

At the mention of a bed, I turned my head to take in the space around us. Just like the other tent, carpets covered every inch of the ground. Two chairs and a low table were set up on one side. On the other side stood a single wide bed, covered in furs and blankets.

I looked between the bed and Anson. "We're both staying here."

The words came out somewhere between a statement and a question but he knew what I was asking. He knew I was looking for confirmation that we would really need to share this tent tonight and for every night of this campaign.

"Yes, it would be most irregular for a Consort to request his own tent."

I blinked at him. Annoyingly, while I felt dust-covered and crumpled from a day on the road, Anson looked impeccable. Not a hair was out of place. His dark clothes did not seem as disheveled as mine. His eyes seemed clear in their luminosity, unlike the blurred sleepiness in which I looked at him.

And he was right. The two of us had agreed to put on an act with this marriage. Even to the Lords and Ladies of the court, we were now selling the idea of a settled—if not entirely loving—match. And while a royal couple might keep separate chambers in the palace, they would not have separate tents in the austerity that was a campaign.

I looked at the bed again. Then I looked back at Anson hesitantly. "You're right. It wouldn't do."

"No," Anson replied quietly. I watched the column of his throat shudder as he swallowed.

The silence stretched on between us, and I lifted my gaze to his. He stared back.

I wished he would say something. Where was that smirking, teasing Lord now when I needed him to cut the awkwardness?

Instead, Anson looked at me as if I was a snake ready to strike.

I stared back at him in the same way.

I cleared my throat awkwardly, determined to say something. "Erm. That's fine. It's not ideal but it's fine."

"Agreed," Anson bit out.

And for the millionth time I wondered at how much he hated me that the thought of sharing this tent seemed to put him in physical pain.

"We can share the bed," I offered.

It was warm in the tent and I worked at my cloak's closure at my throat. It had the added benefit of being a distraction.

"No, thank you," Anson replied shortly.

My eyes snapped back up to his. "Don't be silly. There's nowhere else to stay."

He watched me for a moment. Just as he parted his lips to speak, the tent flaps opened. I spun to find Kaiht and Mara.

"Our apologies for keeping you waiting, Your Majesty, Consort," Mara said as both women bowed. "Shall we help you undress?"

Kaiht's eyes were fixed on Anson. Mara's cheeks had the slightest blush as she looked between the Consort and me.

I turned questioning eyes on Anson. "Erm…"

But he was turning away. From over his shoulder, he called, "I'll leave you to it, Your Majesty. Have a good night."

"Anson," I called after him. He stopped but did not turn back to look at me.

My gaze flitted to the expectant faces of Kaiht and Mara, then back to Anson's broad shoulders.

I cleared my throat, "Anson," I said again. "You're welcome to stay. It's fine. We'll figure it out."

I was not sure what compelled my tongue to form those words. Maybe it was the wine. Maybe it was the exhaustion of that first long day on the road. Maybe it was all of the reading, and with it a dawning understanding that there was a depth to Anson I did not fully know.

Regardless, I was instantly mortified to have said the words and nervous at what I had just offered. I looked at the frozen Kaiht and Mara—both silent and watchful as they took in this painful scene. I wanted to tell them to leave so Anson and I could discuss this without an audience. I wanted to tell them to leave so I could have a moment with my husband.

Anson had other ideas. "Thank you, Your Majesty. But I will see you in the morning," he said without missing a beat.

Then he ducked out of the flaps and was gone.

I stared at the wavering flaps, both willing him to come back and grateful that he had not stayed. I did not want him here yet I suddenly felt guilty that he was the one to inconvenience himself in this sham that was our marriage.

And the fact that I felt bad about that surprised me.

I shook my head as Mara and Kaiht came up alongside me, one on each side.

"How odd," Mara said softly.

"I thought he would stay," Kaiht added. She lifted my wrist to start at the buttons of my sleeve.

I just shrugged. "I don't know."

It was the truest thing I could say.

I did not know anything when it came to my husband.

32
jealousy

I DID NOT SEE ANSON FOR THE REST OF THE NIGHT. IT was only the next morning when I headed for the Great Hall that I found him sitting at the high table beside Lord Grimly, drinking something steaming from a rudimentary mug.

I wondered where he had slept. He certainly had not come back into the tent after he so quickly left the night before. I had collapsed into the pile of blankets and furs on the bed and risen at dawn, undisturbed.

I eyed him as I approached the high table, as the Lords and Ladies in the Great Tent all stood and bowed. And then I scoffed to myself. Wherever Anson had ended up, it had not been outside in the cold or the dust. He wore a new set of clothes. His hair looked freshly combed. He rose from his bow with clear, alert eyes that told of peaceful sleep.

Regardless of how much I wanted to ask, I could not— not with the entire Senior Council taking their seats beside me.

"Good morning," I said to them as I settled into my wooden chair. I wore a traveling gown of deep, burnt orange. The skirt was narrow, the material coarser than the fine court gowns I had grown accustomed to, and the feel of it was oddly comfortable.

"Good morning, Your Majesty," Lord Ivan said. The other members of the Senior Council echoed it. Anson notably kept silent.

A servant came forward with my own earthenware mug. The steam that rose from it smelled of *rooibos*. I nodded my thanks to him before asking the Lords, "Do we have a plan for today?"

Over his fork, Lord Grimy nodded. "Certainly, Your Majesty. We made good time yesterday and covered more ground than we anticipated. If we can maintain this pace, we can be at Barrick Castle the day after tomorrow. Then the border one day after that."

That meant we could be facing Trina Cheile's army in three days.

My brows rose at the realization. "We initially planned for five days to a week. Will the rest of the Lords' troops be able to adapt to that timeline?"

I could not imagine troops mustered from every region of the kingdom would be able to make it in such short time. But I watched Lord Marcus incline his head confidently. "Yes, Your Majesty. Most of them were tasked with getting to Barrick Castle even before we arrived. We've sent missives about our progress. I am confident that they will still beat us there."

"Alright," I exhaled. There was no putting off the inevitable, no reason to delay the battle to come. I nodded at Grimly. "Let's try for the shortened time frame. Less time on the road would be best for everyone, I think."

I looked at Anson pointedly but his eyes were trained on the plate before him. He lifted a mound of *pap* and scrambled eggs to his mouth, completely oblivious to my staring.

A servant laid a plate before me, and I turned my attention to it.

The rest of breakfast was notably quiet, as if the reality of the road had finally settled onto the courtiers who traveled with us.

I finished my plate. I drained my mug. And as soon as the Lords of the Senior Council and I rose from the high table, the servants began breaking it down.

It seemed we were on the road again that soon.

I took the opportunity to find Kaiht and Mara once more and have them help me with a "bio break" as a Humanrealm professor had once called it. When the three of us resurfaced from the woods, the tents had all been broken down. The carriages were nearly packed, and the Senior Council Lords were already loading themselves into our carriage.

I spotted Anson off to one side of the disbanded camp, in conversation with Lord Walsh. I sent Kaiht and Mara off as I headed in their direction.

"Your Majesty," Walsh said with a bow as he spotted my approach.

Lord Anson turned to me with one raised eyebrow.

I threw an overly large smile at Walsh. "Good morning, Lord Walsh. If you wouldn't mind, I'd like a word with my husband."

"Of course," Walsh bowed again. "Excuse me."

I watched Walsh's back float off into the bustle of travel preparations. Then I turned to Anson. "Is everything alright?"

Anson looked at me with shuttered eyes. They said pointedly too little. "I'm not sure what you mean, Your Majesty."

"I mean you stormed out of the tent last night without us finishing our conversation. You were silent all through breakfast." Then suddenly a thought hit me. I leveled a look at him. "Is it about where you stayed last night?"

"No."

I suddenly felt stupid for prying into this topic. It was something I certainly did not want to ask about and something he certainly did not want to speak of. Heat rose in my cheeks as I quickly continued, "Because I don't care. I think you're being silly in not staying in the tent. You can have the bed and I'll set up a pallet on the floor, or vice versa—"

I do not know how long I would have gone on blubbering in my embarrassed state but Anson cut me off before I could get much further. "Don't worry about me, my Queen. I was fine last night. End of conversation"

"Anson."

"Your Majesty," he replied in the mirrored admonishing tone of my own.

I crossed my arms on instinct but then dropped them when I realized the court could see. Instead, I pasted that fake smile back on my lips. I wanted to say more but my attention snagged on Grimly waving to us.

The zebras were saddled. The Lords were climbing into their assorted carriages and onto their various zebras. It was time to travel. The time for talking was over.

"This conversation is not done," I said quietly as Anson and I moved towards our carriage.

"Oh, I think it is," Lord Anson replied.

I glared at him as he handed me up into the carriage.

Another day on the road passed with little excitement. That was a good thing, even if in sheer boredom I could have almost wished for a zebra to throw a shoe, a missive to arrive, an enemy soldier to appear—anything really to disrupt the endless hours of open roads and rocking carriages.

We stopped for food once, and to take care of any personal needs. And then we carried on towards Barrick. The Lords showed me on the map once again the relative distances, and I nodded thoughtfully as I took in the wide expanse between us and the southern border. It looked so far, yet no distance could ever be too great with Trina Cheile there and waiting.

Like the day before, we pulled into an already set camp as the sun sank past the horizon. The same arrangements of Great Tent and residential tents circled a central fireplace. I followed the Senior Council Lords into the Great Tent for dinner, and again we ate roasted meat, vegetables, and whatever else our hunters could find along the journey.

Apparently *every* night on the road held an element of entertainment. Music and dancing kept the spirits high, I was told. I doubted that was how the war path went—that there was anything that could keep spirits up when days grew brutal and nights grew cold—but who was I to stop an Izweian tradition.

Queen or not, I would not take it from the soldiers and advisors and camp followers. As such, I once more sat in a makeshift Great Hall on a makeshift throne, and I watched the men and women of the Court pretend we were home in the palace.

I had to admit it had a certain charm, threadbare though the affair was. It allowed you to pretend that you were elsewhere, if only for an hour each day. Even I could appreciate a saccharine dollop of escapism.

I begged fatigue to get out of dancing myself. Anson sat patiently beside me and whether he wanted to dance or not, he did not comment.

Yet, someone seemed to want him to dance. Someone had their eye on him as a partner even if I did not. I watched as Lady Madeline of Ingonyame approached our makeshift high table with a charming smile and glittering eyes.

Her dress was fine, cut in a style that showed off her curves through the deep green of the *chitenge* cloth. I wondered how many servants this Lady had brought with her on campaign. While I felt crumpled and creased and dusty from the road, Madeline never looked it.

It did not help that with her porcelain skin, her dark ebony hair, her wide, full mouth, she was always effortlessly beautiful.

Lady Madeline curtsied low before us. "Your Majesty. My Consort."

"Lady Madeline," Anson replied in greeting. Something about his voice warmed at her approach, and I caught myself turning to see his face.

A smile graced his lips—a genuine smile, one that I had hardly ever seen on that face.

An odd, deep part of me felt my hackles rise.

Madeline had an answering smile on her own painted, burgundy lips. "May I beg a dance with the Consort?"

My eyes widened at the same time they spun to watch Anson nod his assent. "Certainly, Madeline," he said as he rose in a fluid motion from his seat.

I forced my eyes to return to their normal size. I forced my brow to lower.

A tent of people were watching my every move and the last thing I needed was a rumor that I felt slighted or threatened by Lady Madeline.

Because that was *not* how I felt. I had no claim on this man besides duty. Still, as Anson moved around the head table, made small talk with Madeline, and then took her into his arms at the first beat of music, I felt a strange pinch in my throat.

And I hated my reaction.

Just as I hated this arrogant, stupid man.

I had long suspected that Madeline was Anson's mistress, or had been fairly recently. I had seen them together over and over in my time in the Alterealm. Yet he had denied it the first and only time I had pointedly asked him about her.

I shook myself. This was a ridiculous thing to think about. None of it mattered. Anson did not matter to me. I did not own his affections, nor did I want them. Whoever he shared his heart—or whatever other things—with was none of my concern.

At least that was what I told myself. That was what my head yelled at my body.

But my body would not listen. Perhaps it *could not* listen. Not as I watched Anson lead Madeline in a twirl that was composed of laughter and bright eyes. Not as I watched Anson dip her and then bring her back up with a gentleness that belied the Anson I knew.

I realized my hands were bunched in my lap, the nails biting little crescent moons into the palm of my hands. I forced my hands to relax and for my fingers to extend. Unconsciously, I reached for Finn's bracelet on my left hand. I spun it around and around as I watched Anson and Madeline with a carefully neutral face.

I wanted this song to end. I wanted to jump up and march out of this tent. I wanted to be anywhere but here, watching Anson dance with Madeline.

And at the same time, I demanded, *why, why, why?*

Why did any of this matter to me?

I took a deep breath and purposefully picked up my glass of *konstans*. I was reacting this way because in whatever sick part of my brain, I had come to see Anson as mine. It was not about his affection. It was that *I* was the Queen and he was *my* Consort.

That meant Madeline was encroaching.

Slowly, too slowly, the song wound to an end. Anson and Madeline smiled at each other once more and then she dropped into a low curtsy before him. When she rose, he touched her upper arm and said something quietly to her. Then he made his way back to our head table.

I allowed my hands to clench and unclench once, twice. Then I downed the rest of my wine and prayed my face was inscrutable.

Settled back in his seat, Anson reached for his glass. I took a bite of my food just to have something to do with my hands.

Minutes ticked by. The musicians played more songs. At some point, Lord Grimly came by to ask Anson a question about the particular needs of our cavalry troops.

But I did not speak to Anson. I did not trust myself to say anything good or logical in this moment.

Anson had other ideas.

"What's wrong?" he said behind the rim of his glass as we watched two courtiers make their way back to their seats after a dance.

"There's nothing wrong," I replied. I hoped my voice was believable.

From my peripheral vision—I certainly was not going to meet his eye now—I saw his brows lift. "You're practically simmering. Granted, you and I do not usually have the liveliest of conversations but this is strained even for us."

"There's nothing wrong," I replied again. I set my fork down decidedly. "I'm just tired. I think I'll call it a night."

I rose from my chair, followed by the rising and bowing of all the men and women in the tent. I did not say goodnight. I just wanted to be alone.

And to ponder what was wrong with me.

I kept my head tall, the court smile on my lips as I left the festivities. My own tent had been set up a few feet away and I threw back the entrance drapes.

Only then did I hear the footsteps behind me.

I made it two steps into the tent before I whirled at the sound. I watched as Anson threw back the flaps and followed me inside.

"What?" I asked shortly.

"*What?*" he replied incredulously. "You say nothing is wrong yet you storm off in the middle of dinner."

"It was hardly the middle," I quipped back. I crossed my arms over my chest.

"I'm not here to discuss how many people had finished their plates or not. I want to know what is wrong, Your Majesty."

"And I told you at the table—nothing. Nothing is wrong."

"You were fine before I danced with Madeline. When I came back, you were stiff and cold. Did something happen when I was away?"

I pointedly looked at the desk set up in the corner of the tent, the line where the hem of the tent met the carpets that made up the makeshift floor. Anything to not meet Anson's eyes while I told a boldfaced lie. "Nothing happened."

Anson's answering scoff was loud.

But I had nothing more to say. I made to turn from him, searching for the pitcher of *konstans* that had to be somewhere, a glass of water, really anything to distract from this.

I did not make it far.

No, Anson reached out and grabbed my hand, keeping me turned towards him.

I froze. My eyes rose to meet his of their own accord.

His green gaze looked back at me questioningly, searchingly. It was as if he would puzzle out the insides of my mind, every wavering, insubstantial thought swirling behind my eyes.

I did not care, not as my hand heated at his touch.

"Your Majesty, tell me what's the matter," he said quietly. His tone brooked no argument. It sought answers. It meant to be obeyed.

And while I hated it, something in me told me to answer him. And to be honest.

I took a deep breath and let the words fall from my lips. "I got upset at Madeline asking you to dance. That's all."

Anson's eyes narrowed but he did not let go of my hand. I could feel the press and heat of each of his fingers on my palm. Awareness rippled out across my skin. "You were upset at her *asking* me to dance or the dance itself?"

I blinked but did not dare look away from his gaze. That alone would say too much. "The asking," I replied calmly.

Anson scoffed again. "You're a terrible liar."

"No, I'm not!" I cried indignantly, like a child.

"You say one thing but I can see right through your words. You were upset at me dancing with Madeline. Why?"

"Will you please let go of me?" I asked. The proximity was too much. The heat scalded me.

As if he was shocked he was still even holding it, he abruptly dropped my hand. He took a step away before replying. "Well?"

I squeezed my warm hand into a ball. "I…I don't know," I finally admitted. My gaze broke from his. "Regardless of what your personal relationship is with Lady Madeline, I—"

"My personal relationship?" Anson interjected. He looked at me incredulously, a little line crinkling between his eyes. "I've told you before but I'll gladly reiterate. I have no *personal relationship*, as you so politely call it, with Madeline. We were raised in the same House and have been friends since childhood. That is it. There is nothing happening now or ever with Madeline."

I listened to it all, my shame building and building within me. "I'm sorry," I replied. "I have no right to be upset, and I have no right to pry."

Yet Anson shook his head. An earnest line creased his forehead. "You have no reason to apologize. And you are entitled to ask. We are married after all."

"But not a couple."

"Aren't we?"

"No," I replied resolutely and without pause. We most certainly were not.

Anson ran a hand through his hair, a gesture I was coming to know marked his frustration. "My Queen, whatever physical relationship you and I have has no bearing on the fact of this marriage. I would never dishonor you by being unfaithful to the crown."

I shook my head, the absurdity of this conversation warring with the absolute *necessity* of it that I felt in my bones. "And that's fair of me to demand that of you? You should be free to do whatever you like," I countered. And I meant it. I had never envisioned Anson or me faithfully spending the rest of our lives in celibate disharmony together. I had always assumed we would outwardly be a couple but privately and quietly be welcome to do as we liked.

It seemed Anson had other ideas. "When I married you, I took an oath of fidelity and service to you. I intend to live by that for as long as the God and gods allow."

I had no words to say to that. I just stared back at him with questioning eyes.

"I have no right to ask that of you," I eventually said. I swallowed.

Anson shrugged. "You never asked. I offered it when I agreed to become Consort. Now, it's my turn to apologize. I did not mean to offend you with the dance."

I waved a dismissive hand. "Stop, please. I was overreacting."

Yet Anson merely leaned in an inch. "You are the Queen. I do not wish to upset you. And if dancing with other women does that, then it is settled. You and I will have to dance together to every song at every ball until we're old and decrepit."

I raised my brow at that. "That is not what I meant."

"But that is the trade you will have to make," he said with a shrug. I noticed the glimmer was back in his eyes.

But for once, I did not mind his teasing. It was a welcome distraction to whatever aberrant earnestness permeated the air. I smirked back at him. "Deal."

His eyes traveled my face as if searching for something. A moment passed and another. Then, as if he found whatever he was looking for, he nodded to himself.

"Good night, my Queen," he said. He took a step backward towards the tent flaps.

"Good night, Consort," I replied.

LIKE THE NIGHT BEFORE, I HAD NO IDEA WHERE ANSON went once he left my tent. I did not dare ask him as we sat at the high table for breakfast. I simply pretended, as he pretended, that we had spent the entire evening in each other's company.

It was for the best since Grimly, Lucas, Marcus, and Ivan all joined us. They were always with us. There was too much to discuss. Between battle strategy the Lords debated—and then turned to me for final opinions—or decisions of where to stop for the evening, it was a necessity that we were together nearly all hours of the day.

It was not until we were loading into the carriages that I realized that today was different. Today, I watched as the Lords of the Senior Council climbed onto zebras. Meanwhile, Anson stood waiting for me near our usual carriage.

I approached with my question written across my face. "They're not riding with us?"

Anson pushed a set of tumbled locks out of his face as he extended his hand to me. "Not today."

I took his hand, pointedly ignoring the heat of his fingers, the memory of the feel of them last night. He boosted me up into the carriage. "Why not?"

Anson did not reply at first. Rather, he climbed in after and shut the door. He settled on the bench across from me, and I instantly wished he had chosen to sit beside me. Then at least I would not have to look at him.

"They wanted to give us some privacy," he replied.

I raised an eyebrow at him in surprise. "Why would they do that?"

"We *are* married."

My brow rose higher. There was more to this story, I was sure of it. "Anson, what did you say to them?"

The carriage started moving and Anson settled into his seat, leaning back so that the crown of his head rested on the carriage wall. He looked at me down the bridge of his nose. Then he winked at me. "That's for me to know."

I scoffed. "You're a ridiculous person."

His mouth hitched up into that smirk of a smile, and without meaning to, I caught myself smiling back.

I quickly dropped the corners of my lips into a frown. "Also, why are you so happy?"

I had not realized it at first but he was in a good mood. He had been all morning.

I let my gaze sweep across his face, the green gleaming of his bright eyes, the tousled, almost playful sweep of his hair. I took in his clothes and the polish of his shoes. It was everything and nothing. But there was something…jaunty about him this morning.

And it made me nervous.

Anson laughed as if my question was funny. "Am I not usually happy?"

"Certainly not."

That only made his smile grow wider. "Oh, I think I am, my Queen."

"Not around me. Or maybe I pull the grumpiness out of you."

He laughed again. "No, that's not it either. You just don't know what a good mood is."

"I think I do," I huffed. I settled further back in my seat as I looked at him.

He laughed again. "No, my Queen. I'm not sure you do."

I tapped my foot against the carriage floor in irritation. "Regardless, stop trying to change the subject. What happened today that put you in this mood and made the Lords decide to not ride with us?"

"Maybe I wanted the pleasure of your company."

I leveled a sharp look at him. I would not even dignify that with a response.

"Fine, my Queen. I'll tell you," Anson finally said. His head still angled back, he looked out the window. "I'm in a good mood because we're close to Barrick Castle."

I tapped my foot again. The soft movement echoed around the empty space of the carriage. "And that's exciting, why?"

"Because it's my home."

My foot halted mid-tap. "I'm sorry. What?"

Anson turned his gaze from the acacias outside, the proteas that lined the road. Then he smiled at me. It was a soft thing. It was an aching thing. It reminded me of the smile he had bestowed upon Madeline the night before. Goosebumps rose on my arms at the sincerity of it.

"I said it's my home. I was raised in Barrick. It's the seat of Ingonyame."

My lips parted slightly as my mind raced through the pages and pages of history and geography texts I had read in the many months since my arrival in the Alterealm. In my mind's eye, I could see the passages now. I could visualize the map with their county names, the names of the Houses, as well as the location of the seat, or the main residence, of the Lord there.

I could see the page clearly now. I could make out the map with the little bit of eidetic memory I had. Ingonyame was located in the south of Izwe, its boundaries making up a good chunk of the southern border—the same southern border we were heading towards. Near the northern edge of Ingonyame, I recalled a large dot which demarcated the seat of the region. And now, clearly, I could see the lettering on the map. That lettering said Barrick.

I turned wide eyes back to Anson. "Why did you not say that your home was right in the line of attack?"

Anson being Anson merely shrugged. "It did not seem relevant."

I balked at him. "Of course it's relevant! It's your home. Your people are in the path of an army. Your parents!"

Infuriatingly, Anson shrugged again. I wanted to jump out of my seat and slap him for being so nonchalant in a moment like this. But then the words he uttered next stilled me. "I have no family."

He said it so simply, so normally, as if he were remarking on the comfort of the carriage seat or the way my emerald riding dress complimented the dark circles under my eyes. I searched his face for emotion.

"What do you mean?" I asked hesitantly when it did not seem he would offer more.

"It means I'm like you. Both my parents died long ago. I never had any siblings, so it is just me."

I blinked at the image that appeared in my mind of a young boy with dark, tousled hair and sharp green eyes. I could see a tiny version of his cheeky smile. And I could make out how he was alone, because I had been alone.

Oh, I had had Eliza and Roland for many years, but even then, I knew somehow that I was on my own in this world. It was a lonely existence. It was one I did not envy, even for a man as insufferable as Anson.

Anson continued, lost in thought. I wondered if he even knew I was still here. "Lady Madeline is from my House. Our mothers were close friends so we were raised together. I was a young man when my parents died and I did not need a new set of parents, but her family took me in regardless. I was always welcome in their home, and I spent many nights under their roof. They still keep a chamber for me, for whenever I am in Ingonyame."

I listened, enraptured. And suddenly all of my strange jealousy from the night before, all of my wondering about Madeline and Anson seemed silly. She was the sister he never had. And I was the woman who would strip him of that bond.

"Anson, I'm sorry," I said through frozen lips. "I had no idea. And last night—"

"There is no need to discuss it," Anson interjected with a wave of a hand, as if he could bat away the scars of his heart with the flick of a wrist. "There are no apologies needed. I only meant to explain that Madeline's family is the only 'family' I truly have left in Ingonyame."

"Of course I care about my people, but my people are led by Madeline's father, Lord George, now that I have become Consort. I trust him with them. It was an easy decision of who should lead Ingonyame in my stead. I sleep better at night knowing he is preparing for whatever may come."

I nodded, my face running over the sharp planes of his face. I could not look away. "It's why Madeline is here, too," I mused aloud. I had wondered if she only followed us on campaign because Anson was here, when really it was her home that was immediately in peril.

"Yes. When we got word of Trina Cheile's troops, she asked me if she could travel with us. She wants to be with her family, you see. And if there is going to be war on her doorstep, she wants to fight."

I nodded again. I had judged Madeline since the first day I had seen her. Her beauty had disguised her strength, and I suddenly saw a new version of her through Anson's words. Because I would do the same. If my family was in danger, I, too, would do whatever I could to reach them and fight alongside them.

I opened my mouth to say as much but Anson beat me to words. "As for us being alone in the carriage today, I asked the Lords to give us some privacy. They can decide amongst themselves the reason for my request, but my intention was to give us the space for me to explain this all to you. And to show you my province, just the two of us."

My eyes narrowed but the action was not in malice or disbelief. It was in confusion for why he would be so thoughtful, why he would want to share anything willingly with me. "Thank you," I said simply, dumbfounded.

Anson pulled his head away from the carriage wall. "Don't look so shocked, Your Majesty. I am capable of kindness."

The joking was back in his voice, and I was grateful for that. I knew how to deal with joking Anson. I had no idea who this thoughtful Anson was. I was not sure I liked it.

I let my own smirk rise to my lips. "Sure you are."

His eyes gleamed at me as he leaned forward. He rested his elbows on his bent knees. "By the end of this carriage ride, maybe you'll think differently."

I let my head tip back as I laughed.

That was a good one.

We were several hours away from Barrick Castle and, true to his word, Anson used our privacy in the carriage to point out landmarks and explain landscapes. We stuck our heads out of the windows as we passed granite mountain peaks. They were plateaus really, similar to the one I had seen on my journey to Ukuwela several months ago. I laughed as the branch of a silver tree nearly slapped me across the face, and I pulled my head back in the carriage so fast I almost gave myself whiplash.

As I laughed, and Anson's warm laugh joined in, I pushed back the question of how this was even possible to be so lighthearted with *Anson*. Instead, I thought about how Eliza and Roland would admonish me for sticking my head out of a moving carriage. It was most unqueenly. I said as much to Anson.

His eyes crinkled in humor. "Lucky for you, they are not here. There is no one to see you besides the *hadedas.*"

I chuckled and proceeded to stick my head back out the open window.

As we rounded bends in the packed red dirt road, I let Anson explain the name of one peak and then the next. The country was more rugged here in the south. The peaks were gray but studded with green plants in a rough patchwork. Even from a distance, I could make out the pink bursts of proteas, the blues and oranges and yellows of strelitzia.

At one point, our carriage slowed, and I stuck my head out further to see what was going on. To my surprise, an elephant stood in the road.

I pulled my head in abruptly. "There's an elephant."

I had been in the Alterealm for over a year and had seen all manner of antelope and zebra and birds. I had seen Anson command a group of lions on cobblestone streets. Still, I knew from the stories that Manelesi brought more animals with him, but I had never seen them.

And now…now there was an elephant in the way of our war party.

Anson chuckled at my surprised expression. "Yes, they are quite common here in Ingonyame. Lions, too, of course."

"Just out in the wild?" I asked, even as my mind's eye conjured up the image of a little carved lion held in a child's palm.

"Yes," he replied slowly. "Where else?"

I shook off the mental image as I shrugged. Then I stuck my head back out the window. "It seems dangerous to have predators walking around wherever they please."

I could not see Anson's face but I heard his muffled response from inside the carriage. "They're no more dangerous than humans."

"Hmm," I murmured, too distracted at the scene unfolding before me.

Two Vikela broke away from our party and galloped forward on their zebras. They gently herded the tall elephant off of the path, and when its flapping tail and long tusks had disappeared into the trees lining each side of the road, the Vikela rejoined our party.

The carriage began moving forward once more.

We traveled on for what must have been another few hours. We came across more elephants. At one point, a pack of lionesses sat and watched us pass from the side of the road. Their placid, deep yellow eyes tracked our movement, and I was convinced one was watching me specifically.

Anson told me I was imagining things. I would have believed him, had the lioness not blinked at me just then, as if to say "Oh yes, Queen. Listen."

I was ashamed to admit it but the hours in the carriage with Anson passed quickly, so quickly. Our bickering eventually morphed into real, genuine laughter. I was ashamed to admit it but every time he spoke, I listened eagerly for another piece of information about the landscape, the mountain range that rose up around us. I listened for another piece of his story.

And I reminded myself to stop. I was not supposed to enjoy this ride or this conversation.

This was Anson.

This was Anson.

But like when we danced together at the festival, my head and my heart seemed to have different ideas. If Anson was not being cruel, it was hard for me to maintain my coldness towards him. It was hard for me to recall all of the ways he had humiliated me and made me feel *less than* before my court. It was hard to remember that I had once suspected him of sending me out into the garden that night on my twenty-first birthday.

At one point, just outside the bounds of Barrick, I pulled my head in to make sure my crown was still attached. Anson took the opportunity to stick his head out the window. I watched as his chest expanded deeply. He took in a breath of air, a breath of home.

And I looked at him with confusion. For the millionth time, I wondered again who it was I had married. Who was this excited, *happy* man?

I did not have the heart to ask, even as dozens of questions rose to my lips. Instead, I merely watched his face peel into a smile as the towers of Barrick Castle peaked above the horizon.

My own eyes widened at the site. Like so many other places within Izwe, the estate was ringed by a wall but that was where the similarities ended.

Instead of plaster rondavels and thatch roofs, the estate that rose before me was something out of a medieval painting. A gray stone wall ringed the estate and beyond this border wall, a veritable castle rose. Matching gray walls flowed into pointed spires. Slim windows that looked to be filled with stained glass dotted the walls.

Truly, it was more of a fortress than an estate. I wondered how old it was, how many generations of Warbeck had used it as their home and their court. It was foreboding, yet in looking at Anson, you would think it was as quaint as a small country cottage.

His earnest smile said nothing to the contrary.

As we approached the great stone-and-mortar walls, the iron gates swung open to admit us and our traveling party galloped into Barrick.

Cobblestone clattered under the wheels of the carriage as we circled a wide courtyard. We stopped before a tall wooden door, carved with roses. Then a servant opened the carriage door.

Anson climbed out first. His head lifted to take in the far-reaching points of the turrets. Then he turned back to me and extended his hand. "May I help you out, my Queen?"

I took his extended hand and let him assist me as I climbed out. "How long since you've been home?" I asked him.

His eyes swept across the courtyard before coming back to me. "Several years. There has been no time for homecomings of late."

"Except now."

"Except now," he agreed.

Motion behind Anson caught my attention, and I turned to look as an elderly man came forward, gray hair brushed back from his face. Two younger men followed behind.

"Welcome to Barrick Castle, Your Majesty. Welcome home, Consort," the older man said. He bowed formally to me but when he turned to Anson, his hazel eyes twinkled in recognition and warmth.

"Lord George," Anson said as he stepped up to the man and grasped his shoulder in greeting. "Must I remind you that family need not use my title?"

"It would be improper, especially when meeting Her Majesty for the first time."

They turned to me at the mention and I smiled warmly at Lord George. "It is a pleasure to meet you. The Consort has told me much about you," I said.

That made the man's smile widen. "All good things, I hope."

"Only the best," I replied. The man's genuine warmth was infectious, and I could well imagine a young Anson finding refuge and peace in his family.

"Father!" A voice called from across the courtyard, and I watched as the usually restrained Madeline bounded up. She threw her arms around the older man.

George patted her back like a father pats the back of a toddler. Then she pulled away but remained clinging to the crook of his elbow.

"Welcome, all of you," George said again. "Welcome to Barrick."

The two men took the gap in conversation as an opportunity to step forward. "Your Majesty. Consort. May we request a moment of the Consort's time to survey the soldiers?"

"Of course," I replied. Anson looked at me as if he would say something but I waved him off. "Please, go. I'm sure someone can show me to my room."

"Certainly, Majesty," Lord George said with another bow. He gestured towards the castle door.

Kaiht and Mara and I made our way through the halls of Barrick Castle on the heels of a servant and several Vikela. It was like entering the Alterealm and the palace of Izwe all over again—the curious looks, the deep bows, the whispered words. I had almost forgotten what that felt like in the many months since I had arrived in this world.

Yet here it was again, a whole castle of people curious and seeking me out. I gave them all wide smiles. I touched a few people's hands as they reached out to me. And it reminded me anew that even in this far-flung region of the kingdom, there were people who cared for me, who wished me well.

Just as there were people who thought the opposite.

I wondered how many of the traditionalists resided in Ingonyame. It would be a natural fit after all, for people who wished to see Warbeck restored to live in the province that once ruled over Izwe. But if the people who kissed my fingers and looked at me with tears in their eyes thought this, they were amazing actors.

Our footsteps echoed in the halls of Barrick Castle. The same stone walls outside were mirrored inside, continuing the feel of a fortress more so than a home. Banners hung on the walls and suits of armor periodically stood empty as if invisible sentries lined the halls.

This was a military castle. Every mace and sword, every painting of war that served as decor told of this.

The servant guided us up a set of stairs and then another. Then a set of doors stood before me. He opened them.

"We took the liberty of bringing your belongings up, Your Majesty," he said as he motioned around the room. Like everything else in the castle, it was wide and echoing and filled with gray stone. Two windows were set into one wall. A stately bed rested along another. A third wall held another door—one I assumed must lead to a bathing chamber.

He bowed again. "If everything is suitable, Your Majesty, I am sure you would like to get ready for dinner."

"Yes, thank you."

The servant silently retreated back out of the door and I turned to find Kaiht and Mara pulling out gowns. They were speaking quietly to themselves, and I approached to see what they were so fascinated with.

"What's all the fuss about?" I asked.

Mara looked up at me with her soft eyes. "We were debating which of your gowns would be most suitable for tonight."

"What is tonight?"

"The banquet, Your Majesty," Mara replied pointedly.

I raised my brow at that. "Meaning?"

"Our apologies, Your Majesty. We forget you do not know all of this," Kaiht began. "It is tradition in Izwe that, if possible, there is a banquet when the monarch is in residence at one of the provincial seats. There will be music and dancing and feasting, and your people will be honored to be in your presence."

I blinked at the two women. "Even though we are on the cusp of war?"

The two women looked at each other before Mara responded. "It is an important tradition, regardless of our purpose in being here."

I nodded, for the millionth time accepting that my logic did not always coincide with Alterealm logic.

Kaiht rose to her feet with a gown of deep plum in her hands. "If there are no objections, I believe this gown would be ideal for this evening."

I looked at the gown, seeing and not seeing it at the same time. I reached out and ran my fingers across the material. It was not my finest dress, made up of coarse, functional linen as it was. It would hardly do for a banquet in the palace in Izwe. But here on campaign, I had little options. "Sure. Yes, that's fine," I finally said.

I let Kaiht and Mara strip me of my dust-covered clothes and lace me into the gown. They brushed out my frizzing curls with scented oil until each ringlet again looked defined. They nestled my crown into my restyled hair.

Kaiht and Mara slipped satin shoes onto my feet—ones I had no memory of packing. Then there was a knock again at my door and the Vikela told me the banquet was starting. I let them guide me to the festivities.

And all the while, my mind spun and spun. I wanted to slow down time. I wanted to stop each second and make it so we were not moving to the front tomorrow. I did not want people to die, not for me, not for anyone.

But I did not have that much power. Not even Manelesi had the sort of power it would take to stop time from ticking on.

As the doors to Barrick's Banquet Hall opened, I wished it were so. I closed my eyes. I took a deep breath and wished, futile though it was.

But then music was floating through the doorway. Laughter bubbled out. I opened my eyes and walked into the space with my head held high.

A Queen could not spin out. At least, that was what I told myself as I pasted a smile on my face and said "Rise" to the hundreds of bowed heads before me.

As the crowd rose, my eyes immediately found Anson. He stood at the head of the room, near a raised table that sat atop a dais. Candelabras set into the stone walls cast flickering light across the space and toyed with the rich color of his hair.

He moved towards me as if led by a magnet and I stood still, just over the hall's threshold, waiting.

"My Queen," he said as he drew near, weaving through the throng. "Would you like to join me?"

I did just that.

I walked along his side as we moved slowly through the room. The musicians began their tune again, and though the room looked like something out of medieval England, the same marimbas and *umtshingozi* flutes and *djembe* drums beat out just like they did in the palace in Izwe. It was a strange combination but I had come to accept strangeness. It had been my steady companion this last year in a new world.

I moved with purpose towards the head table, just as I would have in Izwe. Yet it seemed Anson had other ideas.

"There are people who would greet you," he said simply as he motioned me towards one edge of the room.

I nodded and changed course. Only then did I see a head of curls too like mine, and another with blonde hair the exact shade of a morning sunbeam.

Eliza and Roland.

Despite all of the tension that had existed between us since my marriage, I had to stop myself from running up to them. I had to stop myself from flinging my arms around them.

I was the Queen. A Queen would not run. But I did hurry my step, and a wide grin broke across my face.

"Your Majesty. Consort," they bowed as we neared.

I reached out a hand to each of them as they rose. "Eliza. Roland," I exhaled. "I did not realize you'd be here."

A new sort of horror was dawning on me. My elation slowly gave way to realization that if they were here, if they had traveled all of the way from their estate in the north, then they meant to fight. At the very least, they were here to lead a fraction of the army for me.

Roland saw the thoughts flit over my face. He always could read me like an open book. "When we learned of your plans, we began gathering men at Chez Eliza who would fight. It took us a few days longer than we hoped, but at least we caught up to you here."

Eliza looped her arm into the crook of mine. Despite our last interaction, I did not pull away. Not now, not as she added, "Your army will need every man it can spare. We do not know what Trina Cheile plans."

I looked between them both and tears threatened to cloud my vision.

I had not asked them to come. As far as I knew, no letter had been sent to them ordering them to meet us, unlike other Lords who now gathered in this hall. They did not need to be here. They did not need to bring whatever men they could. They did not need to risk themselves by coming this close to the front.

But of course they had. Of course it is what parents did—risk themselves over and over again for their children.

I blinked back the haze that clouded my vision, and I felt Eliza's hand squeeze my arm. I turned my head to smile at her. "Thank you."

"There is no need to thank us," Roland replied.

I fixed him with a serious look, and I said words I should have said long ago, "There is. Thank you. For everything."

Roland nodded somberly back at me and Eliza squeezed my arm once more.

I cleared my throat and only then did I realize Anson was still there. "I'm sorry. We're being rude and excluding the Consort."

"No, no," he replied in a tone more patient than I expected it to be. "I would never presume to get in the way of a family reunion."

"You're part of this family now," Eliza added.

I leveled a questioning look at her but it was Anson who responded. "How could I forget?"

Yet while I would expect those words to come from Anson in the most mocking of tones, it almost sounded serious, accepting. My surprised gaze turned from Eliza to him, but before I could say anything, Anson fixed his attention on me.

His arm stretched out, back toward the wide room filled with new faces "I apologize for having to pull Her Majesty away, but dinner will begin soon. Shall we be on our way?"

"Of course," I said. Then I turned to Eliza and Roland. I took their hands again in mine. "Enjoy the meal. And thank you again."

And then Anson and I were walking away, and for some reason I felt like a small child, reluctant to let her mother's skirts go. I glanced back at Eliza and Roland but already a set of Courtiers had swept them up in conversation.

I turned back to the room, and I let Anson guide me to our table at the front.

Dinner unfolded quickly after that. Where I had grown used to the kudu and yams and greens that so often frequented Izwe's tables, Barrick's fare was slightly different. A whole roasted pig was carted into the center of the room amid cheers. Choice slices were cut directly from the body and brought to Anson and me.

Then potatoes—not yams or sweet potatoes—came out in great steaming heaps. Bread rolls and green salads followed after. And again, I marveled at how in the south, not so far from Izwe's heart, this region had somehow retained vestiges of its original roots.

I said as much to Anson as we hungrily ate. Days on the road had left everyone ravenous, it seemed, as I glanced at Lords more focused than usual on their plates.

"Yes, well, Ingonyame has a nostalgic streak. Of course, it has adapted to the customs and traditions of Izwe but it also retains a sort of pride at once being the seat of kings. The people show it through their food, among other things. It means no disrespect, my Queen."

"Oh, I would never presume that," I replied quickly. It was the truth. I had wondered at the differences but I had not felt slighted. Perhaps I was too lenient of a Queen but I accepted that one could live happily in a world while still cherishing a different personal history.

"Good," Anson said around a bite of pork. "I could have them kill an elephant quickly and put it on the spit if that would make you feel more at home."

I gaped at him. "What?"

The skin around Anson's eyes crinkled. "That was a joke, my Queen."

I looked at him a moment longer before I scoffed. "A terrible joke."

But Anson did not seem to mind. He merely shrugged and took another bite.

As the meal wound down, as the pig's carcass was carved nearly to the bone, the musicians picked up their tune. The notes blended together to form an exuberant melody, and I watched as courtiers drained their glasses of wine and took to their feet.

A partnered dance was beginning and I watched in interest as the couples moved in a quick, upbeat set of steps. It reminded me of the swing dances I had been taught in elementary school in the Humanrealm and the sudden memory of awkward childhood limbs and bad folk music made me smile.

I tried to forget the impending battle. I tried to focus on the dancing and the memories. Just for a moment, I tried to be happy.

At some point, Anson turned my way. "Come with me," he said.

I looked between him and another dance just beginning. "Are we expected to join them?"

Anson shook his head, even as he folded the napkin on his lap and set it on the table. "No, I'd like to show you something."

The background chatter quieted as Anson stood. I looked between the watching courtiers and Anson as I hesitantly rose to my feet. In a hush, I whispered, "Wouldn't it be rude for us to leave?"

"No," he said simply.

I opened my mouth to argue, to insist we stay. But the look on Anson's face was somewhere between excited and hopeful. It was earnest in a way I had so seldom seen. It intrigued me.

"Alright," I replied.

Several Vikela followed us at a discreet distance as Anson and I slipped out of the Banquet Hall amid paused conversations and bowing. I caught Roland's questioning eye and gave a little shrug.

I followed a step behind Anson as we wound out of the stone-walled fortress. Night had descended already, and the glow of the stars cast the gray stone bright. The darkness did not seem to faze Anson. He knew where he was going.

Where my palace's gardens stretched out from the central residence, Anson's estate was more manicured lawns than exotic botanicals. We walked across the grass, past low patterned hedges. I peeked into a dark stone fountain positioned at a juncture in the path. Then we headed towards the edge of the lawn where a shadowy forest rose up like an impenetrable fence.

Anson did not stop at the trees' edge but strode through. I glanced back even as I followed after him, lifting the skirts of my narrow gown as I maneuvered over the uneven forest floor.

But soon, surprisingly soon, the trees gave way once more and we stepped out into a clearing.

It was a meadow. And luminous as the moonlight was, I could make out a field of proteas shining white like millions of clustered pearls.

There were so many proteas that I could not see any path. That did not stop Anson. He stepped right into the mass of flowers and then turned back to me.

The corners of his lips lifted. "They don't bite."

I looked at the substantial petals, the fibrous stalks and could have argued. Instead, I dropped my skirts and stepped out into the sea of flowers.

"What is this place?" I whispered as I drew up beside him. My head swiveled as I took in the luminous expanse around me.

"We call it Yekela, though that is its new name."

I mouthed the word to myself, trying to get the feel of it. "Yekela. Why do you call it the new name?"

Anson took a few more steps into the meadow and I followed after. Far above, a shooting star arced across the sky. "We call it that because it had another name once. Long ago, before Manelesi arrived, this meadow looked very different. It was the last Warbeck Queen's rose garden. It was a beautiful place, and though it was the Queen's, she opened it up to her people to come and picnic and walk the paths. The people cherished it. Many made pilgrimages to it.

"When Manelesi arrived and won the crown, he could not allow the garden that had become so symbolic with Warbeck to remain. He did not tear it apart, but he used his magic to transform it. Where the red rose of Warbeck flourished, he unleashed the protea of Izwe and he called the space Yekela, which means 'forgive.'

"Many traditionalists have come to see this place with anger, as if Manelesi had spit on a symbol of Warbeck. But I have always seen it differently. To me, this is a place of transformation. Manelesi could have razed this garden to the ground. Instead, he changed it: removed the paths and made the garden wild, allowed a stronger flower to prosper. To me, the space is better for it."

I ran my finger over a protea as I stepped deeper into the meadow. Moonshadows lengthened the space around each shimmering bloom. An ocean of constellations stretched out above us. A gentle breeze whispered through the branches of the trees.

It was beautiful. But of course I would think that. It was my flower. It was my story, my ancestor's tale of conquest. For Anson to find it beautiful when it was his story's erasure…I struggled to comprehend the harsh reality of that.

"How could you not hate a place like this?" I asked.

Anson lifted bewildered eyes to me. Even in the dark, I could make out his face. "Hate it? For me, it is simple. My father and mother loved this place. They taught me that nothing dies; it merely transforms. They taught me the lesson of forgiveness that was required of me, being who I am, before I could serve the crown. Because of all that, it is a place of great meaning to me. It is a place of loyalty not because it is easy or because it is ideal, but because it is right."

Anson chuckled then and the expression transformed the serious look in his eyes. "Of course, I had no idea I would one day marry the Queen of Izwe. That adds a different dynamic to it, doesn't it?"

"I suppose," I replied quietly.

Hearing the uncertainty in my voice, Anson turned to me. The proteas reached mid-thigh on him and their bleached appearance stood out starkly against the near-black of his clothes. "This is a place of reconciliation, my Queen."

I could not speak the words that came to my mind, the ones that told of injustice and conquering and colonization. Ones of deep friendship and respect and loyal service in spite of that. Those were not my words to speak, and if Anson did not voice them then perhaps I should let them lie where they belonged: buried under these flowers where the roots of the protea mingled with the dormant seeds of the rose.

I nodded at him instead.

His gaze settled on my face and he seemed to be searching for something, some anger or peace or triumph in this place. But as the night's breeze lifted strands of his dark hair, as the moon reflected in his bright eyes, I did not know what I felt. I was confused at this place, at this story, at the man before me whom I had once sworn to hate.

Whatever he was looking for in my face, I was not sure he found it. But it did not make any difference, not as Anson looked towards the sky.

"We should be getting back," he eventually said.

"Yes, I think that's best."

And so Anson led us out of the protea field, back through the forest, and past the hedges of the sprawling lawn.

We made our way back to the palace in silence. He leveled one look at me before we reentered the banquet. I met it with my own, filled with questions and uncertainties.

But his gaze did not provide any answers.

34
tiny stars

THE NEXT MORNING DAWNED TOO SOON. I HAD PASSED a fitful night, filled with the dread of battle, my questions about Anson, my wondering at a complicated history that seemed all the more real here at Barrick.

I wanted the time to work through my thoughts. But of course time was not something I had. Today we moved to the front.

Anything besides the harsh reality of what we would face there would have to wait.

I climbed from my bed and moved to the little table where a pitcher of water sat.

I felt the vessel's side: cold. I breathed in, letting my eyes shut momentarily, willing heat into the water. And the pitcher's side heated.

I exhaled a long breath. I wanted the water to become cold, and it cooled.

I was not sure how long I stood there, changing the water according to my will. Time seemed to take on odd forms when my magic was at play. On a whim, I envisioned arcing, graceful whirls of water shooting upwards towards the ceiling. The water took on that shape instantly.

A knock on my door shocked me out of my thoughts. The water fell back into the pitcher in a messy splash. I took a step towards the sound but then realized Kaiht and Mara were there. Kaiht went to open the door while Mara draped a substantial shawl over my nightdress.

I pulled it tighter around me as I faced the man in the doorway.

"Good morning, my Queen," Anson called.

I looked at him warily, the way his dark clothes fit each inch of him with grace, the way his hair was pulled back so his green eyes gleamed all the more brightly. "Good morning." Then, because he did not add anything else, I asked, "Erm, would you like to come in?"

He stepped into the room and pulled the door shut behind him.

I motioned to two chairs set beside the small windows. "Is everything in order?"

Anson made his way to one and sat. "Yes, everything is ready for today. Or it will be, as soon as they finish their preparations this morning."

I sat in the other chair, tucking my bare feet under me. The look of them reminded me that I was in my nightdress and a pang of self-consciousness rattled through me.

Anson watched the movement but did not say anything.

I ran my hands over my gauze-covered legs. I cleared my throat. I felt exposed in my thin nightdress. That awareness that Mer had once told me about, that I had wondered about with Joachim, it hung heavy in the air around me. It felt like a hot, shuddering breath along the bare skin of my throat.

Desperate to cut the lingering silence, I said the first thing that came to my mind. "Did you come here for a reason?" I asked. "Or merely to take in the wonder of me first thing in the morning."

Mirth twinkled in his eyes and he winked. "Oh, the latter, certainly."

I huffed as I hugged the shawl closer. My free breasts pressed back at me. "Please be serious."

"There will be much that is serious today."

When I did not reply, when I only lifted my brow expectantly, Anson nodded. The humor left his eyes. "I did come here for a reason, actually. I wanted to show you one more thing before we departed for the front."

"Alright," I responded hesitantly. "How much time do we have?"

"Perhaps a few hours. I came to see if you were ready for breakfast and then we could leave from there. Obviously I came too early," he added as he stood from his chair. "I'll see you in the Hall."

I nodded but did not stand. Anson departed and I stayed seated for some time. I took in the look of the room, the cold stone walls and floor, the darkness that said more about the architecture than the time of the day.

I do not think I had ever missed the palace of Izwe but I did now. I was grateful for the light from the wall of windows and the warmth from the polished wood and thatched roof. It felt like home in a way I never expected it would.

And I wondered if I would see it again.

A battle was looming. Not all of us would return from it.

Dressed in my navy riding habit, I joined the court for breakfast. Apparently I had slept in compared to the rest of the courtiers, for most people had already cleared their plates when I appeared.

Seeing my approach, Anson and the Lords cleared the maps and papers laid out across the head table. I nodded to them with gratitude as I sat.

I accepted a steaming mug of black tea and a scone. I would have been surprised at the fare but a nervous buzzing had settled in my chest. I wondered if I would be able to stomach even the few bites before me.

For the most part, the Lords let me sit in silence. They filled me in on logistics of the final approach today: how Anson, the Lords of the Senior Council, and I would all be on zebraback rather than in a carriage; how all of the troops would travel together; how anyone not actively needed at the front would stay behind at Barrick and make ready to receive casualties or, God and gods forbid, a retreating army.

They informed me that our latest spies had returned from the front early that morning; Trina Cheile had not moved its army. We discussed the merits of why an army would approach and then carefully dig in its feet on the border land, but it was useless to try to read the mind of our enemy. We could not puzzle out their reasons any more than we could understand why peace to them was something to destroy.

Still, I was grateful. A settled army meant that we could approach on our own terms. Accordingly, we decided we would leave just before lunch, which would give us a few hours before we had to be on the road.

I finished my tea and the last bite of the scone. Anson's eyes found mine expectantly and I remembered he wanted to show me something.

"Are you ready?" he asked as the Lords discussed riding formations among themselves.

"For what?"

But Anson just smiled. And again I remarked at the easy nature in which he held himself in Barrick. It made sense, I figured, that the space in which you were raised would have an effect.

"A place I used to spend time as a child," he said.

I do not know what I had expected but it was not that. Slowly, I nodded at him. "OK. Lead the way."

We rose from the head table amidst bows and promises to meet the Lords at the carriages soon. Like the day before, we left the castle, crossed the courtyard, and escaped into the manicured lawn. But instead of delving into the trees towards that strange field of proteas, we went the opposite direction.

The path led us around the backside of the castle, skirting the tall walls. I lifted my face to the midmorning sun as we walked. Only the sound of our footsteps—mine, Anson's, and four Vikela—accompanied us.

We moved in easy silence until we came to a fork in the path. Anson motioned to the left with his hand. "This way."

We turned down the new path and the site of a tower of sorts rose before me.

I took in its gray walls, its lone round window near the top, the pitch of its steep slate roof. "What is it?"

This path was narrower and so Anson had to turn his head slightly to reply. "Historically, it was a lookout post. It has not been used as such for quite some time."

From up close, I could see it was made out of the same stone as the wall around and within Barrick Castle—gray and stately and cold in a foreboding way. A single, unassuming wooden door was set into the side of the tower. That was where Anson headed.

It must have been years since anyone had been in the tower. The handle seemed stuck and it took Anson a moment to wiggle the lever. Just when I thought it would not budge, the handle turned downward with an ancient creak.

"When was the last time you were here?" I asked him with a raised brow.

Anson pushed open the door, and I watched warily as disturbed dust and lint floated inside the dark space. "Like I said, I used to come here as a boy."

I stepped inside hesitantly, wiping away a cobweb that immediately found its way to my hair. "And not since, obviously."

Anson chuckled, seemingly delighted with my uncertainty. "No, not since."

"Hmph," I grumbled. But as my eyes adjusted to the dark, as the deep gray took on forms, I began to see the shape of furniture. A couch sat along one edge of the room, a set of chairs and a table in the center. A winding staircase moved upwards in the corner.

"What was this place to you?"

Anson left his spot by the door and walked into the room. He ran his hand over dust-covered surfaces. And while I could not make out his face, I imagined that it looked wistful.

He took his time looking around. Then he turned towards me. "As a child, I took over this dilapidated space and pretended it was my own castle."

I raised one brow, not that he saw it in the dark. "But you had a castle. Barrick."

"Yes. Well, my parents did. But I wanted something of my own. I've always been independent."

I wished I did not care about his words, his childhood. To my surprise, I found that I did. I caught myself leaning in as I asked, "Were you not close with your parents, then?"

I could just make out his headshake. "I was. My parents— both of them—were kind."

On reflex, I bit out snide words. "Then what happened to you?" Yet even as they left my lips, I knew they were empty. The need to fight Anson, to counter his words, to be bitter and mean, was not there. I was not sure where it had gone, or when it had left.

He turned towards me sharply. "I lost them."

I let his words hang in the air. The sting of them seemed to echo. I struggled against an unfamiliar urge to apologize.

But Anson was used to my cruelty, just as I was used to his. He let the words wash over him and carried on. "I think it was their kindness that made me come here. Kindness is wonderful but when it takes on the level of smothering…a boy struggles to accept that much gentleness. He wants to run and hit and get pushed down. He wants to flex his burgeoning will. My parents did not understand."

"And so you came here."

"I came here. I was able to fashion it into whatever place I wanted it to be. It could be harsh and cold. But if that's what I wanted, it could be that.

"I think my father understood that more than my mother. It took her longer, but eventually they let me run this place as my own little boy hovel. I loved it as I had never loved anything up to that point."

"Cobwebs and all," I added, glancing at a particularly intricate one dangling above me.

"Yes," Anson replied. I could hear the smile on his voice. Then he moved towards the spiral staircase. "This way."

Anson began climbing and I followed after. We passed two levels before the stairs ended.

This floor had more light than the others. A large, round window filled with dusty glass sat in one wall. At the other was a bedframe with no mattress and a simple side table, set atop a rug that perhaps had once been burgundy in color.

I wandered to the round window as if drawn like a moth to the light. This time, it was Anson who followed. He stopped alongside me.

The sun filtered through the clouds, light in dappled beams shining down. I raised my left hand to my forehead to shield my eyes. The motion hitched my sleeve a little higher from my wrist.

"Is that from Finn?" Anson pointed to something and I looked up.

Finn's bracelet.

I dropped my arm defensively, pulling the material back down over my wrist and the silver bracelet that rested there. Then I lifted my chin an inch.

"Yes," I replied cautiously. I was not sure what his reaction would be at my admittance, and I hesitated before choking out the rest. "How did you know?"

Anson's eyes remained trained on the bulge in my sleeve as if he could trace the shape of the cool metal through the thick woven fabric of my gown. "It's not something a Queen would wear," he eventually said. His voice was calm, nearly reverent. "Plus, you never wore it before he died."

Those last words surprised me. I always thought Anson paid me little mind, apart from grasping any opportunity to scoff at my ignorance. My brow crinkled as I gazed at his face, trying to re-see this observant, soft version of Anson—an Anson who would notice and remark on something as innocuous as a bracelet from a past love.

Or whatever it was Finn had been.

"Does it bother you that I wear it?" I asked. It came out more of a whisper, floating across the narrow expanse of air that separated me from him. The light from the round window illuminated dust particles, and if I squinted, I could almost imagine they looked like tiny stars, a galaxy spanning between our bodies.

A small movement caught my eye and I watched as Anson moved his hand. For a moment, just a moment, it seemed as if he were about to reach out and touch my wrist.

But he did not do that. He would not do that.

As quickly as his hand had lifted, he dropped it again. Clearing his throat, he finally raised his eyes to meet mine. "No. This marriage is one of duty. I don't presume to have your heart. And I'd not take from you the last trinket from the man you loved."

There was something wooden in his words, something forced. I tried to pry back the shape of them and peek between the cracks at whatever it was he was not saying. But I could not. Anson's eyes were shuttered to me, and despite the months of calling him my husband, the months of reading between the lines of Bekha's biography, there was so much of him I did not know or understand.

"I didn't love him," I blurted out. I did not know why I said it, why those words slipped past my parted lips. But there they were—one of the parts of my soul I was least proud of laid out before Anson, the last person I ever thought I would tell.

Anson's head tilted slightly to the side, as if he were trying to hear me better. "I'm sorry. I had assumed...You fought for him and for your relationship."

"I fought for me," I answered. If I was being honest, then why stop now. "I fought for my ability to choose something in this realm. It was selfishness only."

Anson watched me a moment before responding. I could nearly feel the seconds pass, like a ticking clock marked each painful moment of that confession hanging in the air. I was not sure why I cared that Anson knew this truth.

Yet I did care, I realized with exquisite, biting shock. I cared what Anson thought of me.

I shook my head as if to push *that* away.

His gaze suddenly felt heavy on my skin and I took a step from him. I turned to face the window square on.

I felt insecure and anxious, and I willed my breath to remain even.

Turned as I was, I felt his eyes skate along my profile as he uttered, "Regardless of what you felt, I'd still not take it from you."

My eyes closed at that.

I needed him to be mean.

I needed him to be wicked and conniving and ugly.

Because I did not know how to deal with an Anson that was anything but. And a tiny voice in my head asked what I might actually feel should I allow myself to believe him capable of anything besides cruelty. Something shifted, skittering in my chest. And the knowledge of the softness there terrified me.

If I could just goad him into something clever, perhaps I could shake the feeling. I thought for only a second before I spoke. "But I'm yours," I said with a sneer, a hearty dose of ironic poking.

He did not take the bait. In fact, he said nothing.

My eyes slid to his unbidden, and the moment our gazes connected, I froze.

He leaned forward a fraction of an inch and my breath caught. Into the dusty space between us, he replied quietly, "You belong to no one but yourself."

The corner of his mouth did not quirk up. He did not smirk or wink or chuckle in that infuriating way of his. No, he was deadly serious as if he were trying to impress upon me the gravity of his words.

That despite being married to him, despite being Queen, despite being out of place in a strange world, I was just as much myself as I had ever been.

I did not know how he had guessed at those deep-seated fears. I did not know how he had read my thoughts so clearly. But he had. And he seemed to know exactly what to say, to assure me that no matter what I had done or would do for this kingdom, I could still find myself.

I blinked against a sudden burning behind my eyes. A wave of emotion I did not know was so tightly bound threatened to loosen in a wellspring.

I cleared my throat as I stepped away from the window and him. I had to put distance between me and…whatever this version of Anson was.

"We should be going," I said over my shoulder as I headed towards the stairs. "It's getting late."

I did not turn to see if he was following me, not as I took the stairs in a hurry, not as I strolled back out of the tower's door, across the lawn, and up to the waiting Lords. I did not turn as I mounted my zebra, and certainly not as I quickly wiped at my too-warm cheek.

I was afraid of what I would see if I did.

35
border

I HAD BEEN TOLD THAT THE FRONT WAS CLOSE TO BARRICK but I had not realized exactly how *close* "close" meant. The entire journey took us just over two hours—two hours sitting on zebra-back, two hours watching the landscape shift from the forested areas around Barrick into the barer, craggy look of the borderland.

Two hours of Anson and me not speaking.

For that last bit, I was grateful. Our interaction in the tower had thrown me. I had no idea what to make of all Anson had said about his childhood. And I certainly had no idea what to make about his easy nature in the carriage yesterday, his talk of forgiveness last night, or the way it felt natural to bare my own heart just moments earlier.

I had not admitted my lack of love for Finn to anyone. I even tried to forget it myself.

In fact, I realized, as I looked down at the reins I held in my gloved hands, I had forgotten to even think of Finn, even feel his bracelet on the skin of my wrist, for some time now. I never took it off but somehow, with everything that happened, the guilt of Finn's death had paled.

A jab twisted in my chest at the thought. I was a terrible person to forget a man, a friend, who had been so dear. He deserved to be remembered. He deserved to not be an afterthought.

I gripped the reins tighter and, with one hand, pulled the bracelet free of my dress' sleeve. I would not hide the last I had of him.

Yet a small voice in my mind asked a different question. It did not ask about Finn but it *did* ask about Anson, and it wanted to know about that moment before the round window. It had almost seemed as if Anson cared.

I knew better. But that voice in my head whispered, *What if he does?*

My gaze slid to Anson where he rode beside me. He looked as deep in thought as I was, and I moved my gaze away before he could feel me watching.

This man did not care, not any more than one loyal cared for the crown.

But that voice again whispered, *no, no.* I shut it down. I drowned it out with doubt. I told it to dream another dream. Anson and I were a dysfunctional team, but to imagine anything more was laughable.

I let my thoughts solidify around that, even as Anson's zebra picked up pace and galloped forward. I watched the angle of his head as he rode. I took in the span of his broad shoulders, the lines of his thighs in the saddle.

In spite of his acerbic nature, he was a suitable consort, a strong consort, a capable consort. And that was that, I whispered back to the voice.

That was that.

Lost in my own thoughts, it took me a moment to realize the trees had begun to thin. They gave way to a clearing and then there was nothing.

Ahead of us, a drop-off loomed.

I could see the sudden *air* in the distance, and then a lower level of the horizon far away and below. I slowed my zebra as I came closer to the edge.

My eyes widened at the site before me.

The drop-off was not merely a cliff. It was not just a canyon. No, at the bottom of the cliff Trina Cheile's army stood waiting. From this distance, I could make out the men like little toy soldiers going about their daily routines: training, making food, repairing tents, shoeing horses.

But there were so many men, so many tents, so many weapons. The reality of this army here, right on our border, hit me as it had yet to hit me. And all I could do was stare in horror and wonder both.

Anson rode up before me, turning his zebra to get a better look. I watched as his jaw set, a muscle ticking on one side.

His eyes swept across the sea of soldiers in the ravine below. He took in their tents and fires and rudimentary structures built in the last week since they decided to make camp on our border.

Then he turned those green eyes on me.

I looked back at him in fear. My heart thudded in my chest. My vision seemed foggy at the edges.

I did not know what to do. I did not know what to say, not in the face of the army below us. Oh, I had heard the reports. I knew the numbers of their troops. Still, nothing could have prepared me for the site of an army in all of its glory. Even from high above, each sword glinted in the sun like warning signs. Each man was a grim reaper, a bringer of death.

My breathing hitched.

"Your Majesty," Lord Anson said, and I brought my panicked eyes back to his. He pulled his zebra close to mine. "Take a breath."

There was a quality to his voice, a compulsion that I had noticed before in similar moments of upheaval. And while I damned him for that voice, that command, I listened to it now just as I listened to it then.

I inhaled a shaky breath and he nodded at me encouragingly. "Good," he coaxed. "Everything is fine."

"How can you say that?" I asked as I threw my head in the general direction of the encampment.

"Nothing about this is new. They have not moved. The count we received looks to be the same as what's below. There are no surprises."

I knew he was right. I knew this visceral reaction had everything to do with my own inexperience, not an actual unknown threat before us.

That green gaze bored into me and I took another deep breath before looking at the enemy army once more.

"Everything is fine," I whispered to myself. "Everything is fine."

I felt Anson's gaze on me a second longer. The heat of it lingered on my cheeks. Then he turned his zebra away and galloped back towards the Lords behind us.

It was a physical task to look away from the army below, but I did. I turned my zebra and moved back the way Anson had gone. He was barking orders, and I only caught the tail end of them as I approached.

"We're making camp here?" I asked incredulously. I took in the rugged ground around us, then the drop off that led to the army.

"Assuming you have no objections to that, Your Majesty," Anson replied, even as soldiers began dismounting and servants began removing boxes from the carriages.

Anson swung off his zebra and I followed suit. I hurried to his side. My hands itched to reach out to him, to grasp his arm where the muscle strained against the dark cloth of his coat sleeve. But I beat back the panic-driven impulses. "But we're so close. Surely we're too close?"

He merely shook his head. "We're in perfect position. With your permission, of course, we will station lookouts on the drop-off's edge—" he paused to look at the sun, the angle of the light. "It's late enough in the day that nothing will happen. But the lookouts can stay on guard through the night. Then, we will have the upper hand—literally—come morning."

"Morning?" I asked numbly.

He quirked a brow at me but the movement was questioning, not mocking. "Yes, we can attack at morning."

I felt sick to my stomach. I wanted to double over and rest my hands on my knees. Perhaps I would breathe better then. Instead, I gaped at Anson. I glanced around me, at the Lords and Ladies and soldiers watching Anson and me talk.

My Court was looking to me for a sign of how to proceed. I could not fall apart. I had to stand strong. I could show no fear.

I took a deep breath and pulled my head higher. Then I nodded at Anson with resolve, even if the look did not reach my eyes. "I agree. It is a good plan."

"Very well. Let's give the Lords some time to get settled, and then we can tell them," he said. Then, he added, "You also should get settled."

I shook my head. "I'm fine."

But Anson pinned me with a hawkish look. "You're not. I can see it in your eyes."

I pasted a stupid, cocky smile on my face. "Yeah, right."

Anson lifted his brow but did not try to call my bluff any more than he had. He turned from me and motioned to someone over my shoulder. I turned to find Kaiht and Mara heading our way.

"Your Majesty. Consort," the women said in unison.

Anson nodded at them in acknowledgement. "The Queen's tent is being set up now. Please help her freshen up before our meeting with the Lords."

"I said I was fine," I retorted but the words sounded like lies even to my own ears.

"Sure," he said simply. He ran his gaze over me, and when his eyes met mine once more, he added, "Get a hold of yourself, and I'll send word when the Lords are ready."

I wanted to scoff in indignation, but I did not have it in me to fight Anson, not now and I wondered, truly if ever again. I was more annoyed that he could see me so easily, that my panic and anxiety were written so clearly on my face.

Really, I was annoyed that I was not being the Queen I should be.

I cast a steely look back over my shoulder at him as I marched off towards where soldiers were erecting my tent. Anson was busy directing men, though. He did not see.

Kaiht, Mara, and I stood together in somber silence as the men stretched the canvass and pounded the final pegs into the ground. Then I stormed through the tent flaps with both women behind me.

Of course there was nothing in the tent. Servants began bringing in my trunks. Another brought a set of chairs and I gladly sat. My elbows landed on my knees and I let my head fall forward into my hands.

"Are you alright, Your Majesty?" Mara asked quietly from somewhere above.

From further away, I heard Kaiht click her tongue. I did not look up as she hissed at her twin. "Of course she's not fine. Did you see that army down there?"

"Well, yes…" Mara began but trailed off.

"Then you know she's not fine."

I let the two women talk over me. I kept my eyes shut. I focused on my breathing. I grudgingly admitted that maybe Anson was right to send me in here.

I could feel the edges of panic, the tightening and tingling that precipitated a full attack. But now was not the time. Panic would not change the fact that an army was camped below us. Panic would not alter the timeline of us marching into battle tomorrow.

And we *would* march into battle tomorrow.

There was no other option, not with that army firmly planted there, not now that my own army had amassed and come this far. We had no other choice but to face Trina Cheile, and our position here would not be tenable longer than one night.

I accepted all of that as I breathed in, held the breath, and breathed out in slow succession. My fate was sealed. This battle would happen. Anson said we would talk to the Lords, but if I decreed this then it would occur.

I knew it was what we needed to do, even if it turned my blood cold, even if every fiber in my being cried out against violence at dawn.

This is what had to be.

I breathed in. I held the breath. I let the breath out.

My eyes remained shut, my head in my hands, but I slowly let my ears become attuned again to the sounds around me. I heard Kaiht and Mara quietly talking about where things should be placed. I listened to the scrape and scuffle of the Vikelas' boots on the rocky ground. There was a sound like a flapping tarp that I guessed was that of the carpeting being strategically placed. A dull thud of wood told me my rudimentary bed was being set up.

I let it all go up around me and I sat there and I tried to breathe.

I was not sure how long I sat there. But with each breath, I let in a little more acceptance. I released a little more fear and dread. When I felt like my head would hold itself up, that my vision would not blacken at the edges, I sat up. I stood from the chair.

My tent was set up around me, and Kaiht and Mara were perched on one corner of the made-up bed. They stood as I turned to them.

Kaiht's eyes were filled with worry. "Feeling better, Your Majesty?"

I nodded, feeling my chest expand easily with this new breath. I could do this. "Yes. Thank you for dealing with the tent."

"Of course," Mara replied. She brought me a bowl of water and a basin, and I let her help scrub the red dust from my face and hands. Meanwhile, Kaiht fetched a thick cloak from one of the chests and dropped it around my shoulders. Even from inside the tent, I could see the light fading outside, and with it, the cold had begun to seep in.

"Shall I replait your hair?" Mara asked me quietly. Her cheeks were wane and I could tell the strain of the moment played on her, even if it was not in her nature to comment.

I glanced at the door but heard no motion. No missive had arrived from Anson that the Lords were ready to meet. I nodded at her. "Yes, thank you."

There was no mirror in the tent, but I felt her every motion as she and Kaiht removed my low crown and undid my frizzing curls from the braids that confined them. Mara dragged a brush through the curls before replaiting them. She artfully wrapped the braids around my head. My crown was placed atop.

Commotion from outside my tent drew my attention and I stood abruptly from my chair. I did not wait for whomever was speaking to the Vikela to enter through the tent flaps. Instead, I strode across the space, pushed back the flaps, and stepped out myself.

Anson and six Vikela looked back at me.

"Your Majesty," Anson said as he took in my newly composed face, my steady hands. When he met my eyes, he looked pleased. "The Lords are ready."

I drew myself up to my full height. "Then let's not keep them waiting."

While I had melted down inside my tent, the camp city had risen silently around me. I took in the wonder of a place born anew as we walked the short distance to the Great Tent. It was situated closest to the drop-off, and as we neared, I took in the look of an army glinting in the low light like a Humanrealm city skyline.

The tent flaps were thrown open and Anson and I walked in unencumbered. The Lords of the Senior Council rose to bow. Behind them, a group of Council Lords did the same. It appeared tonight's discussion would include the wider Council representatives.

"Thank you for coming so quickly, My Lords," I called in greeting. There was no high table or courtier dining tables laid out this evening. No, the Great Tent had been set up like the

Council Chamber. One long table sat in the center with two more elaborate seats at the far end. I took my place there, Anson to my right.

Lord Grimly stood. "Thank you for calling the meeting, Your Majesty, Consort. I believe I speak for everyone when I say this moment is one of mixed emotions. We are here at the border, in sight of Trina Cheile's army. The question now is what do we plan to do about it?"

"Thank you, Lord Grimly," I replied. Then I glanced at Anson. I was the Queen. I knew I could make up my own mind about what to do now that we were here, now that we had confirmed that Trina Cheile had not moved. Yet Anson's words came back to me about fighting at dawn tomorrow and I knew he was right. A childish part of me rankled at the admittance, but there it was.

He was right.

I cleared my throat before continuing. A frog of dread had settled there. "I've considered it, and I believe there is no other option than for us to attack. We've come this far, and if they are not moving then it is up to us to push them back."

"When do you propose to attack, Your Majesty?" Lord Wiley asked from midway down the table.

"At dawn," I responded.

A general murmuring moved through the men. Many Lords nodded. I noticed a few cast furtive glances and shook their heads.

I settled back in my chair and waited. Anson leaned over. "Very good, my Queen," he whispered.

Weeks ago, I would have hissed cruel words back at him, like *I don't need your approval,* or *shove off,* or something equally vicious. But not now. Now, I only looked at him through over-whelmed, grateful eyes. I said simply, "Thank you for explaining the logic in it."

Weeks ago, he would have reveled in being right, in winning a battle of wills. But not now. Now, he nodded curtly, eyes cast down the Council table. There was no pride or peacocking in it.

I turned back towards the Lords. "If there are no objections, perhaps we should proceed with logistics."

"Of course, Your Majesty," Grimly replied. "By our calculations, there are fifteen thousand soldiers stationed below us. We brought thirty thousand of our own, with another ten thousand left behind at Barrick Castle who could act as reinforcements. Consort, do you have a proposed plan of attack?"

From the corner of my eye, I watched as Anson crossed one ankle over the opposite knee. "Yes, Lord Grimly. I've been mulling over our position and our troops. We have the upper hand with the cliffside. If we send twenty-five thousand men down at dawn, we can hold the rest back. And we can pray that we never need to send to Barrick for more."

I watched the Lords around the table nod in agreement. I nodded, as well. "The idea is to hit them with almost everything we have in one go?"

"Yes, Your Majesty," Anson confirmed. "If we can overwhelm them quickly, we can end this attack as soon as it begins."

"I agree. Let's send twenty-five thousand men down. Which men will go?"

As the leader of troops, the Lord of War, Anson again was the one to speak. "The cavalry, the Vikela, and whichever Lords' troops until we've met the twenty-five thousand."

"Is there no reason to hold back some of the cavalry and Vikela?" Marcus called from two seats down.

Anson shook his head. "I do not believe so. The remaining soldiers will be at the camp to defend it against any Trina Cheile soldiers who attempt to make it up the cliffside. Besides that, I believe it is in our best interest to send as many skilled fighters down at the same time."

I found myself nodding. "I agree with the Consort," I said with a glance in his direction. "I want this attack over with as quickly as possible. We'll send whatever we can spare down there in the hopes of doing that."

"And what about those of us around this table, Your Majesty?" Roland asked.

He had been a silent observer since we began this meeting. I had felt his eyes on me, watchful as a father is of a daughter. It was no surprise, therefore, that he asked this question. It was not about the Lords. No, he was really asking about me.

I went to respond but was suddenly unsure. Did the Lords of the Council and Senior Council engage in battle themselves? From my months of research, it seemed some like Anson did while others did not.

I turned questioning eyes on Grimly. "What is typical, Lord Grimly?"

Grimly inclined his head thoughtfully. "In the past, it has been up to the Lords to decide whether they would lead their own troops or not."

"And we are keeping five thousand of those men back," I reminded him.

"Of course, Your Majesty," Grimly replied. Then turning to the larger table. "It is up to Her Majesty and the individual Lords."

But he was missing someone. As my right hand, as my general, it was also up to Anson. I turned to him with the question, "Who do you want on that field?"

Anson steepled his fingers under his chin. His gaze swept around the table. "Lord Lucas, Lord Walsh, Lord Evan. Your soldiers are skilled—nearly as much as the Vikela. They should go in the first wave."

Each of the men inclined their heads and murmured their assent. I tried to assess their expressions, either excitement or fear, but each wore a courtly, artfully trained mask of neutrality.

But Anson was not done. One forefinger tapped against the other as he looked in Roland's direction. I felt my stomach drop out from under me as he opened his mouth. "Lord Roland, I could use your men but they could be equally as useful here. It is up to you."

"I will go, Your Majesty, Consort," he replied solemnly.

My eyes widened. I wanted to cry out and tell him no, to stay on the cliffside, but I could not do that here. I could not show partiality even if every person around this table knew exactly who Roland was to me.

"Very well, is that all, Consort?" Grimly asked.

Anson scanned the table once more. Then he nodded. "Yes, that will do."

"In that case," Grimly continued, "the rest can remain above with the Queen and Consort."

Above?

I turned questioning eyes on Grimly. I opened my mouth and then closed it before his words truly took form in my mind. "I'm sorry. Did you say I would stay above?"

Grimly took me in with curious, wary eyes, almost as if he could hear my mind begin to churn. "Yes, Your Majesty. I believe I speak for all of the Lords when I say it is essential that you stay out of the battle itself."

I blinked at Grimly. I could not fight? Is that what Grimly was trying to tell me?

Since my arrival in the Alterealm, I had learned to wield a sword, to shoot an arrow. I had learned to coax my power out of its shell and, recently, to command it as I needed. We had even summoned Manelesi to do so.

What had all of it been for if now, in the first instance where I would use these skills willingly, I was denied entry to the field?

No, I resolved. I was going into this fight. And to the table of men around me, I lifted my voice and said, "I am your Queen. This is my battle. I will be on that field, alongside my troops."

"Queen Sahle…" Grimly repeated. He tried to reason with me but I would not hear it. I blocked my ears to his words.

He carried on but the words did not take shape in my mind. They babbled like background noise, like the sound of a whirring fan—there but consciously not.

I stood from the table and turned towards the opening in the Great Tent. I could see the lights of our army flickering along the top of the cliffside. Far below, I could see the equally large glow of our enemy's men, camping and waiting.

Many would die tomorrow, on our side and theirs, and it was entirely unacceptable of me to stand aside and allow it to happen. My family had started this feud, albeit many generations ago. If anyone was expected to shed blood, it would be me for the sins of my predecessors. I would be on that field. I swore it to myself.

I was so deep in thought that I did not notice the muffled rumbling of voices as the Lords began talking amongst themselves. I did not hear the sound of someone climbing to their feet.

And then Anson was there, stepping into my line of vision so that I could no longer see the armies' firelight—only his face.

"Your Majesty," he said quietly as he placed his broad hands on my shoulders.

I nearly flinched at the contact. I could count on one hand the number of times he willingly touched me. Although my advisors still sat behind us, this was not a moment that contact was expected, like a dance or assisting me up onto my dais.

My gaze settled on his face and there was something swirling in the depths of his eyes that stilled me. Instantly, I knew what he was going to say.

"No."

"No, what?" he replied, patiently.

"I'm going onto that battlefield no matter what you say to me. This is my fight." I tried to turn from him but his hands held me in place, square to him.

"It is."

My mouth nearly popped open. Was he agreeing with me?

My surprise gave him space to continue. "It is your fight. Your parents, their parents, and their parents before them began this war. It *is* your fight, and you will take your place in it if you wish."

This was what I wanted, but I still stared at him confused. "Why are you agreeing with me?"

He shrugged, and I could feel the motion vibrate along the line of his arms and to my shoulders. "I am and I am not."

When I did not reply, he continued, "As your Consort, I represent your interests, and in moments where you cannot be physically present, it is acceptable for me to take your place.

"I understand your need to be on that battlefield, to see finished what your ancestors started, and I will stand in as Consort. I will be your presence on that field."

"No!" I nearly shrieked at him. "I do not accept that!"

Anson glanced over my shoulder and I turned my head to see what he was watching. The gathered advisors stared back at us.

"A moment, my Lords," Anson said to them simply, and then they were shuffling out of the tent. Roland was the last to leave. I pointedly did not meet his gaze.

Anson did not speak until each Lord had passed us. And when it was just the two of us, Anson moved one hand from my shoulder to catch a stray curl that had unwound itself from my braid.

I froze as he held the curl softly. He ran his fingers around it, seeming to savor the feel of the strands. Then, a moment or an eternity later, he tucked it behind my ear.

The curve of my ear tingled where his fingers had brushed. I shivered.

"Queen Sahle—"

"Anson," I quipped back with a mix of sarcasm and venom. And fear—so much fear.

He smiled that cocky grin at me, but just as fast as it had appeared, it disappeared. Those light eyes grew fierce, pleading in a way I had never seen them. "Please listen to me. I put on a confident face before the rest of the Lords but the reason why I want to send twenty-five thousand men to the field—in spite of Trina Cheile having fifteen thousand at most—is because their soldiers are exceptionally trained.

"The battle will be tough and bloody. Many, many men will die out there. Amidst the flying of swords and spraying of blood, it will be sheer chaos. Mud and death and chaos.

"I know you have trained to fight. In fact, I know you are better with a sword than most men. And your power merely adds to your abilities. But you have never been in battle—"

"We could rectify that tomorrow," I interjected.

"No. That will not change tomorrow."

I stared at him, my gaze steely and hot. "You cannot tell me what to do. I am your Queen. You are my Consort—not my King."

"I am very aware of it, my Queen," Anson replied evenly, not rising to the bait. "I cannot order you to do anything but I *can* beg you. And I am begging you now to let me go out there in your place."

Begging? My mind could not wrap itself around the word.

When we were married, I could have sworn he would love nothing better than to see me killed. It would free him from his obligation to the crown, maybe even give him a path to rule outright. It would free him from the shackles that bound him to me, the most insufferable woman he had ever encountered.

And now he was begging me to stay off of the battlefield?

"Why would you beg?" I asked quietly.

Anson's eyes shifted from my face, flickering momentarily to a spot behind me before coming back. But he did not meet my eyes. There was something nervous in how his gaze stayed at the level of my lips as he spoke the next words.

"You are too important to lose, Your Majesty."

"To you?" I laughed derisively, even though I felt in my bones that this moment was serious.

"To everyone," he replied gravely, eyes still trained on my mouth. "This kingdom needs you. If you go onto that battlefield, it is highly likely that you will not come off of it. And then everything that was promised by your birth—prosperity, unity, peace—all of that would die with you. Your parents' sacrifice in keeping you alive? That would have been for nothing. Eliza and Roland's years in the Humanrealm with you, away from their family and friends in a strange land? All of it would become worthless the instant you fell."

Then Anson lifted his eyes to mine. "And you would fall, Your Majesty. And I cannot let that happen."

I did not say anything for a moment, my gaze locked to his.

I knew he was right, of course. This was my battle, but as Queen with no heir, the country would be in chaos if I died tomorrow. I could concede all of that, but I could sense in my gut that there was more he was not saying.

"And you?" I asked him. "You expect me to let you become just another man dead, another sacrifice, because of a feud my family started?"

He squeezed my shoulders once, then dropped his hands back to his side. He stayed right before me, though. "Yes. When I married you, your battles became my battles. And I promised to protect you and to give up my life, if needed, to keep you safe."

I snorted. "You have a funny way of showing it."

He shrugged, and I watched the pleading earnestness fade from his eyes as the cocky grin came back. "I admit that I can be cantankerous at times."

"Most times," I countered.

He bit out a laugh before continuing, "Now, Your Majesty, I do not think my time has come. I am fairly certain I will walk off of that battlefield tomorrow—my years of training and military experience being what they are. So I ask you officially, will you allow me to stand on the field in your place?"

Despite my protests earlier, my resolve to fight my own battles, I found myself nodding. "Yes, you may stand in my place."

Anson grinned again, and then he stepped away.

"My Lords," he raised his voice to be heard from outside of the tent. And then the advisors were filing past us once more.

Anson met my gaze once more, then bowed. When he straightened, he said, "Thank you."

"Don't thank me," I admonished. "You may very well die."

"Wouldn't you be so glad," he chuckled, as he turned back to the table and motioned to my chair. But the sound was a dark one, a humorless one.

I passed him and sat heavily.

The Lords looked between Anson and me expectantly, and I took a deep steadying breath before addressing them. The words felt like cuts into my skin as I bit out simply, "I agree to stay above. Anson will go in my place."

"Very good, Your Majesty," Roland said. Several of the Lords nodded their agreement.

I watched Grimly rein in his smugness before he said, "The Consort is very experienced in battle, Your Majesty. This is a wise decision."

I did not have the heart to admit it, and so I changed the subject. "Is there anything else to discuss?"

The Lords looked amongst themselves and then back to me with resolve in their eyes. Grimly replied for them all. "I do not believe so, Your Majesty. Consort. We march at dawn."

Those words were the last any of us needed to hear. I climbed to my feet, as did the men around me. As the light had faded and darkness descended, a seriousness had settled over the Lords. No one spoke as we left the Great Tent. No one laughed.

There was no appetite for music or a banquet.

All thoughts were turned on what would happen in mere hours when the sun rose again.

I FELL ASLEEP AMIDST THE BACKGROUND SOUNDS OF A war camp: the metallic slide of swords being sharpened, the raised voices of men, the laughter of women, the clanking of bottles. I let the sound form a cocoon around me, holding me. I convinced myself they were the same sounds that lulled me to sleep as a child: Roland's footsteps in the hallway, Eliza's television show turned down low, the clink of dishes as someone washed up after dinner.

Those were domestic sounds of plenty and love and warmth. And I pretended the ones around me now were the same, rather than a prelude to the thunder of hooves and screams and approaching death blows.

At some point, I fell asleep. Or perhaps it was not truly sleep. I existed in the half-life between consciousness and unconsciousness where dreams and thoughts dance and reality bends like light through a magnifying glass.

In this state, I watched as a silent shadow floated towards my bed. I was not scared. No, I did not fear this shadow because it took the shape of my husband, and in the irrationality of dreams, that was a good thing. That was a welcome thing.

The only light was that which seeped through the thick weave of the tent, a muted glow from the campfires spread around me. But it was enough to make out the tousled waves of Anson's dark hair, the sharp cut of his nose, and shadowy angles of his face.

He stood there for some time, for no time. Nestled in my blankets, I stared back at him and did not move. Then, silently, he sank down to the floor of the tent where the extra blankets I had thrown off the bed were piled. I watched as he laid down on the carpet and pulled one blanket over him and shut those luminous eyes, luminous even in my sleep.

My dream, my consciousness floated then. Perhaps I melted deeper into unconsciousness. Perhaps I finally slid into a sleep so deep there were no dreams. Regardless, hours later, I blinked my eyes open at the growing light and knew it was time to wake. Dawn was approaching. A battle loomed.

And as I sat up from my bed, as my feet hit the blankets thrown from my bed, I remembered that hazy dream-memory of Anson standing there, of Anson laying there. I shook my head against the unreality and stood.

I had a battle to wage.

The sounds of the camp stirring were loud, and I rushed through dressing. I raced the sun. Kaiht and Mara were silent as they loosely braided my hair and brought me my soldier-browns. On top of that, they placed a suit of armor that was made of interlocked panels of metal and leather. A metal helmet topped it all off—the same helmet I had seen while packing. The gold crown was welded onto the helmet's surface and I looked at it with dismay.

The metal felt heavy on my skin. The helmet felt too burdensome, as if it were crushing my neck down into my spine. I readjusted my stance to try and balance the weight.

From behind me, a voice spoke. "You'll get used to the feel of it."

I whirled to find Anson. I pulled a leather-clad hand up to my chest. "You startled me."

"My apologies," he replied with a bow. "I came to see if you were ready."

As he spoke, I took in his own outfit. He was dressed in a similar fashion—soldier-browns with metal and leather armor atop them. His helmet had no crown though.

I said as much.

The face of each of our helmets was open, cut away to expose our full faces. I watched his dark eyebrows rise at that. "No, only yours has a crown."

When I only nodded, he repeated his question. "Are you ready, Your Majesty?"

I did not answer right away. I glanced around the tent. Kaiht and Mara had brought me a mug of tea and a plate of *pap*, but my stomach had felt hollow and ringing since I woke. The food sat cold beside me.

I looked at the two women, and watched as their eyes widened in expectation and maybe a little dose of fear. But there was no reason for fear, I reminded myself. I was not going onto the field today...

Just Anson, I thought, as I turned my eyes back to him.

Only Anson was going onto the field.

I still had not responded to him, and he had begun to look at me with the same concerned look he had when we first arrived at the cliffside. I took a deep breath and nodded, though the motion was short.

"Yes, I'm ready."

He watched me a moment longer, his gaze sweeping from my booted feet to the crown on the top of my helmet. When he lowered his gaze back to my eyes, he nodded with resolve. "Good. Your army is waiting."

I swallowed and forced myself to take a step forward. The pounding in my veins was back and I told myself to breathe. I had rested on the verge of panic since our arrival at the cliffside, but I could not afford to break now.

I was a Queen. I was *the* Queen. My army was waiting.

I said that over and over in my head as I walked up to Anson. And when I was in front of him, he turned and stepped through the tent flaps. I followed.

The sight outside hit me, and I almost stumbled at the near-physical impact of it. All around me, men sat astride zebras in armor and swords. The red and gold standard of Izwe waved in the breeze that lifted up from the cliff's edge. Lines of soldiers waited with quiet purpose.

Anson was several paces ahead of me and I rushed to catch up. I reached out for him and grabbed his hand.

He halted at my touch. He turned to look down at where our bodies joined, where a tingling danced over our flesh. I blinked at my own hand in his. I blinked at whatever emotion had driven me forward to grab him, equally as shocked at my actions as he seemed to be.

He brought his eyes up to mine and I looked back, wide-eyed with uncertainty and anxiety and terror at what was to come. I expected him to push me away, but instead, his grip around my fingers tightened.

"Come on," was all he said as he pulled me in line with him. My hand stayed wrapped in his as we walked to the Lords, as we walked to the last lookout line before the cliff's edge.

The Lords turned to us with a bow as we approached. Roland was there, alongside the Senior Council and a handful of others.

"Your Majesty. Consort," Grimly said in greeting. His voice was stern, serious. It was the voice of one about to watch the world unravel.

"My Lords," I replied quietly as I looked down the cliffside at Trina Cheile's army. Gone were the tents from yesterday. The fires no longer burned. In their place, lines of men stood.

"They're waiting," Lord Marcus said from beside me.

I turned questioning eyes on him. "Why?"

He shrugged his armored shoulders, and though the motion was casual, it communicated the depth of the uncertainty we all felt. "None of us know, Your Majesty. The soldiers on night duty told us that Trina Cheile awoke just before us, lined up, and have not moved since."

"But they had the upper hand," I said quietly. "It makes no sense."

"It doesn't, Your Majesty. Not unless they *want* us to make the first move," Roland answered.

I turned wide eyes towards him. He held his helmet in his hands so I could see his curls were cropped close, almost shaved entirely. He must have cut it in the night. His blue-gray eyes, my blue-gray eyes, looked back at me.

I opened my mouth to speak but a horn sounded behind me. I jumped at the sound, but my hand in Anson's held me steady.

"It's one of ours," Anson said, his voice pitched low so only I could hear. "It's calling the men to get ready."

My heart skipped a beat and I scanned the crowd of men around us. All looked back at me, at Anson with watchful, wary eyes. All of those eyes seemed to say *let's go* and *no please no* and *we are ready, Your Majesty.* They said all of it at once, and I shuddered at the totality of it, the acceptance of it.

The willingness to charge into battle knowing you may not come back out alive.

"They are waiting for you to give the word," Anson whispered into my ear. His hand tightened on mine, and I clung to it. It was a life raft and I was a woman drowning in a sea of emotion, the weight of thousands of lives.

I turned pleading eyes to him. I hated how I must look. I hated how I sought his help in this moment of uncertainty. But there it was. I needed him. I needed Anson.

And I trusted him.

"What do I say?" I whispered.

"Tell them it is time. Tell them anything you wish. You are the Queen."

I knew it but I did not want it. All of those moments when I had railed against my lot in life—railed against being made Queen when all I wanted to be was *just Sahle*—came back to me. I saw Finn's face in my mind. I heard him say that I was the Queen we needed.

And I breathed in those words. I let them surround me. When I breathed out, I looked away from Anson's patient gaze and to the men before me.

"Men, soldiers of Izwe," I called, pitching my voice above the stomping of zebras' feet and the shuffling of boots on red dust. "It is time. Take to your posts and await your Consort's command."

A steady banging began to reverberate through the mass of bodies and I watched soldier after soldier slap their breast plates and stomp their feet. The horn bellowed again, thrumming in the morning air, and I turned to Anson.

"I'm ready," I finally said to him. I turned to the Lords around us. "I'm ready."

They bowed to me and then turned to Anson. Grimly said, "You are the leader on the field, Consort."

With that, Roland turned and marched back to his men. I looked after him, wanting to cry out, wanting to run up and throw my arms around him. Anson's hand on mine urged me to stay, to be composed, to not make a scene.

But then Anson began to pull his hand away, and my grip clamped down. It was not a rational reaction. It was not a logical reaction. It was a gut reaction.

I would not let his hand go.

I would not let *him* go.

His eyes found mine, a sea of gentleness. "Your Majesty, I need my hand if I am to lead."

"No," I replied simply. No, this hand was mine.

Anson merely smiled. He stepped an inch closer. Then he brought our joined hands up to his lips.

And on the back of my hand, he laid a tender kiss. His eyes never left mine, and though his lips remained still, unsaid words turned in those green depths.

My vision suddenly seemed cloudy and I blinked against the moisture in my eyes. "No," I repeated.

"My Queen, I'll see you soon," was his only reply before he slipped his fingers from mine. He strode away with a raised motion of his arm. And then the horn bellowed again and Anson made his way for the cliffside.

A single path led downward into the ravine and to the enemy below. Amid the sounding of the horn, the beat of dozens of drums, the soldiers began to follow him, but I could see his face just before he slipped out of view.

And that face turned towards me. It burned towards me.

And then he was gone.

I rushed forward as if I could keep him safe by keeping my eyes on him. But there was too much brush just below us. There were too many men marching down the path to the waiting army.

I could not make out Anson's form in the crowd. And so I watched them all. I paced back and forth and watched as every armored man moved forward towards this moment, towards eternity.

THOSE OF US ON THE CLIFFSIDE ABOVE HAD WAITED with bated breath as Anson led our twenty-five thousand men down the path to the bottom of the ravine.

I half expected Trina Cheile to rush forward and block the path, but they did not move. Not until the last of our army stepped off the path and faced them.

I had read nearly all the books in the palace's library about warfare. I had discussed battle strategy with Finn more times than I could count. But considering it and actually being a part of it were two entirely different things. It was like being told how to ride a bike and hopping on one yourself. In theory, everything worked the same, but no amount of study could prepare you for the exact moment a rock appeared in your path or a car swerved into the bike lane.

Some things were unpredictable. So was the experience of battle.

From our cliffside perch, I watched as the figure in the lead— Anson—motioned with his arm to the rest of the troops. There was a breaking apart and a lining up of the various battalions.

Then, as Anson swept his arm down in one brisk motion, our army surged.

The noise was instantaneous, and though we were high above the battle itself, I could hear the clangs and shouts as if I were a part of them. And in a way, I was. These were my men. These were my troops. My father and my husband were in the midst of the fray.

I tried to keep track of Anson and Roland, but I lost them as Trina Cheile's army defended, as the lines blurred, as the individual bodies became mere pawns on a chess board.

Beside me, Grimly, Marcus, and the other Lords who had not gone into battle stood. They talked amongst themselves but they did not try to speak to me. I was too preoccupied.

My heart was in my throat and I paced along the cliffside, sticking close to the Lords in case something important occurred. But my limbs itched to move. My sword was strapped to my hip and my fingers twitched towards it periodically. They wanted to grasp the weapon, they wanted to swing it at my enemies. Yet all I could do was stand here like some simpering Queen and wait.

I could feel the magic in my blood singing. It buzzed like bees under my skin. It wanted out and it wanted to fight.

I gritted my teeth against the need.

"Your Majesty," Grimly called. I had paced away from them and I hurried back to the Lords' side at a near-run.

"Yes?" I breathed.

"A messenger has come up the path," Grimly started. He looked with concerned eyes to the others. "He tells us that Trina Cheile's soldiers are barely fighting."

"They're what?" I bit out. Surely I had heard him wrong.

Grimly cleared his throat. "They're barely fighting. That's what the Consort sent up to us."

I glanced down into the ravine before pulling my eyes back to Grimly, to the Lords' expectant faces behind him. "Why would they do that?"

Lord Marcus was the one to reply. "They're waiting for something."

"And we don't know what," I guessed. The quiet, concerned looks around me were confirmation enough.

I exhaled. I did not understand it. None of the Lords did. Why would Trina Cheile bring an army here and then not cross the border? Why would they stand at attention but not attack in the night? Why would they hold us off but not try to get the upper hand?

None of it made any sense and my brain spun on the illogical nature of it. It made no sense unless there was something we were missing.

"Are we not seeing something?" I finally asked. I addressed it to all of the Lords, but none of them replied. They merely looked back at me with cautious eyes.

I turned back to the battle, watching the glint of swords and hearing the chattering of zebras. We were missing something. I was sure of it. I just could not put my finger on what.

Turned back to the battle as I was, a particular set of fighters caught my eye. To this day, I do not know why I looked at that place the moment I did. There were thousands of soldiers on the field, but my eye went right there.

Perhaps it was the way one of the soldiers—our soldier— moved as he dealt blow after blow to the enemy soldier he was fighting. Perhaps it was the way his limbs had a sort of catlike grace even in battle.

Whatever it was, my vision zoned in on the pair the moment before the Trina Cheile soldier sent a glancing blow to our soldier's helmet. The hit caused the helmet to topple off of the Izweian's head, and even from my perch above, I knew that dark hair. I knew that fierce face.

Anson.

My breath hitched as I watched Anson roar his frustration at the enemy soldier. Then he charged the man, swinging his sword in a series of blows. They balanced both aggression and finesse in a way I marveled at. Not even Finn had handled a sword as effectively.

And I marveled even more so as I watched the enemy soldier block each blow effortlessly. That soldier met each swing, almost as if he knew exactly the angle of Anson's next strike. Then, suddenly, his sword drew back. It arced down in a swipe nearly too fast for my eyes to register—nearly too fast for Anson to register.

"Anson!" I screamed futilely. He twisted away from the blade but not even his lithe movements were fast enough. No, I watched the blow land in the space where shoulder met neck. Then, as if his body were nothing more than a sack of gain, he folded to the dirt.

There was no logical thought after that.

There was no choice—not for me.

No, the moment Anson's body hit the ground, my feet moved of their own accord. My body jumped into motion, propelling me towards the cliff path. And I did not wait to see if anyone joined me. I did not watch a moment longer.

Déjà vu tickled through me. I had already lost someone I cared about.

I would not lose someone I loved.

Looking back, perhaps I should have considered that thought. But it simply did not matter in the moment, tangled in the fear and terror at seeing Anson motionless in the blood-soaked dirt that slicked the battlefield. It did not matter, and all that did was that I had to get to him.

I had to get to him.

Distantly, amidst the sound of steel on steel, I heard someone or maybe several someones yell, "To the Queen! To the Queen!"

I was vaguely aware of men running alongside me, weaving down the rocky path that dropped us feet by horrifying feet into the raging battle.

And then we were there, my own unsheathed sword swinging up on instinct as I met the first blow with a block someone long ago had taught me. I laid grown men to waste as I moved. And with the force of my will, my magic, I crippled bodies.

Where once soldiers stood in gleaming armor, husks of burned metal now remained.

A part of my brain moved back to a time not so long ago when my magic had flared the cool white of charcoal. But that thought too had no place here. I fought to see the soldiers barreling towards me, the reality of the dark mud, the splatter on my face of blood or earth—I was not sure which. I fought not to see the eerie purple sky that overlaid the normal, blue one above me.

"Majesty!" someone yelled to my left and I dodged a blow that came too close. I needed to focus. If I had any hope of reaching Anson, I needed to stay present.

I could not see him through the fray, but from my earlier vantage point, I knew roughly where he had been. I battled my way in that direction, taking what seemed inch by inch of ground despite my calculated swings and pointed magical attacks.

I always feared releasing that blinding light. It was one thing to battle Manelesi in the arena. There was limited damage that could be done there. This was another thing entirely.

I did not want to indiscriminately kill. But I reminded myself what Manelesi had said, that my power was my will. I had not hurt Finn that time I killed the creatures. I had targeted my power at Manelesi and not blown the arena apart—at least not by accident. Perhaps it was possible for me to kill in this packed space in the same targeted way again.

It was not hard to focus my anger and fear. Adrenaline and dread raced through my veins at the mere thought of the minutes Anson had been on the ground.

I let the terror climb in me until it felt like a physical presence lashing against my skin. And then I merely *thought*. I willed the enemy soldiers between me and Anson to simply melt away.

And they did.

Where once there were bodies, alive and whole and swinging, there was instantly sludge and heaps of metallic armor. My own soldiers turned their heads in confusion, the blows they had been calculating still ready in their muscles. But then they saw me and they fell aside.

I did not know what they had been told of me, what they knew of me and my gifts. But something must have been written on the exposed skin of my face that told them to move or suffer a similar fate as our enemies.

One by one they cleared a path and with no one obstructing my way, I launched into a run.

The heavy metal pieces I wore across my chest and hips and head clanked at the motion. I willed myself faster as I saw what lay just before me: Anson.

He remained heaped where I had seen him fall. He had not moved and a new worry raced across my mind. I had been so focused on getting to him that I had not considered whether there was anything left to get to.

Without knowing what I was truly doing, I slid into the mud beside his prone form. I chucked aside my sword and yanked the helmet from my head as I reached for him. My hair, sweaty and tangled, tumbled free of its braid and fell into my eyes. I pushed it back angrily. I pulled Anson to me, trying to turn him over so that I could see his stupid, beautiful, infuriating face.

He was heavy, though. I gritted my teeth as I yanked on his arm and managed to only move that one limb. He was a dead weight and the fear running through me ratcheted up a level.

"Help me turn him!" I shouted. I knew guards were around me—they always were—and with that one command, they approached. Two each took an arm and heaved Anson over.

As they placed him back down, the slightest of grunts slipped past his barely-parted lips.

"Anson!" I yelled at him, reaching for him once more. To my soldiers, to the air, I commanded, "Guard us!" I felt a portion of my magic respond, arcing up and forming a dome of spooled, shimmering light around us.

The sound of battle raged on but I paid it no mind. I could only focus on the man before me. "Please, Anson!" I cried.

I ran my hands across his body, for the first time unconcerned about any physical touch between us. My hands found blood—both his and others—and the wound to his neck that bled too freely. I tore a strip of cloth from my brown pants and wrapped it around that deep gash.

Though I wished I could do more, I knew he needed a doctor. I knew we had to move.

With Anson half tugged across my lap, breathing and still alive, sense began coming back to me. I was a sitting duck here, a helmetless Queen holding her fallen Consort. If the enemy had not yet realized I was on the field, they would any second and the might of their forces would turn collectively this way.

I took a second glance down at Anson. My hands were cradling his face as if it were something precious, something worth saving. And maybe it was. Maybe he was. But to find out, I had to move and move now.

I released Anson and tugged my discarded helmet back on. I glanced around and finally took an assessment of the dozen soldiers who had formed a barrier between Anson and me, and the rest of the fighting.

To the soldiers, I spoke. "Soldiers, we need to move. I need you to get the Consort to safety. Grab him and follow me."

Gathering my blade, I staggered to my feet and took off at a hurried pace. The path I had cleared before was no longer clear. Our soldiers and theirs had continued to fight, moving into that space, undeterred by the metal and sludge at their feet.

I was unconcerned about the battle. All I cared about was getting Anson back up the cliff path and to a doctor. I moved with that purpose. Several soldiers rushed forward to engage me but I dodged their blows and continued on, glancing behind only to make sure the Vikela carrying Anson were still behind me.

I had wanted to be on the field. I had wanted to fight.

Now, all I wanted was to heal Anson.

The thought was more terrifying than the blood and gore around me, more horrifying because for the first time I could admit that I needed that insufferable, annoying, perfect man. That despite all of our fighting and bickering, I would crumble if he did not make it off this field in one piece.

From the corner of my eye, I noticed my magic shimmer and retract. I thought it settled over Anson but I could not be sure. I was too busy moving around another soldier who charged in my direction. As I did, a taller one stepped into my path. I stumbled as I dug my heels in, skidding to a halt so that I would not run into this new foe.

The soldier held a sword, but he dropped it to the ground as he looked at me. Then he reached up and pulled off his own helmet.

Indigo eyes that were nearly white looked back, and then pink lips that were almost beautiful smiled. "Good morning, Queen Sahle."

My eyes widened. I froze in my tracks.

I knew that voice. It was the voice that haunted my nightmares. It was the voice that had precipitated the attack and commanded the monsters on the night of my twenty-first birthday.

And without being told, I knew this was the leader of Trina Cheile. This was Falin.

I could feel the presence of the Vikela around me, but I spoke without turning to them. My eyes still trained on the terrifying man, I commanded my guards, "Take Anson back to camp."

"Your Majesty," one started to reply.

I could hear the argument in his voice so I interjected. "That's an order. Take him now. I'm fine here."

There was no movement for a moment. The Vikela did not want to leave me. But a command was a command. They would obey.

They hurried past me with questioning eyes and I watched them closely, making sure that this strange man did not dare lash out in their direction. I needed to see Anson safe.

When Anson and the Vikela had moved past, I turned back to the strange man. His smile stretched too widely over his pale face. "What a brave little thing you are to send your guards away. And all because you want to protect the Consort. Hmm."

My hand tightened on the handle of my sword. But I did not speak. I just waited. The sound of other fighters squaring off seemed distant to me as I stared back. We were locked in our own battle and no one dared disturb us.

"Oh, I forget my manners," the man continued. He bowed at the waist and my brows rose. "My name is Falin. We have not been properly introduced."

My lips felt tight but through them I bit out. "A pleasure."

Falin's eyes twinkled. "What a delight you are. It's a pity I'll have to kill you one day."

My brows rose at that and I took a step to the right, starting to circle. "Not today?"

Falin mirrored my movements, circling in the opposite direction. His sword remained pointed towards his feet. "I considered it, in all honesty. But I think there are more delightful things you and I could do today. We can save the killing for another time."

"That did not stop you last time," I fumed. Spit flew in my vehemence. "When you attacked on my birthday."

"Ah, yes," Falin replied. His tone sounded mildly amused, the voice of one of Eliza's ladies at afternoon tea rather than the tone of a soldier facing down his enemy on a battlefield. "Things have changed since then. Now you've piqued my curiosity."

I lifted my sword so that it forced a barrier between us. "How so?"

"I killed your lover and your anger was glorious. Tell me, Your Majesty, is there more to this power? Perhaps if we bring your Consort back here for some sport, I might catch another glimpse of it."

I did not think as my anger flared. To mention Finn, to threaten my husband. My outrage soared and my *will* exploded out of me with little direction.

But as my magic hurtled towards him, spooling out in iridescent streams, Falin simply lifted his hand.

His hand absorbed my power. Then with a flick, the power rebounded back at me.

I threw my body out of the way on instinct. I tumbled into the dirt, losing my grip on my sword.

Falin stalked towards me but he did not attack. No, he merely tilted his head to the side in an almost alien way. "Very impressive. So you have a handle on it after all."

I seethed up at him. "A handle?"

Falin merely smiled. He reached a hand down as if he would help me up. I scrambled backward on my butt before climbing to my feet.

His smile grew and he lowered his hand. "Yes, I heard rumors that a certain tutor was found for you."

The sound of the battle was a dull roaring behind the sound of my heartbeat. I focused on each thud. I let the sound calm me, focus me. Then I responded, "I don't know what you're talking about."

"No, I wouldn't think you would. Very well. What else can you do, little Queen?"

But Falin did not give me time to consider. In one second he was smiling and in another, his face twisted as he threw his hands wide.

Magic spiraled towards me and I threw up my own block of white light. It arced between us, bulging outward towards him as I pushed his power back.

His look of concentration held as our power played off each other's. He took a step to the side and I followed suit, my entire being concentrated on his will.

I gritted my teeth as I pushed and pushed. I could feel the tether on his power slipping and I yelled out my frustration as I shoved it back.

My light broke through the plane of his own power and he spun out of the way, much as I had moments before. But where

I had looked up at him with vehemence from the dirt, he stood with a pleased smile.

"Interesting," he muttered to himself. He swept that icy gaze from the crown at my head to my boots. Then he said again. "Powers like these are not meant for you, for Izwe."

My knees were still bent, my body prepared for an attack. My fingers tingled with the depths of magic yet spent. And through the sensation, I barked at him. "No? Only for you?"

Falin seemed to find my words funny. His smile widened and it was too big for his face. "Only for me."

My hands balled into fists, and I realized that somehow I must have picked up my sword as I sat in the dirt. My fingers flexed around the pommel and while Falin smiled, pleased at his own words, I launched myself at him.

One second I was standing there and in another, I was inches from him, my sword sunk deep in his chest.

But Falin merely looked down. In the space where my sword had stabbed, there was no blood. Instead, the space turned to gray shadow around the blade, floating as if stirred slightly by a breeze.

"Tsk, tsk," Falin chided, and I brought my shocked gaze up to his. "That wasn't very nice."

I opened my mouth once, twice. I did not understand. Men were supposed to bleed when a sword was put through their chest. Men were supposed to cry out in pain.

Men were supposed to die.

But this one did not.

This one merely looked at me with disappointed eyes. Then he leaned forward and whispered with words that sounded of sharp nails scratching over an icy window, "I'll be seeing you, little Queen."

His form turned murky, his eyes began to blur, and just before he disintegrated into shadows, I watched as he raised a blurry hand up and snapped his fingers.

Then his form was gone, disappearing into the very air around us. I spun, looking for him. Only then did I realize that the soldiers, too, had begun to take the shape of shadows.

They continued to fight as their forms became insubstantial. Then they were gone.

And it was just me and my army out on that field.

As I looked at the men around me panting and bloodied, the men around me cold and still on the ground, I realized a sickening thing.

It had all been a test.

38
luminosity

"WHERE IS HE?" I CALLED AS I STUMBLED OFF THE PATH, back on the cliff ledge once more.

No one had to ask who I was looking for. They all knew.

I was looking for my Consort.

"The Great Tent," a soldier called to me over the bustle of bodies moving off the path.

I pushed through them, hurriedly moving through the crowd. The Great Tent loomed ahead and I ran the last few paces. I threw back the flap, dodging soldiers entering alongside me.

A sea of injured men stretched before me, but I only had eyes for one.

"Where is he?" I repeated.

The soldiers here also knew who I was looking for. One healer raised his head from a wound he was cleaning. "This way, Your Majesty."

I hurried to his side as he passed his work off to another healer. Then he motioned me to follow him.

In the back of the tent, a barrier had been erected. We moved around it and the separate room was filled with beds. I strode down the aisles between them, scanning the faces before me until my eyes landed on the one I was searching for.

My heart seemed to contract. My breath sighed out, and I sank down on the floor next to Anson's bed. Tears rose to my eyes and I hung my head. I wept.

"Your Majesty!" someone called.

I heard the sound of running, shuffling feet but I did not lift my head.

"Your Majesty, he's alive," the healer who had led me here said gently.

I did not need him to tell me that. I had known the moment I set eyes on Anson. His face and neck were clean of dust, and even in his wounded sleep, there was a rosiness to his skin that a corpse would not have.

No, I cried because I had expected the worst. I knew what someone I cared about looked like in death. I had lived that, not long ago.

I cried now because the person I loved had escaped that fate.

I reached up to grab Anson's hand where it lay alongside his body. It was warm to the touch, and as it had been before, it was a lifeline for me.

Seated on the floor of this makeshift hospital, still covered in mud and armor and blood, I held Anson's hand and cried. And I thanked God and the gods above that this man had been spared.

It was not long before someone touched my shoulder. I flinched at the unexpected contact, but it was just Roland—Roland whole and safe and also here after the battle.

He looked down at me with concerned eyes. "Come, Sahle. It's ok. He'll be alright."

There was a truth in his gaze that told me he knew what he was saying. "Did the healers tell you that?" I asked.

"Yes," he replied. He grasped me by the elbow and helped haul me to my feet. "I got here a few minutes before you and they told me the wound will heal. It has already been cleaned. They gave him some pain medication that will keep him asleep, though."

I knew there were others in the room but I did not care, not now. My armor clanked as I looped my arms around Roland and hugged him to me. "And you? You're OK?"

I felt Roland's body move as he nodded. "I'm fine, Sahl," he whispered close to my ear. "Both of us are fine."

I took a deep breath before I stepped away from Roland. I looked between him and Anson as I wiped the moisture from my cheeks.

Roland passed me a handkerchief. "What about you? You have blood all over you. Are you injured?"

I looked down in surprise. As is the way of adrenaline, it masks any sensation not vital for keeping you alive. Now, I took in my blood smeared armor, the tears in the leather, and I began to feel again. I flexed my arms and wiggled my toes, rotated my shoulders.

"Everything feels right," I replied.

But Roland shook his head. "No. Come. Let the healer check you over."

I opened my mouth to protest, to tell him I would not leave Anson's side, but Roland knew that already. "You can stay right here. Just let the healer look at you."

"Alright," I murmured as I turned my eyes back on Anson.

Distantly, I felt hands on my armor, peeling it off me. A red drape was put up around Anson and me, and the healer and his servants pulled my soldier browns from my limbs. The material stuck in a few places and I guessed that those were the wounds. I hissed through gritted teeth at the sharp stinging, but even those bursts of pain could not make me turn away from Anson.

He was all I could see. He was all I could feel.

He was all that mattered.

For two days, I sat beside Anson. The evening after the battle, we packed up our war tents and returned to Barrick Castle. Roland asked me to ride alongside him on my zebra, the triumphant leader galloping back in victory, but I had no interest in the vision in his mind. Instead, I rode in the carriage with the wounded. I sat right next to Anson, holding his hand, gazing at the way his dark lashes rested along his cheek.

Eliza met us at the gates of Barrick. She took one glance at me, at my preoccupation, and immediately ordered a room put together for Anson. I let the Vikela carry him there, but I followed the stretcher the whole way.

Eliza watched me watching Anson for hours on end. She and Kaiht and Mara were my only reminders that mealtimes came and went, that clothes needed to be changed and bodies washed. I let them dress me like a doll, my mind utterly occupied with the unconscious Consort. I sat by his side with Bekha's book, sometimes with nothing at all. And I waited.

The morning of the third day, I let Mara and Kaiht dress me in a gown of soft yellow. They wound half of my hair up, leaving the rest of my curls springing out past my shoulders. No crown adorned my head. After all, there was no one I would see. I was a wife in waiting. The updos of a Queen be damned.

Bright midmorning light filtered through the small windows set in Barrick's gray, stone walls. A discarded plate of bread and fruit sat on the small table beside me.

I was not hungry. I only had one desire. And it was for Anson to open his eyes.

Healers had come and gone. They had continued to dose Anson with pain medication, but I was grateful for it even if it kept him unconscious. The cut to his neck was deep and it needed to be stitched together. I could not imagine the feel of the procedure awake.

This morning, the same healer I had met in the Great Tent entered. His name was Jonathan, I had learned. He was Lord

George's personal healer at Barrick but had come to the battle on George's bidding.

"Good morning, Your Majesty," Jonathan called as he entered the room.

He was not one for small talk. He immediately walked up to Anson, picked up a wrist to check the pulse, felt the forehead for fever. When he began peeling back the bandage on Anson's neck, I stood from my seat.

I had seen the wound one too many times, and it never failed to make me feel a strange mix of guilt and nausea. A nearly empty water glass sat next to me and I picked it up. I knew the room next door was being used as a sort of staging area, pitchers of fresh water included. On quiet feet, I slipped from the room. I left the door open behind me.

I found the pitcher of water easily. I picked it up, angling it so that the stream flowed into the glass.

Then, from the open doorway, I heard a voice croak out, "Where is she?"

I froze, the pitcher suspended in midair. Registering the timbre of that voice, the gravel nature of one who has not spoken in days, I set the pitcher down in a clatter and ran back into Anson's room.

Jonathan stood between Anson and me so I could not see the Consort's face. But I heard the healer reply, "Her Majesty went for a drink of water. She will be back soon."

"I'm here," I said simply.

Jonathan turned in surprise at finding me there, but I did not have eyes for him. The movement of turning pushed his body out of the direct line from my gaze to Anson's. And when our eyes met, tears rose to mine unbidden.

I walked towards his bedside as if pulled by a magnet. I sank down on the edge of his bed and blinked against my blurred vision. This was not a time for tears, but one of relief, of gratefulness.

"You're awake," I whispered. Distantly, I heard the healer shuffle away. The door snicked closed behind me.

"It would seem so," Anson said, even as he winced. I was not sure if it was because of a dry throat or the knitting wound at his neck. Maybe both.

"Do you want some water?" I asked him. It was a stupid question and I cringed internally. There were more important things to discuss yet I felt awkward and tense, relieved and anxious. I looked at Anson with wide eyes and waited for his response.

He pulled himself into a seated position slowly. Then he nodded. "Yes, water would be nice."

My glass was still in my hand and I passed it to him soundlessly. His fingers curved around the vessel, brushing against my fingers. And my eyes drifted shut at the pulse of energy that flowed between our skin.

I sighed, then raised my eyes to his.

He drank with a strained sort of expression and I watched the muscles in his neck shudder as he swallowed. "Does that hurt?" I asked, for it seemed like the right thing to say in a moment like this.

"Yes. Everything hurts," he replied. He swallowed once more and set the empty glass on the bedside table.

I winced. "I'm sorry."

"There's nothing to apologize for. You didn't strike me down."

I shook my head. "No, but I feel responsible for it all. I'm certain the entire battle was a test to see how my power had developed."

Anson's brows rose at that and he sat straighter against the pillows. "What do you mean? What did you do?"

There was flint in his voice, but for once, I did not mind it. I was past minding his moods. I was only happy he was alive.

"I went onto the field," I replied quietly, not meeting his gaze. "When you fell, I moved. I had no choice."

"What do you mean you had no choice?" he whispered harshly but the quiet belied a certain violence. He was angry in retrospect—a stupid sort of anger.

When I did not answer right away, he reached out and grasped my hand. I looked at him then. I had no other choice, drawn as I was into the green of his eyes.

"I didn't have a choice," I repeated. "I had to get to you."

His brows rose but he did not say anything at first. Then, through tight lips, he asked. "And then what happened?"

"I got to you and ordered the Vikela to take you back up the cliffside. You needed a doctor, you see," I said, twisting the corner of the bedsheet with my free hand. "And on the way, Trina Cheile's leader, Falin, challenged me."

"Challenged how?"

I swallowed against the memory of it, but I recounted it nonetheless. I explained as much as I could remember about what he had said. I had already told the Lords. It was nothing new, though I still wondered at the look in Falin's eye as he told me he would be seeing me soon.

Anson watched me with disbelief. With questioning, accusing eyes, he asked again, "Why did you go onto the field?"

I looked back at him confused. "I already told you."

"You said you had no choice."

"Yes," I whispered, confirming.

"You came after me."

"Yes," I whispered, pleading.

"But I took your place on the field," he said quietly, almost as if he were thinking aloud, trying to rationalize how he had offered himself up yet I had still ended up in the fray. Almost as if none of it made sense in his mind.

And it did not. None of this did.

Yet everything did.

He was still holding my hand. His fingers around mine felt warm and right, and I let the sensation of that surround me. I accepted it.

And with that thought in my mind, I asked the question that had burned a hole in me for the past days as I had sat at his bedside. "Why did you take my place?"

"I told you the night before the battle. Your kingdom needs you."

But I shook my head slowly. I had heard *this* already. "No," I breathed out. "Tell me why, really."

He would not look at me. He stared at the sheets, at the door across the room of his convalescent chamber—anything but meet my gaze.

And I knew it was bad. This was Anson, the man who would look me in the eye as he mocked my failings, who I could always count on to point out my flaws and not have a single qualm about it.

Yet here he was, shy and avoiding, for the first time since I had met him. "Now you clam up? After all of the terrible things you've said to me? After years of saying whatever you please no matter who it might offend?"

That caught his attention, and his eyes flicked to me for a moment before moving abruptly away.

But there was a seriousness in that gaze that I had never seen before. It was similar to the way he had looked at me as we danced, as he told me he would take my place on the field. There was something more; there was something he wanted to say and I could see the words swirling unspoken as if they turned around and around in his mind, just behind his eyes.

"Anson, spit it out."

"I can't," he ground out and I saw his knuckles go white as he grasped the sheet in his lap tightly.

"You've never shied away from a single thing, at least not when it comes to me. Do me the courtesy of carrying on that trend."

His eyes gleamed with annoyance, but it was a front. I could see that clearly. Underneath it was hesitation and fear and… something warm. He cleared his throat, and as if he had made a decision, he spoke.

And he said the words I never thought I would hear. "I loved you the moment I saw you seated on that *stupid* dais last year, looking confused and afraid and overwhelmed. I took one look at you and knew I was doomed, that the prophecy was right. And I did not want it."

I froze. My ears rang with the impossibility of the words. Through motionless lips, I uttered, "I don't understand."

He looked at me for a moment. His gaze swept my still face and he nodded slightly, imperceptibly to himself. As if deciding this was the moment to tell his tale, he began. "To understand any of this, I have to go back some years—twenty-one years, in fact—to just before you were born. You've already learned that your mother and I were close. She was my dearest friend, apart from Madeline. Many supposed that I loved her and I did, but only platonically.

"When she chose Otto as Consort, I was very happy for her. And when you were born, she invited me to meet you in private, just her and Otto and myself. I walked into her chambers—your chambers now—and your soul stilled me in my tracks."

I felt my brow crease. "My soul?" I asked, sure I had misheard him.

Anson nodded, eyes fixed far away as if reliving the moment again. "Yes, you know I have minor magic but I've never shared my ability with you. Well, it's that I can see the soul of a person. It's not something they can hide. It's like peeling back all of their layers like an onion and seeing the true core within.

"Every soul is unique. Like a fingerprint, no two are the same. They shine with a specific sort of light. Their edges take on different forms. The grooves and swirls are as individual as the person they make up. But when I saw you, your soul shone platinum. It had ridges like a topographical map of the highest mountain ranges. The edges were fanned, woven, almost like the finest lace. It looked just as mine does. They *matched* in every way, and they seemed to recognize each other.

"In all my years, I had never seen that. Nor have I ever since. But I knew then that it meant something, that there would be some connection between us.

"I never told anyone, not even Bekha, though I always thought Otto suspected. He watched me interact with you with wariness, as if he could see some intangible link between us. You seemed to stop fussing when I was near. Your eyes always tracked me in a room. I did not know what it meant then but maybe Otto did. Perhaps he could see the future written out before him. Wielders do not discuss their power with others, after all."

Of all the things I could ask, I murmured, "You never knew what his was?"

Anson shook his head but continued. "Some time later, you had been presented to the court and were then brought before the oracle to discern what they would see in you. You know your prophecy. You've seen it written out so I won't repeat that. What's necessary to know is that when it was done, we all left the chamber. Bekha realized you had dropped your toy lion and asked if I would go back for it. I did.

"Oracles are mystical creatures. They're alive but not. Their consciousness spans this realm and others, the plane of the living and the dead. And they take on the appearance of the dead until they have something to say. This one had fallen back in her lounge once she had finished your prophecy. Her skin had taken on a bluish tinge. Her cheeks had gone waxy and too-still. Her eyes were shut.

"But when I entered the room, she sat back up. She came alive with rosy cheeks and bright, feverish eyes. It was just me in the room and she fixed me with a hysterical gaze. Her chapped lips cracked as she smiled widely. Then she said, 'Anson of Ingonyame, of Warbeck, there are things even you cannot change. She will be your leader, your *umlilo*, as you will be hers. You will burn for her.'"

I had heard this part before, weeks, months ago. Still, I listened to every word. I barely breathed, afraid the slight whispering noise would distract Anson from his story.

He continued, "She said those words and, just as quickly, closed her eyes once more and drifted back off. I was shaken and stared at the sleeping oracle, trying to figure out if I had imagined it. Then, I heard a noise from the hall outside and I hurried out.

"It was Wiley. He had overhead—he admitted that much—and I forced him to swear an oath of silence. I have often wondered whether that was the right choice. I wonder whether my honesty could have resulted in a different outcome for your parents and this kingdom, but the prophecy was so much about me that I did not think it mattered then.

"I would stare at you in your crib, bouncing on your father's knee, eating smashed bananas from your fingers, and I questioned day in and day out what it all could mean. Your matching soul mocked me. It boggled me. I thought about it constantly…until the day your parents were killed.

"I was one of the first in the room that night. I killed several of the attackers and then rushed to where you were, crying in your crib. Eliza and Roland were just behind me and they hurried to your parents, but I knew it was too late. I could see Otto's soul was gone and Bekha's was fading quickly. I knew Bekha would want her daughter protected, and so I picked you up and made sure you were fine and then I took you to your mother.

"I tried to give you to her but she said no. She told Eliza, 'Keep her safe.' But then she looked at me as if she *knew*—as if she knew what the oracle had said, as if she knew that our souls were the same and that she wanted me to protect you.

"I cried as Bekha's soul faded, and I hugged you to me. At some point, Eliza took you from my arms and I let her." He scoffed, a sad, derisive sound. "Who was I to hold you?"

"When the Lords met next and decided what to do, I was the loudest in wanting to send you away. You needed to be far from this world, far from the death that stalks the palace. I watched as Eliza and Roland took you away in that dome of borrowed light, and I felt your soul leave like a piece of mine had suddenly been ripped away.

"I wanted you safe. I mourned the loss of you. And for your sake, as well as your mother's, I did everything I could to make sure you never returned to this place.

"But then you did. Despite twenty years of my arguing and conniving and scheming, you did."

Anson paused, rubbing a hand over his mouth before he continued. "I thought I was prepared for it, but there was no way to be. Not when I *felt* your soul snap back into this realm. Not when I walked into the Council Chamber and saw you sitting there as Bekha had once sat.

"You looked everything like Bekha and nothing like her. Oh, the features were your mother's but they were put together in a way that was entirely your own. You were the most beautiful woman I had ever seen. You took my breath away.

"You stared back at me with a mirrored sort of wonder. Your soul blazed brighter the nearer I drew. It fairly blinded me all over again in its luminosity, in its pure, incandescent light. Mine answered. And, after twenty years, I knew exactly what the oracle had meant by burning. I could see it play out before us like some fated, written-in-the-stars love where our souls called to each other, wanting the twin pieces to fit back together. Where we were just going through preordained motions.

"And I couldn't have it. You were young. You were new to the Alterealm, your life, your responsibilities here. I could not bear to watch every decision taken from you in a single day. I swore then I would do everything in my power to stop it."

"Stop what?" I breathed. Caught in the story as I was, it made no sense. Was it even possible to stand in the way of destiny?

But Anson plowed on as if he had not heard me. "I didn't want it for you. I had no claim to you, regardless of what some oracle said or how our souls played off each other. I wanted you to be free. But I *could* protect you, as your mother wanted me to.

"I could help you more from afar, from the place of impartial advisor. I had no right to feel the way I felt when I looked at you up on that throne—"

"With love?" I asked incredulously, disbelievingly.

Anson's gaze snapped to mine and he nodded, honestly and without reservation. "And heat, and longing. Those are all messy emotions, and I knew I could help you more if I put them aside, if I fought the urge to become your friend.

"Just as a healer cannot operate on a sibling or partner, I could not be an objective, rational advisor if my feelings were in the way. I feared I could not make the right choices if I was bound to you."

"But I don't understand. If you loved me..." I began.

"Yes?" he urged simply.

"Your needling and your harshness—" But then, it was like a puzzle piece snapped into place. In the space of silence, I could almost hear the audible click. "It was an act. You thought you could hold me at a distance with your viciousness."

Even before I saw the mingled acknowledgement and shame pass over his face, I knew it was true. I suddenly had the answer to why this man had always been cruel.

My eyes shut of their own accord as I let loose a long breath.

He had never hated me. Quite the opposite. He had loved me and had feared that love, and so he pushed me away in the only way he knew how.

I opened my eyes as Anson began anew. "But the oracle was right. I could not stop our souls from singing to each other. I could not stop myself from burning for you. Whether in anger or love—"

"It's passion. It's all heat. It's burning," I broke in because I understood now. Everything finally made sense—the words of his prophecy, every action and reaction when it came to Anson.

"Yes," he said with a wistful smile. "Each time I pushed you and you fought back. When we danced at the high holiday and your skin heated under my fingers. No matter how I acted, no matter what I did, I could not change it. I could make you hate me or befriend me and our souls would still call for each other. Your beauty would still defy logic. All paths would still lead here, to you as Queen and me as your Consort. I would burn for you irrevocably.

"And there you were in the middle of this. You had no choice in your life, your position of power, anything. The last thing you needed was a man saying you also had no choice in who you ended up with—that you were his by some strange twist of fate. I wanted you to have a choice."

I blinked at the words, at the scene that flashed before my eyes: me summoned to Council to answer for Finn, and Anson, my sole champion there. "That's why you supported me with Finn."

He swallowed and I watched the strong column of his throat shudder. "Yes, though it nearly killed me. You were making that choice for you, despite what any of the Lords thought. I was proud of you, though the idea of you with a soldier…" He took a steadying breath. "Let's just say I was not a personal fan."

I shook my head. "Not that you ever said."

"No. Why would I?" he asked. There was genuine confusion in his green gaze. "It was my problem to deal with—the love I felt for you, the burning. Besides, I hoped that your relationship with Finn and then with Joachim would put distance between us.

"But I couldn't seem to stay away from you. Our souls were drawn like magnets to each other. I found reasons to speak to you, and then hated that I did, hated that I pushed and taunted and upset you. But that too was my burden. As long as you were living the life you wanted with whomever you chose, that was enough for me."

I stared back at him, captivated. "You say you could not bear to see my choice taken away, but what about your own? The oracle said you would burn for me and you burned. There was no choice in it for you."

He gave a resigned shrug. "No, there was never a choice for me. There never has been. From the moment I was born, I was meant to be an agent of the realm, a Lord and servant to the crown. But I had hope for you. I wanted more for you than obligation."

"You wanted love of my own free will."

He blinked at me. "Yes, always. Can you not see that? So much has been taken from you. I refuse to take more, no matter what I feel."

"And what do you feel?" I asked slowly.

His eyes locked on mine, and for the first time since I met this man, I felt like I was truly seeing him. This was the Anson that Ruth had always known, the Anson who had been my mother's best friend. This was the boy who had grown into a man among the proteas of the Yekela. The man looking back at me was the real Anson, without mockery or jests. It was just him, earnest and honest and completely laid bare in his vulnerability.

"I already told you, Majesty, I loved you the first moment I saw you on that throne."

I swallowed. "And now? After all this time?"

The room stilled. The very molecules of air seemed to freeze, waiting for his response.

"And now, nothing has changed for me."

I stared at him and he stared back. My mind spun as I tried to take in what he was saying.

This man who had mocked and needled, defended and helped—here he was baring his soul to me and all I could think about was the way, even now, his hair folded over itself in gentle waves, how the bridge of his nose rose sharp and defined above his cheekbones, how his luminous green eyes searched mine as if every answer he could seek was there.

And perhaps they were. I realized suddenly the power he had given me in this knowledge. With his confession, he handed me the tools to ruin him or make him the happiest man alive.

More importantly, he laid out that knowledge with no expectation. How I responded was a choice, and I could see that he would live by it no matter what my decision was. He would live by it no matter how much I hurt him.

Because I could hurt him now, really and truly hurt him. I could scoff in his face and tell him I hated him. I could stand up and walk away and refuse to speak to him again. I could yell that he disgusted me.

But none of that was true.

The truth was something I had tried to deny for the many months I had known him. It had been easy during that time, while he was cruel and jeering, but that feeling had been there all the same. Perhaps that was why he had always irked me so, because despite everything he had ever said to me, he was a good man. I knew it deep down, and I respected it.

The truth was that a part of me *had* lit up the first moment I had seen him, as if my soul had turned to his and said, "Oh, there you are." In the months since, I had tried to forget that because it made me feel ashamed and weak and silly to be so taken with a man who was so obviously not taken with me.

But not anymore.

Now I looked at Anson and saw him—not the act he had put on for me, not the needling Lord with a wit sharp as knives, not the snide Consort who always seemed to know more than I did. There was just Anson staring back at me, and I could see the hope that shone in his eyes even though I knew he was trying to keep control of it.

And so I moved closer to him, scooting along until I was sitting with my thigh pressed against his.

I did not think. There was no room for thinking now. Instead, I just felt.

Anson stilled completely as I detangled my fingers from his. But instead of pulling away, I put both hands on his wrists. I watched his face for any sign that he wanted me to stop, but instead of wariness, there was a sort of disbelief as if he had dreamt of this moment for too long—and had never thought it would come to pass.

He was wearing a long-sleeved white shirt, but even through the woven fabric, I could feel the heat of his skin as I dragged my hands up his arms. My fingers skated over his shoulders, strong and solid with lean muscle.

I paused only momentarily as I bracketed his neck, avoiding the healing wound there. One by one, I allowed my hands to cup his face as I had done on the battlefield.

His green gaze was trained on mine but I felt a shiver echo over his skin as my hands settled around his jaw, the angles of his cheekbones.

I did not think. I just felt. And I whispered into the few inches that separated us, "You loved me then." I phrased it as a statement, a confirmation of what he had told me just moments before. But really it was a question as vital as the very oxygen I breathed into my lungs.

"Yes," he said softly. Close as I was to him, the word seemed to float on the warm air, caressing my cheeks.

"You love me now," I whispered.

"Yes," he repeated.

I let the words wrap around me. They were both foreign and familiar, as if my innermost being, my soul, had always known this to be true despite the months of bickering and tears and anger.

My mind skipped back to that battlefield, to the moment Anson had fallen, to the single thought that had raced across my mind—that I could not lose the man I loved.

And I knew.

I knew that thought, that immediate gut reaction to his fall, had not been a mere fluke.

I meant it, and I sighed out as I let the feeling of it take root within me. My eyes filled with tears despite my best effort to keep the swell of emotions at bay.

"My Queen?" Anson asked, his beautiful eyes narrowing in concern.

But I could make no words pass my lips. I could not tell him that I loved him, too. And so I did the next best thing.

I closed the gap between us as I brought my lips to his.

It was like kissing the moon, pressing my lips to something mythical, something I had yearned for but not known I had yearned for.

A single tear fell, skating down my cheek and mingling with our lips. Anson groaned, a slight sound yet there nonetheless. As if the tear had woken him, he suddenly moved from his frozen, shocked state.

He threaded his hands into my curls, pulling me more securely against his mouth. His tongue darted forward, stroking the seam of my lips and asking for entry.

And who was I to deny this man? This beautiful, kind, selfless man. This man whom I loved.

I opened to him and sighed as his tongue met mine.

In all of the months I had spent with Finn, all of the years of dating in the Humanrealm, I had shared plenty of kisses with plenty of men. I knew the anxiety-filled moments of a hesitant first kiss. I knew the taste of a sloppy, drunk-at-three-in-the-morning kiss. I knew the comfort of a Sunday morning kiss over coffee, and the rush of a kiss that kicked off a one-night stand.

Yet I had never shared a kiss that felt like *home*, that both settled into my bones in an ultimate rightness and lit me up as if I had taken the strongest drugs. I had never felt a kiss that tingled across my skin in the same way my magic did.

This one did.

Even as Anson carefully lowered me down so I was half laying on the bed under him, I shivered at the thought that an innate part of me recognized him.

He pulled back, propping himself up by his uninjured side. "I'm sorry. Did I do something wrong?"

I let my hand stroke through the strands of his dark hair as I shook my head. "No, you didn't."

"Are you sure?"

"Yes," I breathed. And then I smiled. My words were back and so I finally said, "Yes. I love you."

Anson looked at me as if I had just told him he had won the lottery. But his hesitation lasted only an instant. Then he lowered his mouth to mine once more.

We drank each other in as if we were drowning, as if the taste of each other's lips alone could save us. But hours or seconds later, Anson stilled. He pulled away as he angled his face towards the door. Then he was helping me sit up, rearrange my smashed curls, realign my dress where it had gone askew.

A knock sounded at the door. I knew my cheeks burned with exhilaration and I prayed that they were not visibly red as Anson called, "Enter."

Grimly and the members of the Senior Council came in, with Roland in the rear. I felt myself blush more furiously as I set eyes on my father. His eyes settled on me, and as they flickered back and forth between Anson and me, I realized that I might have put my hair and clothes back in order but I had not moved to the chair. No, I was still seated next to Anson on the bed, our thighs pressed unconsciously together.

I wiggled a fraction of an inch away from Anson, but Roland's eyes tracked the movement.

If Roland wanted to say something, he bit his tongue. He sank into a low bow alongside the other Lords. "Your Majesty. Consort," they said in unison.

"My Lords," I replied. "To what do we owe the pleasure?"

Grimly was the one to answer. "Healer Jonathan informed us that the Consort was awake. We wanted to take the opportunity to speak to him and you, Your Majesty."

"About what?" Anson asked brusquely. My gaze turned to him at the tone. He was not pleased at being disturbed.

I bit my lip to keep from smiling at the thought that he was annoyed at us having to break our kiss.

The Lords seemed to incline their heads in supplication at Anson's tone. "The battle, Consort," Lord Marcus alone braved.

Anson sighed but I felt the bed move as he sat up straighter. "Fine. Go ahead."

I moved away from the bed, taking the water glass with me again. I had heard all there was to hear of the battle. The Lords had frequently come to report and fill in details as I sat next to a silent, unconscious Anson. I had no desire to hear it all again.

I left the room on quiet feet. And this time when I made it to the pitcher, this time when I poured water again into my glass, a smile broke wide and dawning on my face.

ANSON WAS NOT THE ONLY SOLDIER INJURED. NO, OF the twenty-five thousand who went down into the ravine to meet Trina Cheile's army, two hundred ten had been killed. Five hundred sixty-two had been injured.

I found the numbers staggering in their sparsity. The Lords and Anson did, too. We had sent more men to the field than Trina Cheile, but still, we had expected to suffer graver losses. The simple fact that we had not solidified my belief that none of it had been real.

Oh, it was a real enough fight. Swords had clashed and blood had spilled. But Trina Cheile had not truly meant to fight *for* anything. They were merely there to coax me out. They had meant to get me onto the field and test what my powers could do now.

It did not slip my notice that Falin knew I had a trainer, that I had been developing my gifts these last few months. The Lords had paused at that when I recounted our fight, looking amongst themselves silently. It had been so quiet I could have heard a pin drop.

Even now, days later, those words sent a shiver up my spine—not for the words themselves but the *how* implicit in them. The only way Falin could know about Manelesi, when even most of the Lords did not, is if he had a spy in the palace estate.

A spy somewhere close, on the Senior Council or in the Yesonto.

I had mulled that thought over as I sat beside the unconscious Consort. I brought up each Senior Council Member's face in my memory, then each of the Masters'. None of those earnest, sharp men could truly be working with Falin. Right?

I alternated between worrying about it and forgetting it, remembering it anew and worrying again. Every word I spoke, every look now held a tinge of suspicion. It was not in the forefront of my mind, but like a ghost lingering in my peripheral vision, like a whispering wind, I kept asking *who*.

Consciously, I also knew Falin was powerful, so powerful in fact that perhaps he could sense our channel. Perhaps none of my subjects had communicated with Falin. Perhaps he had merely sensed the shift of power in the land much as the Masters had.

I clung to this thought, hoping beyond hope that it explained everything Falin had said. I was too weary, too exhausted to the bone to truly consider the depth of betrayal that Falin implied.

I would have to deal with it. I knew that. But all I could handle now, all my mind could wrap around was Anson.

Our kiss had been a singular affair. After the Lords had left, Jonathan had returned with two other healers at his heel. They had all poked at Anson's wound and conferred while I stood silently by. At last, they came to the conclusion that for the Consort's quickest recovery, he should be put back to sleep.

Anson had looked at me then, wonder and disbelief and a strange sort of fear flitting across his face. But I merely brushed aside his hair from his forehead as I told him softly, "I'll be here when you wake up."

The days continued to pass in Barrick Castle and I found the strength to pull myself from his bedside. The realization that that was what I was doing—pulling myself away—shocked me.

I knew what Anson and I had shared. I knew the words we had spoken, the taste of our kiss. But the force of my attachment to him continued to surprise me.

Yet I was Queen, and there were more injured men to see and logistics to consider. And so I reluctantly left Anson's chamber and headed to the Great Hall which had been repurposed as a hospital for those still in need of tending.

With Eliza at my side, I walked the aisles between the beds. I reached out my hands and placed them on feverish cheeks. I held the hands of the injured. I murmured my thanks to any man who would listen.

I knew the Lords watched me. They took in my actions with distaste. It was not long ago that I was told I should never let the people touch me.

I had thrown that idea away quickly, first at Ukuwela, then at Finn's funeral and my wedding. The list went on. It was instinctual to me. I was Sahle, but I was also Queen Sahle. I was my own person, but I was also their monarch. If my touch and kind words could give them comfort, then I would give it.

It was the least I could do for men who had fought and bled for me—for the test that this battle had shown itself to be.

Slowly, as the days ticked by, more of the injured men were discharged from the makeshift hospital. The Lords began insisting we travel back to the palace of Izwe, and I agreed. I wanted to go home. I wanted to take Anson home.

And so, nearly one week after the battle in the ravine, we loaded the carriages and took to zebras. We bid Barrick goodbye and we made the journey home.

Three days on the road blurred into a series of camps and cold nights and sore muscles. Anson never woke but I kept his sleeping, healing form close by. And then, the palace of Izwe was mere hours away, and like a horse close to the stables, I could feel the energy, the drive to move go through the traveling party.

This time, when Roland urged me to leave the carriage and join the Lords on zebraback, I agreed. That was how, seated astride a tall zebra, flanked on both sides by Lords and standard bearers, I rode through the streets of Izwe with my crown atop my head, stray curls streaming in the air behind me, the skirt of my gown billowing. My people lined the roads, clapping and throwing flowers. They reached out their hands to touch my skirts. They called, "Queen Sahle! Queen Sahle!" They called, "Queen and Conqueror. Queen and Warrior."

I was not sure about those monikers; I had not done nearly enough to deserve them. I had stayed on that cliffside too long, waiting until I could not wait any longer. But my own inner monologue did not matter now. The people wanted a conquering queen, a warrior queen, and I sat up taller to play the part.

The palace gates opened before us and I sighed in relief as I galloped into the courtyard. I sighed in relief as I slipped from my zebra, as I joined Roland and Eliza on the steps leading up to the palace door.

Their eyes shone with some emotion I could not place as they watched my approach. "Queen and Conqueror," Eliza said as she and Roland bowed.

"Not you, too," I murmured.

But they only smiled. Pride and respect shone across their familiar faces.

Courtiers packed the hallways as we entered the palace. They bowed and called my name. I inclined my head but I was too distracted by the stretcher behind me, the man who laid upon it: Anson. I wanted to get him into a proper bed as soon as possible.

The Vikela helping support Anson began to turn down the hallway which led to Anson's rooms one level below mine. I froze in confusion for only a moment, not understanding what was happening. Then I called, "This way please."

"Your Majesty?" the Vikela asked, confused.

"You can bring the Consort to my chambers," I explained.

Kaiht and Mara were already in my rooms as I entered. They were fluffing the bed and unpacking trunks and pushing dust from surfaces that had been in disuse for days.

I smiled in homecoming at my room. The wide wall of windows looked out over the forest around us. The *hadedas* glided and cawed. The warm, woodsy scent of the thatch roof above wrapped around me.

I sighed to myself before turning to Anson and the Vikela, now entering the doorway. "You can take him to the bed," I called.

And I watched as the Vikela settled Anson there. His clothes were dirty from the road but I did not care. I wanted him here, with me. That was all that mattered.

Two days passed and Anson stayed in my chambers. Kaiht and Mara had made up a second bed, next to my overly large one. I slept in that second one. I did not want to move or jostle Anson. He needed all the rest he could get.

Jonathan, who remained with us on Lord George's insistence, came to check on him a few times a day. He dosed him over and over with the medicine. I would have asked if it was strictly necessary but even I could see that the wound was almost completely closed. I marveled at the speed of the healing, and Jonathan informed me that for people with magic in their veins, sleep sped up the process beyond that of a typical person's healing time.

On the second day, Jonathan returned and removed the bandage from the sleeping Anson. The wound was pink but the skin had smoothed over. No more medicine would be needed. He had healed.

And now, he only had to wake up.

THE SUN ROSE AND SET IN EQUAL CYCLES. I ROSE FROM the cot next to my bed each day and dressed, heedless of the sleeping Anson mere feet away. The Lords had much to discuss with me—going over the battle dozens of times, asking again and again exactly what Falin had said to me, wondering what our next move should be.

I entertained their questions and noted the particular emphasis in Falin's words. But at the end of every session with the Lords, I turned to the empty Consort's chair beside my throne. Then I told the Lords that I would not make a decision until Anson woke.

The Lords eagerly waited for Anson to wake.

I waited for Anson to wake.

The entire palace waited on bated breath.

This morning, Kaiht and Mara dressed me in the soft tea dress with vining protea flowers embroidered across the skirt. They slipped little satin slippers onto my feet. Then they sat me down before my dressing table to do my hair.

"Up or down, Your Majesty?" Mara asked as she separated the curls into sections in her palms.

I studied her gentle face in the mirror. "Down, I think. Maybe a low braid or something simple?"

"Certainly, Your Majesty," Mara replied. I felt her fingers begin the plait and I relaxed into the soothing feeling. Behind me, Kaiht re-emerged from the wardrobe with a few crown boxes.

"Do you have a preference today, Your Majesty?" Kaiht asked as she set the boxes on the dressing table.

I went to shake my head but halted mid-action, afraid to ruin Mara's work. "No. I don't care about the crowns. You can pick something."

From behind me, a voice murmured softly, hoarsely, "Could I pick?"

I spun in my chair, rising to my feet in a hurry. Mara's braid was entirely forgotten.

I crossed the distance from the dressing table to my bed, Anson's bed, quickly. "Anson," I breathed out in relief as I sat on the side of the bed, facing him.

"You did not let Mara finish your hair," Anson said.

Already, I could feel the ends unfurling, the braid coming loose in springing coils. I did not care, not now that Anson was awake, not now that his eyes were open, his lips moving.

"It doesn't matter," I replied. Both his hands rested at his sides and I picked up the one closest to me. "Do you need anything? Water, food, the bathing chamber?"

"Water would be nice," Anson answered. This time, I did not have a glass already in my hand.

I turned to seek out the pitcher Kaiht and Mara normally kept on the small table near the fireplace, but Kaiht was there before me. She held out the full glass and I took it from her gratefully. "Thank you, Kaiht."

"Of course, Majesty. Consort," she replied, dropping into a curtsy before us. When she rose, her knowing eyes shifted between us. "Shall we leave you?"

I nodded at her. "Yes, please."

I watched Kaiht and Mara slip out of the servants' entrance. Then I turned my gaze back to Anson. His had never left my face, even as he sipped at the glass of water before him.

"How long have I been out this time?" he inquired.

I rubbed a consistent circle into the back of his hand. "Just under two weeks."

He nodded thoughtfully. "The medicine?"

"Yes, George insisted Healer Jonathan travel with us back to the palace. Jonathan wanted to keep you asleep so that you would heal faster."

Anson lifted his free hand to the injured spot, moving the neck of his shirt away to feel the new skin. "Good," he finally said.

As if he was only now taking in his surroundings, his vision slowly expanded outward from my face. He turned his head as he looked around the room, as he noticed the tall four poster bed he was laying in.

"This is your room," he said slowly. "How did I get here?"

"We brought you here," I replied simply, matter-of-factly.

Anson nodded. "But why? Why not take me to my rooms?"

I smiled at him, a small thing, a shy thing. My gaze dropped from his face and to our joined hands, softly resting atop the downy blankets. "I told them to." Then I lifted my eyes back to his face. I told myself to be brave. "I did not want to be away from you."

Anson's eyes narrowed as he looked at me. He did not say anything, not for the space of four heartbeats. Just when I was about to draw away, when I was beginning to fear that I had imagined the closeness between us, Anson parted his lips. "Then it was not a dream," he murmured more to himself than to me.

"A dream?"

He blinked at me, seeming to remember I was listening. "I thought perhaps I had imagined our…conversation."

"And our kiss?" My voice came out huskier than I intended.

His eyes dropped to my lips. "Yes. That, too."

The cup was empty and I reached out to take it from him. The glass was cool under the pads of my fingers. "It was very much not a dream."

Anson did not respond, and the lack sent a pang of anxious nerves through me. I slipped my hand from Anson's as I moved to set the finished glass on the side table. But I felt his eyes on me. It tracked my movement, and I imagined, for one second, that the force of his gaze could see every last muscle stretch and contract, every blood cell flit through my veins.

When I settled back on the bed, when I looked at Anson once again, I could not place the emotion on his face. Did he regret our kiss? Had I imagined the depth of feeling he and I had shared?

I knew I had not, but perhaps I was too hasty in believing everything had changed for him. Perhaps it had only changed for me.

That much was true. As I had sat on the makeshift hospital floor and cried in relief at him being alive, I knew my world had shifted forever. The force of my feelings was a new gravitational pull, pressing me into the space around Anson.

But then he spoke. "Good."

It was a simple word, and though I wished for more, I knew I had to be patient. His body had been put through hell.

I had to be patient, and so I changed the subject even though he looked like he might say more. I did not want to push. I did not want to pry. There would be time for more words later.

Anson was alive. He was awake.

"Would you like to bathe?" I asked him.

If he was surprised at the change in conversation, he did not let on. "I would appreciate that."

I nodded before I climbed to my feet. "I'll give you some space. Feel free to use anything in the bathing chamber."

"Thank you," he replied. He folded back the blankets and stood from bed slowly. He did not move forward for a moment, and I guessed he was testing his balance after so long horizontal.

Then he disappeared into the bathing chamber, the latch clicking shut behind him.

I let out a long exhale as I turned away from the door. I should have asked him if he needed assistance. I should have asked him if he needed new clothes.

He probably did. And that thought sent me heading to the door where I knew the Vikela would be stationed. I asked them to go to Anson's chamber and bring a fresh set of clothes. Then I waited.

I paced before my wide wall of windows. I ran my fingers along the ferns set against the wall. I toyed with my hair, braiding and re-braiding the loose ends of my curls. And I asked myself why I was so anxious. My body seemed to buzz like an electric current had been set to my skin and could find no release.

The sound of water being poured and splashed slipped under the door from the bathing chamber. With each sound, my mind envisioned Anson scrubbing at his hair, wiping a soft cloth over muscled arms.

I shook my head. I was sick. The man was recently injured and bathing for the first time in weeks. Leave it to me to make it into something it had no right to be.

Luckily, the servants' entrance opened and Kaiht returned. She carried a set of folded items and I recognized them as Anson's dark clothes.

"Thank you, Kaiht," I said, breathless, as I rushed up to her.

Her eyebrows rose. "Are you alright, Your Majesty?"

"I'm fine," I replied, though I took a deep, steadying breath.

She lifted the clothes slightly. "Would you like me to bring these to the Consort?"

I debated taking them from her hands, but I could not bring myself to do it. I nodded instead.

She inclined her head as I turned back to the windows. I watched wispy clouds float by, high above, offset by the startling blue of the Izweian sky. The silver trees below moved gently in the breeze and I breathed in, imagining the wind whip past me and through me.

Imagining what I would say and do when Anson stepped back out of that bathing chamber.

Some time later, I heard the door to the bathing chamber open once more. I turned slowly to find Anson. His hair was damp and combed back from his face. His dark pants were cut to show the way his lithe muscles moved as he walked towards me. The neck of his white shirt was open to the throat, and as he approached, my eyes took in the line of his collarbone, the rise of his pectoral muscle just barely visible at that opening.

I swallowed, despite myself. Then I forced myself to meet Anson's gaze. "How are you feeling?"

Anson stopped beside me, casting his gaze out of the windows as I had been. The sunlight streaming in played on his dark hair, glinting a rainbow of reds and silvers and browns as it reflected.

He rotated his injured shoulder a few times. "A little stiff but surprisingly well, given that I was almost cut in two."

"I wouldn't go that far," I replied, despite myself.

He glanced at me in surprise, a gleam of the old Anson in his eyes. "No, you're right. It was merely a paper cut."

The corner of my mouth lifted. Here was the Anson I knew, the relationship I had come to expect. "Exactly. Stop being such a baby."

Yet even as I relaxed into our bickering, even as I said it, even as Anson winked one green eye at me, I knew it was not the same. Where there had been heated animosity before, there was playfulness now. And under it…under it there was a sea of emotion.

We only had to jump in.

"Sahle."

I stilled. My eyes widened. The sound of my name on his lips was the sweetest sound I had ever heard. It was sweeter than his laughter, sweeter than that stupidly perfect scoffing sound he made at the back of his throat when annoyed.

It sounded like bells, like the singing of angels.

It sounded like joy.

"Say it again," I breathed, my voice barely louder than a whisper. Without conscious thought, I turned, bringing my body closer to Anson's.

His head tilted in confusion. "Say what?"

I smiled a sweet smile, a wistful smile. "Say my name again."

And the answering smile he gave me was not coy. His eyes did not glimmer with malice or teasing. No, the smile he gave me rose to his eyes and told of love—just love.

"Sahle," he said simply.

I stepped into him. "You've never called me by my name."

He shook his head. "I have. You probably don't remember, but I said it that night I found you and Finn after the attack."

And just like that the memory returned to me. But it was a hazy memory, a half memory. It was clouded and fuzzy by fear and jittery adrenaline, horror, and confusion.

And it had not sounded like this.

At least, not that I could remember.

"You haven't since," I replied. Close as we were now, I could smell his skin. It smelled clean, of the soap I kept in the bathing chamber. But underneath it, it smelled like a crackling fireplace on a cold winter night, like thick blankets that kept the chill out. It smelled like Anson.

I let my eyes close at the rush of emotions.

I opened my eyes when he spoke.

"It was not our relationship then," he said simply.

"And it is now."

He looked down at me, his green eyes sure and steady and…kind. Then he said, "It is all I have hoped for since your return to Izwe."

I laughed the smallest laugh. "You had quite the way of showing it."

"I had my reasons."

"Yes, you've said."

I expected him to tease, but he did not. His eyes were serious as they bore into me. "But you haven't told me. Not really. Is this what you want, Sahle?"

"I thought I made it clear the other day," I replied.

As if he needed to hear it again, he asked, "Will you say it for me? Will you tell me what you want?"

And so instead of leaning forward and kissing him, I held back. I looked up into that green gaze and I said the words I never thought I would say.

"Anson, I want you," I spoke into the space between us.

His eyes shut momentarily. And then he opened them and a new emotion shone there. Fire looked back at me. Smoldering fire that wove around the love. Fire that burned a heat I had not seen nor felt for a long time, maybe ever.

Without conscious thought, I lifted my arms and wrapped them around his neck. And as I drew his lips down to mine, I said, "You once told me you'd never touch me, not until I asked."

His lips just barely brushed mine. Against my lips, he spoke. "I did."

I exhaled against his warm skin. And on that exhale I let float the words I never thought I would say, not to him, not to anyone ever again. "Then touch me. Please."

As if the fire in his eyes was merely an ember waiting for a gust of wind, my words ignited an inferno.

Anson's lips crashed into mine. Where there was gentleness and hesitancy a moment before, there was nothing but fierceness now. I met each kiss with an answering one of my own. I let my lips open to him and I answered each stroke of his tongue with a mirrored caress.

Then Anson's hands were on my hips. They hitched me up and somehow through the thick skirts of my embroidered dress, I managed to wrap both legs around his waist.

He moaned at the feel of me pressed against him, and I felt him begin to walk. Then abruptly I was falling.

But I was not afraid.

No, I trusted Anson as I had never trusted anyone.

When my back hit the downy blankets of my bed, I smiled up at him. Then I reached out a hand to guide him to me.

His body covered mine, nestling into the space between my thighs. His lips found mine again and it was my turn to moan as he ran his hands along my waist and across my breast.

There were too many clothes, too many layers between us. But he seemed to sense it in me. He knew what I wanted without me having to say.

We shed layer after layer. I freed the buttons of his shirt. Anson pulled the laces of my dress free. He ran his fingers through the unraveling sections of my hair until my curls sprung wild and free around my shoulders.

And then he pulled my dress away from me, and I was naked and bare to him.

But unlike so many moments when I felt exposed to this man, this was different. His eyes raked over my naked chest. They swept over the swell of each hip, the angle of each calf.

He leaned his forehead against mine with a shuddering exhale. "You are more beautiful than I could ever imagine."

I let my eyes close at the words. I let them wash away my insecurities, my uncertainties. And then I drew his lips back to mine.

He needed no more encouragement, not as he kissed his way down my neck. Not as he took the peak of one breast in his mouth, teasing the nipple. Not as his deft fingers found their way to my core.

I whimpered at the contact. I opened my legs wider to him.

I had no control when it came to him. I had always known that. I just had not known the many ways that it would and could manifest.

"God and gods, you're perfect," Anson breathed out.

I had no other words but please. And so that is what I said. I begged him as I never thought I would beg anyone. And I was not ashamed.

"Please. Please, Anson."

He knew what I was asking for. He was only too happy to oblige.

He positioned himself at my entrance, and I looked up at him in expectation.

"Please," I said once more.

"I love you," he whispered back. And then he watched me with that green gaze as he seated himself inside me with one deep thrust.

I arched back. My moan rang out somewhere between a cry and a plea.

Looking back, I often wonder whether we rushed this first moment together, whether we should have taken our time, ran our fingers over every ridge and hollow, kissed every inch of skin. But that was not Anson and me. Our relationship had never been soft and easy. We had never been patient. Nor were we in this moment.

As he moved in me, as I rose up to meet every thrust, I could not believe that this was how this story, our story, went.

This was the man I hated. This was the man I loved.

The friction rose between us. The vastness of my love drove me to the edge.

And just like that I broke so fully and deeply that my breath was gone. My eyes shut. I turned my face into the pillow beside me and cried out. I was not sure whether the sounds were moans or screams, not as sensation ricocheted through every inch of my body.

"Don't turn away," he growled against my neck. Deep in the throws of passion as I was, I only half registered him pulling me up so I was seated on his lap, straddling him. "I want to watch as you come apart in my arms."

I had nothing to say, not as I gasped for air, my head tipped back as the waves of ecstasy thrummed through me. As I floated back down, I felt his kisses on my neck, hot and open-mouthed. A shivery ripple ran through me.

Anson had slowed his pace as I came, but he increased it once again. I opened my eyes to find his face just before mine. His green gaze burned into me and I could not look away.

His hands gripped my hips and he helped me raise and lower myself at an aching pace. The muscles of his shoulders and arms stood out, bronzed and strong. I do not know what came over me but as he increased his pace further, as my own pleasure ratcheted up once more, I leaned forward and bit his shoulder.

It was a small bite, more of a nibble really, but something about it seemed to push both of us over the edge. Maybe it was the sheer animalism of it. Maybe it was the lack of control I felt, wrapped in Anson's arms—the one man I thought I would never, ever fall willingly into bed with.

But, as if the completely lowered inhibitions heightened the pleasure of *us*, I broke again. I muffled my cries in the newly-healed dip where his neck and shoulder met, but I heard his groans. I felt his shudder as he pumped up into me, spilling himself deep.

I shut my eyes against the sensation, the full heat of it. I let myself go boneless against his chest. My breath whooshed in and out in quick tempo. My body hummed in tired contentment.

But above it all, I felt *peace*—deep and abiding peace. And as Anson drew back to look at me, as I watched his wonder-filled eyes track over my flushed face, he smiled.

"I love you," he whispered. His voice was coarse and out of breath. "I have loved you."

The back of my eyes burned, tears threatening to rush forth, but I held them back. I brought one of my hands to his forehead. I brushed away strands of dark hair that stuck to the sweat there. Then I completed the sentiment.

"And I will love you. Always."

It wasn't Queen Sahle saying it. It didn't feel coerced or pulled out by guilt. It was just Sahle. It was me.

I loved him, and I meant every word.

41

awake

IN THE BURGEONING AWARENESS THAT WAS NEW-MORNING consciousness, I felt his arms wrapped around me. But I did not startle.

No, as I sank back into my body, I felt at home.

It was a dizzying thing to feel at home in his arms.

Anson's arms.

Yet the smell of his skin, the comforting weight of his body settled me. I did not want to move but I had to. I cracked open my eyes and angled just slightly to catch a glimpse of his beautiful, everything face. And he looked back at me.

"Good morning," he said into the dawn-encrusted light that sank in from the wall of windows.

"You're awake," I replied.

"I have been for some time. I did not want to disturb you."

I nodded, transfixed by those luminous eyes I had spent so long hating, those soft lips I had spent too long dreading.

We watched each other for a few minutes, lost and found in the feel of our skin resting against the other's. The quiet stillness of morning wrapped around us like a cocoon.

Then Anson smiled at me and my heart leaped in response. It was not a sly look—gone were the smirks, his winks, his crooked brow. It was an earnest smile, and I felt my own lips form the mirrored expression.

"We should get up," I said.

"Undoubtedly," he answered.

"There's much to do."

"Without question," he replied.

"But maybe just ten more minutes like this?" I asked.

"Certainly, my Queen."

His lips met mine and I let myself fall a little deeper into him.

acknowledgements

If I thought writing my second novel would be easier than the first, I was sorely mistaken. It was just as thrilling, just as fraught. And I can honestly say I would not have made it through the process without the support of the following people:

My husband, Hannes. Thank you for always being the source of my strength. It can't be easy being married to a writer, but you take it all in stride. You ground me, and you remind me to eat and sleep and step away from the computer. Thank you for your unconditional love, your willingness to be my first reader, and your surgical (but constructive) criticism.

Whitney, my wonderful second reader. The joy in your late night texts made me believe in the beauty of this book. Thank you for your praise and your keen eye for movement and physical details. No one catches an errant third hand like you do.

Emily, my incredible editor. Thank you for your patience, your skill, and your expertise. You have a knack for seeing both the big picture and the smallest details, and I'm so glad I signed on to work with you and the entire Fractured Mirror Team.

Allison, my design guru. Thank you for another gorgeous cover. I will forever admire and covet your artistic skills.

My ARC team. Thank you for being the best cheerleaders a girl could ask for. Your excitement, fan theories, and outrageous DMs always make me smile.

My family and friends near and far. Thank you for always asking about my stories, and for not getting upset when I miss your calls because I'm deep in a fictional world. Your love and support mean the world.

And last but certainly not least, my wonderful readers. I started writing Sahle's story as a challenge to myself. But each time one of you reaches out to tell me how deeply you resonate with her, it reminds me that the real value of writing and sharing stories is connection. It's been a pleasure meeting you across these pages.

about the author

C.P. DU TOIT was raised in Northern California but spent six years as an expatriate in Scotland, South Africa, and Australia. A born storyteller, she has been writing poetry and short stories since she was a child. She currently lives in Philadelphia with her husband and their two black cats. The *Light Trilogy* is her first published series.

www.ingramcontent.com/pod-product-compliance
Lightning Source LLC
Chambersburg PA
CBHW030333010826
48973CB00004B/987